CW01666539

G.M.HAGUE

VOICES OF EVIL

PAN
Pan Macmillan Australia

First published 1996 in Pan by Pan Macmillan Australia Pty Limited
St Martins Tower, 31 Market Street, Sydney

This edition published 2001 by Hinkler Books Pty. Ltd.
17-23 Redwood Drive, Dingley, Victoria 3172 Australia

National Library of Australia
cataloguing-in-publication data:

Hague, G. M.
Voices of evil.

ISBN 186515 6426

I. Title.
A823.3

Typeset in Sabon 10.5/12.5 pt by Post Typesetters, Brisbane
Printed in Australia

Also by G. M. Hague in Pan

Ghost Beyond Earth
A Place to Fear

Graeme Hague was born in 1959 and now lives in Queensland. When he's not writing he alternates between being a professional musician and working as a technician in live theatre.

ACKNOWLEDGEMENTS

This story has taken several different shapes and forms since its beginning and the final manuscript needed careful reading by various friends to assure me that the whole thing still made sense—and that I could finally leave the novel alone and call it complete. So, thanks go to Jocelyn Cooper (who had the worst task of waiting months for the final chapters, because I wouldn't tell her how the story ended), Anthea Dennis and Karen Crawford for their time, encouragement and support. Also, thanks to Selwa, who was just as involved as myself in nursing this project through all its different versions and ideas to an end. It was, in fact, our first.

FOREWORD

This is a ghost story—not a war story. But a large part of the tale in this book is located during the allied invasion of the Dardanelles in 1915, better known to Australians as the Gallipoli campaign and significant in our national folklore. As it's likely this novel will be read by some people unfamiliar with the Anzac legend, a brief explanation is in order.

The amphibious landings and subsequent battles for the Dardanelles Peninsula—for tactical reasons too vast and complex to be dealt with here—were an attempt to reach Constantinople and knock Turkey out of the Great War. For the first time in history Australian armed forces were deployed overseas in significant numbers and, more importantly, under their own national flag. Combined with troops from New Zealand, they became known as the ANZACs (Australian and New Zealand Army Corps). After training in Egypt, the

Anzacs, some 30 000 in number at the initial landings, were given their own specific part of Gallipoli to invade. Because of this, their story is often looked upon separately, and with little reference to the other nearly half-million British and French troops who saw action over the next eight months attempting to capture their own objectives on other parts of the peninsula.

The entire campaign was a failure, doomed in the first hours by bad luck (when, due to strong tides, the Anzacs were landed on the wrong beach and faced impossible terrain), then by the sort of bureaucratic bunglings, hopeless strategies and needless waste of lives that became synonymous with the Great War in almost every theatre. However, the legend of the Anzac soldier was born, as they fought courageously against a determined and clever enemy, a difficult country and a hostile climate. The reputation of the Australian 'Digger' as a fighting man was established. Those same soldiers weren't to know that at the same time they were also forging a national identity. And, in the end, when the High Command decided to withdraw from the Dardanelles, in a brilliant manoeuvre the entire Anzac force removed itself from what had become known as Anzac Cove (a name officially recognised in a gesture of goodwill by the Turkish Government years later) without suffering a single casualty and without the Turks ever realising they were leaving.

It is an enormous part of our Australian history

and one that should never be allowed to fade from our memories—not the least reason being the 9000 Australian soldiers who lost their lives fighting what they believed was a just fight for their new country. I hope this novel will make its own contribution to keeping the Anzac traditions and legend of Gallipoli alive.

And, of course, being a ghost story, I hope it keeps the reader awake at night.

Graeme Hague
Mackay 1995

1

It looked like a normal room, but it wasn't. Although somebody had lived here for over sixty years, like a vacant motel room, it was bare of personal touches. A careful observer might note the room mainly had a lack of small things—in particular, small, *sharp* things. Dangerous things.

The room's occupant was supposed to be watched continuously, but over the last few years he had become frail and vague with age, needing constant care and attention rather than guarding. In the past, his sudden screaming fits and violent attacks on unwary staff were commonplace, although he was always more intent on hurting himself. It was when the nurses tried to stop him—maybe calm him with a needle—that he turned his clawed fingers against them. They purposely kept his fingernails trimmed very close. For a while, too, they'd been forced to give him his false teeth only at meal times, then take them away again when he finished eating, because he went through a stage of attempting to bite anyone who restrained him. But some shred of dignity surfaced through the mist of madness inside his head and one day he promised to stop biting. It was one of his few lucid moments and rated a special mention in his medical file. Usually, there wasn't that much to write about him. Apart from the effects of normal, physical ageing, the old man's condition hadn't changed much since the day he was admitted to the Home sixty long years ago.

On that very first morning he'd tried to kill himself. Sitting in an office as they processed his induction, he'd snatched a pair of scissors from the doctor's desk and tried to stab himself, but weakened by injuries and slowed by bandages he fumbled the attempt and a nurse was quick to pin him down. When it became clear his suicidal urges were a constant state of mind the special 'safe' rooms he was put in became his permanent home.

Within those walls there was nothing sharp. There were no loose light fittings where he might bare the cord and electrocute himself. Instead, the ceiling lights were flat squares of perspex mounted beyond reach, flush with the suspended cork panelling. He couldn't have a cooling fan, even during the worst heat of summer, in case he hurt himself in the blades. Years after he arrived they installed an air-conditioner, but by then it was too late and he didn't seem to care if it was on or off. There were no drugs or any poisons. Not even strong detergents or household cleaners which he might mix into some sort of lethal cocktail.

The staff at the Veterans' Home were very efficient about these things. They were trying to help him, they said.

Once a year, on 25 April, they dressed him in his best suit, pinned his campaign medal to his chest and let him go to the monument and see the parade. On these outings they had to watch him very carefully. Of course, it would have been simpler to leave him behind, but they could hardly do that. The old man was becoming a living national treasure and he knew it. He possessed a sly cunning that surfaced through the insanity for getting the things he wanted, and this annual excursion was something he expected. Any suggestion he might miss a year brought on a terrible tantrum. He knew that the older he got, the more precious he became—on 25 April anyway—and he could get his way. But once he arrived at the parade he would become deeply withdrawn. Over the years, despite the differing attitudes of the crowds and the times of violence like the Vietnam War protests, his manner didn't change. He would be propped up in his wheelchair and stare sightlessly at the passing pageant. Often, the nurses wondered what all this fuss had been about and if the old man noticed anything, even time, passing at all.

The two small rooms he lived in had been his world for so long. With nothing ever changing, it wasn't surprising that the first thing senility took away from him was an awareness of the years slipping past. But the nursing staff beyond his walls weren't too concerned. It was a common symptom in many of the older residents. More importantly, he was safely locked away from harm and prevented from hurting himself, and that was all that mattered.

But they were wrong.

If someone were to ask the old man, he would tell them they'd locked him *in* with the most dreadful thing. They'd caged him with a beast—a monster. A being who tormented him with cruelty and violence because the demon, in turn, was a prisoner of the old man's insanity.

Today the fluorescent light in the ceiling wasn't working. The maintenance man had come to fix it, removing the frosted panels in the ceiling and the neon tube, and replacing it, only to find a faulty starter was the problem. Now he'd gone to get a new one—leaving his tools behind.

With a trembling hand the old man picked up a screwdriver. He caressed the metal shaft with the tips of his fingers. The feel of steel was so alien to him now. The flattened end wasn't as sharp as a knife, but he knew it could cut—eventually, with enough force. Suddenly there was a strange shifting of the air around him and he looked up, fully aware of what he would see. He wasn't surprised that someone else was standing in the room with him now—someone who had appeared out of nowhere. It was an insane-looking figure wearing odd clothing and it watched the old man silently, grinning at him with mad, dancing eyes. The old man stared back a moment before speaking.

'Now I can do it,' he croaked, his voice ruined with age and lack of use. He tried a triumphant smile, but that was something else he rarely did and the result was a horrid, rictus grin. 'I can get away from this place—and get away from *you*, you godless bastard. You can go back to where you came from and rot.'

The figure said nothing—did nothing, and kept watching him with a hungry stare like a predator awaiting the moment to kill.

The maintenance man would return soon. Anxious that his chance would be stolen from him, the old man hurried to a small writing table he never used because pens and pencils were considered too sharp. Sitting down and grasping the screwdriver in his right hand, he lay his left arm, palm and forearm upwards, on the table. The smooth, soft white skin below his wrist looked particularly vulnerable.

Without giving himself another moment to think, he swept the tool in a short arc and plunged it into his own arm.

The pain was enormous. He tried to scream, instead making only a harsh, guttural sound. Waves of nausea swept over him and he nearly slipped from the chair to his knees, but he held on with a desperate strength. His arm throbbed and burned, quivering with nervous spasms.

Fighting back the dizziness, he opened his eyes and inspected the wound, plucking the screwdriver out and leaving behind a bruised, round hole in his forearm. It seeped blood, a crimson line dripping down the skin and pooling on the table—but only seeping, not the arterial gush he wanted. He had to try again. Sobbing with pain, he stabbed the metal shaft down a second time, but made the mistake of closing his eyes at the crucial moment. This time he missed his arm altogether, the blade glancing so unexpectedly off the polished surface of the table that the tool nearly flew from his grasp.

He spat an obscenity. Dropping the screwdriver would have been a disaster. He knew he wouldn't have had the strength or will to pick it up off the floor. Stricken with the pain, he glanced at the doorway, expecting the handyman to return at any moment.

He must finish now, before it was too late. It was the only way.

This time he kept his eyes open, fixed with a wild, staring obsession on his forearm. He watched the tip of the screwdriver plunge into his own flesh. He almost blacked out from the hammer-blow of agony that travelled up his arm. The whole room seemed to move and sway as he sat immobile, fighting off the swooning faint, until he could focus his eyes again. He was rewarded by a gout of blood spurting up, again and again, splashing red on the formica surface. He'd hit the artery.

He allowed himself to collapse away from the table and slide to the floor. Mists of pain obscured his vision, but he could see the demon figure with its maniacal grin still watching him impassively. Blood pumped out over the linoleum floor in a wide stain. It ran against the old man's scalp, congealing in his thin hair.

The last thing he saw were many pairs of hands, rising up through the floor and grasping at his body. They clawed at him, claiming him for their own. He was too far gone to feel any fear or surprise.

He didn't take long to die—not counting the sixty years he'd waited for the chance. The clutching hands captured his spirit and dragged it to another hell just as unimaginable. At the same time, another spirit escaped from the room. This was an evil spirit, freed by the old man's death to wander the earth again and wait for someone new to be caught within its spell. It wouldn't take long—it never did. Still, the spirit was impatient.

Even for it, an immortal thing, those sixty years were a long time to wait for its prey to fall.

2

Brendan Craft surveyed the dusty, cluttered room and began changing his mind. Cleaning the place was looking like a long, dirty job and a bad idea.

'This is madness,' he said, trying to sound authoritative. He sneaked a look at Gwen beside him and saw her face setting into a determined expression. She opened her mouth to argue and he quickly went on, 'There's really no point in sorting it out. Perhaps we can put the whole bloody lot into garbage bags and take it down the dump. No one's been in here for years. There can't be anything useful.'

'Hey, this is *your* family history, not mine, pal,' Gwen said. 'But you never know—there might be something valuable among all this junk. A few priceless antiques maybe, or just rich in memories for you.' Her smile slipped as she took a second look at the mess. 'Somewhere in there, anyway.'

'It's my family rubbish dump,' Brendan snorted. 'Rich in spiders and cockroaches and God knows what else. What happens if I get bitten? Are you going to save me?'

'I'm a nurse, not a doctor. And besides, I'm not on duty until nine o'clock tomorrow evening. If something sinks its fangs into you, you'll just have to survive until tomorrow night and drag yourself down to the hospital. Otherwise, you might sue me if I get it wrong.'

'What about just a piece of sticking plaster and a bit of sympathy—or do your union rules cover that, too?'

Gwen wagged a finger at him. 'We know all about you journalists. The smallest injury and you'll blow it all out of proportion. Your bit of sticking plaster will be front-page news in the morning and we'll be fighting it out in the courts for years.' She shook her head. 'I'm sorry, but if you hurt yourself, you're on your own. Don't come crying to me.'

'Compassionate as always,' Brendan muttered, while she grinned cheekily at him.

'Look, you're the one who wanted the room cleared, so stop complaining and let's get on with it. You can't just throw it all away, either. You have to at least *look* for anything valuable.' Gwen flicked her long braid of black hair over her shoulder—it reached nearly down to her waist, then she pulled a pair of rubber gloves from the back pocket of her jeans and tugged them on. 'Come on, start doing something useful.'

He sighed and moved further into the room. Tentatively, he began flipping back the lids of the cardboard boxes to see what was in them.

Brendan and Gwen were in one of the upper rooms of Brendan's family home. He'd moved back in recently, after his mother died. With her passing, the place was empty. Brendan was an only child and his father had passed away ten years before. Since then, despite many attempts to move his mother into something smaller or into a retirement home where she might find some company, the old lady had stubbornly refused to leave and spent several years alone in the big house. Brendan had often felt guilty, giving her the lonely existence while he pursued his own life. He'd promised to himself to move back in when she got too old to be left alone, but the decisive moment never seemed to arrive and now it was too late. His guilt swelled, too, after choosing to live in the house after her death, but it was the most practical thing to do. There was a picture of his parents on their wedding day, framed and sitting on the lounge-room mantelpiece. Sometimes Brendan would study his mother's image, wondering if she understood and forgave him.

Brendan's usual memories of his childhood home were of a house filled with a horde of his mother's relatives, occupying the place as if it were their own. It was a very big house, even by local standards, and had at one point in its history been used as a small repatriation hospital for soldiers returning from the Second World War, before being sold cheaply to Brendan's family. This room was used to store the slow accumulation of belongings and junk that built up over the years, unclaimed or unwanted by the passing relatives—many of whom had since died. Looking at the mess surrounding him, Brendan recalled his mother telling him about hearing voices, saying in a calm and unconcerned way that her dead family came to visit her. This room, he suddenly decided, would be full of those ghosts.

'I'm going off this idea,' he said, running a finger across a shelf and screwing his nose up at the caked dirt.

'It's going to be fun, Bren.'

'No, it's not. It's going to be hard, horrible, shitty work.'

'Just think of it as a grown-up's treasure hunt,' Gwen said, picking her way around some obstacles to the far side of the room. 'You'll love it.'

'I won't, you know. Let's go down to the beach instead and hire a surfcat—have some real fun.'

Turning to face him, Gwen cocked her head to one side and gave him a look.

'Oh-oh,' he said, backing off.

'Are you going to get serious about this, or fool around all afternoon?'

He knew to give in immediately. 'Actually, I can't wait to get started,' he told her meekly.

Gwen had shifted into the big house, too, so they could be together more often. It was an unspoken act of commitment between the two of them, but also a practical move, because their separate careers often kept them apart enough as it was. She was a nurse working at one of the city's bigger hospitals. Until recently, Brendan was a journalist at a daily newspaper, but he'd taken the plunge and resigned, going freelance to give himself more time to tackle some ideas he had for a novel. The idea behind clearing the room had been to set up an office for him. Brendan had a powerful computer which needed a lot of space and he wanted to create a proper work environment.

Still teasing himself with visions of the beach and lazing in the sun, he took in the room with a sweep of his hand. 'Just look at this bloody mess. What a load of shit to inherit! Where's the money hidden in the mattress? The priceless family heirlooms?'

'You won't find them by standing there complaining.' Gwen was now searching through the drawers of a small school desk.

'I don't know why you're so damn keen,' he grumbled. 'What if I worked at the kitchen table?' he tried one last time.

'Don't be a lazy bastard. Come on, it could be interesting. You never know what we might dig up.'

He sighed again, moving forward and gingerly opening the lid of another box. The tired cardboard boxes were spilling their contents onto the floor. Several suitcases lay in a corner, promising mildewed contents, musty odours and sour mothballs. Thick dust was covering everything and cobwebs stretched their tenuous strands across the room, the thin lines gleaming silver in the afternoon sunshine coming through a single grimy window.

Gwen picked up a book and scanned the cover. 'Hey, look! This might be valuable. It's *old*.'

'Gwen, if we're going to go through all this garbage, we're not going to just shuffle it around the room and end up keeping everything. Anything less than the crown jewels goes straight down the dump. I don't care how old it is—I *know* it's all old.'

'But we have to give the books to the Good Samaritans, or someone,' she said, still flipping through the pages.

'Whatever—I don't care. As long as they don't stay here.' Brendan pointed a finger at the floor.

'My! Two minutes ago you wanted to go to the beach! Now, you're the boss.'

'I am—and I still do, but you're not going to let me.'

'You're a rotten grump,' she told him good-naturedly.

'And I love you, too,' he shot back.

Brendan moved about the room and gave everything a quick inspection. He discovered several boxes he could dump immediately. One was a carton of old curtains, faded and moth-eaten. He carried it downstairs and loaded it into the back of his station wagon. One trip like this was enough to convince him the stairs were going to be too awkward. Glancing back up at the house and the window above, he figured out a plan. He went back inside, getting the car keys on the way, and returned to start the car, edging it further down the drive. Then, when he got back upstairs and into the room, he shoved the window as far open as he could and started unceremoniously tossing the other boxes out onto the lawn below.

'Hey, don't kill anyone,' Gwen said, amused.

Another box went, followed by a splintered hatrack, a collection of rotting magazines and a tailor's dummy complete with half-finished frock. Brendan then laboured downstairs twice with loads of books, staying the second time to pack the lot into the car.

Returning to the room once more he pointed at two suitcases. 'Just these, I think, and that'll be a full load.' He picked one up and shook it. 'Light as a feather,' he said. 'Must be clothes.' With a flourish he tossed it through the window. The second case was only slightly heavier. 'Clothes *and* the family bible,' he guessed, grinning.

Out it went.

'You *have* a family bible?' Gwen asked.

'Only kidding,' he admitted. 'I can't remember any of the Craft family ever going near a church—

except to get married, of course.' He absently picked up an ancient, broken vacuum cleaner. 'I'll do a trip to the dump, drop off those books at the Good Samaritans and be back in half an hour. Want anything while I'm out?'

'Grab some coke, or lemonade, will you? This could turn into thirsty work.'

'Damn, that means I'll have to go to the liquor store. I might as well grab a six-pack while I'm there.'

She rolled her eyes at him.

'Well, it's Saturday, right?' He tried to appear hurt when Gwen didn't look impressed.

He stomped down the stairs again, struggling to see his way past his laden arms. Soon Gwen heard the car start and move off down the driveway. She rolled her sleeves up and determined to get as much done as possible before he came back.

When Brendan returned, Gwen was a mess. She was wearing light-coloured clothing, which hadn't been a good move. Her shirt and shorts were stained by the dirt from the room and there was a brown smear across her forehead after wiping a weary hand over it.

'About time,' she said, as Brendan came in carrying a frosty bottle of lemonade and two glasses. 'I suppose you've been skulking around the corner, hoping I would finish before you got back.'

'You look as beautiful as ever,' he said, putting his arm around her shoulders. Gwen was short with a firm, lithe figure and she ducked easily away. 'Forty minutes!' Brendan went on. 'You know, there was a queue at the rubbish dump? Can you believe it?'

'That's urban living for you.'

'Then let's move to the country—hey, you've done wonders!' he gestured at the room.

'That burning smell is the incinerator choking to death on your family history,' she said wryly. 'There's just the one box with stuff I thought you might keep, or at least check before I threw out. The rest of the bags are full of garbage. You can probably leave them out for collection this week.'

'Great. What about that cupboard?'

'I haven't looked. I thought I might leave that for you, lazy-bones,' she grinned, sitting on the floor. Leaning back against the wall, Gwen poured herself a drink.

'Thanks a lot.' He pulled a face and went to the cupboard. Opening the door provoked an avalanche of moulding linen. 'Yuk!' he backed away. 'More rubbish, that's for sure.'

'Out the window, too?'

'Damn right. I'll stuff it into bags downstairs.' He began feeding the linen outside. Next he discovered a pile of crushed and worn shoes at the bottom of the cupboard. He threw those, too. Lastly, Brendan pulled a tin box down from the top shelf and made to toss it out without bothering to check inside it.

'Hey, wait,' Gwen called out, hearing it rattle. 'There's something in it.'

'Who cares?' Brendan was poised in mid-throw.

'I do. Let's have a look.'

He looked at it more closely. It was about the size of a shoe box. He gave it a shake and something clattered inside. 'It's almost empty,' he told her. 'Have a guess.'

She thought for a moment. 'Ammunition?'

He frowned. 'What makes you say that?'

'It's sort of *army* green, don't you think?'

'I suppose so, now that you mention it, but we haven't had any soldiers in our family for generations. Dad was too ill and his father was in the medical corps, I think.'

'Well, let's have a look!' Gwen said, impatiently.

'Okay, hold your horses.' He squatted down beside her.

He struggled to force his fingernails under the lip of the tight-fitting lid. Finally the top sprang off, falling to the floor with a loud, metal clanging.

'Got it,' he said unnecessarily.

'See?' Gwen said. 'I said it looked military.'

Inside the box, lying loosely, were several cloth badges, a military-looking medal and the Rising Sun hat-pin of the Australian Army.

Gwen looked at him excitedly. 'Whose are they?'

'I don't know.' He raised his eyebrows in surprise, then shook the tin so the contents slid around. 'Oh,' he said, his eyes going wide.

'Wow!' Gwen made to grab something from the tin, but Brendan deftly snatched it away from her reach.

'Wait a minute,' he teased her.

She dug her fingers into his ribs.

The moving badges revealed a gleaming, two-dimensional figure about five centimetres long and made of a golden metal. It was in the shape of a hyena, or a wolf, rearing high on its two hind legs. One eye, in the form of a bright green stone, glared malevolently.

'What is it?' Gwen asked breathlessly. 'Brass?'

Brendan plucked it out of the tin and examined it closely. A small node of metal melded to the back with a hole drilled in it had a necklace of stained leather thonging threaded through it.

'I think it's gold,' he said, unsure. 'I suppose brass would have tarnished by now.'

'Gold! Are we rich?'

Brendan laughed. 'I don't think so, but it might be worth a few dollars, I suppose.'

He turned the pendant back and found himself staring into the single green eye. Brendan frowned when he thought he detected a faint glimmer within the stone. When it didn't happen again he dismissed it as a trick of the light.

The golden metal and strange emerald eye twisted back and forth in front of his face, dangling from the strip of leather. The late afternoon sun, still coming through the open window, reflected off the charm and sent dancing pin-points of light chasing around the walls of the room. Brendan held the charm up and stared at it a long time.

He found the charm mesmerising—fascinating,

drawing and pulling at his mind with seductive insistence. Then it was the jewelled eye absorbing all his attention, pushing back the rest of the world until only the green stone filled his vision. Brendan's ears echoed with a dull roaring, blocking out any other sounds, and the periphery of his vision blurred to indistinction.

He had only ever fainted once in his life, after getting up too quickly one morning following a heavy drinking session the night before. Now a small, distant voice warned he might be about to do it again.

'Brendan!' Gwen snapped, bringing him back to reality with a jerk. 'What's wrong?'

Brendan shook his head and tried to clear away the dazed feeling. 'Hell, that was weird,' he said, forcing a smile. 'For a moment I thought I was going to faint.' He pinched the bridge of his nose with his fingers.

'Did you glug down a quick beer in the car, on your way back from the dump?' she asked him ominously.

'No!' he protested. 'I—I bought a six-pack, but they're in the fridge.'

'Then maybe you're coming down with something,' she said more gently, putting her hand on his forehead. 'You feel a bit hot,' she decided, after a moment.

'No, I guess I—ah, haven't really eaten all day. That's probably it.' He shook his head and rubbed his forehead, then asked, 'Want to see this?' He offered the golden figure. Surprising him, Gwen drew back.

'No, thanks,' she said hastily, 'It may be worth some money, but it gives me the creeps. It looks nasty, with that horrid little green eye.'

'Yes, well—' Brendan was momentarily at a loss for words. He dropped the pendant back in the tin and replaced the lid. 'We might look it up at a later date, hey? See what it's about.' Inexplicably, a feeling of relief came over him once the thing was out of his sight. He stood and placed the tin back on the high shelf. 'I'll probably do something about it when I organise this cupboard. I suppose I'd better leave a shelf or two for Jeneatte, in case she wants to leave some of her stuff here.' Jeneatte Beason was a girl who did research for Brendan in her spare time and occasionally typed first-draft articles into the computer from his scribbled notes. 'But it won't be for a while,' he added. 'I want to get the computer settled in first.'

Gwen was surprised at how quickly he was dismissing the tin and its contents. 'But what if it's worth a lot of money?'

'The charm? Oh, I don't think it will be,' he said with a wave of his hand. 'It's probably gold plating, not solid gold, and just cast alloy underneath,' he added, ignoring in his own mind the weighty feel of the pendant.

'Oh,' Gwen shrugged, looking about to make more of an issue over it. She was interrupted by the telephone ringing.

'Do you want to get that?' he asked. He grinned, watching her curse and scramble to her feet in the rush to answer it. Once she'd left the room Brendan's smile faded and he used the time to rest his head back against the wall, closing his eyes. There was still a slightly fuzzy feeling inside his mind. He was still like that when Gwen returned, putting her head through the door.

'I have to go out,' she said. 'Hey, are you okay or not?'

'I'm fine,' he said quickly. 'What's wrong? Where do you have to go?'

'That was one of my trainee nurses. She's studying and I promised her some of my reference books. It's not far and I want to drop them over—so I'll do a quick trip.'

'Can't I do it for you?'

'No, there are a few things I want to point out to her—some pages I think she should read. It won't take me long. You can keep going here,' she added smugly.

'Thanks a heap,' he said.

'Don't worry, you've still got your six-pack.'

He brightened. 'Now, there's an idea.'

Gwen sighed and looked at him with mock exasperation. 'At least try and do something, will you? Just get the cupboard finished, okay?'

'Yes, master,' he replied solemnly. 'The car keys are on the kitchen table.'

Gwen disappeared, calling out that she'd be back soon. Brendan went to the single cardboard box she left for him to check and began rummaging through the contents, taking them back out and spreading them around himself on the floor as he dug deeper. It was mainly a collection of tattered childhood toys and trinkets which Gwen must have assumed to have sentimental value. Brendan didn't agree, wrinkling his nose at the musty smells coming from the box. Near the bottom of the carton were more books and some old photograph albums. Brendan was flicking through one of these, glancing at sepia pictures of people he didn't recognise and who were probably long dead, when he heard the car start and reverse away. He dropped the album and went over to the window, leaning out just in time to see Gwen waving up at the house to him. He waved back as she accelerated down the street.

Leaving the window Brendan stood, strangely undecided, in the middle of the room. After a moment he figured nothing in the last box held any interest or value for him, so he thrust everything back inside. This only took a minute, leaving him again feeling at a loss what to do. His eyes strayed back to the open cupboard and the metal tin on the upper shelf. Without really knowing why Brendan pulled the box out again. This time the lid flipped off easily. His fingers found the leather thonging and he lifted the charm out, looking at it as he absently placed the tin and its lid on one of the lower shelves. He stepped away from the cupboard and into the sunlight. Like before, the light caught the shiny metal and reflected back away again in thin rays of gold, catching motes of dust floating in the air. The small green stone of the figure's eye glimmered prettily in the sunlight, making Brendan hold his breath. A long time passed, as he stared at the charm slowly turning in front of his face.

Suddenly, Brendan's fascination turned to a cold fear when he became aware of a change around him. The narrow beams of reflected sunlight coming from the charm were now cutting through a thin mist filling the room—a mist which was becoming noticeably thicker. Brendan tried to twist around and see if it was smoke coming through the door from another part of the house. His muscles responded slowly and unwillingly. He was somehow being prevented from moving through the white haze. Brendan could only stand there—his hands fallen to his side with the charm dangling unheeded close to the floor—and watch the mist close in. His fear was making him shiver as with the chill of disease and he wanted to run from the room—but he couldn't take a single step towards the door.

When a voice whispered in his ear he cried out, startled. The words were unintelligible, the sound a sibilant hiss. It came again, this time from the other side. Brendan desperately wanted to look all around him at the same time and guard against whoever it was, but he moved sluggishly, like a drunkard beyond controlling himself properly. The mist quickly became full of whispering voices coming from all directions. Some instinct told Brendan he should be very frightened of what the voices were trying to say, so in desperation he clapped his hands over his ears. Closing his eyes tight he didn't feel the charm bouncing on its leather thonging against his arm. The mist seemed to press against his face, caressing his skin.

And something else was trying to work its way inside his mind. A louder whisper, insisting Brendan should listen to it. Trust it. And obey it.

Gwen found him leaning back casually against the open window. He was drinking one of the beers and obviously congratulating himself on a job well done. The room was completely empty, the cupboard closed.

'How are you feeling?' she asked, going over and giving him a kiss, before plucking the beer can from his fingers and taking a drink herself.

'Good, now this is done,' he said, satisfied. 'How about you?'

'Linda makes hard work of studying. She needs to learn how to concentrate on the right subjects, instead of spending too much time on things that are irrelevant for the moment. Still, I think she's going to go far, if she sticks with it.' Gwen changed the subject. 'Anyway, what about us? What are we going to do?'

'I was thinking about a pizza and going to the movies. A treat after our hard day's work.'

'Sounds good, but what about your little turn this afternoon? Don't you think you should have an early night?'

'My little turn—?' Brendan stopped. 'Oh, that. I'd forgotten about it already. I'm sure it's nothing to bother about.' He affected a worried look. 'Hey, please don't make me go to bed early, Mum. I want to go to the pictures.'

Gwen looked at him for a moment, making up her mind. 'You're an idiot,' she said affectionately. 'Okay, let's do it—even if *I* did most of the work in here,' she added. 'That means you can pay for the pizza.'

The movie was good, taking their minds right away from dusty, spare rooms and trips to the rubbish dump. If Brendan gave any thought to the green tin and its contents, and what happened when he opened it a second time, he didn't mention it. As far as Gwen could tell, Brendan seemed fully recovered from his earlier dizzy spell.

Later, with their bellies full of warm pizza, they decided to call it an early night. It was only after settling in bed awhile, with Gwen's slow, rhythmic breathing next to him, that Brendan suddenly remembered the box and what it held. Still, he didn't recall the swirling mist or the whispering, frightening voices, but only the metal tin with its badges and medals inside. He stared at the dark ceiling and pondered on the life of the man who must have owned them, probably risking his life to earn the medals, only to have the recognition of his bravery buried amongst the unwanted relics of a family junk room. It seemed so sad. Sleepily,

Brendan frowned to himself, thinking there might be an angle for a story in it. He tried to concentrate on the idea, but found he was too tired to keep the effort going.

He drifted into a deeper sleep and he allowed himself to fall into the beginning of a dream with its unbidden, flickering, images racing across his mind's eye. Without warning, a scene came to him with such clarity that Brendan stirred and nearly awoke with surprise, his eyelids fluttering, but the dark room kept him sleeping—and the dream ran on.

Long rows of men in khaki stood under a burning sun, a hot, coarse sand under their feet. Brendan was a part of the long lines, sensing the other people standing each side of him and continuing on into the distance. Everyone was dressed the same. He could even feel the heat of the sun through his clothes. Then, before he could make any sense of it all, the dream changed and now Brendan lay under a sky of brilliant stars, more brilliant than ever he'd witnessed through smoggy city nights. Again, other men were all around him in a great gathering. There was a constant murmur of conversation, but Brendan was alone. It was a weird, unsettling feeling to be surrounded by so many other people, yet be somehow alienated. As he lay there, trying to understand, Brendan felt something stir in the sand beneath his legs and he raised himself on his elbows to look down the length of his body.

To his utter astonishment and horror, a hand thrust itself up through the sand and began groping blindly in the air. In the bright starlight, he could see the flesh was cracked and mottled with decomposition, the fingernails rotting and ruined.

Before Brendan could react, the hand grasped the calf of his leg, the loathsome fingers gripping strongly. He tried to pull away, but the hand held on tighter. He yelled for help, but the sound came out as a terrified croak, so he hacked out a cough, clearing his throat, and shouted again in a high, wavering voice.

No one took any notice. The indistinct shapes around him carried on their muted discussions.

Brendan scrabbled to get a grip on the loose sand and drag himself away. He dug trenches on either side of his body, getting nowhere. His terror was mounting, turning him frantic. Jack-knifing forward, Brendan struck out with his closed fist at the hand, but it was difficult to deal an effective blow without hurting himself. A putrid stench was rising out of the ground now. Gagging, he hammered at the hand again. In his fear, Brendan missed and painfully struck his shin. He didn't hear his own pitiful crying for help.

He felt himself being sucked down, drawn into the sand. The hand disappeared beneath the surface, taking his leg with it. Like quicksand, Brendan was being pulled under to drown in the dirt and join the dead thing already under the soil.

In seconds he was up to his crotch, both his legs buried. Filtering through his panic Brendan felt a second hand beneath the ground grip his other leg and the process accelerated. The rough sand parted like thick mud and took him to the waist. Giving up any pretence of fighting the thing that held him, Brendan began grappling instead for anything to stop himself being drawn under, but his grasping fingers felt only the loose, useless sand. His clothing was riding up over his body, the legs of his trousers pushed up above his knees. His shirt was wrenched out of his waistband. Brendan sank to his chest and he pathetically started imitating a swimmer treading water, thrashing at the sand with his arms with wide, circling motions. Without knowing it, he began uttering over and over again meaningless half-words, his fear robbing him of coherent thoughts or words.

With a final, vicious jerk, stretching his spine agonisingly, Brendan's head was dragged beneath the surface. Gritty sand forced its way into his mouth and pushed against his eyelids. A choking pressure against his chest forced the air from his lungs. With his limbs held rigid by the surrounding dirt Brendan put his last strength into a wailing, despairing scream.

'Brendan! Brendan! For Christ's sake, wake up!'

Someone shouting in his face penetrated the facade of the nightmare and slowly brought him back to the real world. The blackness of the suffocating sand turned to harsh electric light. The weight on his chest became Gwen, professionally straddling him and pinning down his thrashing limbs. His face stung sharply—she'd slapped him more than once. With a groan he slowly relaxed, the tension of the dream leaking from his body and leaving him weak. He focused on her concerned face.

'What the hell was that all about?' she asked, her anxiety making her angry. Beads of sweat lined Gwen's upper lip and spotted her brow. For the moment he couldn't speak. She went on, 'At first, I thought you were having a bloody fit, then I realised it must be a nightmare—and a damn good one at that. You were throwing yourself about so much I was sure you were going to hurt yourself.' Gwen released his arms so she could lean back.

'Sorry,' he whispered, feeling a harshness in his throat.

Gwen gingerly massaged a hot, red mark on her upper arm. 'You got me once,' she said ruefully.

'Ouch,' he said for her, reaching out and tenderly touching the mark with his fingertips. He used the moment to chase away the last shreds of the nightmare lingering in his imagination.

Gwen asked softly, 'What the hell were you dreaming about? Can you remember?'

Brendan hesitated, unwilling to deliberately re-open his mind to the images. 'I was being buried alive,' he said simply.

She looked at him, surprised. 'Good nightmare.'

'Top class,' he agreed with a shaky sigh. He nodded at her perched on top of him. 'Hey, that's a good hold, too.' He tried a smile.

Gwen rolled off, collapsing on her back beside

him. 'I've done enough time in the looney ward. Some of those folks can come out ready to take on the world. Mind you, I didn't have to hold anyone down on my own.'

'Yeah—well, sorry about that,' he said again.

'No, don't be silly. You couldn't help yourself.' She frowned and looked at him. 'Have you done it before? You haven't since I've known you.'

'I don't think so. Maybe as a young kid, but Mum and Dad never mentioned it.'

A connection came into her mind and Gwen opened her mouth to remind him of his strange affliction that afternoon. She stopped herself at the last moment—it would be best left until the morning. Instead, she said, 'Too many beers this afternoon.'

'Bullshit.' This time his grin was more like his old self. 'I'd only had two before we left for the movies. Too much pizza, more like.'

'Okay, so give them both up.'

'No way. Be unhealthy and happy, that's my motto.'

Gwen checked his face once more. Satisfied he was shaken, but not actually ill, she stretched across and flicked off the bedside light. With a start, Brendan found he wasn't so comfortable in a dark room any more. He reached out, pulling Gwen closer.

'Come on, are you really okay?' she asked seriously.

'Yeah, just a bit shaky,' he admitted.

'Want to leave the light on?'

'No!' He tried to sound offended. 'I'm a big boy now.' He felt her shrug.

'Just asking.'

Brendan kissed Gwen's shoulder to wish her goodnight. She turned over and gave his thigh a squeeze. He felt a sudden, strong urge to make love and immerse himself in her comfort, to block out the disturbing nightmare and the ominous darkness pressing in all around him. He began running his hand over Gwen's body, searching for the places he knew aroused her. They were both naked, the way they always slept except for the coldest part of winter. She started to respond slowly, sensing his need and growing steadily more excited until they were both wide awake, fervently caressing and kissing. Brendan used a sort of desperate strength he never had before, surprising Gwen, but she didn't complain. And he tried to make it last as long as he could.

When they were finished he was quiet, but Gwen mistook it for the usual comfortable silence that followed their love-making and soon fell asleep. Brendan lay there a long time, listening to the old house creak and groan around him. They used to be familiar, comforting noises.

Now they put him on edge.

3

February 1915, Mena Camp, Egypt

Ben Hamilton was chewing thoughtfully on his thumbnail and regarding the nearby pyramids with one eye. 'How do you reckon they built them?' he asked of no one in particular.

Loel answered. He was a small, dark man who had emigrated from Malta to Australia to find a new life. Delighted with his adoptive country, he'd enlisted at the outbreak of the war, only to be sent back to his native part of the world to fight. He spoke with a strong accent and a command of the English language which often left a lot to be desired, as did his understanding of some other things Australian. From somewhere, during the months of training, he had earned the nickname 'Squibby'.

'The blacks,' he ventured. 'They would've used the blacks, right?'

'The blacks?' Adrian Galther tipped the brim of his hat back so he could stare contemptuously at Loel. Galther was a short, wiry man, normally surly and ill-tempered. 'They don't have blacks in Egypt, you fool.'

Loel looked hurt and Hamilton offered gently, 'They didn't have blacks—not like we do, anyhow. But they did have a sort of system with slaves at the very bottom of the ladder. They rated them about the same as we do our blacks—worse, really.'

Loel stared at the pyramids and pursed his lips. 'Big job,' he decided eventually, making Hamilton laugh.

Galther was pulling a wry face as he threw a handful of desert sand into the air. 'God knows why anyone would want to build anything here anyway.'

The others watching agreed silently. The seven soldiers of the Australian Imperial Force sat in a bored circle on the sand, their rifles carefully stacked together close by, the muzzles pointing skyward. The sun beat down remorselessly, but there was nowhere to go for respite. The flat, featureless desert was spread out around them, broken only by a few low, sandy ridges and the jutting, almost intrusive ancient pyramids. There was no shade at all, and no tents available for the troops. No one in the High Command back in Australia had realised tents might be needed, while the administration already in Egypt to meet the arriving soldiers assumed tents would be standard issue. At least the men didn't have to suffer the killing heat of the northern summer—yet.

The morning had been taken up with repetitive exercises and marching drill. Another hour was wasted standing in the long kitchen queues for the midday meal. Two ladles of thick stew and a handful of hard biscuits for lunch, followed by a mug of strong, sweet tea. While the food was far from wholesome or appetising, many of the men came from poorer homes and thought themselves to be eating well.

For the seven men, now there was the afternoon to endure. Someone had realised that training manoeuvres in the heat did more harm than good, the toll exacted on the men through heat exhaustion and dehydration too high. The High Command's solution was to reduce the daily hours of training from eight down to five. Meanwhile, the men were advised to rest and conserve their energy, which usually meant a mass exodus in the direction of Cairo for long nights of drinking and patronising the local brothels. Some regiments were required to stay in the camp to act as security—as these soldiers were on this day. But in the evenings the troops on duty often sneaked away too, and were rarely missed.

'So, where do you reckon we're going?' another of them, called McAllen, asked hopefully, reviving the endless discussion of where the fledgling army would be deployed. McAllen had become notorious for starting this same conversation almost daily.

'I told you, it's *got* to be France,' someone declared.

'Where else?'

'They're saying the Western Front is like a miller's wheel, using men for grist,' Galther said morosely.

Hamilton was shaking his head. 'But it doesn't make sense.'

'Who knows? It's just what I heard.'

'No, I mean France. Why train troops in the desert, if you're going to send them to France? We'd be better off training in England.'

'This ain't training,' said Nick Story, the youngest. 'All we do is march around in circles and shoot at bits of wood. I've been doing that since I was seven, without the bloody marching.'

'But you're not prepared for the bits of wood shooting back,' Gordon Rogers told him, pointing the stem of his pipe at him.

'I'm used to ducking my old man's fists. That's good enough.'

Rogers looked at him soberly. 'The German is a good fighting man, make no mistake about it. All those countries in Europe have been squabbling with each other for centuries. Their armies are made up of professionals, see?' Rogers had been a teacher before he joined up and this, along with his extra years, meant his opinions were regarded highly. 'Mark my words, boys. If we get into this new trench warfare we keep hearing about, we'll be lucky if half of us here come out alive.' He looked ruminatively at his pipe for a moment, as if regretting what he'd said.

There was an uncomfortable silence, broken by Story. 'But the war'll be over before we even get there! Everyone says so!'

'That was *last* year,' Rogers sounded almost apologetic. 'God knows how long it will last now. Some people are predicting years.'

'Years? Are we going to be camped in this damned desert for years?'

'We should be so lucky! No, I'd say we're going to be in the thick of it sooner than we think. This rumour about Turkey might have some value, I'd say.'

'Half of us, you say?' someone asked. His name was Oakley, which had immediately earned him the nickname of 'Annie'. He looked at Rogers, his face worried. 'Half of us will be killed?'

Rogers opened his mouth to reply, then stopped and shook his head unconvincingly. 'Probably not. I'm just an old bastard who worries too much,' he smiled reassuringly.

Story grinned, 'Then I say we should all go into Cairo tonight and paint the town red! Just in case Teacher here is right. What do you say?'

They all brightened at the idea, except for Hamilton.

'We've got a long march tomorrow,' he reminded them. 'And a night on the rot-gut will mean my water bottle will be empty far too soon for my liking.'

'You don't have to drink,' Oakley said. He was a family man, constantly fretting over leaving his loved ones for the army, but at the same time enjoying this second chance at his youth, free from the responsibilities of home.

'With you fellows? You must be joking!'

Hamilton influenced the others more than he knew, except perhaps Rogers. They all considered the wisdom of the long hike into Cairo, followed by a bout of drinking, when there was some hard training to follow in the morning.

'Well, it's early days yet,' Story decided, wisely backing down while support was weak. 'So, are you blokes coming to the pyramids? Some fellow has a wager he can be the fastest to climb to the top. I'm going to have a look.'

Everybody rose from the sand, brushing the clinging grit from their clothes. It was either go and watch, or succumb to the boredom of the afternoon and stay in the small square designated their area by simple, coloured flags driven into the sand.

It took several minutes walking the distance across to the base of the nearest pyramid. Apart from Loel, who possessed the squat and swarthy stature of a southern European, the men were typical of the Australian soldiers. Tall, lean and dark-skinned from a lifetime in the sun. Only Galther was physically shorter than his companions and he made this worse, walking with a slight stoop.

No one knew who the ancient pyramid tomb was dedicated to, nor did they care, aside from a passing expression of interest made by Rogers. From a distance they saw a small crowd already gathering at the foot of the sloping stonework. On closer inspection two men were furtively taking bets.

'It's no big deal,' Oakley said, looking up at the peak of the pyramid. 'I've been up to the top of this one myself.'

'If you're careful,' Hamilton reminded him.

There were five runners in the competition, spreading themselves evenly along the base of the stone and ready to climb. The seven had arrived just in time to see the race. A brief flurry of final betting was occurring, but the crowd and contestants alike were starting to get restless. One of the climbers took off his shirt exposing a tanned, muscled torso. The others followed his example and removed theirs too.

'Are you going to have a bet, Ben?' Galther looked at Hamilton with eager eyes, but Hamilton shook his head.

'Nah, I don't know any of these blokes. They all look pretty even to me. It could be anyone's race.'

Oakley sidled up close and said quietly, 'I know one. That man on this end was at my basic training camp, and I saw him climb the ropes like a monkey.' When Hamilton raised a doubting eyebrow, Oakley added, 'See the tattoo on his arm? The anchor? I reckon he's ex-navy, or something.'

'Just because he can climb a rope, doesn't mean he can climb a wall,' Galther said sceptically, although the chance of some inside information was exciting him. Oakley shrugged and moved casually towards one of the bookies. This was enough for Galther, who hurried after him. The competitors were still impatiently waiting for a start, while the bookies milked the crowd for every last wager. Galther and Oakley managed to have their bets accepted.

'Come on! Let's get on with it!' one of the climbers shouted.

Reluctantly, the bookmakers waved away any more punters and moved to the base of the pyramid.

'I'll give you a "steady" and a "go",' one called aloud. 'First man to the top wins. No interfering with another competitor.' This brought some ribald laughter from the spectators. The bookie stood back and raised his hand.

'Steady!'

He waited until all five were ready, crouched over, their feet in the sand and their hands poised above the stone.

'Go!'

A roar went up from the crowd. Four of the climbers immediately threw themselves at the stones, scrabbling and slipping their way several feet upwards. The fifth, the man with the tattoo, calmly set off placing his hands and feet carefully. He moved smoothly and quickly overtook the others, who were soon panting and gasping from their exertions. Often they needed to pause and catch their breath properly. The watching crowd greeted these with laughter and raucous encouragement. Shortly, only one man apart from the tattooed soldier looked to be in the race and this was only through stubborn determination and the strength of his youth, not any climbing skills.

'This is a one-horse race!' Galther cried exultantly, above the shouting.

In the bright sunshine the sunburned figures shrank in size as they gained height, becoming like dark insects against the sandstone of the pyramid. The soldiers below shouted themselves hoarse, urging on their own favourite. The climbers responded and struggled on. A minute later the leader neared the top. He knew he was well ahead of the others and paused to look down. Only the youth was close, having scaled nearly three-quarters the distance. The remaining three, struggling for breath between gasps of laughter and too exhausted to go on, were clinging to the stone around the halfway mark. The crowd began calling for the tattooed man to finish the climb and bring an end to it. The youth, though, took it as encouragement and put in a last burst of effort, clawing at the stone.

Then he slipped and fell several feet to a narrow ledge.

At first it looked like he would save himself, as he managed to hold on and keep his balance, but he writhed and clutched in pain at his body. A good-natured 'whoa!' went up from the spectators, then the men fell silent, realising things were more serious than they looked. A few began yelling a different, anxious encouragement, but the young soldier rolled off the stone towards the ledge below. Only this time he kept falling. He started tumbling terribly and screamed over the dreadful cracking sound of a limb breaking. An instant later his head struck the stone and he plunged head-over-heels down the uneven slope like a rag doll. One of the other climbers below cried out with alarm when it appeared the falling body would strike him on the way through. The man scrambled frantically sideways and, for a moment, nearly lost his grip too.

By the time the youth's body reached the ground he was cartwheeling and bouncing sickeningly off the stone. He rebounded once off the hard-packed sand at the base of the pyramid and landed at the feet of the watching soldiers, who by then were quickly stepping backwards.

The boy's head and face were a mess of blood. From the angles of his contorted limbs it was obvious both his arms and possibly one leg were broken.

And there was no doubt about his neck.

Shocked, everyone stared down at the body. Hamilton was close and he felt sickened, looking at the dead boy's face. The spell was broken by somebody running off, screaming for a medic. The bookmaker who started the race stooped down next to the corpse. The bookie was a leathery, experienced sergeant who'd seen action in South Africa.

He shook his head sadly and called aloud, 'No point in yelling for a medic. The boy's dead.'

For several minutes they all stood helplessly until two men with a stretcher pushed their way through. After taking a quick look they lifted the body onto the litter and threw a blanket over the youth's chest and head.

'Make way,' the lead bearer called gruffly. The watching men parted, allowing them through.

A sombre silence fell over the soldiers.

'Hey, look,' Galther tapped Oakley on the shoulder and pointed. The tattooed soldier was perched on top of the pyramid. They could see from the way he held his shoulders and stared helplessly down that the scene below had shaken him badly.

'It doesn't matter,' Oakley shrugged. 'I don't think I want the money now.'

'I reckon a bet's a bet.' Galther waited for some support, but Oakley didn't offer any. 'Well, I'm going to see him, anyway,' he muttered, looking at the ground as he shuffled towards the bookmaker. Several other soldiers were drifting around too, unsure of what to do about their money.

Hamilton led the way around to the opposite side of the pyramid. The sun had fallen appreciably into the west now, finally creating an area of shadow which grew out from the base of the stone.

'Poor fellow,' he said, sitting in the sand and leaning back against the lowest block.

Story was pale. 'Yeah, what a way to go—and he misses out on seeing some action, too,' he added oddly. 'Still, I suppose we'd better get used to seeing that sort of mess. Dead bodies, I mean.'

'Just make sure *you're* not the one that's in the mess,' Rogers told him gravely.

'Hey, I'll be right,' Story shook his head quickly. 'I know I won't get shot.'

'Shot?' Hamilton looked at him with wry amusement. Witnessing the death of the climber was making him feel particularly mortal. 'What about getting blown to pieces by a shell? Bayoneted by some Prussian? Or run over by a gun carriage? Wars are great places for accidents, you know.'

'And disease,' Rogers added unkindly. 'We've already lost about two dozen blokes to pneumonia, I heard.'

'Pneumonia! How the devil do you catch bloody pneumonia in this heat?' Story laughed, then stopped when he saw Rogers was serious. 'Well, I don't care. I haven't come all this way just to get knocked by some stupid German whose breath stinks of sausage, or to get sick, either. I promised my mum I'd bring her home a medal or two. I'll be a hero, that's what.'

They couldn't help laughing at his youthful exuberance, the pall of gloom caused by the climbing accident already fading. Hamilton figured Story would be fairly typical.

It's always the other fellow who's going to get killed, never yourself, he thought, glancing sideways at the youth.

Loel was waving his arms and saying, 'Well? Are we going into Cairo tonight, or not?'

'No, I don't think so,' Hamilton said, but looking undecided. 'That march tomorrow will bloody kill me, if I'm sick from being on the grog. Besides, I'm getting a bit tired of Cairo. It's all the damned same, I reckon.'

'See how you feel after the evening meal,' McAllen suggested, his eyes sly.

'I can see you blokes will nag at me like old women until I change my mind.' Hamilton grinned at him, then shrugged. 'Okay, we'll see.'

A passing soldier was calling out that a cricket game had started near the main camp entrance. As they got to their feet to follow, Galther appeared after settling his claim with the bookie.

'Any blood on the money?' Oakley called out harshly.

'A bet's a bet,' Galther said again. 'That bookie would've kept my money, if that tattooed bloke hadn't won, right?'

'Maybe.' Disgusted, Oakley dismissed the subject with a wave. 'I don't give a shit, anyhow. We're going to play cricket. Are you coming?'

Galther nodded and trotted to catch up.

With so many men involved, it wasn't a normal

game of cricket. Half-a-dozen balls circulated, meaning the batsmen at both ends faced up to a barrage of bowls. They only ran between the wickets for the fun of it, forcing the fielders to scramble for the struck ball. When a batsman was dismissed he was replaced by the man responsible, such as the bowler or perhaps a fielder taking a catch.

The game broke up when the kitchens opened for the evening meal. The men wandered casually over to their packs and got the tin dishes they used for all their meals unless they were eating rations straight from the can. Waiting in line, Hamilton found himself standing behind Oakley.

'Look at that, Ben,' Oakley nodded at something in the distance. 'I never thought I'd see it in the middle of all this bloody desert.'

Hamilton followed his gaze and blinked with surprise. They'd all been so absorbed with the cricket no one noticed a line of ominous, black thunder clouds filling the horizon.

'Next thing you'll be telling me is that it's going to rain,' Oakley said.

'It looks that way.'

'It *never* rains in the desert,' Story called from further back in the line.

'Of course it does, you bloody idiot—just not very much,' someone nearby told him amiably.

Darkness fell. Apart from in the direction of the storm-laden horizon, the sky presented its usual stunning display of stars, paling only near the half-full moon. It wasn't long after dusk that the lightning started in earnest. Jagged lines of blue-white light stabbed at the earth, bringing to the soldiers rolling booms of sound which many imagined, because of their circumstances, might be similar to the sounds of a distant battle. The men sat in small groups, taking time over their meals and watching the approaching clouds. The storms moved quickly closer, the lightning vivid and bright as it crawled across the sky. The thunder became startling, explosive cracks.

Hamilton managed to resist his friends' urging to walk the five miles to Cairo, preferring instead to watch the sky. So everyone stayed, sitting on the sand and swapping yarns about cyclones, storms, droughts and anything else to do with the weather. The first stirring of a breeze laced with the smell of rain brought an air of expectancy. The vanguard clouds of the storm now blotted out the stars above and the lightning seemed to strike the ground so close it made the earth tremble. The flashes of light revealed a towering, threatening bulk of angry cloud above. On the ground, in the storm's path, the swarming multitude of soldiers shown in hard black-and-white relief with every lightning flash seemed to be wavering in fear. But in fact many of the men were dancing and fooling about in anticipation, waiting for the clean, cooling rain.

'I think we're going to get wet,' Oakley announced unnecessarily.

'Who cares?' Loel called back happily.

'Where are we going to find cover?'

They all looked at each other for a moment, then simultaneously burst into laughter with Rogers yelling, 'We don't!'

They all added together, a chorus of shouting, 'Because there's *no bloody tents!*'

A strange rumbling sound began to grow, interrupting their laughing, and it was McAllen who pointed, calling, 'Look!' His shout started a ripple of excitement through the ranks. 'Wait for the next lightning.'

The next burst of brilliant light showed a fog-like bank advancing towards them across the desert.

'It's a fog!' Galther cried, amazed.

'No, it's not, you dumb bastard. It's rain!'

It was a wall of rain, falling so hard the men were hearing it pound into the sand. The sight triggered a hive of activity as men belatedly began trying to protect their packs and kits of extra clothing. No one possessed an oilskin or anything similar. Some men buried their things in the sand. Most were concerned with keeping dry their stocks of tobacco and matches.

The first drops of rain were large and gentle, plopping down and bringing cries of delight. Then a curtain of near-hail swept over the soldiers, soaking them instantly and changing their cries to yelps of pain as the rain stung their exposed skin. Still, some of the men danced with pure joy in the downpour, linking arms and swinging each other around with wild energy.

'Bloody marvellous!' Loel bellowed at the others

above the noise. It was one of his favourite Australian expressions.

'Bloody marvellous,' Hamilton agreed, slapping him on the back. Rivulets of water streamed off his hat and down his face. They both had their shoulders hunched against the rain. The storm crackled and exploded around them. Lightning hissed through the air, making some men duck instinctively.

The storm continued for over ten minutes, lashing at the soldiers as they made futile attempts to seek cover. Some of them ran to the pyramids and huddled against the stone. Everyone expected the rain to abate as fast as it appeared, but only the shattering thunder and lightning moved away from the camp, leaving behind a steady downpour that quickly lost its novelty value.

'This is all very well,' Rogers said to Hamilton as he plucked his shirt away from his body. 'But what do we do now?' They were huddled together in a tight group, having to shout to be heard. Along with coping in the storm, the men were thrown in pitch blackness, the countless fires of the camp instantly extinguished by the downpour. The lightning tended to be more a blinding hindrance than a help. The surrounding sand was now a hard-packed crust with pools of water everywhere.

'How should I know?' Hamilton asked good-naturedly.

'There's only one place that's warm and dry right now,' Oakley announced, a mischievous grin on his face.

'It's already dark, and it's five bloody miles!'

'So? Are you gonna sleep? It's pissing down with rain, for Christ's sake.'

'Okay, okay,' Hamilton relented. 'Anyway, maybe with the rain they'll call off tomorrow's training.'

Oakley cheered and gave him a thumbs-up.

They left the camp and began walking towards Cairo, tramping down the narrow road that had become a main thoroughfare since the army arrived and was now a muddy, difficult track. The roadway was busy. Soldiers swarmed in both directions and there were several mounted Lighthorsemen trying to corral loose horses alarmed by the storm. Senior officers dashed to and fro on their own animals, or in carriages, finding some sort of panic in the change of weather. They shouted meaningless orders which everyone ignored, while the horses' hooves sprayed huge sheets of mud and water.

The hard training of the past months allowed the seven men to maintain a fast pace, despite the clinging, wet sand and the constant interruptions to their rhythm caused by other traffic. Soon the lights of Cairo sparkled through the rain, beckoning them to even greater effort.

'Where are we going?' Hamilton called breathlessly. They were walking in single file to one side of the track. The lightning, accompanied by long grumbles of thunder, was still close enough to illuminate the terrain for miles around.

'The Wozzer, of course,' Story threw over his

shoulder. He had to dodge to one side as a horse-drawn guncarriage, the gun litter crowded with drunken artillery men, splashed past on its way back to Mena.

'Why don't we try and get into Shepheard's? Everybody's soaking wet, so they might not notice the difference.'

'And bump into one of our own officers? We're on duty, remember? Not bloody likely, mate.'

'I forgot we were the duty mob,' Hamilton sighed as he walked. So it was going to be the 'Wozzer' again—short for Haret El Wasser, which was as close to a red light district as anything in Cairo came. They carried on in silence, saving their breath for the brisk walking, and hurrying with a quiet urgency, as they looked forward to the first drinks.

The transition from rural areas to urban dwellings happened very quickly. A line of white houses announced the beginnings of the city and the cramped, high-density lifestyle of the civilised Arab. Soon, the soldiers were filing their way through narrow alleyways on a familiar route. In the darkness around them, naked children played in the rain. Most of the buildings were lit by oil-lamps or candles, the warm glow spilling past closed blinds and shutters and reflecting off the slick, wet stonework. Hamilton felt safe in the company of so many companions. Normally, his eyes would be searching the dark shadows for any would-be attackers hoping to snare a soldier with a fat purse.

Tonight he took the time to peek, as they passed, at the Arabs through any uncovered windows.

They were, he decided, a poor lot indeed. Even the advent of rain hadn't seemed to have cheered them up any.

The bad weather had little effect on business in the Wozzer. Haret El Wasser was a combination of dozens of drinking houses and a red-light district of extremely dubious hygienic quality. There was also a bazaar of hundreds of stalls selling everything imaginable. The bars each offered their own brew of wine, often more toxic than alcoholic, but the friendly invasion of soldiers drank it anyway. It got you drunk, which was the desired effect, regardless of how close it came to poisoning you at the same time.

The Wozzer, as always, was a press of people. The soldiers pushed their way through the crowds, Arabs harassing them and shouting in their faces every step of the way. The rain added a new dimension to the stench of so many bodies close together. A mildewed, sour smell filled the air. Normally the street was well lit, but the rain had doused many of the open flames and left a lurid, eerie glow from the surviving lights as they threw dancing shadows across the walls.

'I don't care where we go, as long as we get there soon,' Story called. 'Follow me!' He plunged through the crowds, aiming with great determination for a particular doorway. Most of the bars had been renamed by the Australians for their own convenience. Thus the one they were heading for, while it had an indecipherable Arabic sign across the portal, was known as 'The Post Office', because of the predominant red paintwork.

The inside was packed with soldiers. It seemed everyone was roaring a yarn or an insult at somebody else. The noise was tremendous, the air thick with tobacco smoke and the smell of wet woollen clothing. While the others stayed close to the doorway, Oakley and Story fought their way to the counter, returning eventually with seven crude bottles of wine.

'Cheers, gentlemen,' Oakley distributed the bottles. 'Ain't this better than sitting in the rain?' They answered him by drinking long. All of them finished with pained expressions on their faces, but only Rogers bothered to comment.

'Christ, Annie! What the hell is this shit?'

'I beg your pardon? What sort of bloody language is that from a schoolteacher?' Oakley shot back. 'Hell, don't blame me.'

'Well, what do you expect? Are you trying to bloody poison us?'

They laughed and Story said, peering into his bottle, 'I don't know. I don't reckon it's all that bad.'

'How the hell would you know?' Galther scoffed at him. 'You'd never even seen a drink until you got here. You've never had a *real* drink.'

'Maybe not.' Story unwrapped one finger from around the neck of the bottle to point at him. 'But you can be bloody sure I'll have a couple when I get home.' They all loudly agreed with that, nearly drowning out Story who added, 'Which reminds me. I have to do something about that, before we go back to camp tonight.'

'Do what?' Hamilton squinted at him. He'd had to wait while Oakley cajoled Galther into going and buying another round, on the strength that he'd collected his wager from the bookie that afternoon. 'What are you going to do, Nick?' Hamilton pressed.

Story looked uncomfortable. 'I want to buy something, that's all.'

'Buy something? What?' They all leaned closer to hear, sensing some fun at the younger man's expense.

'Well,' Story squirmed, then changed to become stubbornly defensive. 'I was just thinking about what Teacher here had to say about how many of us might come back, you know?' They looked blankly back at him. 'You know—he reckoned only half of us might survive the war, right? Well, I thought I might pick up something to help me out. Get me home. Just something—' he shrugged.

'The pox?' Loel asked, delighted. 'You want to get the pox so they send you home?'

It was true the authorities, in an effort to rid the ranks of an unruly minority, had taken to punishing any appreciable misdemeanours by simply shipping the offenders back to Australia for immediate discharge. Catching a venereal disease, aside from the health complications, qualified a soldier for this, although the regulations were primarily aimed at more serious offences.

'Get fucked, Squibby,' Story growled. 'I'm going to be up there fighting with the best of them. I *am* going to be the best of them!' He poked himself in the chest, 'I told you, I'm going to get a medal or two.'

'So what are you talking about?' Hamilton asked.

'I don't know,' he shrugged again. 'A good luck charm—a rabbit's foot, or something.' He waited for the inevitable jokes, but his friends were more interested than amused.

'You don't believe in that sort of stuff, do you?' Hamilton couldn't keep a smile off his face.

'Why not? Sometimes I do. Haven't you got a lucky number? Or a lucky colour?'

Hamilton was taken aback. 'When I was young, I suppose. I don't think of it much now, though.'

'Well, there you go.' Story looked relieved he'd come out of the matter with his pride intact. Galther interrupted, arriving with seven fresh bottles of wine. Oakley nudged him as he struggled to hand them around without dropping any.

'Nick here reckons he's going to get a good luck charm tonight—to get him through the war in one piece.'

'What a load of shit,' Galther grunted.

After finishing this round of drinks, they changed bars—and kept changing, working their way from one end of the Wozzer to the other on the same side of the street, before repeating the feat on the opposite side to return to where they started. They got very drunk, but adrenalin and the euphoria of their new, exciting lifestyle kept them going. However, Hamilton judged their successful return to the 'Post Office' was a good time to start heading back to Mena Camp. The prospect of the morning's forced march was finally getting some serious consideration. The others grudgingly agreed and after a last drink they all trooped outside to begin the journey back to camp. Then Story stopped them as they left the fringes of the bazaar.

'Hey! Hey wait! I wanna ask this fellow about a rabbit's foot.' He stumbled toward a ragged stall set apart from the rest near the end of the street.

It was little more than an old tent thrown across a sagging wooden frame. Water was pooling in parts of the canvas, threatening to bring the structure down. Two small lamps sputtered in the rain, which was now a steady drizzle and drifting in the sides of the tent. The vendor's wares were scattered across three splintered packing crates, tended by an old man perched on something low, its identity hidden by his flowing Arabic clothes. He regarded the approaching soldiers warily.

'You speakee English?' Story demanded, wobbling uncertainly in front of the crates. The old man answered him with a curt nod. Story gestured at the modest collection of merchandise. 'You got a rabbit's foot? A rabbit's foot? Understand?' The Arab regarded him blankly.

'Do they have rabbits in Egypt?' Oakley asked Rogers, settling down on a doorstep to wait.

McAllen stretched out on the ground and fell instantly asleep. Only Hamilton wandered over for a look.

'I don't think so,' Rogers replied. 'Otherwise, we'd probably be eating the bastards.' Oakley nodded slowly at the wisdom of this.

A few yards up the street Galther was throwing up in the shadows, while Loel patted him sympathetically on the back. He was thumping him too hard, but Galther was too busy vomiting to protest. He flapped his hands ineffectively behind his back at the grinning Maltese.

'A good luck charm?' Story was trying again. At this the Arab smiled and nodded. He stood, revealing he'd been sitting on an ancient sawhorse, and rummaged through one of the piles of goods. He produced a stone scarab beetle.

'This one very lucky,' the old man claimed in fractured English. 'And very old. Very, very old.' His voice was painfully husky and Hamilton, listening from the side, thought it must have been the result of a lifetime's haranguing in the bazaar. The Arab showed his years with deep, tired lines on his face and a bowed back, but his eyes sparkled clearly.

'Shit,' Story pulled a disgusted face. 'You can get these things anywhere, and you all say they're *very, very old*,' he mimicked.

'It is real!' The Arab looked suitably mortified.

'Yeah, yeah, right.' Story took the amulet and tossed it up and down. 'But is it lucky?'

'It will bring the smile of any god,' the old man said, smiling slyly and sensing a sale.

'Where I'm going he'll want to be laughing his fucking socks off, mate, not just smiling.'

'The world is full of old soldiers,' the Arab reminded him gently.

'Right.' Story inspected the beetle more closely. 'How much?' he asked, finally.

Hamilton looked on with amusement, intrigued Story seemed so sincere in thinking he could purchase good fortune. When money eventually changed hands and Story walked away, satisfied, Hamilton made to follow. Then he noticed Galther was still being ill in the shadows. Not wishing to go too close in case it triggered a similar reaction in himself, he decided to pick through the goods on display while he waited for Galther to finish.

'You wish to purchase one, too?' the Arab asked quietly, once Story was out of hearing.

'No,' Hamilton answered absently, his eyes idly searching through the merchandise. 'I don't believe in that sort of thing.'

Hamilton purposely kept his gaze away from the Arab in an effort to discourage any tirade of salesmanship. He didn't see the man's eyes turn more sly and hard, his tongue flickering quickly over his lips before he uttered, 'But you saw a man die today, I think. It so easily could have been you. These are matters of luck and you need—what is the word?—*protection* from such things.' The old man's voice was soft, yet strangely insistent. An acquired skill, Hamilton thought. It took a moment for him to realise what the Arab had said.

'Yeah, but that was a stupid race up a pyramid, not a—' Hamilton began, and stopped abruptly. 'Hey, how do you know what I saw?' he asked, a cold feeling growing in his stomach. It was an instinctive thing, the hair on the nape of his neck was creeping, too. The lack of light made everything unreal and suddenly threatening. Hamilton couldn't stop himself glancing quickly towards his mates for reassurance. Then he stared hard at the Arab, who smiled sadly and spread his arms.

'I see it in your face,' he explained. 'And in your friend's face. Death leaves its mark on all of us, does it not?'

Hamilton eyed him suspiciously, fighting against his initial reactions of fear and mistrust. Common sense won through and he decided it was probably just a good guess on the part of the Arab. Disease and accidents were claiming the lives of the soldiers almost every day—the official term in the army was 'natural wastage'. Still, the queer sensation in Hamilton's gut didn't go away. A light seemed to burn behind the old man's eyes for a moment—a feverish gleam. It was like a second personality, totally different and malignant. It alarmed Hamilton, then, just as quickly, he wasn't certain he'd even seen it.

Unsettled, Hamilton's own voice was harsh. 'Then why the hell aren't you a rich man? With so many bloody lucky charms, I mean?' He waved at the laden packing crates.

'*My* charm keeps me strong when I am old. I can still see my enemies from a great distance and I have all my teeth,' the Arab added proudly. He bared his gums to show him.

Hamilton's fears suddenly seemed foolish and imagined at this slightly ridiculous display. The old rogue was obviously using every trick in his book to get another sale. The alcohol in Hamilton's veins was running strong, making him bold, and now he had an urge to prod the Arab and teach him the lesson that not everyone was a complete fool.

'Okay, so what sort is it? What's your charm then?' Hamilton asked carefully.

The Arab looked wary again, but as Hamilton guessed, the salesman knew that to refuse a customer anything was a step in the wrong direction. Because of his age and the strength of the younger men in the prime positions in the bazaar, he could ill afford to lose any sale these days. Reluctantly, he pulled something hanging around his neck out from under his clothing. He held it out for Hamilton, leaning closer, to see.

'It is old, and not pleasing to look upon, but it is very powerful. I know such things.' The stench of the man washed over Hamilton as he leaned closer, trying to see, in the poor light, what the Arab held. The seller's voice dropped lower. 'I can sell you something of your own. Something as good. You will need it on the battlefield.'

Hamilton didn't know why he acted as he did next. Later, he told himself perhaps it was a new confidence, or arrogance, coming with the uniform and rifle. Maybe it was just his drunken desire to demean the old man, who had no qualms about preying on a soldier's inner, unspoken fear of never returning from the war—using that fear to sell them useless trinkets for 'good luck'.

Certainly, Ben Hamilton would never remember the curious, green gleam coming from the man's hand, escaping between the Arab's fingers—a radiance which seemed to beckon for his total attention.

Jerking forward, he went to snatch it from the Arab, intending to simply keep hold of it in a childish taunt.

'Let me see,' he exclaimed, darting his hand forward and wrapping his fist around the dangling golden charm. In the rush of the moment, the world around Hamilton contracted to only himself and the salesman. His face was so close to the Arab's that he felt and smelled the other man's foul breath against his cheek. Everything else around him was an indistinct blur.

But the Arab reacted far more violently than expected. With a shriek he jumped backwards, stumbling on the sawhorse and falling. The fine chain around his neck snapped easily, leaving Hamilton holding the charm. Shocked, he stared down at the thing in his palm without actually seeing it, his mind filled instead with the wrong he was doing. Then Hamilton snapped out of it.

Confused and ashamed of his behaviour, he went to step around the packing crates to help the old man to his feet. Behind him he heard some of the others calling out to check he was okay. Hamilton waved them to stay where they were.

'Shit, I'm sorry. I didn't mean—' Hamilton tried to apologise, but the Arab leapt upright with amazing agility for one so old and went scuttling into the darker shadows at the rear of the tent.

His voice croaked from out of the darkness. 'A thief! I should have known the *Setris* would find one, in time. I should not have shown you!'

'The what? Who? What the devil are you—look, have it back. I don't want it.' Hamilton offered the charm, but the Arab laughed derisively. When he spoke his voice was harsh, his eyes glittering angrily in the unsteady light.

'You cannot give it back,' he snarled. Then he puzzled and frightened Hamilton by adding, 'You don't know how, you foolish *kafka*. Even if I told you how, here and now, you would not understand. So, it is yours, thief—and you must keep it!'

'But I wasn't stealing it, I was trying—'

'Pah!' the Arab interrupted, spitting dryly at him. 'But it is yours now, *thief*.'

'I don't *want* it!' Hamilton took another step forward and stopped when the Arab gasped. The man's eyes shone again, but this time Hamilton thought he could see fear mixed in with the madness. Hamilton held up a calming hand.

'Look, mate. I'll leave it right here on the

counter, and here's some money in case I broke anything, all right?' The words stuck in his throat, a part of him still suspecting he was being tricked into parting with his money.

A tense silence followed. Hamilton broke it by searching his pockets for some coins to leave with the charm. He put a handful of change down.

'There you go. There's enough there to buy half your bloody shop, see?' Hamilton was more concerned the authorities might get hold of this stupid misunderstanding and ship him back home. Otherwise, the crazy Arab could go to hell. At the sight of the money the old man stopped his worried, frantic movement and looked long at the soldier. Something like pity crept into his expression.

'It may be you are just a fool, and not a thief,' he said, softly. 'And maybe you are like the moth drawn to the light,' he sighed. 'It is too late. What is done cannot be undone.'

'Hey, I've just given you some money.' Hamilton was getting angry and he turned away, calling over his shoulder as he walked, 'I've got witnesses here, too. Don't start complaining to anyone, because it won't work. You're not going to get *me* sent back home!' He didn't care that this would probably mean nothing to the Arab. Hamilton threw one last look over his shoulder before he reached the others. The old man now seemed shrunken and pitiful.

Oakley and Rogers grinned as they rose from the doorway. Oakley asked, 'What have you been up to? Did he try to rip you off?'

'Stupid wog reckons I tried to steal something,' Hamilton grated. 'It was just a bit of harmless fun. I gave the bloody thing back and gave him some money to shut him up!' He walked straight past them as he spoke, heading back to camp. 'Christ! I hate fucking Cairo! When are we going to get into some fighting?'

They laughed and followed, kicking McAllen awake as they went.

The track back to Mena Camp was churned into an impossible quagmire. The men found it easier to walk on the high mound of sand directly next to the wheel ruts, although it was difficult to maintain balance in the dark and the men's drunkenness was not helping them. Frequently, they toppled off back into the ruts to squelch in the rain-softened clay, which was the base to the desert's drifting sand. A heavy drizzle fell without respite. Low cloud erased all the stars and the soldiers could barely see where they were going. They were assisted by a line of bobbing lights in front and behind made by soldiers returning to camp who, before they left Cairo, had the presence of mind to obtain some covered oil-lamps. The only sounds were the trudging of feet and the soft patter of the rain falling into puddles. Occasionally there was the rattle and jingling of a horse-drawn carriage as animals with their loads passed, the wheels making little noise in the mud. Otherwise, in the stillness of the night the men could hear the murmured conversations of others doing the same journey.

'Reckon we'll be marching in the morning?' Galther called weakly. His stomach was sore from all the retching.

'They don't stop the war when it starts to rain,' Rogers said.

'Ah, but do the officers know that?' Hamilton shouted hopefully from the lead.

As if to rebuke him the sky opened up and a deluge swept over them. The men groaned and cursed, the heavy rain pounding down on their heads and shoulders.

'We could double-time,' Hamilton suggested. He experimented by jogging ahead for the next ten yards. Then he jumped onto the ridge of sand between the wheel ruts to see if it was any easier walking there.

'What's the fucking point?' Oakley snarled. 'There's no bloody shelter at the—'

He stopped in shock as something thundered out of the rain and darkness, rushing straight at Hamilton.

It was a two-horse team pulling a flatbed wagon. Hamilton heard the snorting of the horses, the ringing of their harness and the racket of the bouncing wagon before he saw the menacing shape racing towards him. It was a large, moving blackness barely discernible against the distant wavering lamps. He hardly had time to shout a warning when a strong arm swept him to one side. He crashed, grunting at the impact, face-down in the gritty mud. The horses plunged past, spraying water and sand with their hooves. Instinctively,

Hamilton tucked his legs into his chest in case they went under the wheels.

As fast as it began, it was over. The team and wagon crashed past the others, who also had to throw themselves sideways. Then the noise of its passage was quickly fading into the distance, swallowed by the heavy rain. Stunned, everyone lay where they fell for some time. They vaguely heard more alarmed shouts coming from down the track, marking the wagon's progress.

'Jesus Christ, that was close,' Hamilton muttered, slowly pushing himself into a sitting position. He was shaking and out of breath. 'Thanks for that, whoever it was.'

'Thanks?' Story groaned, from a similar position. 'I'll kill the bastard if I ever meet him!'

Hamilton frowned at his dark shape. 'Who the devil are you talking about?'

'The fool on the bloody wagon, of course. Who are *you* talking about?'

'Whoever it was who shoved me out the way. I was a goner, just standing and staring like an idiot at the damned thing coming straight at me!'

'Well, it wasn't me,' Story admitted. No one else took credit either.

'*Somebody* saved me,' Hamilton insisted.

'Why was the bastard going so fast? How could he see where he was going?' Galther asked, amazed. The others began to pick themselves up, too. Loel had to feel around on his hands and knees for his hat.

'Well, you may have been luckier than you think,' Rogers said gruffly. He was patting his pockets, making sure he hadn't lost his pipe. 'At a guess I'd say that fellow had a third horse tethered to the front of the team, leading them along the track. I've seen it done before,' he added, musing. 'I'd say that's what shoved you off the track, Ben. But still, you got hit by a horse. You might have been run over.'

Hamilton was very doubtful. 'It didn't *feel* like a horse—and why wasn't I trampled?'

'Just a brush with the shoulder,' Rogers shrugged in the darkness. 'If it was leading the team, it would be a good animal. Probably saw you long before you saw it.'

'I didn't see the bloody thing at all!'

'Well, I must say, too, I've never heard of it!' Oakley burst out.

'Not common,' Rogers agreed. 'Not in the bigger towns, anyway,' he added cheekily and being rewarded by Oakley's snort of derision. There was a friendly rivalry between men who came from the towns and those who journeyed in from the bush to enlist.

After a moment Hamilton asked, 'Well, it can't have been anything else, right?' He was answered by a long silence. Eventually he said, 'Well, okay—come on, we'd better get moving again. We won't get back until dawn at this rate.'

Considerably more sober and subdued, they continued on towards Mena. No one knew what time they finally arrived. They were so tired, nobody cared to find out.

The exhaustion, combined with the alcohol in their systems, brought sleep to them almost instantly as they huddled together on the damp sand, all of them trying to stretch extra inches from their wet blankets to cover themselves completely.

Hamilton awoke sometime in the night, confused and uncertain what had stirred him. A drizzle was falling again. His face was already wet from the dampness soaking through the blanket he'd pulled over his head, which in turn made him hot and stuffy, too. Exposing himself to the fresh air, the rain was a chill breath against his skin, waking him quickly. There was no glow in the east, so Hamilton figured he hadn't been sleeping long. Looking around, he saw no one else had been disturbed. His comrades were darker shapes spread across the black ground, the scene barely lit by scattered covered lamps kept alight for men trying to make their way to the latrines in the night without treading on anybody.

He carefully stood, hoping not to wake the others, and picked his way to the clearway, a wide path running through the multitude of sleeping soldiers marked by white tape. Without knowing why, Hamilton began to walk towards the pyramids. Men snored and grunted all around him, and to one side he glimpsed the red pin-point of a covered cigarette. Nobody called out or questioned what he was doing. Reaching the edge of the main camp, Hamilton heard a whispered conversation, alerting him to two sentries standing close together. They turned towards him as the crunching of Hamilton's boots on the sand gave him away.

'Can't sleep,' Hamilton called softly, before they had a chance to challenge him. 'Maybe a walk will help.'

'How can any bastard sleep through this, without any bloody tents?' one of the sentries replied gruffly, waving him on.

Hamilton took his time, strolling with his hands deep in his pockets. In front of him the black pyramids grew in size as he got closer, the hard, angular edges visible against the slightly lighter sky. While he walked, Hamilton let his imagination wander, hoping a few answers might come unbidden to him, but his mind stayed strangely blank. He still had no idea why he'd awoken or what reason he had for going to the pyramids. It was like an urge, a longing to do something in particular, and it was simpler and easier to satisfy the urge without asking himself why, exactly, he needed to do it. Besides, too many questions only invited a vague confusion to take over from where it lurked on the edge of his consciousness.

Soon he found himself standing at the base of the nearest pyramid. Hamilton nodded slowly to himself, acknowledging it was the same structure the men had climbed in their race the previous day. He waited, expecting that somehow his reason for being attracted here might reveal itself, but nothing happened. After a while Hamilton moved around to the opposite side of the pyramid, the side hidden from the camp. It was darker here too, shadowed from the faint light coming from the moon trying to pierce the thinning rain clouds. Hamilton stood in the darkness, scuffling his feet in the sand. A thought came to him and he reached into his shirt pocket, pulling something out.

It was the good luck charm he'd taken from the Arab trader. Hamilton didn't feel any surprise that he still had it. He held it out, at arm's length, studying it. The green jewel set as the creature's eye gleamed slightly—almost imperceptibly—and Hamilton twisted the charm backwards and forwards to see if it could catch more light.

Without warning, a dizziness hit him and he held his breath, waiting for the spell to fade, fighting to keep his balance while the night spun around him. The attack didn't last long, and it left him feeling weak, but unexpectedly mentally more in control.

'What the hell am I doing here?' he asked aloud, annoyed at himself for giving in to the odd whim which had brought him there. Dawn couldn't be far away and Hamilton knew he needed to get some sleep. Now he looked down, bemused at the charm in his hand. Then a voice answered him, coming out of the darkness and startling him.

'Why don't you climb the pyramid?'

Hamilton spun around. 'Who's there?' he

snapped, his nerves jumping. 'What the hell do you think you're doing, sneaking up on me like that? Do you think it's damned funny?' No one replied, but Hamilton thought he could see someone sitting on one of the lower stones and he moved closer.

'I climbed it. I climbed it today. It's quite easy, as long as you don't try to go too fast.'

Hamilton thought he detected an ironic humour, but he was too rattled to let himself become good-natured. He called, 'Who are you? Are you the fellow who won that race today?'

A dry, husky chuckle surprised Hamilton. *'Oh no, I didn't win. I lost.'*

'Then what the hell are you doing here? At this time of night?'

'Why don't you tell me what you are doing here?'

Hamilton was lost for words, torn between justifying himself and telling the man to mind his own damned business. 'I couldn't sleep, so I decided to walk—' he began unwillingly, but the other man cut him off.

'Actually, I'm waiting here for you.'

Hamilton was startled. 'What?'

'I'm going to give you some advice.'

'What are you talking about? How did you know I was coming here? *I* didn't even know!'

'Have you got your good luck charm? Show it to me.'

It was then that Hamilton realised something very strange and frightening was happening. His blood ran cold. He didn't know what to do—and he couldn't run. It was as if he was frozen, trapped where he stood. Still he grasped the charm in his hand and found himself holding it out.

'See? It brings you luck. It brought you to me.'

The young soldier's fear grew when he noticed a white mist rising from the sand around him. It touched his skin with a clammy feeling making the hairs on his arms bristle. It brushed against his cheek and Hamilton wanted to twist his face away, but there was nowhere to turn. It surrounded him, growing thicker. The mist glowed slightly, throwing light onto the stone of the pyramid and between its drifting tendrils, revealing the other man.

It was the youth who had fallen and died during the race.

Hamilton's throat went suddenly dry and raw. He whispered, 'Jesus Christ, it's you. How can it be? What in God's name is happening here?'

'Climb the pyramid, Ben. Climb it, and come back down the way I did. Go to the top and just let yourself go. You won't have to go to the war, then you won't need any luck.'

The other soldier's figure was still bloodied, his uniform torn and hanging from his boyish frame. The skin was a sickly white.

'No! This is a dream! It *must* be a dream!' Hamilton said, grating the words out between his clenched teeth. 'This isn't *real*.' He closed his eyes tightly, but he could still feel the mist caressing his skin and face. He thought of the wine they'd drunk and tried blaming that, fixing on the idea with a desperation.

'It's not a dream, Ben. It is real, and you would be wise to take my advice.'

Hamilton still couldn't move. He realised that his muscles were tensed to the point of locking, trapping himself. He tried to do the opposite, letting himself go and expecting to fall to the ground. For a moment nothing happened, then he felt himself slipping downwards and the darkness became complete again with grains of sand pushing against his face. Groaning, he rolled over and looked towards the pyramid. A figure still sat there, staring down at him, but now Hamilton wasn't sure it was the youth. It looked like someone else—someone different that he didn't know. Someone more frightening. The swirling mist made it hard to see. He told himself he didn't *want* to see and with an effort closed his eyes again.

Someone repeated, *'Climb the pyramid, Ben.'* It was another voice, not the youth's.

Hamilton didn't answer, but screwed his eyes closed even tighter and now tried to concentrate on nothing except the tiny grains of sand rasping against his cheek.

All he could see in his mind was the broken, dead youth sitting on the stone of the pyramid, waiting for him to climb it.

Telling Hamilton to throw himself to his own death.

The next morning, under a dull, leaden sky, Hamilton sat with the others and searched his sodden kit in the hope a few pairs of clean socks might have somehow stayed dry. The march was on, much to everyone's dismay. He was worried his wet boots might dry and stiffen, rubbing his feet raw, and wearing two pairs of socks could make all the difference. Hamilton was in luck, discovering some socks at the bottom of his kitbag that were only slightly damp.

As he sat on the sand tugging his boots off, something in his pocket dug into his thigh. Hamilton searched the pocket for the offending item. Pulling it out, he was utterly confounded to see the Arab's charm lying in the palm of his hand. In the daylight he could see it was a golden dog, or some sort of wolf, standing on its back legs and lifting its open jaws to the sky. The brilliant green gem represented a single eye.

'I gave it back,' he said, aloud to himself. 'I'm *sure* I gave it back.' He closed his eyes and tried to remember every detail of the moment. He was rewarded by an aching head. 'Well, I know I was pretty drunk, but—' he admitted to himself. 'Damn it, I suppose I *might* have picked the bloody thing up again,' he added, knowing it was really a lie. Then he recalled the near-accident he'd had with the wagon.

'Maybe you *are* a lucky charm, after all,' he said, pursing his lips thoughtfully. 'But I'm damned if I can remember—'

'So, who the hell are you talking to? Yourself?' Oakley interrupted, sitting down next to him. 'Are you sick? You spent half the bloody night at the latrines, I know.'

Hamilton squinted at him. 'Me? No, I didn't. I slept like a baby. It's all that grog you forced into me.'

Oakley was surprised. 'I'm sure it was you. You're the only bloke who worries about treading on everyone when you get up. Every other bastard steps on your head and doesn't give a damn.'

'Then someone else must be getting considerate, because it wasn't me, I'm telling you. The first thing I knew after we hit the sack last night was that bloody sun burning my eyes this morning,' he said, although the overcast sky above them belied this.

Oakley looked at him strangely for a moment, then apparently thought it better to change the subject. 'Dry socks, eh?'

'Get your eyes off 'em. They're mine.'

'Wouldn't dream of it.' Oakley looked pained.

Hamilton put up with the expression for several seconds before he snarled with mock disgust and threw one of the pairs at Oakley. 'Here, you bastard. Don't say I never give you nothing—and if I get a blister today the last thing I'll do while I can still walk is kick you up the arse!'

'Thanks, Ben.' Oakley grinned and retrieved the socks. He began to tackle his own boots, but he was cursing almost straight away, having broken a lace. 'Damn,' he muttered, looking helplessly at the broken end.

Hamilton groaned and searched through his kit-bag again. He handed over a new bootlace.

'I'll make it up to you, honest.' Oakley gratefully accepted it. He stripped the old one from his boot and went to toss it away.

'Hey, hang on a second. Give that to me.' Hamilton clicked his fingers at the piece of leather. Oakley stretched out, picking it back up and passing it over. Hamilton threaded it through the hole in the charm, then tied the leather around his neck.

'What's that?' Oakley frowned.

'Sort of a good luck charm, I think. It's not really mine, though. I'll have to give it back, when I get a chance.'

'Right,' Oakley nodded, but not understanding. 'I reckon you're going as silly as Nick,' he decided, and left it at that. He had more important things to worry about, such as marching for ten miles across the desert before lunch.

Hamilton didn't get back to Cairo for a week. The soldiers' training reverted to eight, and sometimes ten, hours a day. At the end of it the men could only collapse under makeshift shelters to avoid the rain and sleep like the dead. Nobody even considered the long hike into Cairo until the day when they were given an entire Sunday off.

The Arab's stall was missing. Hamilton tried to ask several nearby traders what had happened to it, but they ignored his questions and tried selling him something instead. He decided to knock at the doorway where Oakley and Rogers had waited. The door was answered by a thin Arab who looked at Hamilton suspiciously. Slowly, Hamilton explained what he wanted, asking him if he remembered the stall, or what happened to the man who owned it.

'He has gone to Allah,' the man said shortly.

Hamilton was shocked for a moment. 'Hey, but he was fit as a bull—he showed me his teeth and everything,' he added stupidly. The man was silent, not offering anything more, but not moving. Hamilton realised he was expecting to be rewarded for his information. Retrieving a coin from his pocket, he flipped it at the doorway. The thin Arab caught it deftly and, without another word, slammed the door closed.

Hamilton stood on the worn step and stared at the door. He was tempted to knock again and demand more of an explanation, even though his common sense told him there was no reason why the Arab should know anything more. The stall-owner's death would be common street gossip and little else. Still, something nagged at Hamilton, as if he were missing an important point.

His indecision was solved for him by Story yelling for his attention. He had found a photographic stall with an ancient camera and an aged Arabic photographer. It looked doubtful that any of the equipment would work or that Story would get his money's worth, but he was insisting all of them pose for a picture together. Hamilton shook his head, half-amused and half to rid his mind of the strange doubts, and walked back to his friends to oblige Story with his photograph.

4

Brendan was moving down a dark corridor. Stone walls ran straight out in front of him into a blackness beyond the glow of a burning torch he was using to guide his way. The shadow ahead was menacing and more than equal to the challenge of the flickering flame.

He had no idea where he was or what, in particular, he was doing. Only that he must keep moving—searching for something, perhaps—he didn't know. And that he had to keep looking, because there was no other way to end this, except to find what he was searching for. There was no other way *out*. Brendan felt as if he was trapped, like a laboratory rat running endlessly through a scientific maze. The urge to give in to his fear and panic—simply let himself go—was strong. It was difficult to keep thinking logically and try to find an escape. He stopped for a moment and examined the wall next to him. It was made of a coarse, pale sandstone, shaped and fitted with painstaking skill. It didn't give him any clues where he might be. Reluctantly he began moving forward again, dragging the fingertips of one hand along the wall as he walked, keeping his balance. The stone was cool and dry to his touch, the porous quality of it soaking up any sounds rather than echoing them back. The noise of his scuffling feet had a curious flat nature. He could feel the heat on his scalp from the torch, but he was already holding the brand as high as the ceiling would allow. Holding the flame more directly in front would ruin what little sight he had.

A greater sense of awareness grew in Brendan as he kept moving along the passageway, like he'd been in a daze and was slowly coming out of it. It helped in pressing back some of the fear. The questions began clamouring inside his head. What was he doing here? Where the hell was he? A thought came to him and he stopped, holding his breath and listening intently. But he couldn't hear anything. There were no clues for him there, either. He was helpless to do anything except press on, hoping the answers lay somewhere ahead.

But when the short arc of the torch's glow finally revealed an archway, with a bigger blackness on the other side suggesting an end to the corridor, Brendan hesitated. *Come inside, said the spider to the fly,* he thought grimly.

After the close, stifling walls on either side and the low ceiling, the prospect of a larger room was so welcome, so inviting, that it may be *too* inviting. Edging closer so the torch would throw some light past the arch, he could see the passageway opened into a wider area, like a chamber. He waited to see if the flame's light attracted any movement. Nothing happened. He concentrated again on listening hard, but the loudest thing in his ears was the nervous pounding of his own blood. That left nothing else to do but go forward, because Brendan instinctively knew that turning around and retracing his steps was not an option. Tensing himself, and ready for anything, he walked through the arch.

He found himself in an enormous room. The ceiling was only slightly higher than in the corridor, but even raising the torch still didn't let him see the other end of the chamber. Worried about losing his bearings, Brendan put a hand to the stone again and started making his way around the walls. Immediately he discovered niches everywhere, created by omitting one or more of the masonry blocks. The spaces were filled with all sorts of things, like small and unusual ornaments, but mainly there were delicate figurines made of a dull metal or carved wood. Many of the wall spaces between the alcoves were decorated with hanging mats woven into simple designs, some with hieroglyphics painted on, others portraying prancing, angular caricatures of men.

Brendan edged along the wall, peering at each new item. The small statues had a strange, chilling effect on him, the feeling made worse by the darkness at his back. Someone could be standing in the middle of the room watching him, waiting for the right moment to reach out with clutching, clawed fingers. He turned around often to check, once whirling quickly and making his torch sputter dangerously close to extinction. Each time he expected to see movement lurking just beyond the light of the burning torch, but he didn't see anything. Still, the feeling he was being watched persisted. His fear played tricks with his mind, stopping him from concentrating on a familiarity with the statuettes and figurines which was nagging at him for identification. The answer just wouldn't come.

The next niche in the wall was much larger than the rest, shaped like a sentinel's box.

And it was occupied by a man.

Brendan gasped at the sight, just stopping himself from drawing quickly back. The glow of the torch revealed the figure of a man standing, legs braced, with his back to the wall. It was more than just an average man, for he stood almost two metres tall with powerful, muscled shoulders. Brendan took a moment to recover his breath and wind his courage back up, then he leaned forward carefully, examining the figure. It was so realistic, so human, it was impossible to determine what it could be made from. The skin on the face and exposed arms had a parched, leathery look. The clothing was a smock with intricate patterns woven through it, tied around the waist with a thin braided rope. He wore a tall, pointed cap laced with the same delicate embroidery. The figure stood with his hands clasped to his chest. Blank, staring eyes were levelled at some point above Brendan's head.

An effigy of a high priest, or a God-figure, Brendan thought. *Or one of their demons.* He had to admit to himself, too, the thing scared the hell out of him. It looked so alive.

And evil.

Another idea came to him. *Mummified.* But that would suggest, Brendan realised, he was looking at the corpse of what was once a living being—a man over six and a half feet tall. Ancient men, he knew, were generally a lot smaller than their modern-day counterparts. Even the Biblical Goliath, should he actually have existed, needed only to be more than six feet in height to be considered a 'giant'. It meant the figure he faced now would have rated as a true, freakish giant amongst men.

Then he saw the priest's eyes had dropped and were staring directly at him.

Brendan cried out, a strangled, choking sound that echoed around the walls of the chamber. It was not just the movement of the eyes, but the look within them. A glare of hatred and wicked corruption of the soul. Brendan stepped backwards, holding the torch up to keep the figure away. Then he heard groans of fear from behind him, from within the darkness in the middle of the chamber, and he spun around. The wavering light of the torch reflected off a mass of swaying, ethereal forms. They were hard to see in the flickering shadows, but Brendan recognised them through some inner knowledge that was all a part of his nightmare—he was *supposed* to know. They were the tormented souls of men, bound together with a common consuming terror. He suddenly understood they'd been following him as he'd wandered in the dark passageways. He had been their unwitting guide, leading them to—what? Brendan twisted back around. The high priest had let his hands fall to his sides and there was a faint gleam of amusement within the terrible glare.

The giant's mouth slowly opened to a sickening gape. Strings of saliva stretched between the lips like a spider's web. Broken, rotting teeth glistened in the firelight. Impossibly, the head of a serpent appeared in the dark maw of the mouth. It slithered uncaring between the priest's lips and lowered itself carefully towards the ground, the muscled body of the snake controlling the fall with strength and grace. The sight triggered a reaction in Brendan, an overwhelming urge to retch. Only his paralysing fear prevented it. His mind was refusing to accept the evidence of the man's torso jerking spasmodically beneath the loose smock. The snake was nearly five feet long. It had to pause and judge the final drop, its tail whipping from the priest's mouth as it fell, slapping to the stone floor and instantly coiling into a defensive posture. The priest seemed to look upon the serpent with grim satisfaction.

The moaning of the multitude behind grew louder to a keening note filling the chamber. The snake fixed its attention on Brendan and began to slide slowly, purposefully, towards him.

'No,' Brendan whispered, edging backwards more. *'No!'*

The mental effort of wrenching himself from the nightmare was so intense it overflowed from his mind to become a physical movement. Every muscle in his body tensed and threw him into an upright, crouched position, hugging his knees to his chest. He rocked unsteadily on the bed, his forehead buried in his arms while he waited for the frightful, sickening images to fade.

'God *damn* it,' he groaned softly, his stomach churning.

'Bren? What's wrong?' Gwen was instantly awake and sitting up beside him. Then she sighed knowingly and reached out to put a soothing hand on his cheek. The bedroom was barely illuminated by streetlights coming through the curtains, but she could see a sheen of sweat covering his skin. A feverish heat radiated from him.

Finally, he spoke. 'Just another nightmare,' he said quietly.

'Another one? Come on, Brendan! This is getting beyond a joke.'

'It's not my fault,' he said wretchedly. 'I don't understand it, either.'

'I know, honey.' She started rubbing his back. 'I just think it's time you began thinking about seeing a doctor. It's been a week now. Most people are lucky to have one nightmare a year.'

'Lucky?'

'You know what I meant.'

'And what do you mean, a doctor? Don't you mean a shrink?'

'No, I mean a *doctor*. You never know, it could be a diet thing, or a bump on the head.'

'How about a brain tumour?' He tried to be funny, but it didn't work.

'Don't say things like that,' she shuddered, 'I mean, it's just not *right*—that you should have all these nightmares all of a sudden.'

In the darkness he stared bleakly at the sheets between his feet. Gwen kept rubbing his shoulders and they stayed silent for some time. She found herself guiltily suppressing deep yawns. Then Brendan spoke.

'I remember what this one was about,' he said carefully.

'You do? Well that makes a change. Maybe it will give you a clue what's causing them.'

'Well, I don't know all that much, but I think I was in a tomb.'

'Tomb? Like a—a crypt?'

'More like a dungeon. I think these figures I saw, little statues and wood carvings, were Egyptian. Like that exhibition we saw last year. There were patterns on the walls, too.' The memory came to him clearly now. Brendan wondered why it hadn't been so easy while he was dreaming. The first answer that occurred to him was startling—and frightening.

That would take all the fun out of it.

Gwen was trying to remember. She said, 'Gold of the Pharaohs? With all those golden death masks? And that big wooden coffin thing.'

'Sarcophagus,' he offered absently.

'Yes, that's it. So, do you think you were inside a pyramid?'

Brendan was still immersed in his own thoughts and it took him a moment to realise what Gwen asked. He said slowly, 'Now you say it, I suppose I must have been, though God knows why I'd be dreaming about those sort of things.'

'It's weird. Why would you be having nightmares about pyramids and mummies, or whatever? Are you reading something?'

'No,' Brendan answered shortly, because Gwen's mentioning of mummies brought back a strong image of the tall figure, disgorging the snake from its mouth.

'Sorry, only asking,' Gwen snapped back.

Brendan ran a tired hand across his face. 'No, look—I'm the one who should be saying sorry. I wasn't snapping at you. You reminded me of something bad in the nightmare, that's all.'

'What was it?' Despite her interest, Gwen submitted to another huge yawn. Brendan shook his head. He didn't want to try and decipher the crazy, frightening images of his dreams now. He hated remembering them at all.

'It's too much to explain.'

'Try me.'

'Gwen, you have to start work early in the morning. Why don't you go back to sleep and I'll tell you about it later? Anyway, I'm getting over it now. I'll drop off myself in a second.'

She looked at him doubtfully. 'Are you going to see a doctor?' The question caught him off guard, as it was meant to.

'Look, I—' he held his palms up and shrugged. 'I just can't see any value in it.'

'So now it's *Doctor* Brendan Craft, is it? Besides, when was the last time you had a check-up?' As Brendan opened his mouth to protest Gwen continued, 'Or a tetanus shot?'

'I haven't had time,' he excused himself weakly, knowing he was already beaten.

'Well, you have now. You're a self-employed, self-made man, right? So why don't you humour me? Make a doctor's appointment, get your check-up done, have a tetanus shot—and just mention the nightmares. See what he says, okay? It can't hurt.'

'Tetanus shots can kill you,' he grumbled.

'Don't be a coward. Injections don't hurt,' she scoffed mildly. '*Dentists* don't hurt, these days.'

With a groan he collapsed backwards onto the pillow. Eventually he said, 'I'm not going to a bloody dentist, that's for sure.'

'Idiot,' Gwen said, poking him with a finger, before throwing her arm across his chest. 'Just go to the doctor, all right? I'll keep the monsters away the rest of tonight.' She yawned again. 'Let me know if Boris Karloff turns up. I've always wanted to meet him.'

'Thank you for your concern and comfort,' he murmured. Suddenly he felt exhausted, the urge to sleep sweeping over him like a wave. He hardly heard Gwen's reply.

'Anytime,' she mumbled back.

Doctor Bridges walked back around the desk to his chair, pulling the stethoscope from his neck. 'You appear to be in the peak of condition, Brendan, except for those bags under your eyes. Or were you looking for a day off?' he smiled.

Brendan struggled to put his shirt back on without standing. 'I've gone freelance these days, Doc. I'm a self-employed businessman now. No more newspaper stories covering cats stuck up trees or community bingo nights. Strictly the exciting stuff from now on.'

'That's very admirable, but can you pay my fee?' The doctor laughed away any need for an answer and became serious. 'Okay, so are you putting in a few hours?' Bridges settled into his chair. 'Because if that's the case, I'd say there's nothing wrong with you that a couple of good nights' sleep wouldn't fix. You look a bit burnt out.'

Brendan paused in the middle of fastening a button. 'Actually, there was something I was going to ask you about.'

'Ask away. That's what I'm here for and it's bound to be more exciting than taking stitches out.' At Brendan's puzzled look, he nodded at the doorway. 'My next patient.'

'Oh, of course.' Brendan hesitated, unsure how to start. 'Anyway, I've been having nightmares,' he said casually.

'Stay off the spicy foods,' Bridges said quickly.

'Really? Does what you eat make a difference?'

Bridges raised his eyebrows. 'Are you that serious?'

'Look, it's a bit hard to explain. Maybe I'm asking the wrong person.' Brendan shrugged an apology and looked like he wanted to leave.

The doctor gestured for him to be patient. 'I'm sorry—so, how often do you have these nightmares?'

'I don't have the same one all the time, but it's always a bad dream of some description.' Unaware he was doing it, Brendan rubbed his hand tiredly across his eyes. 'Enough to wake me up and scare the shit out of me.'

'That's what nightmares do,' Bridges said mildly. 'So what? Once a week? Once a month? Does there have to be a full moon?' he added, smiling. Brendan didn't see it. He was still rubbing his eyes.

'Every night this week, so far,' he admitted reluctantly.

'Really? It's Friday, you realise,' Bridges blinked, taken by surprise.

Brendan frowned, then nodded wearily. 'Yeah, Sunday night was the first.'

'What are they about?'

It was Brendan's turn to smile, wryly. 'Why? Are you a psychiatrist too?' Without waiting for an answer he went on. 'Well, I don't remember what they're about, except for the one last night. All I know is they're damned frightening and—' he stopped, daunted as always by the idea of describing the broken, strange images. 'Does it really matter?'

Bridges tapped his teeth with a biro for a moment, choosing his words. 'It might,' he said. He sat silently for some time, thinking. 'Okay, I'll tell you what I can, but bear in mind that for every piece of advice or consultation you hear in regards to matters of the human mind, you'll always find ten other people who'll disagree, or at least offer a plausible alternative. And no, I'm not a psychiatrist, so all I can give you is an educated opinion and some information I do know—or don't know, depending on how you look at it.' He offered Brendan a quick smile. 'And I can refer you to a shrink, if you like,' he added. At Brendan's encouraging look he swung his feet from behind the desk and relaxed more in his chair as he warmed to his subject.

Brendan listened without interrupting.

Bridges began, 'The human brain is still very much a mystery, right? But we have found out a few things—Pavlov's dog, Freud, all that nonsense.' The doctor waved a dismissive hand. 'Still, there's so many *everyday* things we don't really know about. For instance, it's entirely possible eating spicy food will give you a nightmare, but it's more likely that the pain of the indigestion is the cause, which means that your bad dream could just as soon be triggered by a cut finger, or a twisted ankle, understand? So, unless you know you suffer from painful indigestion, I wouldn't bother racing home and changing your diet. But then again we *don't know for sure,* right?' He ticked the possibility off one of his fingers. 'Next, we have your imagination associating with something that's happened to you during the day or, in your case, something that happens every day. Are your nightmares populated by people you know? Places you go?'

Brendan shook his head, sensing the doctor wasn't about to tell him anything he hadn't already figured out and rejected for himself.

'Then, what about something you're reading? Or a movie you've seen lately?'

Again, Brendan shook his head. Bridges half-shrugged and looked apologetic. He stood, taking an optical device out of his top pocket, and walked back around to Brendan's chair. The doctor leaned close and for a second time peered into each of

Brendan's eyes through the instrument. He looked for quite a while in each, before stepping back suddenly as if he were startled at his own behaviour.

'Hmmm,' he said vaguely, then was silent as he walked back to his own chair, pocketing the device as he went. 'That's about all I can tell you,' he went on, ignoring the examination. 'If you can't readily associate what you experience in your nightmares with things in your waking moments, I can only suggest a psychiatrist. They might be able to dig a little deeper into your head and find something hidden, or suppressed.' Bridges now seemed uncomfortable. Brendan figured it must be because the doctor was venturing into realms beyond his own qualifications. 'Mind you, my own personal opinion is that you have to be totally honest with a psychiatrist, or not go at all. They can only make a valued judgement with all the information at their disposal.'

'I'm not hiding anything.'

'No, I'm not suggesting you are, but some people do—and waste their time and money for years. I'm just trying to impress upon you that going to a shrink requires a serious attitude.' Bridges then added gently, 'And it doesn't mean you're going crazy, by the way. Don't get hung up on the idea.'

Brendan nodded again. 'What did you just see in my eyes, by the way? You looked worried.'

'What? Oh, nothing. No help there at all, I'm afraid,' Bridges said, before adding lamely, 'I, ah, was only annoyed at myself for looking twice. A good doctor never has to look twice.' He quickly changed the subject.

'I should tell you there's another possibility, but I'm getting right out of my league. There are *diseases* of the brain which can cause all sorts of different symptoms in different patients.' He made a small, frustrated motion with his hands. 'Of course, it's way out of my experience, but I'm not too far short of the mark if I say your brain can become ill, or diseased, just like your liver, kidney,' he shrugged, 'or even your heart, really. These diseases can be healed, or at least controlled by various drugs, but they do have side effects. Again, you'd have to have them recommended by a psychiatrist, who would then decide whether or not they were going to do you any good in the first place,' he finished, spreading his hands almost in apology.

'Are you saying I could have something wrong with my *brain*, which can give me nightmares?' Brendan asked. In a way, it was the sort of explanation he'd been looking for, but now he was faced with the reality of it, it was unwelcome and frightening.

'Really,' Bridges backed off, 'you'd have to hear someone more knowledgeable explain it. Do you think you want to see a psychiatrist?'

'No.' Brendan pulled a wry face. 'I think I'd like to give it some more thought first. You can't think of anything else?'

'Short of your being on a bad drug habit, which

I hope I'd discover with a normal examination.' Bridges pursed his lips in a suppressed smile. 'Or perhaps you've been possessed by the devil, which is just as unlikely—then no, sorry. There's nothing I can think of, of any value. For the record, my professional opinion at this point is to recommend a psychiatrist.'

Brendan shrugged slightly, 'Thanks, anyway.'

'No problem.' The doctor idly glanced at his appointment pad, obviously wanting to finish. 'Anything else? They're probably piling up out there, dying in my waiting room. It's bad for business.' He watched Brendan hesitate and summon up some courage. Bridges wondered what it might be this time.

'I'm supposed to get a tetanus shot. I haven't had one for years.'

Bridges laughed. 'Is that all? Don't worry, they don't hurt too much.' He stood, gesturing Brendan towards another door. 'Go into the dispensary there and I'll have a nurse come and jab you in a minute—look, hang on a second,' he said suddenly, stooping over his desk and quickly scribbling something. He handed Brendan a piece of paper. 'Here's a prescription for a pretty hefty sleeping pill. Don't use it unless you really want to, and then don't take any more than you think you need. Certainly don't go over the prescribed limits. These things should knock you out into a deeper sleeping state where dreaming normally doesn't occur. And let me know how things go, okay?'

Brendan looked dubiously at the prescription. 'Right,' he nodded.

Two of the tablets were expected to make anybody sleep. Three were recommended for patients suffering considerable pain. Brendan was experimenting with four tablets only days after filling out the prescription. Only then did he experience a dreamless, timeless sleep which began with a fading consciousness and seemed to end barely seconds later. He knew the night had passed, because of the morning sunlight silhouetting the bedroom curtains, but the pills gave him a shallow, unsatisfying sleep. He didn't awaken feeling properly rested. Brendan, desperate to ignore a dull exhaustion soon accompanying every hour of his day, held tightly to his sense of humour.

'Time to shut down all systems,' he'd mutter to himself, using a glass of water to swallow all four pills at once. He did this in the bathroom where Gwen wouldn't see. She knew about the sleeping tablets, but would have been horrified at how many he was taking.

Otherwise, the nightmares took over again. At least now, with the dreams such a regular, terrifying occurrence, he could recognise them building in his mind and sometimes he could wake himself in time. A tiny voice in his mind, like an unwilling, helpless spectator, would warn him. The nightmares were filled with the same scenes of ancient Egypt with leering, golden masks, poisonous serpents and indistinct, yet terrifying, creatures inhabiting the dark stone passageways. The high priest was always there too, like the ringmaster of a dread-filled, terrifying circus, overseeing the haunting of Brendan's mind. One night Brendan dreamed he was being pursued by the Minotaur, a mythical figure with the body of a man and the head of a bull. As he fled through the stone corridors, twisting around to see how close the thing was getting, Brendan would see the beast's slobbering, wet snout glistening in the light of the torch, or its red, glowing eyes burning in the darkness with an insane hunger.

So Brendan took the tablets.

He didn't realise the pills had their own deadly, whispering voices until it was almost too late. Once, after lying on his bed for only a few moments before his mind filled with images of tortured bodies and large pits packed with dusty corpses, Brendan quickly got up and went to the bathroom. Opening the medicine cabinet he took down the bottle of pills, noting that already his supplies were getting low. He unscrewed the cap and used his thumb and finger to pull out the wool gauze, then he tried to tip four of the tablets into the palm of his hand. But his hands were shaking and almost the entire contents of the bottle fell out. Over a dozen pills shone up at him in the hard fluorescent light.

It would be so easy, Brendan suddenly thought, *to just take the lot.* All his problems would be solved, even if it meant leaving behind a few of the good things too.

Constant exhaustion and frustration were leaving him feeling wretched. He knew he was a simple act away from solving everything. Put all of the tablets in his mouth and drink the glass of water. Then he would sleep like he'd never slept before and there would be no more nightmares.

He kept staring down at the collection of white dots in his trembling hand. Everything else around him seemed to retreat to a distance, leaving his concentration fixed solely on the tablets. A roaring noise filled his ears. Beneath that, insistent voices hissed encouragement. Something beckoned to him—an idea of peace and contentment.

He needed only to take the tablets.

A knock on the door shattered the moment. 'Bren? Are you all right?'

Badly startled, Brendan let several of the pills fall from his palm to bounce spectacularly off the tiled floor of the bathroom. He made awkward attempts to catch them, cursing as he did.

'Shit, ah—yeah, sorry. I've dropped the bloody sleeping tablets everywhere.'

'I'll give you a hand.' Without giving him a chance to protest Gwen pushed the door open and came in. She immediately stooped to the floor, picking some pills out from under the basin. 'Here you go,' she offered, holding them up.

Brendan held out the bottle and she dropped them in, the tablets making musical, tinkling noises as they struck the glass. Not a flicker of surprise or concern crossed Gwen's face as she saw the pill bottle was nearly empty and any that weren't on the floor were in Brendan's hand. But he knew what she would be thinking.

'I've been taking four each time,' he blurted out, in a rush of honesty.

Gwen looked at him, her face more sad than angry. 'Four? Bren, that's ridiculous! And dangerous, too.'

He looked miserable. 'Anything less doesn't work.'

'You're not giving them enough time to work. Instead of waiting until you start to fall asleep and seeing if you have a nightmare, you should take them before. Give them half an hour to work.'

'Maybe,' he nodded, sounding despairing.

'Tomorrow night I'll give you two just before we go to bed, all right?'

'You'll *give* me?' He raised his eyebrows. 'Don't you trust me?' He tried to sound bantering, but an edge crept into his voice.

Gwen hesitated, then looked pointedly at the handful of tablets still in Brendan's hand and said, quietly, 'No, Bren. I think it might be better if I gave them to you every night.'

He looked back down at the pills and took a deep breath. 'Yes,' he said, eventually. 'Maybe that's a good idea.'

Brendan had plenty of time to think hard and rationally about his problems. He still believed there was a perfectly normal explanation for it all, one which would manifest itself eventually and show him the cure. At least his visit to the doctor had opened his mind to different possibilities. While he didn't consider for a moment his being possessed by the devil—one extreme of Doctor Bridges' possible explanations—he didn't so quickly dismiss the idea he was suffering from some type of contracted, or induced, disease. The problem was, all the symptoms pointed to a mental affliction—whether through disease or not—and the emotional barriers Brendan suffered when he tried facing the fact he *might* be losing his sanity were too much. Instead, he preferred to look for explanations ranging from practical to ridiculous. He regularly refused the sleeping tablets in favour of some scheme to prove the source of his ills. Their bed, for instance, underwent a close examination to ensure he really was comfortable lying on it. He tried laying hard wooden boards under the mattress. Brendan also considered his nightmares could be stress-related, although he knew he wasn't under any real stress. His work was going smoothly, his personal relationship with Gwen couldn't have been better and his financial status was enviable, with substantial savings and equity in the old house.

Still, he deliberately gave himself three days off, ignoring his work completely and lounging around the house reading books and watching television. On the third night he went to bed late without taking any sleeping pills, having stayed up and watched television until he felt very tired. But like a predator seeing a chance to pounce, the nightmares came sweeping into his head as soon as Brendan began drifting to sleep.

He made efforts to track down allergies, though he'd never suffered an adverse reaction to anything in his life. He tried shutting out any outside influences which might be subconsciously upsetting him and lasted one entire night without turning on the television. On that occasion Brendan and Gwen's attempts at keeping themselves amused eventually made them laugh—they were so used to watching television in the evening. At least, it was an opportunity for Brendan to hang on to his sense of humour.

And whenever he experimented with each new 'solution' he would go to bed that night and wait, nervously, for the first signs it wasn't going to be different after all. Usually, it began with an unsettled feeling in his gut—an anxiety that wouldn't leave him, even though sleep began to take over his body. Next, he saw nonsensical images unconnected with his conscious thoughts, telling him his mind was switching from the controlled, ordered behaviour of his awake persona, to the erratic and random thoughts of a mind falling asleep. But then the first frightening images would come into his mind and Brendan would admit defeat, rising and prompting a quiet, sympathetic sigh from Gwen, who would be waiting just as anxiously to see if the nightmares would stay away. Brendan began taking the two tablets like a man resigning himself to a life-long habit.

And still, it didn't seem right.

Like Gwen suggested, taking two sleeping tablets earlier helped. But rather than getting a good night's sleep Brendan still felt he simply lost large chunks of his life. He yearned for a normal sleep with a pleasant dream and a slow, gentle awakening into the real world in the morning. Not this loss of consciousness, followed by a snap awakening into the new day. Gwen could see the toll it was taking on him, but sensed it was something Brendan had to face and defeat on his own—for the moment, at least. Harassing him into more positive action, she guessed, would only bring more unwanted pressure to bear. So, instead, she tried to ease his worries by distracting him with extra loving attention.

The restaurant was a large converted house. The separate rooms were made into booths for two or three tables each which, while not being completely private, created an atmosphere of intimacy. A small, efficient staff glided through the rooms, chatting informally to the patrons. Candlelight flickered off the walls.

Brendan and Gwen were enjoying a pre-dinner glass of wine.

'I guess I owe you some sort of apology,' he said, looking at the tablecloth.

'Don't be silly, Bren. You're tired—you may even be ill. For Christ's sake, don't start apologising just because you're not the best of company lately. I only wish I could help you a little more.'

'So do I, but I honestly can't work out what's going wrong. These nightmares don't make any sense.' He paused guiltily, because the snatches of terror he'd seen before the sleeping tablets took hold perhaps didn't make much sense, but they had that same theme which didn't change, so they did, in fact, make a sort of sense. 'But I can't chase them away, unless I take so many of those damned drugs I end up a zombie for the rest of the next day.'

'What about Doctor Bridges? All those things he had to say?' Gwen asked, although they'd already discussed this in detail.

'So I'm either sick, or crazy,' Brendan smiled at her ruefully. 'Or both,' he added. 'Don't get mad at me, but I don't want to talk about that sort of stuff tonight.'

Gwen sighed, 'Anyway, I have to agree, I don't think you're going crazy.'

'I'm *not* going crazy,' he said, in an urgent whisper. 'Christ, I'd *know* if I was going crazy, wouldn't I? I'd—I'd be—' He gave up, muttering desperately, 'I'd just know, that's all.'

Gwen took his hand. 'Don't get upset, Bren. They're only nightmares, after all. Something that happens when you're asleep, right? Listen, if you start standing on your head in the bathroom or something, I'll start to worry, okay?'

'But I can't understand why it's something I can't *control*,' he gestured helplessly. 'Or at least *do* something about. What's happened to modern medicine, for Christ's sake?'

'They're just nightmares, Bren, remember?'

'But they're so fucking *real*,' he grated, betraying a growing desperation she hadn't seen before.

'But when you wake up, they're gone, right?'

'Right,' he agreed wearily, then shrugged an apology. 'I'm sorry.'

'You should tell me more about them. Sharing things can sometimes help, you know.'

'Okay, I will. But not now, okay?'

It was a small concession, but Gwen was happy to leave it at that. Until now Brendan had been reluctant to say anything about his nightmares except in the broadest outlines, which told Gwen almost nothing. Brendan claimed most of the things were too fantastic or macabre to describe. She changed the subject.

'Entree?'

'Yeah, great idea,' Brendan said, relieved to get off the topic.

The next hour passed pleasantly. The food was excellent, the wine mellowing. The couple had little trouble chasing away Brendan's woes and becoming deeply involved in a hopeful conversation centred around their future plans. Entrees came and went, with Gwen and Brendan opening a fresh bottle of wine while they waited for the main course. Another couple occupying the only other table in the room stood and left. Brendan felt himself beginning to relax for the first time in over two weeks. He didn't mind admitting it was probably due to the alcohol. He could feel muscles in his neck relaxing, creating a pleasant soreness which told him they'd been stressed for some time. Gwen made a comment, making him laugh.

'You haven't laughed so much for weeks,' she told him encouragingly.

He pulled a face and indicated the glass of wine. 'Maybe if I drink a bottle or two of this every night I could chuck the sleeping pills in the bin.'

'I think the long-term effects might be a problem,' Gwen smiled. A fleeting expression crossed her face, which she caught before Brendan could see. *Drugging yourself to sleep for the rest of your life isn't exactly the greatest, either.*

'What the hell,' Brendan raised his glass towards her. 'We'll experiment with the theory tonight, anyway. We came in a cab, didn't we? We might as well take advantage of the fact and get romantically as drunk as we want.'

'We've run out of booze again,' Gwen protested, not very hard.

'That's easily fixed.' Brendan leaned over and plucked a wine list from the nearby vacant table. He only looked at it for a second before changing his mind, handing it to Gwen. 'Your turn to choose.'

'But I don't know the first thing about picking a wine!'

'Either do I, so what's the difference?'

Gwen made an exasperated noise and started studying the list. Brendan occupied himself by swirling the remains of his wine as perilously close to the rim of the glass as possible.

Then he saw the beetle.

Brendan was amazed, then revolted. The insect was huge, its body about the size of a large egg, the long, spiky legs scraping uncertainly on the unfamiliar surface of the tablecloth. It crawled out from behind the candle holder and moved towards Brendan's side of the table. The creature shone blackly in the candlelight, a tiny drop of moisture glistening on the tip of its rhinoceros horn.

'What the hell—' Brendan choked. Clamping down on his loathing, he acted without thinking. He snatched the napkin from his lap, smothering the insect with it, then picked up the bundle of cloth and threw it hastily into the corner of the room. He knocked over Gwen's wine glass in his haste, the small amount of drink she had left causing a dark crimson stain on the white linen.

Now trying to rescue the glass, Brendan didn't notice the napkin fluttering to the floor, empty.

'Why on earth did you do that?' Gwen cried with outraged amusement, jerking the wine menu aside to see.

'There was a big insect—a beetle-thing, on the table. It was bloody enormous.' Brendan's voice was thick with disgust.

'A what?' she laughed.

'A beetle, like a huge Christmas beetle, on the table.'

'So, what did you do? Kill it?' Gwen leaned forward, inspecting the table.

'I picked it up in my napkin and hurled it over there,' he pointed.

Gwen looked at the crumpled napkin on the floor. 'I can't see any beetle.'

'Well, it's probably still caught up in the cloth,' Brendan defended himself confidently. 'It had a big spike on its head—'

A waiter hurried in, asking calmly, 'Is there a problem?'

'It's okay. There was a big insect on the table, that's all,' Brendan explained, beginning to feel a little foolish.

'An insect? You mean—a roach?' the waiter arched his eyebrows and looked suitably worried.

'No, it was a big beetle type of thing. It must have flown in through a window.' While the waiter looked relieved, Brendan felt obliged to add, 'I'm sorry to cause a mess. I suppose I overreacted a bit.' He looked around to see which window must have allowed the insect inside the restaurant. A frown touched his face when he saw none were open.

'We'll change the tablecloth, sir.'

'No—no, don't bother,' Brendan stopped him. 'I'd rather not suffer the inconvenience.'

'I still can't see any beetle, Bren,' Gwen announced, eyeing the crumpled napkin.

'Look, I'll show you,' Brendan offered, with more bravado then he felt. He imagined the spike on the beetle might possibly deliver a nasty sting. Still, he rose and stooped down in the corner, picking up one edge of the napkin. He drew quickly back, pulling the cloth with him.

But it was empty of any entangled insect and the carpet beneath it was bare. Brendan blinked in surprise.

'Cute little critter, isn't he?' Gwen said.

'There *was* a beetle, I tell you! It was huge!'

'Yes, Bren. I'll bet it was,' Gwen mocked, smiling. Brendan clicked his tongue in annoyance and sat down again, puzzling over it and looking about the floor. Gwen turned to the waiter, who observed it all with mild amusement, and said, 'While you're here, could we have another bottle of wine? This one, here?' She placed her finger on the menu. The man nodded easily and left the room.

Gwen listened sympathetically while Brendan retold the details of the beetle—the size, colour and how it simply appeared on the table. His frustration grew as she gently humoured him, nodding and suppressing her smiles. Slowly he began to see the funny side himself, but he kept the game going, comically insisting he hadn't imagined the whole thing. A shadow darkened the doorway and Brendan looked up, expecting to see the waiter returning with the wine.

Instead, in that moment Brendan's world became a totally different and terrifying place.

Standing, staring at him with insane, burning eyes, was the high priest figure of Brendan's nightmares. The dusty, ancient Egyptian clothing and the drawn, parched skin looked just the same in the dim candlelight of the restaurant. The broken teeth gleamed in a mirthless grin.

With a cry Brendan leapt to his feet, his chair toppling over backwards behind him. He stood and stared, unable to tear his eyes away from those of the figure.

'Brendan, what is it?' Gwen gasped, her own eyes round with alarm.

The sound of her voice dragged Brendan's attention towards Gwen. He could tell by the way she was looking at him, in between throwing puzzled but unfrightened glances at the doorway, that she didn't see anybody standing in the doorframe. Without answering he returned his shocked eyes to the nightmare figure.

'What in God's name do you want with me?' Brendan whispered, his voice hoarse. He heard Gwen ask him what he was talking about, but he ignored her.

The priest, his maddened glare fixed on Brendan, slowly raised one hand. Brendan flinched, seeing he held a crude knife and he momentarily believed he might somehow attack him. But the priest used his free hand to cup his own chin, tipping his head back. With a single, deliberate stroke he slashed his own throat. Bright red blood spilled from the wound with a gush to soak his lower neck and the top of his rough garment. Still, the dancing eyes remained staring into Brendan's, watching with impossible amusement for his reaction.

Too late, Brendan jerked his head away trying to avoid the dreadful sight. His gorge arose uncontrollably in his throat. Bending over double, clutching at his stomach with both hands, he vomited a stream of red wine and partly digested food onto the floor. Through the daze of his illness and a roaring noise inside his head, incredibly a voice insinuated itself into Brendan's consciousness.

'It's a way out. After, there is nothing. No more nightmares, no more fear.'

Brendan groaned. The voice was his own.

The waiter, hurrying as much as decorum would allow, rushed into the room. His appearance burst the spectral figure like a soapy bubble, making it disappear instantly.

'What's going on in here—oh!' The waiter's face fell and he gave Brendan an angry look. 'Perhaps we shouldn't have that third bottle of wine, *sir*,' he said, barely stopping himself from spitting out the last word.

Brendan collapsed weakly into his chair and held his head in his hands. 'I think you'd better take me home,' he begged Gwen weakly, without looking up.

'No, I think *you'd* better call an ambulance,' Gwen snapped at the waiter, turning his expression of disgust to one of proprietorial concern. 'He can't possibly be drunk. He's sick.'

'I hope you don't think it's food poisoning!' the waiter said, becoming alarmed.

'Just call the damned ambulance!' Gwen was on her feet and moving around the table to comfort Brendan. The waiter hurried out the door.

'No, stop him,' Brendan said, waving a feeble hand at the doorway. 'Stop him, Gwen. Please.'

'You're sick, Bren,' Gwen told him gently. 'You can't be drunk, you haven't had enough. You need a doctor.'

'No, Gwen.' He raised his head and looked at her with a sad and sickened expression. 'This has got nothing to do with doctors. Just take me home. Stop him from calling an ambulance.'

Gwen took time to check his eyes and temperature, then walked quickly away to find the waiter, a shallow lie involving medications and allergies forming in her mind. The decision made, she didn't dare dwell on whether it was right or not.

'I'm usually walking through these dark, stone passageways, like I'm in a dungeon,' Brendan explained in a dull, despairing voice.

They were back at home, a single table lamp giving the lounge room a low, warm light. Brendan's eyes kept flicking into the darker shadows of the room, searching.

'Like being inside a pyramid—remember what we said before?' Gwen asked. Brendan made a helpless gesture.

'I guess it must be. I'm always holding a flaming

torch of some kind, and I suppose I'm looking for something.'

'Looking for what?'

'I don't know, but I can't seem to stop myself from looking.'

'For a way out, perhaps?'

Brendan shrugged. 'And there's another thing,' he said, suddenly remembering. 'I'm followed by a whole bunch of other people. At least, I *think* they're people. All I ever see is this mass of—of,' he struggled for a word, '*wraiths*, I guess you'd call them.'

Gwen leaned back on the couch and sighed wearily. 'Well, you know the ancient Egyptians used to kill anyone menial associated with the construction of the pyramids, to keep secret where all the treasures were stored and how to even get inside the thing. In fact, I'm pretty sure they didn't even bother killing the slaves, sometimes. They just sealed them inside and let them die of thirst or hunger, whatever would get you first. Maybe that's who they are,' she added doubtfully. 'But it's all a bit *definite* for a dream, don't you think? Dreams are supposed to be disjointed and not make any sense.'

'Not these nightmares.' Brendan shook his head and closed his eyes, tiredness sweeping over him. 'Most of the things I see are as clear as day.'

'What's so frightening about them? I mean, can you be more specific?'

Brendan paused, before answering. 'There's

always this person, this figure, who I find in the dark. He always does something terrible, which makes me want to scream. One time, he vomited out a huge snake, but normally he just looks at me in a way that makes my flesh crawl.' He shook his head again. 'It's so hard to explain.'

'Do you know who he is?'

'No, but I think of him as some sort of high priest—I don't really know why. Maybe just because of the clothing he's wearing. Then again, he's probably just the opposite. Like, an ancient sorcerer or something.' Brendan shook his head at his own words. 'Who the hell knows? I haven't a damn clue.'

Gwen asked quietly, 'And what happened tonight? In the restaurant?'

Brendan took a deep breath. 'He was there. That same person, standing in the doorway and staring at me. He had a knife.'

After a stunned moment, she said, 'You saw something from your dreams, standing in the restaurant?' She tried to keep her voice flat and unemotional, but a trace of scepticism still crept through. 'What did he do? Did he say anything?'

'He cut his own throat. But Christ, Gwen, that didn't stop him staring at me! Blood went everywhere. That's why I threw up.'

'He cut his own throat?'

Brendan was despairing at the tone of her voice. He wished he hadn't told her anything. 'You just had to see it.'

When Gwen spoke next, she tried to sound sympathetic, but firm. 'It was an illusion, Bren. I couldn't see it. *You* didn't even really see it.'

'No—' he stopped himself and took a deep, shaky breath. 'I don't know what it was, but *it wasn't in my mind.* I saw it. It was standing in that doorway, cutting its own fucking throat.'

Gwen suddenly burst out, 'But *why*, Bren? Why should you be seeing all these things and having all these nightmares now? Are you ill? Are you losing your mind?' she added, before she could stop herself.

'I don't know anything anymore,' he said. 'Except that I'm scared. I'm scared all the time of what might be waiting for me next time I fall asleep, and now I don't think I even have to be asleep! What's worse, sometimes I feel I'd do almost anything to get away from it all,' he said in a dreadful voice.

'What do you mean—anything?' Gwen asked sharply.

He said quickly, 'No, forget I said that. I'm not thinking straight.' He sneaked a guilty glance at her.

Gwen looked at him long and hard, but decided not to press him any further.

The next day Gwen left Brendan at home. He convinced her he was fully recovered from the night before and quite capable of spending a normal day. He intended working more on the spare room, setting up his computer properly and maybe erecting some shelving on the walls.

'I'm fine,' he told her. 'I've been thinking about last night and I've got a theory. My guess is that I always have residue of the sleeping tablets in my system and they don't like strong alcohol. Those pills are pretty heavy stuff, you know.'

'I know. So, what are you saying? You hallucinated?'

'Did *you* see anything?' He smiled at her, but it was a crooked smile.

'No,' she admitted, after a moment. She went over and hugged him, then kissed him affectionately. 'I've got a nine-to-fiver today in the maternity ward. Want to cook some dinner? I should be home by six at the latest.'

'Sure,' he shrugged. 'When do you go into Emergency? Soon, isn't it?' Gwen's hospital rotated experienced nurses through the more demanding, or traumatic, departments such as Emergency or Intensive Care.

'Next week, for a two week stint.'

'Lonely nights for me,' he kidded her, then realised what he was saying when a look of concern appeared on Gwen's face. He became serious. 'I'll be okay. I'll get on top of this thing soon and besides, I've always got the tablets,' he added, pulling a wry face.

When she was working normal hours Gwen liked to take a bus into the hospital, rather than driving her small Toyota. It saved a lot of money otherwise spent on petrol and parking. It also let her read, or simply sit and think over things. She didn't mind the press of other commuters, easily shutting them out of her mind.

Now she sat silently, her face touching the window, but not seeing the cityscape slide past in front of her. Brendan's problems were beyond her experience, but she slowly decided there must be someone at the hospital who might be able to throw a little more light on things. In fact, someone immediately came to mind and she resolved to track down this person during her lunch break and try to get some information.

One of her first jobs when she arrived at work was to find someone sympathetic to tie up her braid into a more acceptable bundle. Today it was one of the administration receptionists, who never failed during the task to click her tongue and lament she was never able to grow her own hair so long. Gwen chatted with her for a while, then idly asked, 'Is David Mooreson on today?'

'Starts in an hour and goes through till six.'

David Mooreson was a specialist in head injuries and probably had a greater knowledge of the workings of the human brain than anyone else in the hospital. Gwen knew him well from her shifts in the Emergency Room, where he was often called in to examine accident victims. During a coffee break Gwen telephoned him and he readily invited her to join him for lunch, eating, as he did, over his desk in his small office.

'Some of the Admin staff are horrified at the stains that appear on my paperwork,' he added with a chuckle, over the phone. 'One day I'll put their minds at rest and explain they're only beetroot or tomato sauce.'

She called again before leaving to see him, asking if she could bring him something on the way. Gwen ended up backing through his office door balancing two cups of coffee in addition to her own sandwiches.

'How's the kiddie factory?' Mooreson asked, rising to help. He took one of the coffees, then with his free hand unceremoniously swept a pile of papers to one side, inviting Gwen to sit in a chair and use the space to eat her lunch.

'Production's slow today,' she told him, sitting down gratefully. 'But it doesn't seem to stop the mums from having me run around like a mad woman all morning.' She went on to ask him about the progress of several mutual patients, then they discussed the latest gossip circulating through the building. Finally, Mooreson screwed up the wrapping from his sandwich and lobbed it expertly into a wastepaper bin in the corner.

'Now,' he said seriously. 'You obviously have something you want to ask me, so you'd better spit it out.' He smiled encouragingly. He was a handsome man in his early forties, with a dark, full head of hair only just beginning to show tinges of distinguishing grey.

'Well, I'm not quite sure what I want to ask.' Gwen laughed to cover her uncertainty about what she was doing.

'Try, and see what comes out.'

'Okay.' Gwen took a deep breath. 'What can cause hallucinations?'

Mooreson blinked in surprise, 'Oh, I thought you might be chasing some career type of advice.' Gwen could see him mentally adjust his thinking. 'Okay, what sort of hallucinations?'

It was Gwen's turn to be surprised. 'How many sorts are there?'

'For a start, there's the sort that are on the periphery of your vision, like almost feelings that something's there, but when you look at it directly it disappears. Then there's the type that's as solid, seemingly, as you are to me sitting there.'

'The solid ones, then.'

He smiled, 'I had a feeling you were going to say that.' Mooreson settled into his seat. 'Well, the first, most obvious cause of a hallucination can be a drug-induced state of mind brought on voluntarily. You know about those sorts of drugs, in one way or another. It is possible, too, for the same sort of effect to occur through an unplanned, or unforeseen, reaction to various prescribed medications. It's a nasty fright for the patient, of course, but often soon pinned down and remedied. It's certainly not very common—'

'What if you're not on any drugs?' she interrupted him.

'Then you have to look at a natural mental disorder.'

'Someone going crazy, you mean.'

He smiled again, this time gently, as he sensed Gwen was harbouring a genuine concern. 'For want of a better word—yes.'

'Are there any other possibilities?'

Mooreson looked at her for a moment. 'I think you'd better tell me who we're talking about here and exactly what they're seeing. It would help, you know.'

'Brendan, my boyfriend,' Gwen said reluctantly. 'He's been having nightmares and seeing—ghosts, I suppose you'd call them.'

'But something you see in a dream could hardly be called an hallucination.'

'Well, that's the problem,' Gwen said hesitantly. 'Last night he says something straight out of one of his dreams walked through the door of a restaurant we were in and stood there, cutting its own throat—'. Gwen's voice trailed off as she realised how strange it sounded. 'That's what he said, anyway,' she added, reluctantly. Mooreson merely raised his eyebrows.

'I see. No drugs? No bonks on the head lately?'

'No, none that I know of—and I'm almost certain I'd know.'

Mooreson looked apologetic and spread his hands. 'Obviously this is not a time for snap judgements, but I'm afraid if these things are happening and continue to happen, you might have to seek professional help. Perhaps even psychiatric help.'

Gwen was crestfallen. 'So he *is* going crazy?'

'Well, there is one other possibility, of course.'

'Really? What's that?'

'That the apparition exists, that there *is* something there.'

Gwen was amazed. 'Are you saying I should believe in ghosts? Do *you* believe in them?'

'Personally, I don't believe in ghosts, no, because I've never seen one, but let me tell you something interesting.' He paused to take a sip of his coffee. 'I was looking at a book one day in the library, just whiling away the time until the kids picked what they wanted to read. It was called something like *350 Famous Ghost Pictures*, or whatever.' He waved his hand, then held up a finger. 'But the point was, in the beginning of the book there was a foreword and in it, the authors claimed they had researched the authenticity of every photograph to the best of their ability, but couldn't ever declare any of them to be proven one-hundred percent genuine. Then they added—and this is the interesting bit—that of all the 350 possibles, if just *one* of those photos was genuine you'd have proof that ghosts exist. Put that way, the odds are pretty good, don't you think?'

'I see what you mean.' Gwen was reluctantly impressed.

'So, your Brendan is either on drugs you aren't aware of, going crazy quite naturally, or being haunted. Which do you prefer?' Mooreson smiled to take the sting out of the question. Gwen, however, considered it quite seriously for a long time.

'Pass,' she said finally, shaking her head wearily.

Mooreson was watching her. An uncomfortable

expression came on his face and after a moment he said, 'Look, I do know someone else who might be able to help you, if you want to go that far. It's a bit, ah—unusual, I suppose you'd say.'

'Who?' Gwen was puzzled. Mooreson was normally so sure of himself. Now he was writing a name and address on a piece of paper for her. He handed it across the desk. 'Warden Anthony,' she read. 'That's a different name. Who's he?'

'He's sort of an expert on ghosts,' Mooreson explained. 'I don't hand out this sort of advice every day, you realise. I'd appreciate it if you didn't tell too many people about it.'

'You're kidding.' Gwen looked doubtful. 'A ghost hunter? Like in the movies?'

'This guy's no ghostbuster, or some weirdo freak, believe me. He's actually a leading software programmer. Ghosts are just a hobby,' he added with a small shrug.

'I don't know if he could help, David. Someone like this might just aggravate the situation.' Gwen read the note again. 'I doubt anybody could help, to be honest.'

'Put it this way.' Mooreson said, spreading his hands. 'Warden's about the best man you could talk to about it and, more to the point, he would be your best chance of discovering whether somebody's playing tricks on you.'

'Playing tricks? What do you mean?'

'You know, maybe someone's trying to scare you out of your house—that sort of thing.'

'They're doing a bloody good job, if they are,' Gwen said quietly.

'So, give him a call. I don't think you can lose, do you?'

'No, I suppose not.' She put the note in her pocket, hoping Mooreson wasn't offended that she hadn't leapt at this chance. 'And thanks.'

'Do you think Brendan's capable of getting violent?' he asked, startling her.

'I—I haven't even considered it.'

'I don't want to alarm you, but if he has a developing mental problem, it could be the next symptom to manifest itself. You should be keeping a very careful eye on him for that sort of thing.'

'I'll remember that,' she nodded, nervously.

Mooreson's warning stuck in Gwen's mind and nagged at her for the rest of the day. She didn't feel better about it until, later in the day, she signed out two ampoules of sedative and some syringes and packed them to take home. That evening, as she tucked them away at the very back of their refrigerator so Brendan might not notice them, Gwen guiltily considered that she might be overreacting. Still, it felt better to be safe and have the sedative there, if it was needed.

5

Jeneatte Beason badly wanted to be a journalist and regarded Brendan as the perfect role model. She was more than a little infatuated with him too, but Brendan tried not to notice. She had arrived early in the morning and he was showing her his new office, the computer blinking at them from his desk.

'It's nearly set up the way I want it,' Brendan was telling her. 'I want to get a small stereo up here, too. Maybe a bar fridge for milk and coffee, that sort of thing.'

'It's great,' Jeneatte said, looking around with sparkling eyes.

'It's better than working in the kitchen.'

'What do you want me to do today?'

Brendan flipped open a manilla folder lying next to the keyboard. 'Okay, these are all articles I had published more than two years ago. The original serial rights are expired, so I can resell them to a different publication now. Just to be safe, I want to try selling them overseas to a British or American magazine,' he said, rifling through the pages to show her. 'See? All of them are carbon copies of the originals, because I didn't have a computer back then. I want you to type some of them in for me—but not all of them. Some are too topical and outdated. The others I can update and make relevant to today. I figure you've probably got a more objective point of view, so I might let you choose which ones I should do,' he added, knowing she would enjoy the responsibility. Eagerly, Jeneatte picked up the top paper and scanned the text. He added, 'You can do any editing you think's worthwhile, too.'

'Can I? Are you sure?'

'Sure you can,' he said, smiling. 'You normally proofread my other stuff. This isn't much different.'

'Okay, great.' She looked around the room. 'Where are you going to work?'

'I have to go out and do some things. That's why I asked you here. You may as well be working on the computer while I'm not here.'

'Oh,' she murmured, looking disappointed. Brendan managed to keep his face straight. She was only seventeen and very pretty—so good-looking Gwen often grumbled half-seriously about he and Jeneatte being in the house together, alone. Sometimes Brendan told himself Gwen might have good cause to worry, especially when Jeneatte wore the tight stretch jeans and T-shirt she had on today. He saw her eyes going to a pile of books and bulging files scattered across the floor in one corner.

'That's the stuff I want stored in the cupboard there,' he instructed her, 'I'm going to try leaving a shelf free for you, for anything you might want to keep here.'

'What are they?' she asked, poking with her foot experimentally at one of the crooked piles.

'Current serial rights I can't touch, or articles I couldn't sell. There's some reference books too, things like that,' he said, shrugging. 'I'll work out some sort of system, one day.' Jeneatte seemed shocked at the idea Brendan could actually write something no one would think was worth publishing. He didn't notice, staring at his watch and calculating his movements. 'I'll be gone for the rest of the day. Stay and work as long as you want. Stick around for dinner tonight, if you like. Gwen will be home around six—me too, I guess.' Ducking down, Brendan gazed through the window. 'They're forecasting afternoon storms again. I suppose it's that time of year,' he added, and gestured at the computer. 'Don't forget to shut down this thing if a storm gets too close.'

Jeneatte was nodding absently, already thinking about work. She sat down in the office chair. Brendan stood silently for a moment, running over everything in his mind to see if there was anything he'd forgotten. Satisfied, he touched her shoulder and said goodbye. Jeneatte murmured a farewell as he was walking out the door. Already she had picked up the first file and started reading, deciding if it might be used again. A few minutes later she heard Brendan's car start and move off down the street.

Brendan needed to go into the city centre. He suffered patiently through the inner-city traffic, finally turning into a multi-storey carpark. He was relieved to see no 'Carpark Full' sign and, pulling to a stop, he took a ticket from the machine. The boom arm rose and Brendan edged his car forward. Facing a choice of trying the six upper levels or turning left and searching the two basement levels, he chose the latter, plunging the vehicle down a steep concrete ramp. The tyres squealed on the smooth concrete as he did several circuits of the carpark, dropping down to the lowest level. At first, the basement was looking like a bad choice, then he found an empty space near the very end of the last section. Brendan glanced at the car's clock before he turned off the ignition. He would just make his first appointment in time.

Jeneatte worked diligently, surrounding herself with manilla folders, reference books and instruction manuals for the computer's software. She created a filing system within the computer and began typing in the old articles. She finished two, before rewarding herself by going downstairs to the kitchen to make a coffee. While she was standing next to the stove waiting for the kettle to boil, something through the window caught her eye.

Clicking her tongue with annoyance, she moved closer to see. A part of the horizon was being slowly consumed by a mass of grey-black cloud. She couldn't see any lightning yet, but outside there was an uneasy calm. Jeneatte figured she had at least an hour until the storm came close enough to worry her. She went back upstairs, carefully carrying the coffee. Back inside the office, she decided to finish the drink away from the organised chaos of the desk, so she wouldn't be tempted to start working again. Jeneatte was determined to give her eyes regular breaks from the computer screen, so she stood, sipping the coffee absently. Her gaze fell on the pile of material Brendan wanted stored in the cupboard and, reaching out, she opened the cupboard door to see how much space was available.

Only two shelves were used so far and these were only half-filled. The others were empty—but no, she corrected herself—there was something on the very top shelf. She put the coffee cup down and, standing on tip-toe, she pulled down the thing from the uppermost shelf. It was a metal box, green in colour and about half the size of a normal shoe box. Intrigued, and ignoring the feeling that she was prying, Jeneatte rattled the tin. Things bounced around inside.

'He won't mind,' she decided aloud. 'He wanted me to organise the cupboard, so I've got to know what's in there.' Moving back to the desk, Jeneatte sat down and put the box on her lap. She nearly broke a fingernail trying to get the lid off but, after resorting to a letter-opener, finally the tin lid popped away.

She raised her eyebrows at the military badges. 'Interesting,' she murmured to herself, stirring the contents around with a finger. A gleam of gold made her draw a sharp breath. Jeneatte pushed aside the medals and picked up the charm by its leather thonging, letting it dangle in front of her face. The green, jewelled eye seemed to wink at her invitingly. 'Wow, check this out,' she whispered. Like Brendan, Jeneatte found the charm instantly captivating. She figured it was possibly made of gold, judging by its weight. Suddenly, she was snapped out of her reverie by a cold shiver sweeping over her.

'Damn.' She turned to look out the window. The storm was closer—much closer—and she still had work to do. Jeneatte dropped the charm back into the tin regretfully and pressed the lid back on. Something about the charm niggled at her for recognition and the notion annoyingly occupied her mind. Another shiver brought goose bumps out on her forearms. Jeneatte hadn't brought any more clothing, but she thought it would be okay to borrow something from around the house.

She walked out of the office and along the short hallway to the main bedroom, peeking cautiously through the door, before going inside. The place was neat and tidy, the bed made. Jeneatte started having second thoughts, unsure about going so far as to open any drawers in search of a windcheater or woollen jumper. Then she saw a sports jacket hanging on the back of the door and decided that would do. The sleeves came down past her wrists and the hemline to the backs of her legs. Jeneatte caught sight of herself in a full-length mirror, with the double bed showing behind her. A fantasy suddenly presented itself in her mind. Brendan would be lying on the bed, waiting for her. Jeneatte would be wearing nothing except the jacket, standing right there in front of the mirror and teasing him with glimpses of her nakedness between the lapels, or bending slightly, making the coat ride up over her buttocks.

She giggled to herself, feeling a warm flush at the thought. And a little guilty, too, because she thought Gwen was such a nice person. To break the mood, Jeneatte hurriedly left the room, returning to the office. Just as she was about to sit down an idea about the charm and what it reminded her of struck her. Jeneatte went back to the cupboard, pulled down the tin and easily flipped the lid off. She gazed down at the golden figure where it lay between the medal ribbons. Studying it for some time, she waited for the answer to come, but only a teasing notion came to mind, leaving her puzzled and a little annoyed. On a whim, Jeneatte slipped the charm into one of the side pockets of the jacket, in case another moment of inspiration arrived and she needed to look at it. She put the lid back on the tin and slid it back onto its shelf. Satisfied now, she turned her thoughts back to work, and returned to the desk. Her coffee, she noticed without much regret, had turned stone cold. It didn't occur to her to wonder how much time must have passed for that to happen.

After a longer-than-usual lunch with a colleague, Brendan hurried to make his next appointment at the bank. Walking briskly along the footpath, he saw that beyond the skyline a tropical afternoon thunderstorm, common at this time of year, threatened to sweep in from the south-east. Already the wind was picking up, bringing a scent of rain and sending dead leaves and litter whirling along the pavement. He put his head down against the breeze and hunched his shoulders. The wind was unexpectedly chilly.

An hour later and the bank was closing when Brendan finished. A junior clerk let him out a side door. Immediately Brendan smelled the rain in the air and felt the sense of urgency everyone carried, trying to get themselves home or into the shelter of their transport before the weather broke. He eased into the stream of pedestrians, letting himself be swept towards the carpark, hoping along with everyone else he'd make it without getting wet.

The rain began with a few brief flurries, then quickly changed to big fat drops plopping steadily onto the pavement. Looking up, Brendan saw a curtain of rain marching down the street towards him. He heard groans of dismay from the people around him. Many began dodging into stores and doorways. Brendan, however, could see a major traffic jam happening in the late-afternoon storm and decided to brave the rain in order to get his car out of the city centre quickly.

He was soaked immediately when the deluge reached his part of the street and swept over him. Putting his head down lower and gasping at the coldness of the rain as it plastered his clothing against his skin, he plodded determinedly on, wary of the now-slippery pavement. The heavy cloud and rain reduced the late afternoon to a murky near-twilight.

At the carpark Brendan was grateful to hurry into the small alcove for the elevator. He pressed the call button, but after a minute or so the lift still seemed unwilling to leave the uppermost level, the illuminated numbers above the door staying on '6'. Feeling cold now because he wasn't moving, Brendan shrugged and decided it would be easier and quicker to use the stairs.

The concrete stairwell echoed his footsteps. Something pushed at his mind and he recognised similarities between moving down into the belly of the building, and his nightmares of walking through the caves and catacombs.

Emerging from the stairs into the carpark the

nightmare-like quality of the place grew as he saw how many of the caged fluorescent lights were broken, making the basement darker than he expected. There was no one else in this section, although there were still plenty of cars parked in their silent rows. From above him, coming muted through the mass of concrete, the sounds of other vehicles moving in the building filtered through like the roars of distant animals. Shivering—a reaction not wholly prompted by his wet clothing—Brendan walked quickly towards his car.

Without consciously realising he was doing it, Brendan began searching the distant shadows as he walked, watching them nervously. It was why he missed the black patch of slick oil directly in front of him, as he placed one foot right in its centre and felt his leg shoot out from underneath him. Crying out, Brendan didn't fall, but barely managed to stay upright. The effort he used to keep his balance caused a wrenching pain in his back. He stopped, frozen in the twisted posture that prevented his fall. He was panting for breath and he knew, if he held his hand out, the fingers would be trembling.

'Take it easy, Bren,' he said aloud, the words slapping off the hard concrete around him.

Fumbling for keys in his pocket, he arrived at the car. As he was fitting the key into the door a strange, yet familiar odour came to him. Brendan automatically took a deep breath through his nose, frowning as he tried to recall. Then, suddenly his gut began to lurch as he recognised the smell.

It was the stench of the burning torch he carried when he wandered the catacombs of his dreams.

'That's impossible,' he told himself shakily, hurrying now to open the car door. He rolled the lock over and pulled the door wide, the action causing a lance of pain to shoot up his injured back and starting a bad headache at the base of his skull. Before he lowered himself onto the driver's seat, Brendan took a last, nervous look around.

In the distance a figure was walking—no, *limping*—along the concrete. Within moments Brendan could see it was a man, hobbling like a cripple with his head bowed. The face lifted towards Brendan, but it stayed teasingly unrecognisable in the shadow as the figure shuffled beyond the circle of light from a working neon. Brendan saw an arm rise, beckoning him, and a disembodied call echoed through the carpark. He didn't understand it, but the hairs on the back of his neck and forearms arose. Something about the approaching figure scared Brendan badly—he didn't know why.

'I don't like this—I don't like this at *all*,' Brendan whispered to himself, a panic rising up inside him. Without knowing it, he put one hand to his neck, unconsciously grasping for something. His fingers groped vainly. He wasn't wearing anything. The headache stabbed at him more sharply, making his vision blur a moment. He juggled the keys into the ignition, started the engine and revved it hard, slamming his door closed at the same time. Quickly, he made sure the other three were locked, then he swung the car violently out of the parking space, the tyres screeching now on the concrete, and accelerated fast down the laneway towards the exit ramp.

Straight for the figure.

'Get out of the fucking way,' Brendan grated through his teeth. He didn't have the courage to stop. He *had* to get out of the carpark.

Remembering to turn his headlights on at the last moment, he saw for an instant a ruined corpse dressed in a rotting uniform, staggering along the concrete in the car's path, before vanishing just as Brendan's vehicle would have struck it down. Brendan cried out in fear and shock, recovering just in time to wrench the car towards the exit ramps. He hadn't felt any impact. He glanced in the rear-view mirror. In the darkness behind it was difficult to tell, but Brendan would have sworn the driveway was empty. There was no body lying sprawled on the concrete. He hadn't run anyone over.

Clamping on his fear and slowing down, he drove the remaining distance to the toll booth in a sickened daze, looking repeatedly in his rear-view mirror to see if the corpse was somehow following. There was a queue of cars waiting to pay and while the delay made Brendan feel trapped, expecting a ghoulish tap on his window at any moment, it also gave him valuable moments to recover. He kept one eye on his mirror and the other on the line of cars, willing them to get out of his way. The parking attendant took his money, giving him a doubtful look, but Brendan automatically depressed the floor pedal and sped off under the boom.

As the car emerged from the carpark, a deluge of rain instantly blanketed the windscreen, blinding Brendan. He had an impression now of being trapped in his car underwater, at the bottom of a deep pool, and he fumbled for the wiper control. A face suddenly pressed itself against the windscreen and Brendan cried out, jerking backwards in his seat. The face was only there for a moment, distorted by the thick film of water, then it was gone, but Brendan had seen it was the face of a young girl, her fair hair splaying out around her head in a halo, as if he were staring up at her corpse, floating on the water's surface above him. She was dead—drowned. Her dead eyes had stared down at him accusingly.

The first swipe of the windscreen blades cut the water off the glass, removing the last shreds of the hallucination and letting the real world back inside. It was a world of pouring rain and slow-moving vehicles. Sodden, hunch-shouldered pedestrians walked by on either side, looking enviously at those lucky enough to be in cars and out of the weather. Brendan kept driving mechanically, blinking in a mild shock at the images he'd seen. He focused on controlling the car, forcing himself not to dwell on what happened. It helped him to keep his sanity, stopping him from going over the mental edge.

*

Jeneatte worked for another half-hour, keeping a watch on the storm's approach through the window and twice pulling the metal charm from her pocket, staring at it as if the act itself would explain the strange attraction she felt for the thing. Then, one exceptionally loud crack of thunder rattling the window told her it was time to shut down the computer. Any power disturbances within the suburb might damage the system. She risked another few minutes, printing out her work so far, then turned everything off. Quickly, she began shuffling the papers into order. Jeneatte had done a lot of editing of her own and she was impatient to see how it would come out in print.

After reading only a few pages she felt an unexpected despair. Her own writing seemed awful. She could clearly see where her own work imposed itself on Brendan's original writing. Her words were like blemishes on a good painting. It made her stop and think—and she didn't like the thoughts that came crowding in.

Who the hell did she think she was? What had her believing she was capable of improving Brendan's articles? In fact, what in God's name made her think she could write at all? With a sudden, uncharacteristic harshness Jeneatte told herself she must be some sort of conceited fool.

Tossing the sheaf of papers onto the desk, she stood and began pacing the room. Rain started lashing at the window, but the occasional flash of lightning and rolls of thunder were still quite distant.

As she walked awkwardly within the confines of the office, Jeneatte had one hand in the jacket pocket, fingering and rubbing the metal in there. Feeling exasperated, she turned to the pile of material to be stored in the cupboard. *It's something I can do without too many stupid mistakes,* she told herself savagely. Opening the cupboard door, she began stacking things on different shelves, reading what they were and deciding their rightful place as she went.

But after several minutes of this Jeneatte concluded she was achieving nothing useful after all and, in a fit of temper, slammed the door closed again. Returning to the desk, she tried reading her work once more. Again, the words looked wrong, jumbling together with an amateur syntax of primary-school standard. Staring down at the page, Jeneatte felt tears spring into her eyes. She threw the sheets down, then realised how she was behaving and took a deep breath, trying to calm herself. She was startled to hear it coming out as a sob.

There was something she could do—should do. Something that *would* help her relax.

She put fresh sheets of paper on the desktop and took the charm out of her pocket, laying it on the surface in front of her. Using a pencil, Jeneatte began a detailed copy of the charm, drawing in every nick and scratch on its golden surface and even flipping it over to sketch the back with its drilled node of metal and the stained leather thonging threaded through. She made four attempts at each side, rejecting her efforts every time and pushing them impatiently aside in favour of a blank page. On the fifth drawing, the pencil point ripped through the paper. Her wrist and fingers ached from gripping the pencil.

Another mood change swept through her. She suddenly, desperately, needed a walk and some fresh air to clear her mind, believing it might let her come back and try again. Try anything—writing or drawing, it didn't matter. As long as she got it *right* next time. She didn't care about the rain drumming against the house or the rolls of thunder making the walls vibrate. She *had* to get outside. Without thinking about it, Jeneatte dropped the charm back into the jacket pocket as she got up from her desk.

She walked along the hallway towards the stairs, passing the main bedroom. Pausing for a moment, she remembered her earlier fantasy of seducing Brendan, wearing nothing but his jacket.

Stupid bitch, a voice whispered in her mind. Jeneatte agreed, believing now that Brendan Craft wouldn't find anything attractive about her at all. She was too young and not half as pretty as Gwen. And he would probably be angry at what she'd tried to do with his articles. Feeling tears coursing down her cheek, she turned on her heel and went downstairs to the front door.

Outside, stinging rain forced her to shade her face. Strong gusts of wind tore at her clothing. Still wearing Brendan's jacket, she kept one hand in the pocket, touching and rubbing the charm. Striding resolutely down the street, her body bent against the storm, Jeneatte was uncaring where she was going, her mind filled with bitter recriminations against herself for her recent behaviour, her lack of ability and her foolish fantasies. Two streets later she turned onto a main four-lane road. Early homeward-bound traffic rushed past in a constant stream, throwing up sheets of water from deep puddles and coating Jeneatte with filth, adding to the soaking she suffered from the rain. Another voice—her own voice, she vaguely realised—warned her she was turning numb. From the rain, or the cold—she didn't know which. Jeneatte ignored it, walking on.

The first voice, the insistent one dragging her deeper into a despair, continued its sibilant hissing, strangely clear despite the roar of passing traffic, urging and feeding her inner anger. Jeneatte was nodding and mumbling, accepting what she was being told. Once, she stopped in front of a large, plate-glass window and looked for a long time at her reflected image. She should have seen a beautiful young girl. Instead, she saw a bedraggled and mud-stained woman, staring back with a gaunt, haunted expression.

Ugly, someone said in her head.

Jeneatte nodded jerkily.

She stumbled on for nearly an hour, the storm unrelenting. Until finally she understood she'd arrived somewhere. Somewhere good.

The bridge was high, old and narrow, crossing a

major tributary of the city's supporting river system. It had been closed to vehicles for over a year, the timber sinking too much with age, crumbling the road surface and getting too dangerous for cars. A long barrier pole at one end ensured no one was tempted to run the gauntlet. Dodging around it, Jeneatte stepped onto the walkway built along one side of the bridge.

The protective railing sagged alarmingly now, only reaching waist-height. Nobody fished from there anymore. The water below was too polluted from factories upstream. But children were known to ignore the painted warning signs and in the summer months swam out from the banks to jump off the concrete bases of the supporting pylons. In a half-hearted gesture, the town council had erected barbed-wire fencing, jutting out at right angles, less than four metres above the concrete to at least stop the swimmers from jumping off the top railing.

Jeneatte stopped in the centre of the bridge and leaned out, looking down at the water far below. It moved sluggishly, an oily scum on its surface frothing to white with the heavy rain. She hardly saw it—she hardly saw anything—mesmerised by the whispering voice in her mind.

There is a place where you need no one. No pressure. There's no need to succeed. No writing. No drawing. No problems.

For the last time, Jeneatte agreed with the inner voice.

No one saw her. Torrential rain and the isolation of the closed-off bridge hid everything. Her stretch jeans allowed her to straddle the railing easily and stand resolutely, both legs on the wrong side, her feet spread and her hands holding the railing behind. Releasing her grip on the railing, she let herself topple forward into space. Jeneatte didn't scream as she fell, though she let out a grunt of agony as she tore into the rusty barbed wire, taking most of it with her down to the water. Although the wire broke her fall, it cut into her badly. The pain stunned her and she couldn't fight the chill shock of the water closing around her, pressing past her lips and filling her lungs.

Jeneatte drowned in the filthy water, her staring eyes unable to see the thick tendrils of her own blood which she was sucking down her throat.

Back in Brendan Craft's house, the green metal tin in the cupboard shifted slightly, as if a live thing inside were stirring briefly. Then it became still.

6

24 April 1915, Aegean Sea

An armada of ships pushed their way through a gentle swell. The men were crowded tightly together on the decks. Murmured conversations carried above the whisper of the ocean sliding down the ship's side. An occasional bray of laughter seemed unnaturally loud. In other circumstances the mass of bodies forced together might have been uncomfortable, suffocating. This night, it was different. Underneath the excitement and bravado there was a mutual need for moral support, each man reaching out for the feeling of strength and unity that came from sharing these moments. The soldiers stayed close to each other, densely packed until they were all rubbing shoulders, but still always making room for one more, if someone were to join their group. Cigarettes glowed everywhere, pin-pricks of red heat swelling and dying, illuminating the tense, concentrated faces of the smokers.

Galther pushed his way through the press of bodies to where Hamilton leaned against a lifeboat davit. Hamilton didn't notice Galther's approach. He was staring down at the black water churning past as he drew quick, almost desperate pulls on a cigarette. He hadn't smoked when he first arrived in Egypt. Now it seemed he was rarely without a smouldering cigarette between his fingers. In the light of a setting moon his face was drawn and pale.

'Can't sleep again?' Galther asked.

Hamilton started and twisted around. 'Jesus! What are you trying to do? Scare me into falling overboard?' He turned back towards the ocean and flicked his stub over the rail. It fell in a glowing arc and disappeared.

'They reckon submarines can see that sort of thing for miles,' Galther said worriedly, nodding at the water.

Hamilton shrugged. 'The officers haven't told us not to smoke topsides. I guess with so many ships and the moon it doesn't make much difference. There's probably a whole pack of bloody submarines lining us up right now. They could hardly miss, could they? Still, they reckon there's safety in numbers and you'd have to be unlucky to cop a torpedo among all this lot,' he added, gesturing at the ocean filled with craft, large and small, sailing purposefully in the same direction. 'I don't suppose too many blokes will be sleeping. We'll be boarding the boats soon, I would say.'

'Some of the navy swabbies are going around waking everyone. They're handing out tea and hot grub, too.'

Hamilton was tempted to mention something about condemned men receiving their last meal. Instead, he said, 'Well, there you go then. They'll be mustering us to our boarding places after we eat.'

'Did you sleep at all?' Galther had been struggling with thoughts of gunfire and bloodshed all evening. It was now just past midnight. Soon after dusk the troops had been advised to get their heads down for some rest.

'Not really. I've been having some pretty crazy dreams.' Hamilton paused, immediately regretting telling Galther this and trying to dismiss them with a wave. 'Anyway, I keep dreaming about bloody Cairo and the pyramids, I think. I'm not sure,' he ended lamely. But the truth was, he *was* sure. His nightmares were populated mainly by strangers in strange places, yet there was one face that continually came into his mind—the young soldier who had been killed in the pyramid race. Hamilton didn't understand this at all. He only knew that the pale, dead face staring at him in his dreams, sometimes from a crowd, was more frightening than the other inexplicable creatures inhabiting his nightmares.

'Dreams? You mean, nightmares?' Galther asked.

'Sort of,' Hamilton replied reluctantly.

Galther raised his eyebrows in the dark. 'I haven't had a nightmare since I was a kid,' he shook his head.

'Take my word, you don't want 'em,' Hamilton said wryly.

'Pretty bad?'

'Bad enough.'

Hamilton was saved the pain of further description by a disturbance in the troops. Officers and Non-commissioned Officers were passing amongst the men, ordering them to eat their last hot meal and form up in their allotted disembarkment positions by 1.00 a.m.

'Here we go,' Hamilton said quietly, pushing himself away from the davit. 'Let's go eat and grab a mug of tea. It might be the last one we get for a while.'

'It might be the last one ever,' Galther couldn't stop himself uttering the words. Hamilton stopped short, then gave him a friendly slap on the shoulder.

'Hell, I wouldn't worry too much, Galth. I reckon the poor bloody Turks will shit themselves when they see this many blokes camping on their beach in the morning. They'll run away screaming, you watch.'

Galther shrugged unhappily and began easing his way into the queue of soldiers going below decks. 'So, do you think they know we're coming?' he asked, over his shoulder.

'Nah,' Hamilton lied convincingly. 'We'll be in Constantinople before the Turks know we landed. What do you think all that hush-hush lark back in Mena was all about? How we weren't supposed to talk about anything, or even try guessing where we were going to fight? *We* didn't even know where we were going until we got on the boats. It's my guess you probably won't get to fire your rifle. There'll only be a few Turks minding the beach, and they'll surrender as soon as they see our whole bloody army dropping by—wouldn't you?' he added, almost believing himself.

Galther nodded in reluctant agreement.

An hour later they stood in regimented squares painted on the upper decks. The soldiers had practised this routine on many occasions during the voyage. An officer quietly spoke to each group, repeating instructions they had all heard several times before. They were interrupted by a solemn moment—the sound of the ship's engines slowing to an idle. It seemed an age before a naval officer signalled the ship had come to a halt. When everything was ready, the troops filed steadily and silently to the rails, climbing over and descending rope ladders into the boats waiting below. Weighed down by their packs and carrying a rifle, the climb was not an easy one, but the weather was being kind and the men had practised this manoeuvre, too, several times before.

'Hey, Ben!' a voice rang out, loud in the disciplined silence. It was Oakley, straddling the rail and preparing to board a different boat. Among his friends, Hamilton had only Galther in the same craft as himself.

'Good luck,' Hamilton called back, ignoring a stern, disapproving look from one of the officers.

'See you on the beach.' Oakley gave him a thumbs-up before disappearing towards the dark sea.

'Let's keep it quiet,' an officer growled belatedly. Some friendly, muttered jibing answered him.

The landing area was still over the horizon. The plan was for the ships to tow the troop-laden boats closer to the shore, then smaller pinnaces would take over and pull them within the last thousand yards, which would be rowed by crews of navy ratings.

Sitting in the boat, Hamilton looked up at the immense steel wall of the ship passing by as the tow rope was handled back to the stern. Craning his neck, he could make out against the night sky above the dark shapes of those men still aboard the troopship, leaning over the rail and staring down at the soldiers. Hamilton started nervously when one figure in particular stood out from the others. It was a small, pale face that seemed to be staring directly at him.

Hamilton felt himself go cold.

Something told him it was the same dead face he saw in his nightmares, even though he knew it was impossible.

He whispered, 'For God's sake, it can't be!'

'What?' Galther asked jerkily. He had been watching the black water, heaving close enough to be touched now, as if something might rise out of the depths and snatch him out of the boat. 'What did you say?'

Hamilton tore his gaze away from the face above and looked at Galther, who was staring at him with wide, frightened eyes. 'No, it's nothing,' he said quickly. Before Galther had a chance to answer, Hamilton looked back up towards the deck again. The face was gone. Hamilton suddenly wondered if he were going mad.

The next two hours were spent bobbing in the wake of the troopship, four boats per ship attached by a single line. Like baby ducklings faithfully following their mother, they moved across the ocean under the vast panorama of northern stars. The sky was mostly unfamiliar, missing many of the familiar constellations of the southern hemisphere. But the stars were a comfort anyway. They suggested a gentleness and normality, something that could be depended upon, when everything else in the world was about to go insane.

Nobody smoked and conversation was minimal. Everyone was lost in their own thoughts of what the dawn might bring. The moon had set an hour before. Landfall was a broken, uneven black mass rising slowly in front of the more discernible shape of the troopship towing them. The jagged outline of the Gallipoli Peninsula eventually dominated the horizon, looming above the ocean, silhouetted against the bright stars.

The pounding of the troopship's engine died away to a barely discernible rumble, the sudden quiet showing how much the noise had been a part of the soldiers' night. In the distance other engines from the fleet could be heard dropping away to an idle, too. From their own troopship came the noises of the pinnace being lowered. There was the grating of a winch and the groan of a davit taking the strain. Muted commands floated across the water. A soft splash was followed by the starting of a much smaller motor, and the pinnace began to make its way to the stern of the ship to transfer the towline. Meanwhile, the four boats drifted with the inertia following the lack of towing. They clustered together, allowing comments to pass between the boats as they drew close enough. Then a gentle tug on the towrope announced the pinnace had the line. The boats were pulled in a shallow curve towards the land.

That was when Hamilton realised he could *see* the pinnace. The stars overhead were losing their intensity as the eastern horizon, directly ahead, began to pale. The silhouette of the peninsula sharpened.

Minutes later, at a signal from the stern of the

pinnace, a sailor at the bow of each boat cast off the towline. The navy crews immediately swung out their oars and pulled strongly, keeping time with the quiet urging of the midshipman at the stern holding the rudder. With each dip and splash of the oars, Hamilton felt the tension grow in everyone. Apart from the noise of the rowing, there was an unreal silence.

He thought, *This is it. They were landing on an enemy shoreline. They had been training for it, talking about it, waiting for it for months now.*

He wondered how long he was going to live—Hamilton didn't believe for a moment any of the things he'd told Galther. They were in a war and this was going to be a great battle. *Why else,* he told himself, *would they need such a large army?*

They were less than three hundred yards from the shore now. The sky had become an open mural of blazing pink and orange hues, but the landing zone was still held in dark shadows. The sun hadn't yet appeared above the skyline, but everything on the ocean was clearly visible in a dim golden glow reflecting off the clouds. Countless ships steamed slowly in holding patterns out to sea. Bright pinpricks of signal lights stabbed at each other from the bridges of the command vessels. Between them and the landing craft, the sturdy pinnaces chugged calmly to and from the distant fleet, collecting the next waves of troops.

Hamilton could see over a dozen boats would reach the land before their own. He felt a moment of relief, born from the thought that others might bear the brunt of the enemy's defence first, before overwhelming the Turks. The feeling was instantly replaced by a hot, burning shame.

'Hey, where's the fucking beach?' someone asked hoarsely.

No one answered and Hamilton blinked in surprise when he saw why. The shoreline slowly revealing itself consisted mainly of short, steep cliffs. The ridges were touched with the orange colours of the dawn, but the scalloped areas were still hidden in areas of deep purple shade. Tufts of thick vegetation clung precariously to the slopes. Only a thin line of yellow sand ran between the cliffs and the sea.

Answering a dozen enquiring looks, the midshipman took his eyes off the approaching shore long enough to shrug his confusion at the troops. He cast a look over his shoulder at the naval fleet, as if expecting some sort of a signal to be flashed towards them at that very moment. The indecision on his face changed to grim determination as they heard the first sounds of firing from the shore. A vivid rocket streaked into the sky from somewhere near the top of the cliffs. The crackle of rifle fire bounced out across the water and they watched the first Australian troops disembarking into the water fifty yards short of the beach.

'Wakey, wakey, Turkey,' someone murmured.

Nobody in the boat laughed.

In the half-light they could see khaki figures

struggling waist-deep towards the sand, holding their weapons above the water. From the distance it seemed some of them simply got tired and fell forward to disappear below the surface. The others, reaching the beach, scrambled frantically under the meagre shelter of the cliffs. Some of the men crumpled to the sand and lay untidily, with their rifles, so carefully tended to for so long, thrown or gouged into the yellow shale.

Over a dozen boats landed in a short two hundred yard stretch of beach. It became impossible to concentrate on the fate of any particular one, so much was happening at the same time. Hamilton noticed the water around his own craft was beginning to plop and splash. He didn't understand what it was until one of the soldiers cried out and clutched his chest. Another man twisted violently as a bullet struck his shoulder. Hamilton flinched as a round buried itself in the seat next to his thigh. Stupidly he tried to calculate the odds of the bullet missing both him and his neighbour. He imagined what path the shot must have taken to travel between several soldiers. Then he was shaken from his dazed dreaming by the youthful screaming of the midshipman, cutting through the roaring of rifle fire and the crumping of artillery rounds exploding on the beach.

'Out! Everybody out! Come on, move, you bastards! Get to the shore!'

Almost without Hamilton realising it, the boat had covered the last remaining yards and drawn level with other craft still disgorging troops. Some boats, their task accomplished and with a new mission to return for more soldiers, were pulling away from the beach. Like crippled insects, many of them dragged unmanned oars like broken legs. Bloodied, blue-uniformed figures were crumpled at the rowlocks.

Instinct and training took over as Hamilton, Galther and the other surviving men toppled from the boat into the sea. Here the water was chest-deep, the sand underfoot clinging and dragging at their heavy boots. With the last man out of the boat, the crew feverishly reversed themselves and pulled quickly away from the beach. Hamilton had to duck a wildly swinging oar and he cursed as it forced him to dunk his rifle underwater. The ammunition in his pouches was wrapped in grease-proof paper, the pouches themselves greased and tightly closed, but the rounds in his weapon might not be quite so waterproof.

The wet rifle became the least of his problems as the boat cleared the wading soldiers, leaving them exposed. The air was full of the cries of men and the furious barking of rifles, an incredible noise of hundreds of rounds being fired within the space of each minute. The water around Hamilton still spattered with bullets and he thought it was amazing he hadn't been hit, unaware many would have been almost-spent rounds from the fighting on the cliffs. The deadly chatter of a machine gun added to the cacophony, quickly joined by another. With horror, Hamilton saw he hadn't moved more than ten paces since he left the boat. He'd just been stumbling along, up to his armpits in seawater, awed and overcome by events around him. Most of the rest of his group were ahead, pushing themselves hard through the sea. He held his rifle high and tried to catch up, forcing himself against the water and the weight of his sodden pack. Something caught his eye off to his right and he watched a line of high, leaping spurts walk its way across the water towards him. Here and there it touched men like some deadly magic, causing them to die violently, or quietly sink below the surface. He realised, too late, it would pass right through his own bunch. Before he could cry out a warning the hail of bullets lifted. Oddly, the Turkish gunner had switched his aim to the retreating boat, already nearly a further fifty yards out. Hamilton twisted around to watch, feeling a sudden affinity for the midshipman and his crew. They appeared to paddle out of range unscathed. He turned back towards the beach and forged on, the water still lapping around his torso.

He stepped into a deep hole. The soft sand beneath his feet disappeared entirely, as if he'd stepped into an abyss. He managed a strangled cry before the water swept over his head and Hamilton thrashed in a froth of bubbles pressing against his face. It took a moment for him to realise what had happened, pushing his panic back. Conflicting emotions crowded in on him. He thought, for a moment, it was peaceful down here below the surface—peaceful and safe. In fact, it was tempting to stay there and die the peaceful, easy death drowning was rumoured to be. But then the panic returned at the first sign of his lungs aching with the lack of oxygen. He tried to push himself back to the surface, gripping his rifle and using it to prod for the bottom. His pack rode high onto his shoulders, pushing his head down. Hamilton became frantic as he discovered he couldn't raise his face from the water. His chest bursting, he couldn't stop an involuntary gasp, flooding his mouth and throat with harsh, salty water. A blackness began stealing into his consciousness as he choked and coughed the last air from his lungs. Now he *was* drowning—whether he wanted to or not—but was too racked by pain to do anything about it. Opening his eyes gave him a blurred image of the sandy bottom. Another body was beneath him, the khaki uniform blending with the seabed. The corpse was drifting on its back and its eyes seemed to be watching Hamilton's struggles above it. Through his agony, Hamilton thought he saw something familiar in the white, bloodless face of the dead man below.

The corpse reached up towards him, beckoning and offering Hamilton a hand to join it in the depths. If Hamilton still had a breath of air in his lungs, he would have screamed in terror.

Another pair of hands reached past his face and grabbed the webbing of his pack.

It was Galther. Amid all the racket and shouting of the battle he'd heard Hamilton's despairing cry as he went under. Every fibre of Galther's body told him to forget Hamilton, get to the beach and underneath the cliffs, where there seemed to be some cover. But something else made him turn and struggle back towards the drowning man. Whimpering with his fear, he turned his back on the bullets and the apparent safe haven offered by the beach and pushed himself towards his friend still thrashing at the water.

Reaching him, Galther slipped his arm through his own rifle sling, then ducked low to grasp anything under Hamilton so he could haul his face out of the water. At that instant the machine gun swept back on its return traverse, cutting through Hamilton's group. Over a dozen men were hit. Unaware of this, Galther and Hamilton were saved by their low profile and the protective water.

Galther heaved and Hamilton burst out. The weight of his pack nearly took him all the way onto his back, dragging Galther with him, but the smaller man held on fiercely, his own terror giving him strength. He pulled Hamilton close to him, yelling into his face, while the other man retched seawater onto his arms and chest.

'We've got to get out of the water!' Galther's voice nearly broke into a scream, 'The beach! We've got to get to the cliffs!'

Hamilton could only nod weakly as Galther wrenched him more upright and close alongside.

Hooking his hand into Hamilton's armpit and supporting a lot of his weight, Galther struggled for the shore. They had to push their way past the bodies just hit by the machine gun fire. They were floating heavily, red clouds staining the water around them. Galther began to curse and weep monotonously, heaving his friend through the shallows. Hamilton still held his rifle, trailing the barrel carelessly in the water. It wasn't until they finally reached the sand that Hamilton recovered enough to begin helping himself.

'Come on, for Christ's sake!' Galther screamed above the rifle fire. Zig-zagging through the bodies on the beach he half-dragged Hamilton to the base of the cliffs. There, they both collapsed, gasping for breath with huge sobs, their backs to the slopes. Oblivious for the moment to everything else happening around him, Hamilton retched and spat out more seawater. Finally he tipped his head back and sucked in several lungsful of clean air. Looking around groggily for Galther, he said weakly, 'Thanks—for turning back, I mean.'

Galther didn't reply, but gave him a strange look almost verging on hatred.

Hamilton didn't blame him.

7

It was as if Brendan's mind was a stone wall and someone was dismantling his sanity brick by brick. His life was becoming one long waking nightmare of hallucinations and constant fear.

The hallucinations tormented him—the moving shadows at night or the shifting, fleeting glimpses of something at the edge of his vision, disappearing when he tried to look directly at them. Sometimes he would suffer from something quite simple, such as an unshakeable conviction someone else was in the room with him, or that he was being watched, but the room would be empty.

Other times it could be a more subtle, disorientating attack on his sanity, where he might find himself staring at a piece of furniture or a knick-knack on the shelf, convinced he had seen it shift slightly from the corner of his eye. It was like nothing could be trusted to behave as it should anymore. And each moment of doubt in Brendan's mind, each time he had to stop and calm down or tell himself that what he was thinking and seeing had to be impossible, was another instance of fear chipping away at his rationality and his mental equilibrium, remorselessly pushing him towards some sort of breakdown.

He didn't believe anybody else could help him. This wasn't a time for doctors or psychiatrists, or any of the drugs they might prescribe for him. Brendan felt there were answers he had to find for himself. It was all a puzzle that, for the moment, was beyond the understanding of his bruised and muddled mind, but he knew there would be a key to everything. All he had to do was find that key and open the door to all the answers. No one else could do it, because everything was happening only to *him* or only *inside* him. Nobody else could see what he was seeing, or feel the fear that was sometimes so strong it made him ill. He could tell Gwen about it, but the words always seemed to fail him. In the end there was only one small comfort for Brendan. One small hope that helped him make it through the days. It was why he endured the frightening assaults on his sanity.

He was waiting for a sign, a clue to solve his troubles.

He tried to ignore one answer that was always there. It came with the insidious depression building up in his mind with every frightening event. Brendan loved Gwen and many other things around him, but in inescapable moments of solitude he found himself questioning the quality of his life lately. Sometimes he felt, in the final analysis, that it was all his own fault in some way.

This was something he never discussed with Gwen. He needed to deal with it alone. Often, he remembered the night when he'd stood in the bathroom, staring down at the handful of sleeping pills and thinking that all he needed to do was swallow them all. The memory came with a terrifying, whispering voice in his mind, a voice saying that he'd missed a perfect chance to find his answers. To solve the puzzle.

Brendan had stayed up very late working on the final edits to an overdue assignment, and now he was pacing the bedroom, hoping to exhaust himself to a point where he might sleep without taking the two tablets Gwen allowed him. If he took them, he would oversleep into the morning and the following day would pass uselessly with the residue of the drugs still affecting his body.

Gwen wasn't home. She was doing four straight nights in the Emergency Room, otherwise he would have quite happily curled up next to her and stayed awake until dawn, if necessary. The two of them had eaten alone, then Gwen went to work—Jeneatte had apparently decided against his dinner invitation and left before he returned from the city. This wasn't unusual, as Jeneatte was welcome to come and go as she pleased.

He hated going to sleep on his own. It wasn't just the bad dreams anymore. Now he worried that, one night, one of his nightmares might kill him—and it would be real. The terrifying high priest with his bloodied throat had stepped into Brendan's world now, somehow crossing over the threshold of his dreams. The next logical step for the ancient, evil figure would be for him to reach out and touch someone. Touch Brendan. Perhaps with the same red-stained knife to Brendan's own throat.

It was hard for him not to let his mind mull over the wildest possibilities. In his work he'd encountered many things requiring a second, amazed scrutiny before his senses accepted what was in front of his eyes. Some were simple freaks of nature. Others were the instances of bizarre human behaviour, like acts of anger or stupidity that made people do things which would be otherwise unthinkable. Before now, all of them had been explainable in some way.

Now his senses and appreciation of everyday events, his interpretation of the world around him, had been changed forever. Convincing Gwen that his frightening vision in the restaurant was the result of too much alcohol had only been an attempt to convince himself, too. But when he really thought about it, he knew it wasn't true. The vision had been too vivid—too starkly real. The high priest had been there in the room with them. Or at least, for Brendan Craft, he had been.

Sometimes it felt like the pressure, the uncertainty and the fear were going to kill him anyway—slowly, but as surely, as any malignant cancer.

And sometimes, like tonight, he believed it might kill him with violence.

Brendan stopped his pacing to stare out the window. On the street below, the streetlights stayed on all night. Comforting pools of electric whiteness stepped down his road at regular intervals. Cars were parked in the street, each deliberately placed within the glow of the lights to deter car thieves. Ordinarily, it was a pleasant enough neighbourhood. Old, and full of retired successful people. To Brendan it was still starkly urban and he couldn't wait for the day his dreams came true and he finally wrote a bestselling novel. Then he could afford to move to the country to more gentle surroundings where he could write his heart out. At the moment he needed to live in the city, close to where most of the news happened. As a freelancer he could pick and choose what he wrote, but he still had to be where it happened before he could write about it.

He used to like the night-time. Especially the early, pre-dawn darkness, when Brendan would set his alarm clock and rise, so he could work. It was the quietest time of all. No buses or trucks thundered along the street. No one called him on the telephone. It was a time when he got a lot of work done.

Lately, the darkness and shadows held too many surprises, both real and imagined.

Brendan looked out at the street, thinking of nothing in particular, and waiting for some internal sign—perhaps just a real yawn—that he might be able to sleep. His eyes moved constantly from one area of shadow to the next. It was a habit now. He didn't expect anything to stay normal. He no longer trusted his quiet, suburban street.

Suddenly, he saw a man cross through the circular light of the furthest street lamp. It happened so fast, Brendan only had time to register someone was there, then moments later the figure walked under the next lamp. It was a long way off, but Brendan could see there was something different—something wrong. A ball of tension began to grow in his gut. At the next light he saw enough to make him groan with sick fear.

It was the high priest, striding with a regal bearing towards Brendan's house. Brendan instantly knew that tonight would be the final night. The high priest was coming to torment him, or maybe kill him, just like he'd feared might happen ever since the restaurant. Brendan looked down at his right hand and clenched it into a fist, stabbing his fingernails into the soft flesh of his palm until it stung sharply. He left four throbbing red arcs in the skin.

He didn't wake up. He wasn't dreaming.

The high priest moved into the next pool of light and, incredibly, walked straight through a parked Ford sedan, wading through the vehicle as if it didn't exist. His form blended with the chrome and metal, like the double exposure of a photograph. When he emerged from the other side Brendan saw the car was rocking slightly on its springs.

He snapped out of the trance which held him staring at the approaching figure and started looking around desperately, thinking vaguely of weapons and defending himself, although he knew in his heart there would be no defence against something like this. Perhaps if he hid somewhere? Brendan's fear was veering out of control, threatening to smother him. There could be no hiding from something like this either, he realised. Besides, he didn't think he could bear letting the figure out of his sight.

Should he call for help? Ring the police? *Hello, officer. I'd like to report a ghost, or possibly a figment of my imagination, walking up my street to my house. I think he's going to cut my throat. At best, he's going to show me his pet snake.*

The sound of his own short, hysterical bark of laughter brought Brendan back to his senses. He turned back to the window and supported his weight with both hands on the upper frame. He watched, immobile and with a sense of the inevitable, as the figure walked away from the last street lamp and stepped onto the end of the concrete driveway. The spectre stopped and stared directly up at Brendan. There were no lights on in the room and ordinarily, Brendan knew, somebody on the outside couldn't have seen him. But the figure's eyes bored into his as surely as if they were standing face to face. Brendan felt fixed within that stare, like an animal caught in the glare of a car's headlights. He also felt just as vulnerable, standing there and awaiting a swift and gruesome fate.

A shimmering green aura formed around the figure, blurring his outline. Brendan's mouth fell open when he saw the high priest seem to melt and collapse within the green light. Moments later the figure reformed itself in the shape of a large dog, like a starving hound or a hyena, with the shrunken gut and bony haunch of a desperate scavenger. The animal's tall, pointed ears stood out. Yellowed teeth glistened in the reflected streetlight. The beast was a black, menacing silhouette and Brendan feared the dog would bound up the driveway, leap onto the lower roofing and throw itself though the glass. Again, tearing his gaze away from the window, he frantically looked around for some sort of weapon he could use to beat the dog to death, but there was nothing. Then, just as quickly, a calmness overtook Brendan.

He understood it wouldn't make any difference, somehow—his having a weapon. If the creature wanted to kill him, it would. It was as simple as that.

The animal lifted its muzzle to the sky and let out a horrid, chilling howl. Immediately, all the other dogs in the neighbourhood took up the challenge, but their barking and yapping was frightened and nervous. Brendan saw a light come on in a house down the road. There was the distant sound of a baby crying.

With a last baleful glare towards the window, the black dog trotted away into the shadows. For Brendan it was strangely anti-climactic. His nervous system was screwed up tight as a drum, expecting the worst. He stayed at the window and watched the street for a long time, waiting and expecting either the animal or the figure to spring out of the darkness and hurl itself at the house. But nothing happened at all. The streets continued to echo with the sound of dogs voicing their fear at the intruder.

Finally Brendan knew the show was over for the night. Once more he'd been subjected to something fantastic. Something his fragile sanity clamoured to deny—something so frightening it took away his ability to act, to think properly, to challenge and understand. A familiar despair filled him and he slowly twisted around, pushing his back against the wall next to the window. He sank down until he sat on the floor and began to cry softly. He cried until he fell asleep.

Gwen arrived home less than ten minutes later. Stepping out of the car she frowned, and a curl of fear formed in her stomach. It seemed every animal in the neighbourhood was making itself heard with frightened, panicked noises. Dogs were howling and yapping from every direction, the sounds underlaid by the sleepy cursing of their owners. Cats, too, were making their hideous squalling that sounded so much to Gwen like a young child in pain. In fact, the new baby of a nearby couple was crying as well.

Troubled, and trying to ignore a creeping feeling up her spine, she hurried inside. It came as a shock to find Brendan in the darkened room, huddled on the floor against the wall. Gwen's heart leapt into her mouth as she assumed he was seriously hurt or ill, but she managed to keep her wits and quickly examined him. He seemed only to be in an exhausted sleep, though she didn't dare to guess why he was on the floor. She woke him enough to lead him stumbling to the bed, where she undressed him and pulled the light covers up to his chest. Then she took her own clothes off and climbed in next to him. He felt hot and sweaty, and started to mumble sleepily as she pressed close. His words were at once angry, confused and frightening. Gwen listened. What she heard made her grow cold and suddenly she didn't want to hear anymore. She gently stroked his head and chest, soothing him back to sleep again, whispering that there was nothing to be afraid of anymore.

All the while she was trying to ignore the fear building up inside her own heart, and trying to shut out the noises of the animals still howling in the street.

The next morning Gwen watched him carefully as she finished her coffee, tipping the cup to her lips without lifting her elbows from the table. Despite working the nightshift, it wasn't unusual for her to join Brendan at the breakfast table. No matter how late or how long she worked, she always woke up in the early morning. It was a fact of life Gwen had learned to live with. Doing something constructive until early afternoon, then having a long nap before returning to the hospital, usually brought her body-clock back into line.

They sat quietly as Gwen struggled to function properly on only a few hours' sleep and Brendan, looking pale and drawn, nibbled unenthusiastically at a piece of toast with marmalade. She arose from the table and made herself a second cup of coffee, pouring lukewarm water into the cup and popping it into the microwave. As the carousel hummed into action, she asked casually, 'What happened last night?' Her eyes didn't move from the microwave.

Brendan took a moment to answer. 'I saw him again,' he sighed, his voice cracking a little.

'Who? The same thing you saw at the restaurant?' Gwen tried to keep the alarm out of her voice.

'Same guy, all right.'

'In the house? In the bedroom?'

'No, he walked along the street and came to the driveway.' Brendan flicked a glance at her. 'I'm not being sarcastic—that's the way it happened.' He remembered the way the figure passed through the car, leaving it rocking, but decided it was too fantastic to describe. 'He just stood down there for a while and looked up at me. I was watching him from the bedroom window.'

'You're sure you weren't dreaming?'

Brendan shook his head, 'I was wide awake—well, I was tired and sort of hoping I might be able to go to sleep without taking any tablets. But I *was* awake. This was no dream—' he stopped and looked helpless. 'Hey, do you want to know the worse damned thing about all this? What I'm starting to hate the most?' Brendan's voice rose with his frustration and he became more animated. 'I don't have a damned clue what to do about it! There's this—this thing who keeps popping up in my dreams, and now he's turning up in my *life*, for Christ's sake! He scares the living shit out of me and I can't do a damned thing about it!' He tossed his unfinished toast onto his plate and began to rub his eyes.

Gwen was quiet for a while, her heart going out to him. Then she asked, 'What about the dog, Bren?'

He looked up, surprised. 'The dog? How do you know about the dog?'

'You said something last night, while you were half asleep. I put you to bed, do you remember? I found you on the floor next to the window.'

'I don't remember,' Brendan mumbled. He took a deep breath, before he went on. 'Okay, this man, this thing, that I saw—he stood at the end of the driveway looking up at me. Then there was this sort of light, like a—like—'. He faltered and fluttered his hands in the air. 'Anyway, it was like something out of a Steven Spielberg movie. And the guy turned into this big black dog. It all happened in a second or so and it was over before I knew what was going on.' He looked at Gwen desperately, expecting her not to believe him, or tell him it was all in his imagination.

'What sort of dog?' Gwen asked instead, struggling to keep her voice calm. The microwave rang for her attention and she removed her cup, adding coffee and sugar from the cupboard, before returning to the table. Sitting down she could see Brendan was trying, too, to brings things back down to a sane level.

'It was the meanest son-of-a-bitch dog you've ever seen,' he smiled, but without humour. 'I couldn't see it that well, but you could just tell, even in the dark. I thought it was going to come through the window and tear me to pieces, like in a horror movie, but it just howled at the sky for a while, then went away. I couldn't believe it.' Brendan shook his head and let out a silent whistle. 'I'm telling you, that howl on its own was enough to make you want to run for your life. Every dog and cat in the neighbourhood must've died of fright. You should have heard 'em, all barking and carrying on at the same time.' Brendan picked up his toast again, considered it, then with a grimace put it back down. He didn't see Gwen turn slightly pale.

She was looking at him over the rim of her cup again and she asked gently, 'So, why didn't you run, Bren? Or hide, if you thought this dog was going to come bursting into the house and attack you?'

'Believe me, I thought about it. But then it was like I saw things plainly without being so scared and I figured—what's the point?' Brendan started to look helpless again. 'How can you hide from something like this? Or fight it? I don't even know what it is—or where it is! It might be real, or half-real, or probably just something—' he stopped and made a frustrated gesture with his hand, ending it by tapping his head with his fingers '—all in my head, I suppose,' he finished lamely. 'I guess I just don't know anymore.'

Gwen toyed with her coffee, swirling it around, until she made up her mind on something. 'Listen, Bren. I had a talk with Dave Mooreson the other day, remember him?'

'The head injuries guy? Did he suggest locking me away?' Brendan couldn't stop himself sounding a little bitter.

'That was one of his suggestions, but not the one I'm thinking of—' Gwen replied calmly. 'Look, this is—well, it's hard for me to say this,' she added, bringing a frown to Brendan's face.

'I know, I know,' he said quickly, almost angrily. 'But you think I need professional help.'

'No, it's got nothing to do with you—well, of course it does, but not what you think. It's more something I have to accept myself.'

This made Brendan silent for a moment and he looked puzzled. 'What are you talking about?'

'I think we have to start looking at the possibility these things you see are real. I mean, that you're actually seeing them—' Gwen's voice trailed off. She couldn't lift her eyes from the coffee cup.

'What?' Now Brendan was surprised, almost stunned. 'Are you saying I'm seeing ghosts?'

'Well, what do you think?' Gwen suddenly challenged him, her eyes glittering. 'What do you *really* think? You must have thought about it. How else can you explain it all?'

'Yeah, okay—' he was flustered. 'When I'm scared shitless, I'll believe anything. But in the cold light of day, it's different. You're seriously suggesting I'm being haunted? How? Why?'

'We don't know, but what else could it be?'

Brendan was shaking his head, unwilling to concede. 'No, it has to be something wrong with my head. It has to be something in my *imagination*. The alternative is just too fantastic.'

'I don't think you really believe that.' Gwen leaned closer, her voice hard. 'Deep down, I think you agree with me. It's just that, like me, you find it a bit hard to swallow—and maybe it's easier to keep thinking you're going insane. Hell, I don't know which I'd prefer, either! They're both as scary as each other.'

Brendan laughed weakly at her. 'You've got no idea at all,' he told her. 'And why are you so certain, anyway? What suddenly brings you down on the side of the ghosts and the ghouls?'

'Your dog,' Gwen said simply. 'And all the other dogs in the neighbourhood, for that matter. Not to mention a few cats and babies, too.'

'The dog?'

'You told me that when it howled, every other dog for miles around went crazy. Well, I got home last night in time to hear that. It scared the hell out of me.'

Brendan looked at her dumbly.

Gwen gestured impatiently. 'Don't you see? It's proof that what you say happened, really did happen. Proof enough to me, anyway—' Gwen paused, searching for the right words. 'Look, you're the only one who's seen these visions, right?' Brendan nodded, beginning to understand. 'Even in the restaurant, when this thing was supposed to be right beside me, I still couldn't see it, right? But when that dog howled, *every other dog in the whole damned suburb heard it!* Isn't that what you're saying?'

Brendan stared at her and, for a moment, his eyes shone with a mixture of relief and hope. Then they returned to being dark and troubled. 'That's no good, Gwen. I could just as easily have imagined or hallucinated that, too.'

'You're not listening to me! I'm saying, I didn't imagine it, did I?' Gwen's voice rose with exasperation. 'I heard them, too! No, Bren. We have to draw the line somewhere, and I think I just drew mine. What if we walk down the road together now? Ask a few folks if their dogs went crazy in the early hours of the morning? I think I know what they'll tell us. Do we need to do that?'

Brendan stared at the table top and, after a moment, shook his head. 'No, I guess you're right.' He thought for a while. 'All right, for the moment let's say *maybe* there's something happening here, but there's got to be more to it than—'

He froze in mid-sentence.

'Brendan? What is it?' Gwen said, alarmed at the expression on his face. She was reminded of how he'd looked in the restaurant and a chill ran down her spine. He could only stare at a point in space near her.

There was a soldier in the room with them, standing next to Gwen's elbow, as if he'd just walked through the connecting door. He looked tired, his fixed gaze concentrating on nothing, his eyes framed by the brim of his slouch hat. A cigarette smouldered in the corner of his mouth. He wore a dirty uniform, patched and supplemented by civilian clothing. His stubbled face was grimy and lined by lack of sleep. In the crook of his arm was a rifle, the barrel almost touching the floor. With his free hand, he patted absently at his pockets.

'For heaven's sake, Bren! What's wrong?' Gwen's anxious hiss cut through Brendan's shock.

He kept his voice flat and as calm as he could. He didn't take his eyes off the soldier and to stop a violent trembling he kept his hands, palms down, pressed hard against the table.

'Standing right next to you is a soldier,' he said,

his voice tight. 'He has a gun—a rifle, but he's not going to fire it. He's just standing there, staring at nothing.'

'What?' Gwen jerked her head around, trying to see all corners of the room. 'I can't see anyone! I can't even *feel* anything!' she added, unexpectedly.

'If you moved your right arm out, you'd be touching him.' Brendan's voice had become awed more than fearful. The vision of the soldier didn't seem threatening in any way.

'Brendan, I can't see anything,' Gwen said, speaking slowly and clearly now. 'Can you? Are you really seeing something? Or is it in your own mind? Can't you tell the—' Then she stopped just as Brendan had.

'Oh my God!' she breathed, after a shocked pause.

She'd been looking directly at Brendan, but as she spoke her eye caught something unusual in the window behind him. It was the reflection of the interior of the kitchen, created by the bright overhead fluorescent light. Not a good reflection, because it had the shaded rear yard as a backing, but on the tinted surface you could see outlines of the refrigerator, the kitchen table, Brendan's back and shoulders, and another white blob which was Gwen's staring face.

And somebody else.

The faint shape of someone standing near her. The shape held something under one arm—something long and quite bulky. Gwen couldn't discern any colour in the reflection, but it was unmistakable that the figure wore a hat of some kind. She tried hard to calm her racing pulse and concentrate, trying to glean more detail from the glass image, but it was too hazy and indistinct.

She didn't see what Brendan saw.

The bullet took the soldier high, near his temple. Blood and brains burst in a spray from the other side of his skull. A mist of red cascaded down onto Gwen, but she couldn't see or feel it. Brendan cried out in horror and tried to stand too quickly. He was forced to sit again as his legs hit the underside of the table. He watched helplessly as the soldier slumped to the kitchen floor behind Gwen's seat. Gobbets of bloody stuff, spattered out from the exit wound, covered her, the table and everything on it. All he could see of the soldier was a pair of worn, dirty boots poking out into the passageway.

'Hey, what the *hell* happened?' Gwen asked, ducking this way and that to try and recapture a glimpse of the reflection in the window. She was unaware of the horrible sight she made. Brendan stared at her, aghast.

'He was shot in the head,' he told her, his voice thick with disgust and suppressed nausea. 'You're—you're—' he made a meaningless gesture with his hand, then changed it to fierce rubbing of his own eyes. It seemed to achieve something, for when he looked at her again the gory mess was gone. So, too, were the boots sticking out from behind her chair.

'That was just *incredible,*' Gwen whispered shakily. She reached over the table to take one of Brendan's hands.

'So much for your ghost theory,' Brendan said despairingly, staring bleakly down at her. 'I saw something standing *right there,* and you had no idea! It's got to be—'

'But I saw it, Bren,' Gwen interrupted him. There was a stunned silence between them as Brendan stared at her.

'What?' he said disbelievingly.

'I saw him, too.'

'No, you didn't! You can't have. You were looking—'

'I damn well *saw* him, Brendan!' she snapped, squeezing his hand to make him listen. 'In the window,' she nodded at the glass. 'I saw a reflection in the glass. It was faint, but it was there! I saw a man—and he was carrying something under one arm. Then he disappeared.'

'His rifle,' Brendan explained vaguely. Now he stared at the spot where the soldier had stood.

Brendan suddenly felt light-headed—almost euphoric. He was overcome by a feeling of relief. In the space of the last few seconds everything had taken a sudden about-turn. The rules of the mad game he'd been playing had changed and he immediately began to feel stronger, knowing there was something definite he could question now—something other than his own sanity. The seeds of doubt were fading. Perhaps the fears, the uncertainty and the sapping, sleepless hours full of nightmares were still to be endured, but the possibility that they were all the product of his diminishing, diseased mind was gone. His mind couldn't be creating visions other people could see, things other animals could hear. Even with Gwen only witnessing a reflection, it was enough. It still meant he was being tormented by something *outside* of himself, not the onset of his own insanity. He didn't know who, or in particular why, but right at that moment he didn't care.

'It's fantastic,' Gwen was saying, her voice a mixture of fear and wonder. 'It's like seeing a UFO, or even *God!* All your preconceived ideas about ghosts—all the books, the movies, the stories. They're all thrown into a different light. Now I'm thinking, how many of all those others could be true?'

'You didn't see him shot?' Brendan asked her.

'Shot? No,' Gwen said absently, struggling to come to grips with what she had seen. 'That's dreadful,' she added blandly, looking around the floor as if expecting to see the soldier's body lying there. She was trembling slightly.

Brendan became intent. 'Gwen, listen to me! Something's just occurred to me. I think what we just saw happened a long time ago. We only saw a re-enactment, understand?'

'I—I think so,' Gwen said. 'But what does it mean?'

'Mean?'

‘A soldier! Why are you seeing a soldier?’ Gwen stared at him, and at the same time Brendan suddenly slapped the table with his hand, making her jump.

‘The tin! The tin upstairs! With the badges and that weird medallion of a—’ he stopped, a new thought stealing his voice.

‘A dog,’ Gwen finished for him quietly.

‘I think we’d better take another look, don’t you?’ Brendan decided. ‘Wait here and I’ll bring it down.’

Walking through the house and up the stairs, Brendan couldn’t stop himself from anxiously inspecting the shadowed doorways and approaching each corner half expecting some new vision to step out in front of him. Even without any implied threat, the soldier had been an eerie, unsettling vision. In the office, Brendan went straight to the cupboard and reached up for the tin. As his hand was about to close around it, he hesitated, staring at the green tin. Something about it was niggling at him, and eventually Brendan decided it had been moved. That worried him more than it should have, putting a fresh cold feeling in the pit of his stomach. He looked over his shoulder at the desk and saw some papers which he knew Jeneatte would have been working on. Thinking hard, Brendan told himself that, just because the tin had been moved, it didn’t mean Jeneatte had looked inside it—and Brendan couldn’t understand why he didn’t like *that* idea either.

But it was hopeless to worry about it. He could

only ask Jeneatte what she'd done the next time he saw her. And perhaps it would be best to put the tin out of her reach, too. Hide it somewhere.

Shrugging, Brendan grabbed the tin and walked out of the office.

When he returned to the table, Gwen had made fresh coffee for them both, using the small chore to force her thinking into some sort of normality.

'I forgot all about this thing,' he admitted, prising off the lid with a butter knife. Gwen gave him a doubtful look, but he didn't see it. The lid of the tin rattled on to the tabletop and Brendan tipped out the contents.

'That's it,' he breathed, picking up the golden charm with unsteady fingers. 'That's the dog I saw last night.'

'Hey, humour me,' Gwen said, leaning forward and almost snatching it out of his hands. She put it flat on the table and covered it completely with a plate.

'Come on—you're kidding, aren't you?' Brendan asked, needing a moment to understand.

'No. Don't you remember what happened last time?'

'Yeah, so I was ill. Big deal.' He reached for the plate, but she stopped him.

'Bren, I'm not sure what it was exactly that made you ill, but it happened straight after you gave that nasty little thing a good look. For all we know, you may have absorbed something poisonous through your skin,' she added, with a sudden inspiration.

Brendan paused reluctantly. 'Okay, I hadn't thought of that.' He eyed the plate warily, then turned his attention to the badges. 'Okay, so just for the moment, what have we got here instead?'

Gwen picked up the hatpin. 'A rising sun hatpin. Remember that television series? This is the badge of the Australian Army.'

'I guess there's no doubt about that.' Brendan said, holding up two 'Australia' epaulet badges. There were two other nondescript ones. 'But what about these? And the medal? Which one is it?'

'Victoria Cross?' Gwen said hopefully and with a weak smile.

'I don't think so,' Brendan shook his head ruefully. 'Even among my scattered, confused ancestry, I think I would have heard about any Victoria Cross winners.' He studied the coloured badges more closely. They were a simple oblong shape, divided in half, one bright yellow, the other red. 'These are just coloured. They have nothing written on them,' he complained.

'So we're back to square one.'

'We haven't had another look at the charm,' he reminded her.

'Do we have to?'

'Why are you so afraid of it?'

'Come on, Bren! It's obviously linked with some of the things you've been seeing, don't you agree?' Gwen sounded a little desperate.

'Yes, but I don't see—'

'Like I said before, just humour me, okay?' Gwen

interrupted him. She really had no idea why the golden figure upset her so much. It was an instinctive thing, she realised, which she couldn't put a name to. 'Look, I've got an idea. Wait a minute—and *don't* look at the bloody thing until I get back, promise?'

Surprised at her manner, Brendan could only nod. She left the kitchen and shortly Brendan heard her rummaging around upstairs. He absently stirred his coffee until her footsteps emerged again from the passageway. Gwen was carrying a polaroid camera.

'What are you going to do with that?'

'What do you think?'

'Aren't you overreacting a bit?'

Gwen placed the camera on the table more firmly than necessary. 'Let's think up a few ground rules here—agreed?' she snapped, and continued without giving him a chance to argue, her voice becoming harsher. 'We are dealing with something totally new and unknown, right? I don't know about you, because you've been seeing some pretty scary things, one way or another, for some time now, but *I* just saw a damned ghost in the kitchen window and that's got me confused and more than a bit frightened, okay?'

Gwen stopped and closed her eyes for a moment. Brendan saw she was shaken and he felt guilty. He realised, too, that he *was* constantly too wrapped up in his own problems to notice how they were affecting Gwen. Brendan reached out a hand, but she kept her eyes closed and didn't see it, instead gesturing at the plate concealing the charm. 'The last time you touched that thing,' she continued, 'you had some sort of fainting fit you couldn't explain. Maybe it's because you actually touched it—we don't know, but it makes sense not to touch it again until we know. There are lots of things in this world that can get into your bloodstream through your skin. Ask me, I'm a nurse,' she added wryly, then managed a wan smile. 'So, while we're at it I say—well, hell! Let's go the whole hog and not even look at it, okay? Not you, anyway. I want you to just lift the plate, so I can take a quick snap of it, then we'll put it back in the box. My theory says we can look at a picture of the damned thing all day, if we want to.'

There was a silence as she looked pleadingly at Brendan to agree with her.

'Okay,' he said gently. 'There's no harm in being careful.' He picked up the edge of the plate. 'Are you ready?'

'Wait a second.' She fiddled with the controls for a moment and turned on the flash. It needed a few seconds, making a high-pitched whining noise, for the capacitors in the light to charge. 'Ready,' she decided, checking the glowing LED on the side of the camera.

Lifting the plate aside, Brendan couldn't stop himself looking down at the charm. A golden gleam struck his eyes, a glow suffused with a green core. Once again he felt his entire attention drawn towards the charm like his mind was being sucked into a vortex, but before anything took a real hold the spell was broken by the blinding flash of the camera. Brendan pulled back quickly, startled. Blinking his eyes, he watched as Gwen scooped up the charm, a grimace on her face as she held it gingerly between her fingertips, and dropped it back into the tin. She sealed the lid with unnecessary force.

'There *is* something about the thing,' she declared. 'I can feel it. It—it's *wrong* somehow.'

'I can't feel it,' Brendan murmured innocently. 'I still think it's just an old piece of gold jewellery.'

Gwen again sat opposite him and they put their heads together to watch the photograph develop.

'Is it working?' he asked.

'Yes, it develops the main picture first, then the colours sort of fill in.'

The image slowly formed on the paper. Brendan was the first to comment.

'You missed, you dummy,' he said lightly. 'Where did you learn to take pictures?'

But Gwen wasn't amused—she was looking frightened. 'I didn't miss,' she said unsteadily. 'There's no way I missed. How can you? You just point the damn thing and press the button! Look, you can see the salt shaker and the edge of your plate, so it must have been aimed at the right spot.'

Brendan looked from her to the photograph several times. 'Are you telling me you *can't* take a picture of that thing?' Gwen returned his gaze and nodded slowly.

'Okay, that does it!' Brendan picked up the tin

and stood up with one movement. 'Maybe I have to handle being haunted by a ghost—even one with a rifle—*especially* if I can't do much about it anyway. But I sure as hell can do something about *this*!' He walked from the kitchen through the back flywire door.

Gwen heard the slap of the plastic rubbish lid.

Brendan came back inside rubbing his hands together. 'Collection night tonight. No more problems.'

Gwen was too taken by surprise to disagree. Instead, she stirred the pile of military pieces on the table. 'What about these?'

'Well, I reckon these are different.' Brendan sat down again. 'I suppose we should try and find out who they belonged to.'

'Well, they must belong to that soldier who was here—the ghost.' Gwen picked up one of the badges. 'But how can we find out?'

'My first idea, a moment ago, was to go down the library and try identifying these bits and pieces. I was going to do it while you have your afternoon nap, but I'm not so sure now.'

'Why not?'

Brendan looked uncomfortable. 'Well, after all—things are starting to get a little strange around here and I don't know about leaving you alone in the house. Christ knows what could happen next. Perhaps you should think about moving out for a while—maybe stay with Jodie until we sort everything out.'

Gwen stared at him. 'What? And leave you here alone? Don't be ridiculous! Maybe we can both move out somewhere—but I don't know where. I'm certainly not going to leave you by yourself.'

Secretly, Brendan was relieved Gwen wasn't going to leave him alone, though he knew that was selfish and possibly risky.

'Listen,' he gave her a hard look, 'I don't particularly want to leave the house. I don't believe we'll be able to get to the bottom of things that way, which means you'll be staying here, too. Are you sure you want to do that?' At Gwen's reluctant nod he added, 'Okay, so if you get scared, or feel threatened in any way, I want you to get out straight away, understand? I mean it.' He ended with a smile. 'Anyway, if things get to that stage, I'll be right behind you.'

'Okay,' Gwen smiled back, but it faltered after a moment. 'Brendan, I really don't think I'm under any threat. I think it's you who's going to attract all the attention—not me.'

Brendan sighed and took some time to reply. 'Yes, I think you're right.'

8

After another coffee together, using the time to settle down and think about their situation more calmly, Brendan and Gwen came to an understanding. They couldn't always stay close or live their lives as if every moment might bring another ghostly visitor. There were often going to be times when either Gwen or himself would be in the house alone, and while the soldier's spectre had been alarming, it wasn't particularly threatening. Brendan kept telling himself there hadn't been any real danger. And besides, he suspected Gwen was right and that without his own presence, nothing would occur anyway. He was the catalyst, the cause of the supernatural events somehow. Gwen alone in the house should be safe.

At the same time he realised that whatever demon it was that had come into Brendan's life, bringing the terrifying visions with it—be it with a magical, dog-shaped charm or some ancient poison he'd absorbed through his fingers—it wouldn't go away by itself. Brendan couldn't just sit around the house waiting and worrying what would happen next. He had to *do* something about it, before things got worse. The trouble was, he had very few options.

He decided to start with the library.

A modern building, it had a white, suspended ceiling and metal shelving for the books. Posters hung everywhere, urging people to read regularly. One corner of the building had facilities for viewing videos, while another boasted a large stereo for listening to audiobooks. Computer terminals were scattered around the rooms, their monochrome green screens waiting patiently for someone to enter a query. Considering it was only a suburban library, there was an appreciable maze of books. At least, enough for anyone to comfortably lose themselves in.

Brendan threaded his way through the tall stacks, counting down the catalogue numbers until he came to the section he wanted. The first book he tried was an illustrated volume of armies of the world, but it was an American publication and

Australia hardly rated a mention, being grouped together under the broad heading of the British Commonwealth. A second book used hand-painted figures to illustrate the different uniforms of armies of the world, but the badges and insignia were smudges of colour not supposed to represent anything specific at all. Then he saw on the bottom shelf a group of books dedicated to Australian military history. He bent down, sensing he was getting warmer in his search. He picked out Alan Moorehead's *Gallipoli* and opened it near the centre. He found himself looking at two paintings depicting Anzac soldiers on the beach and their life in the trenches. The pictures were graphic, grabbing his attention, and Brendan began reading the accompanying text. Standing in the aisle with the book in his hands, he quickly became absorbed in the story.

Some movement at the edge of his vision finally distracted him from the pages. He looked up and along the aisle, expecting someone wanting to push past him, but it was empty. Brendan shrugged, thinking it must have been somebody walking past the ends of the shelves. Unexpectedly, the shrug turned into a shiver and he turned back to the book. If it was going to help him at all, Brendan had decided to take it to a warmer part of the library to sit down and read it properly. However, still captivated by the fascinating stories and paintings he discovered on every page, he absently remained standing in the aisle, holding the book in front of him.

After a while his palms became sticky from the protective plastic cover, so he absently wiped his hand on his jeans before turning the page. He was surprised and annoyed to see he left a red thumbprint on the paper and he swore softly to himself, then looked around guiltily to see if anyone heard him. He idly checked the palm of his hand to see where the stain might be coming from and saw his skin was coated with red, sticky stuff. He figured it must be the dye coming from somewhere out of the book jacket, prompted by his sweaty hands. Automatically, he put his hand to his nostril and sniffed.

It was blood.

Brendan jerked his face back, nearly flinging away thc book in a reflex action. He stopped himself in time. Luckily, no one else was in his aisle. He looked at his other hand. That, too, was covered in blood. Twisting around, he could see a dark smear on the back of his jeans where he had wiped his hand earlier.

He went cold inside as he realised what was happening. The book was oozing blood from the cover, coating his hands and leaving him like a murderer with the evidence on his fingers. Brendan immediately started panicking, looking around desperately for what to do. The thought occurred to him, *But is it real? Can anybody else see it?* He stretched out a shaking finger and touched the exposed metal of the shelving. He left behind another smeared red fingerprint. It didn't really prove anything—the blood could still be only his own personal hallucination. But Brendan couldn't take the chance.

On the jacket of the book was a painting called *Soldier*. It showed the haggard, tortured face of a Lighthorseman floating eerily and dismembered in amongst a wash of red. Whether the red was supposed to represent blood, Brendan couldn't be sure—it didn't matter. It was definitely blood on his palms and gumming between his fingers. He stared at the picture and tried to understand what was happening to him when, without warning, he experienced an incredible wash of emotions. Completely against his will, Brendan was overwhelmed with despair and exhaustion. He felt the flesh of his face become heavy and sensitive, and he knew he must have paled and developed the deep, dark rings of fatigue under his eyes, just like the soldier in the painting. His body was aching with bruises and unknown abuse. In his head he began to hear distant noises. The sounds of men screaming in fear and anger. There was a constant roaring noise, like gunfire.

Brendan felt himself being dragged into the soldier's world, living a moment of the man's life.

Even though he knew he was still standing in the middle of a safe, suburban library, he started to become desperate and frightened, not knowing how it was going to end. He had to escape the startling emotional freefall. As if he was drunk, the room started to spin around him and then Brendan thought he was falling, the floor beneath him opening into a whirling vortex trying to suck him down. The voice of common sense, shouting to be heard through the mist of the illusion, told him he had to let go of the book—get rid of it somehow. It should have been easy to push it back into any place on the shelf, but Brendan couldn't focus enough to do it. This simple act was beyond him. He knew he was still standing upright, but the spiralling room was getting worse.

'Mr Craft, are you all right?'

With these words, spoken by someone close by, everything snapped back to normal, but the sudden transition back to sanity was just as shocking and Brendan stood in a daze, blinking stupidly at the girl in front of him. It was Lisa, the library's youngest assistant and someone he knew quite well from his frequent visits. She had come unnoticed from somewhere amongst the shelves and was now looking at him anxiously.

'I—I'm not sure,' he finally managed to reply, his mouth opening and shutting uncertainly.

'Do you want to sit down? You look like you should—my God! Where is all that blood coming from? Did you cut yourself?' She moved closer to help.

'I must have,' he said hoarsely. 'I—I didn't notice, I'm sorry.'

'It's this metal shelving,' she told him, taking him by the elbow and steering him out of the aisle and towards a distant white door. 'They auctioned off all the lovely old wooden shelves. They said it didn't fit in with the modern decor,' she added scornfully. 'Now we're always getting complaints about the sharp edges. Hey, you're a writer! You should write a letter to someone about it.' She nodded at his bloodied hands, which were still nursing the book. 'Goodness, this is terrible,' she said in a matronly way.

'Oh—the book . . .' he tried lamely.

Lisa pushed open the door with her rump, delicately guiding both his arms through the opening so he wouldn't touch any of the white paintwork. 'Don't worry about the book. I'll clean it up later. We cover all our books with plastic, so I'm sure there's been no damage done.'

'I should pay for it.'

'No, really,' she smiled at him. 'We couldn't have one of our best customers doing that, could we?'

She sat him at a table in the staff lunchroom and plucked the book from his hands with her fingertips, putting it next to the sink.

Brendan stood again immediately and had to fight off another brief moment of dizziness, but he could feel the burden of the soldier's emotions beginning to lift from his mind. 'If you turn the tap on for me, Lisa, I'll wash my hands.'

'Are you sure? I was going to bathe it for you. It must be a pretty nasty cut, with all that blood. Are you still dizzy?' she asked, changing the subject and confusing Brendan more. 'I thought you were about to black out back there. You frightened the life out of me!'

You don't know the half of it, Brendan thought wryly. 'No, I'm okay—it happens now and again when I read for too long,' he said, the lame excuses forming in his head as he spoke. 'I really should invest in some glasses, I suppose.' Brendan suddenly realised he had to think of a way he could disguise the fact there would be no wound at all. 'Ah, and could you find me a roll of sticking plaster?'

'Of course. That's what I was going to do,' she said. After turning on the tap she moved away and began looking in a first-aid cabinet on the wall, saying over her shoulder, 'I'm certain there's some in here.'

Brendan didn't answer, but quickly washed his hands clean under the running water. As he had suspected, the flesh of his hands was unmarked. He patted them dry on a towel hanging next to the sink, then pressed his thumb over an imaginary cut in the ball of his other thumb. He turned to find Lisa waiting with a piece of plaster.

'Just put it on the back of my thumb for me, will you?'

'Hold your hand out properly, I can do it,' she argued.

'No, please.' He tried hard to keep his voice calm and nodded down at his hand. Lisa shrugged and pressed the plaster across the top of his thumb. The piece was too large and covered from the tip of the nail right down to his knuckle. With deft sleight-of-hand Brendan smoothed the dressing around his thumb while hiding the supposed injury from the girl. He ignored the strange look she gave him, before she went to the sink and began to clean the book with a damp cloth.

'Thanks a lot,' he said, feeling he should say more.

'No problem,' she smiled, then held up the book. 'See? No problem here, either. All cleaned up.'

'I stained one of the pages with a fingerprint,' he admitted.

'That's nothing. We have people who make notes in the margins, or circle the page number so they know where they are—even in the new books. Do you want it?' She held the book towards him.

The question took him by surprise. It was the last thing he wanted to do. 'What?' he said, trying to work out what to say.

'The book. Do you want to borrow the book?'

'No—no, I don't think so. It didn't have what I wanted,' he added weakly. In fact, he never wanted to touch the book again. The memory of the blood coating his hands—*someone else's blood,* he knew instinctively—made him feel slightly sick.

Lisa prattled professionally on, eager to please. 'Okay, so did you see *The Australian Soldier*? It's in the same section.'

'No, no I didn't,' Brendan said absently, looking around for the means to escape. All he wanted now was to go home without being rude.

Lisa went to the door and held it open for him. 'That book might help you more, though I wouldn't really know. I'm not much of an expert in that sort of stuff. I only thought of it because he's another of our local authors who comes in here a lot. I'm surprised you haven't met him,' she said, still chit-chatting merrily, but dropping her voice down to a whisper as they came back into the library. 'The poor old fellow lives down near the football ground. He always complains that every second week during winter he can never get any work done. You know—home games and people parking their cars on his front lawn and everything,' she added with a quiet laugh.

Brendan had stopped dead, reaching forward to grasp Lisa by the elbow and stopping her from moving further away from him. 'Who?' he asked, confused by her torrent of words, but understanding something important.

'Mr Netthold—Carl Netthold, the author. I thought you realised—'

'A historian? A war historian? He lives near here?' Brendan didn't realise, with his sudden urgency, that he was scaring her a little.

'Well, I just told you he wrote that book, *The Australian Soldier*. I guess that makes him some sort of expert, doesn't it?'

'Can you give me his address?'

'Oh dear—' Lisa looked sorry she mentioned Netthold. 'I don't think I can do that. It's not allowed normally, of course—'

'What about just his phone number?'

'Well—' Lisa squirmed, uncomfortable under Brendan's stare. 'That's the same really, isn't it?'

'I am another writer, don't forget. I'm sure he wouldn't mind.'

There was a moment with Lisa looking trapped, then she finally gestured for him to follow her to the desk.

Carl Netthold had no qualms about inviting Brendan to come over and see him straight away, after Brendan stretched his luck a little further at the library and asked if he could borrow their phone to make the call. Netthold was a studious, bespectacled man of nearly seventy years of age. In his earlier years—and for some time afterwards, Brendan suspected—he'd obviously been a very fit man and he certainly didn't deserve Lisa's description of being a 'poor old fellow'. Once inside the historian's house, Brendan was busy envying the man his study. It was exactly what he hoped to create in his own office. The walls were lined with countless reference books and pictures of a much younger Netthold, the photographs faded to sepia, with their subjects invariably in uniforms of some description. The room had a warm, wooden feel to it. Brendan was surprised it didn't have a log fire roaring in the corner. On a large desk, clashing with the old-worldliness of everything else, a modern wordprocessor hummed quietly.

Netthold saw the direction of Brendan's gaze. 'A necessary evil, I suppose you could call it. My younger son bought it for me for my birthday. I don't understand how the blasted thing works most of the time. I just type in what I want and I know a few rudimentary commands to save my work, but if anything at all goes wrong I have to get straight on the phone and call Jim. Makes me feel like a fool.'

'I know what you mean,' Brendan said. 'They're handy things to write with, but when they go wrong they seem to go wrong in a big way.'

'Exactly!' The older man was pleased. He gestured around the room, inviting Brendan to take a tour. He had a few words to say about almost everything on the walls and Brendan listened with genuine interest.

'Korea,' Netthold said, pointing to a picture of two men, neither recognisable because of a swathe of clothing. They were standing knee-deep in snow. 'I missed out on the Big One because I was too young, but it gave me the bug to join up anyway. They sent me to Korea instead.' He regarded the picture with fondness for a moment, then his expression turned sad. 'Nearly as damned-fool stupid as Vietnam, really. It didn't occur to anyone back in those days, though.'

Brendan sensed Netthold enjoyed these impromptu opportunities to display his knowledge and own rich experiences. He said encouragingly, 'Not many people know we sent anybody to Korea.'

'About 14,000, all up. Lost nearly 350. That's

not bad, I guess, if you think about it,' Netthold added ruefully. Turning away from the wall he waved Brendan to a comfortable lounge chair, sitting himself in his office seat and swivelling it around until his back faced the computer. 'Now, what can I do for you? You're a writer yourself, you say. Is it something you're working on?'

'No, not really, though I suppose I might be able to use it later on,' Brendan replied, surprising himself with the idea. 'Actually, I'm trying to identify someone.'

'A soldier?'

'Yes.'

'Is he dead?'

'Ah—of course,' Brendan said, seeing in his mind the ghostly soldier standing in his kitchen.

'Why, "of course"?' Netthold asked, frowning. He pointed again to the picture of the two soldiers in the snow. 'I'm not dead, right?'

'No, I see what you mean.' Brendan smiled an apology.

'So, what have you got?'

'A few badges and a medal. Nothing more, really.'

'A picture?'

'No.'

Netthold eyed him carefully and leaned back in his chair. 'That makes it a bit tricky,' he said slowly.

Brendan came to an unexpected decision. He'd come to see Netthold with the intention of using a plausible story made up primarily of lies—an imaginary family history and some vague references to the green tin. Anything, in fact, except admit he was trying to trace a ghost. Now, in the face of Netthold's hospitality, it seemed the wrong way to do it. Brendan hated being dishonest and this man, he realised, was surrounded by ghosts of his own. *One more probably wouldn't make a difference,* he thought.

Brendan took a deep breath and said, 'Okay Carl, I guess you can only kick me out again.' He steeled himself to look the other man in the eye. 'I'm trying to track down the identity of a ghost—the ghost of a soldier.'

A tense silence followed with Netthold steadily returning his gaze, until he asked, 'A ghost, hey? Have you seen it yourself?'

'In my house. My girlfriend couldn't see it, but she could see its reflection in a window.' Brendan shrugged slightly. 'I don't understand that.'

Netthold let his own breath out with a whistle. 'All I have to put up with is the blasted television. My wife's addicted to it,' he said, breaking the tension. He shook his head. 'Have you got the badges with you?'

Brendan pulled them from a pocket and handed them over. Before looking at them, Netthold reached into a drawer and took out another pair of glasses, exchanging them for the ones he already wore. Still, he peered short-sightedly through them at the collection of things on the desk blotter in front of him. Immediately, he dismissed the hatpin, saying quietly, 'That's never changed.' He gave the medal only a cursory look too, grunting in a manner that told Brendan he recognised it. Then he turned the coloured badges over in his fingers several times, giving them a more careful inspection.

'These are nothing, yet they are everything,' he said cryptically.

Brendan wasn't sure if he was meant to respond. After a moment he asked, 'What do you mean?'

Netthold held up one of the pieces of cloth. 'In the last two world wars—some people bunch them together and call them the "Thirty Year War", did you know?' he added unexpectedly.

Brendan nodded, because he had heard the term before.

Netthold went on, 'Well, mass volunteering and conscription flooded the ranks with new, raw recruits. Thousands of them. These recruits were often rushed into the front line, or at least bustled through the training process very quickly so they could fight. The point is, they were given no time to develop the sort of *esprit de corps* the peace time soldiers possessed. Oh, don't get me wrong—it wasn't so much they were lacking a sense of belonging or a pride about their battalion's or brigade's history. Far from it, normally,' he corrected himself. 'I'm talking about an ignorance of all the little things—symbols and badges—that were considered important before the war and distinguished them from other units. To the untrained eye they can be quite confusing. For example, there were badges like these and ribbons, even tartans, among the Commonwealth troops, not just the Scots.' Netthold fingered the second badge, now almost talking to himself. 'I'm saying a lot of traditions of the individual battalions went by the wayside until the end of the wars, understand?'

'Sort of,' Brendan said, struggling a little.

'The point is, very few of the conscripts understood the basic hierarchy of the army itself, let alone the old traditions. The men, at best, knew they were part of such-and-such platoon, in such-and-such battalion and such-and-such brigade, and so on, but much of it was beyond a lot of them. So the command johnnies came up with these.' He waved the coloured badge. 'You simply ate, slept, exercised and even fought wherever you saw this coloured badge—in this case—and you knew you were in the right place, see?'

'Simple enough,' Brendan nodded.

'True, and it was. The main idea was at least the men knew when they were in the right or wrong place by comparing badges, even if they didn't know where they were supposed to be, if they were mistaken. Don't forget, the lower ranks attracted a lot of illiterate and uneducated men, so things had to be kept very easy.'

'So, do you know who used this particular combination?' said Brendan.

Netthold shrugged and looked amused, knowing his answer would frustrate Brendan. 'Yes, and no.

This pattern may have been used several times in the past. Like Gallipoli, North Africa or even Normandy, although so few Australian troops took part in the invasion of France the chances are slim there,' he added. 'But that's just to mention a few theatres of war, of course.'

Brendan was disappointed. 'Where does that leave us?'

Netthold picked up the medal. 'This campaign medal, I suppose. It's the Gallipoli campaign, as a matter of fact.'

'But, that's good, isn't it? Doesn't it narrow it down? Couldn't you work out what—' Brendan struggled for the right term. 'What division, or whatever, these things belong to?'

'Probably wouldn't take long,' Netthold murmured. 'Then all you have to do is prove your ghost owned the badges.'

'Of course—' Brendan stopped, suddenly flustered. 'Well, who else?'

'I'm afraid I can't help you there. I don't even know where you found them. In the house?'

'Upstairs, in an old cupboard.' Again, Brendan paused for thought, then he shook his head. 'Carl, it's like Gwen says. I have to draw a line somewhere. I found these badges in a sealed tin box in a junk room in my old family house. Ever since I found them weird things have been happening to me. Mostly they've just been really bad dreams. Then this soldier walks into my kitchen this morning and has his head shot off—just like that. I'm not asleep, Gwen's got all her marbles and at least sees the damn thing in a reflection. Now the penny's dropped and I figure they *must* be connected. The ghost and the badges, I mean.'

Netthold raised his eyebrows. 'You saw this poor fellow get shot?'

'He was standing there, staring into space. He had a cigarette between his lips. All of a sudden his head exploded,' Brendan's voice turned thick with horror, 'and he fell. I figure he must have been shot. It couldn't be anything else.'

'Fascinating, absolutely fascinating,' Netthold said, adding matter-of-factly, 'Sniper, from the sounds of it. That's how they got them, usually. A man just got too tired to be careful, eventually. Sooner or later you stick your head up and a sniper blows it off. They're always there, waiting. Was he wearing puttees?'

'Wearing what?'

'Puttees,' Netthold repeated, gesturing at his own leg. 'They were a long strip of cloth the soldiers wound around each leg for protection. They were phased out before the Second War.'

Brendan thought hard. 'I know what you mean now, but I really can't remember. I suppose I was too stunned by what was happening to take much notice of what he was wearing.'

'Never mind.' Netthold handed him back the badges and medal, then leaned back in his chair. 'I can try and find out for you what battalion, or regiment, they signified in that particular campaign, but you'll have to give me a few days.' Brendan nodded gratefully. 'It shouldn't be too hard, as a matter of fact. Gallipoli was quite a military stuff-up from the very beginning, but I imagine those coloured badges originated during the initial training period in Egypt. The top brass in the Allied forces persisted with that sort of organisational rubbish—badges, tapes run across the ground—right throughout the war, almost. Never learned their lesson, even though every plan was always blown to hell and gone in the first few moments of the battle,' he ended with a sigh. He pulled a blank notepad towards him and was silent as he drew a quick sketch of the badges and made a note of the colours.

Brendan hadn't heard the last half of what he'd said. He was mentally berating himself for being all kinds of a fool. Every Australian was steeped in the Gallipoli tradition from their earliest schooldays and it was just as commonly known the troops trained in Egypt before they left for the battle.

Egypt.

With the ancient pyramids and tombs, and endless stretches of sand that might suck a man down. And myths of ancient spirit-men who could turn themselves into black, howling beasts.

Netthold was asking him something.

'I'm sorry?' Brendan had to bring himself back to the present.

'I said, what do you hope to do with the information, once I give it to you?'

'Oh, I'm not really sure. I imagined I could trace it back and find a list of all those men who served in that section. A listing of casualties would be even better. Then I could look for a family name, I suppose.' Brendan's voice trailed off. Spoken aloud, the plan seemed more than a little optimistic, but Netthold was nodding.

'The Australian War Memorial would probably help you, or at least point you in the right direction. You can get a list of those who served with a notation beside their name if they were a casualty—Killed in Action, Wounded in Action—that sort of thing.'

They discussed this some more, then Brendan stood, preparing to leave. 'Look, how can I thank you?' He gestured helplessly.

Netthold waved a hand. 'I'll just put you in my little black book here. I guess there may be an occasion in the future when you can do a service for me, right?' He winked. 'And you've given me an excuse to stay away from this damned machine for a while.' He let out a bark of laughter, nodding at the computer.

'Anytime I can help, that's for sure.' Brendan shook Netthold's hand and gave him a business card, adding that he could call him at any hour if he had any success. As he stepped out the door he couldn't help giving one last envious sigh at the study.

9

Ben Hamilton pressed his head back against the sand and looked up at the sky. The colours of the sunrise were quickly washing out to an azure blue with grey, scudding clouds racing across. The beach was littered with casualties, the fallen men sprawled beside their weapons. The water boasted more khaki figures, mostly face-down, rolling gently with the waves caused by the landing boats. Too late, the lesson had been learnt from the killing spree the Turks enjoyed when the invading soldiers were expected to wade through deep water to the shore. Now the boats were coming all the way in and beaching, the troops only having to contend with knee-deep water, before moving quickly to the cliffs. The concentration of fire onto the beach had slackened too, taking pressure off those still landing, with some of the troops now tackling the defenders directly, but it was still extremely dangerous out on the sand. As Hamilton and Galther lay there, waiting to get their breath and their bearings, other men ran straight up the beach and began climbing the sandy cliffs. They clawed and dug their way up as hard as they could, showering sand down on those below. Occasionally a body would crash down the cliff-face and thud onto the beach.

The two men weren't alone huddled at the base. Many of the wounded had crawled to the same shelter and were waiting for aid. Others, like Hamilton, were trying to recover from near-drowning before going on. There were some men who waited for the chance to dash back onto the beach after stricken friends, watching the sweeping machine-gun fire and judging their moment. As he sat, gasping, Hamilton watched several attempts. Many succeeded, but some resulted in the rescuer getting himself killed or wounded too, leaving another corpse to add to those already lying in the cheerful morning sun. Hamilton lifted his eyes to the dead floating in the ocean, rocking gently in the slight swell or with the passing of more boats. He remembered the white face and clutching hands that had reached up for him from the sandy bottom and an involuntary shiver passed through him.

Galther's voice snapped him back to the present. He was looking helplessly up at the sandy cliff.

'How the hell are we going to get up that?' he said, as if he couldn't see the men everywhere who were shouldering their weapons and throwing themselves into the climb. All along the short face, like a swarm of khaki ants, the troops were attempting to scale the cliffs. It was impossible, from the base, to fire up at the Turkish positions without risking hitting one of your own men. Now and then somebody dashed four or five steps back out onto the beach and quickly fired off a half-dozen rounds at the upper heights, but the risk was great and the chances of success small.

Before Hamilton could answer, in an avalanche of sand two soldiers deliberately crashed back to the beach next to him. Ignoring Hamilton and Galther, they set off purposefully along the base, looking for a better point from which to climb. It was only when the leading man threw a glance over his shoulder that they stopped and ran back. It was Oakley and McAllen.

'Ben! Galth! I thought you two would never get here!' Oakley grasped each of their hands and shook them. McAllen did the same.

Hamilton was amazed by his enthusiasm. 'Got caught in the rush,' he said meekly.

Oakley suddenly looked around furtively and, seeing no officers nearby, took off his hat. Hidden under the crown was a tin of ready-rolled cigarettes. He offered them around, impervious to the yelling and shooting surrounding them. He cupped his hand around a match.

'Saw you go under,' he remarked conversationally. 'Didn't know if you were hit or not.'

'Galth saved my life. I was drowning. Silly bloody way to die, amongst all this.'

'Well, you saved his life too, I reckon.'

'What?'

'Didn't you see? That bloody machine gun went through your mob like a hot knife through butter. If you hadn't been dilly-dallying in the deep water you probably would've copped one too.'

'Christ.' Hamilton vaguely remembered pushing past the floating bodies. He looked at Galther, who shrugged noncommittally.

Oakley was saying, 'Yeah, well—you win some, you lose some. You can owe each other one, if you like.' He speared a plume of smoke from between his teeth. 'What a fucking mess.'

'What happened up there?' Galther jerked his head upwards nervously.

'Got stopped by an overhang,' Oakley explained. 'You've just got to drag yourself up and, while you're having a breather, take a few pots at Johnny Turk. I reckoned it was easier to come back down and start again than climb over the ridges. It's just asking for it, that way. Thank God somebody got those machine guns.' He threw a glance at Hamilton. 'I think it might have been Nick, being a bloody hero, who got one of them.'

There was a silence while they contemplated the

wisdom of this, then Oakley flipped his butt to the ground. 'We'd better get going, before some bloody officer tries to give us some more damned-fool orders.' He moved away, taking the others by surprise. They ran to catch up. Oakley was dodging the new arrivals crowded against the cliff as he trotted along. At the same time he kept a critical eye on the paths and gullies running up the cliff-face.

'Let's try here,' he decided, slinging his rifle and starting to climb. He totally ignored a body tumbling down, missing him by a few inches.

'Jesus Christ,' Galther breathed. He was the last of the three to follow. 'What's got into him? Does he think he's on a fucking training run? Has anybody told him the bastards shooting at us are for real?'

The fighting in the cliffs and through the rugged country beyond was grim, fierce and deadly. Oakley led the way, followed by McAllen, Hamilton and Galther. The last two watched and learned from Oakley's example of kicking his own footholds in the soft sand, grasping handfuls of the prickly vegetation and trying to distribute his weight as much as possible. The problem was, while they were busy climbing or simply hanging on for their lives, they couldn't return the frantic fire of the defending Turks. Luckily, the very act of clinging to the slopes afforded some cover. It was also impossible to determine the exact location of the front line where the opposing troops came into contact.

'Here's a go,' Oakley called down as a warning, after they'd climbed for a minute or so. He stabbed one toe of his boots hard into the sand, then hooked his other knee over a small shrub. Anchored, he unslung his rifle and worked the bolt. 'See that bush there, boys?' he said, aiming.

'Great,' Galther groaned, 'Which bloody bush?'

Nobody answered him. Hamilton was trying to shoulder his own weapon, but every time he took his hands off the sand he began to slide inexorably downwards, kicking dirt in Galther's face. He found he desperately wanted to start firing his weapon—do his bit in the battle. He flinched as the body of an Australian tumbled sickeningly past. Briefly, he remembered the sight of the young private somersaulting down the pyramid and that, in turn, triggered another memory, but it was a vague thing which he couldn't fully picture in his mind. He wondered if he was trying to recall a dream. The crack of Oakley's rifle snapped him back to the present.

'How do you know who you're firing at?' Hamilton cried, half angry because of his own inability to shoot, but also for letting his mind drift. Finding a target was difficult though, because the slopes were dotted with khaki-coloured troops at all heights in front of them. He cursed, feeling useless as he realised he had no idea what a Turkish soldier even looked like. He slipped another six inches backwards and he heard Galther swear and spit sand below him.

'Really punch your feet into the sand,' Oakley advised him calmly, ignoring the question. 'And start shooting at these bastards.' Beside him, McAllen began squeezing off measured, careful rounds. Galther was looking up at them anxiously without making a move to fire himself.

'How do you know they're Turks!' Hamilton yelled again, furiously kicking his feet until he managed to support his own weight. He pulled the rifle off his shoulder with such frustrated haste he nearly ruined his precarious balance.

'It's easy—these blokes are shooting at *us*,' Oakley said, not taking his cheek off the butt of his rifle as he smoothly sent a full magazine towards the Turks. 'Damn,' he added quietly, popping out the empty clip and replacing it with a full one. In front of them, muzzle flashes continued to sparkle amongst the leaves.

Hamilton looked along the sightline of Oakley's weapon and finally spotted the Turkish dugout. A clutch of dirty brown conical hats bobbed excitedly behind a thick shrub. Feeling very aware of the moment, Hamilton raised his rifle, took aim and pulled the trigger.

A soft click was the only result.

'Shit and fuck it,' he snarled, as he wrenched the magazine full of damp ammunition from his rifle. He fumbled in his breast pocket, forced his fingers past the grease-proof wrapping and pulled out a spare clip. He rammed it home with the flat of his palm, disregarding, like an insect bite, something that plucked at his upper arm, burning his biceps.

Oakley was shouting about out-flanking the position. McAllen was nodding and agreeing, but keeping up a steady rate of fire. Hamilton deliberately sighted on one of the conical hats and squeezed off a round. The rifle barked and slammed into his shoulder.

He was utterly confounded to see his first shot—his first attempt to take another man's life, amount to absolutely nothing. His target didn't fall and the fight raged on around him, unabated.

His next shot was equally unsuccessful, and the one after that. He emptied the whole clip and failed to see any difference. He heard someone laughing and amidst the noise Hamilton knew the laughter was directed at him. He looked around angrily, but no one was even looking his way and certainly nobody was laughing. It was a humourless cackle and he could hear it quite clearly. Suddenly, realising who was laughing, Hamilton's stomach filled with a cold fear that had nothing to do with the deadly battle raging around him.

'Shut up!' he called aloud, surprising himself. He had no idea why he did it, or who he believed he was calling to. 'Just shut the fuck up! Why don't you leave me alone?' he added.

Oakley paused a moment to frown down at him, then turned his attention back to firing his rifle.

The laughter stopped to be replaced by a whisper, loud and clear inside Hamilton's head.

Why don't you stand up, Ben? Show yourself. It won't take long, and then you'll be falling just like I fell down the pyramid. Nothing hurts after that—nothing at all.

Hamilton twisted around desperately, trying to locate where the voice was coming from. Deep in his fear he knew who he was looking for, but at the same time he refused to let himself accept it. Corpses nearby all lay still, but Hamilton tried to watch all of them, expecting one to roll over and reveal itself as the dead youth from the pyramid race. Then he shook his head violently. *What in God's name am I thinking? Am I going mad?*

'This is crazy,' he suddenly cried out, anguished. 'I'm going insane. I must be going out of my *mind.*' His eyes focused to see Oakley glaring down at him.

'Ben, come on, mate! For God's sake, pull yourself together. Keep 'em busy!' he called harshly. Oakley's words seemed to push away the other whispering voice and, for the moment, there was no more laughter either.

Gritting his teeth with determination, using every shred of reality around him to keep himself concentrating on what he was doing—on what was real—Hamilton reloaded his rifle and tried again. On his third shot he would have sworn he saw one of the distant heads kick backwards. He experienced a grim satisfaction, serving to further push away the madness lurking on the edge of his mind. The crack of a rifle near his feet told him Galther had finally started firing. Then he saw the reason why Oakley wanted them to keep the Turks occupied. A small section of Anzacs suddenly rose out of the bushes behind the dugout and poured down a murderous fire. Moments later they waved to the following troops it was now safe, and continued their way upwards.

'Let's go.' Oakley made to sling his rifle.

'Wait!' Hamilton called weakly, holding up his empty rifle clips.

'Right,' Oakley nodded, agreeing. He leaned hard into the sand and began tending his own magazines. Then he called casually, 'Are you okay, Ben?'

Hamilton was ejecting the damp ammunition from his original clip and replacing them with fresh, dry rounds. His mind was only half on the job, while he was trying to mentally reject the memory of the mocking laughter and terrifying, whispering voice. 'Yeah,' he yelled back after a moment. 'I—I just got too mad with these fucking cliffs and got crazy. I'm all right now.'

'Don't blame you,' Oakley said, with a reassuring grin.

Again, Hamilton marvelled at Oakley's poise among the frenzied fighting around them. Taking his example he tried to ignore his shaking fingers and calmly reload his second clip, then he removed and topped up the one in his rifle. Last, he quickly tugged the grease-proof paper away from his extra ammunition in his pouch, throwing it down the slope. Watching it flutter in the air he saw, beyond it, the beach was now teeming with soldiers advancing on the cliffs in a great khaki horde.

'I'm ready, Annie!' he heard himself shout.

'Ready, too,' McAllen echoed. Oakley gave them the thumbs-up and began climbing again. He edged his way towards a stream of men advancing through a gully. Sadly, the safest ways to climb were shown by the different concentrations of casualties strewn across the landscape. In some areas the bodies were literally piled up on top of each other, demonstrating to all how deadly that way could be. Others, like the gully the four were heading for, offered some protection. But still, because of high, flanking positions on both sides of the entire landing zone, the Turks could snipe at most of the attacking troops all the way from the beach right through to the furthest point of the advance.

The terrain beyond the cliffs was a series of sharp, rugged ridges and open gullies. The Turkish defences there had been well placed, but were never designed to cope with a large major assault. Instead, they were more emplaced to deal with minor, flanking movements that might come from the much better landing points to either side of the cliff face—where the Australians *should* have landed. Still, the Turks exacted a terrible toll on the invaders, who threw themselves recklessly towards the Turks' guns until they succeeded in establishing a precarious bridgehead through the sheer weight of their numbers and a stubborn determination. Oakley, Hamilton and the others adopted the same method as most, which meant finding a concentration of the enemy and working hard to wipe them out, then moving on. As they fought their way ahead, they ran through the initial wave of troops who had taken the full brunt of the defending fire and now lay in pitiful heaps, their numbers massacred.

At one stage Hamilton called forward desperately, 'Christ, Annie. What are we supposed to be doing?' He was crouching below a rocky outcrop. Fifty yards to their left a group of Lighthorsemen were edging their way viciously, with casualties, towards a deep Turkish dugout.

'Keep going,' Oakley called back. 'I haven't seen a fucking officer since the beach. It's up to us, I reckon.'

Pressing themselves hard against the sides of a rocky gully, they moved towards a small knoll, which looked like an obvious and advantageous place to be. The Turks apparently agreed, for the Australians attracted a burst of machine gun fire from somewhere close to its base. Ricochets and splinters of rock whined murderously through the gully. It was a miracle that only McAllen suffered a wound, a mild gash in his thigh making him gasp with pain. Learning lessons fast everyone melted into the smallest cracks and gaps in the rocks for cover. The machine-gunner stopped, robbed of visible targets. Hamilton wondered why he didn't keep up his fire and rely on the deadly, ugly ricochets to do the job.

'You okay, Macca?' Oakley yelled.

'Yeah, just give us a sec—' There was a grunting sound as McAllen wrapped and tightened a piece of legging around his thigh. 'Not serious,' he grinned at Hamilton, who was the only one who could see what he was doing.

'We've got a real job, here,' Hamilton nodded at the knoll. Inside himself, he was amazed at his own calm nonchalance. At the same time he realised how quickly men were adjusting to their surroundings, and he was beginning to understand that Oakley's almost heroic attitude on the beach was more the result of the extra crucial minutes he'd spent under fire.

'Fucking machine guns,' McAllen grumbled, tugging at the temporary bandage.

'Did Nick get one? Didn't Annie say so?'

'We reckon we saw him going hell-for-leather straight at a dugout and the boys broke through, but Annie wasn't sure it was him.'

'Hey, what about Squibby?' Hamilton asked, suddenly remembering. 'Has anyone seen him?'

Oakley heard him, answering shortly, 'He's still on the beach.'

'Still on the—?' Hamilton fell silent, suddenly understanding. Briefly, he tried to remember what Loel's dark Maltese face looked like and was puzzled to discover it was difficult to picture him clearly.

'Look,' Oakley said, jerking the barrel of his rifle at the knoll. 'We should go now.' The Turkish gunners had either given up or decided the Australians had escaped the gully somehow. Now the machine gun opened up again in a wide sweep to attack the Lighthorsemen, who had taken the dugout and were trying to re-group before continuing on.

'We can move up now, while they're busy,' McAllen agreed.

On Oakley's wave the four men ducked away from their cover and scampered through the gully. With every step they were ready to throw themselves sideways behind protective rocks and ridges. They got to within fifty yards of the Turks, before Oakley screamed for everyone to take cover again as he saw the traverse of the gun move their way. Again the bullets exploded or glanced off the rocks, turning themselves into misshapen, tumbling projectiles many times more harmful. From somewhere close Hamilton heard Galther groan with fear, but didn't dare expose himself to indulge his mate with a friendly, supportive look.

A slow, thunderous boom rolled across the peninsula. It seemed the entire battlefield paused to listen, before resuming their own fierce noise.

'Hey, it's the navy,' Hamilton realised first. 'They've started bombarding.'

A blast of arriving shells shook the ground, but they were landing miles south, supporting English troops further down the peninsula. The naval gunfire quickly grew to a constant roar.

'Why don't they fire over here?' Galther cried, looking longingly at the machine gun post. Oakley rolled his eyes at McAllen, but Hamilton explained for him.

'Galth, they'd be just as likely to shell us as the Turks. No one knows where anyone else is.'

'What a fuck-up,' Galther muttered uneasily. Somewhere nearby a yell went up as a group charged a stronghold. The men sheltering in the gully clearly heard the steely clash of bayonets and the enraged shouting of men in hand-to-hand fighting.

As if inspired, Oakley jerked his head at the machine gun. 'We'll have to rush this one, too.'

'Are you mad? We'll be cut to pieces!' Galther cried in a strangled voice.

'No, wait until he sweeps in another direction, like before. We nearly made it last time.' The Turks chose this moment to saturate the gully with another prolonged burst. A shower of shrapnel and splinters cascaded down onto them.

'Annie, we could wait until someone else tries to get him,' McAllen ventured carefully. 'Just to get his attention, like, while we run up the gully.'

'But we could wait all day! I say we should do it now. How about the next sweep away?' Oakley asked, trying to sneak a look at the Turks, but having to pull his head back quickly.

A tight silence fell between them as each contemplated the wisdom of charging. Hundreds of crumpled and bloodied khaki shapes around them were evidence of the near-suicide of trying to rush fortified positions.

'Yeah, okay, let's do it,' Hamilton breathed, feeling at once light-headed and terrified.

McAllen thought about it a little longer, then shrugged. 'If we do it right, we'll be okay. The bastards will be watching over their sights, not this way.'

'That's right,' Oakley nodded.

'For Christ's sake!' Galther croaked, but nobody answered.

'Bayonets,' McAllen said quietly. He drew his own from the scabbard on his belt and mounted it to his rifle.

Oakley did the same, watching what he could see of the knoll carefully, his eyes narrowed. The spitting, churning turmoil that was the machine gun's arc of fire turned away from the gully and cut through a clutch of men who, fresh from the beach, had ignored the gruesome signs and begun advancing across open ground. As the first of their number fell, the rest threw themselves to the dirt. They stayed pinned down, the bullets picking at the sand and scrub around them.

Oakley had raised his hand in a gesture of warning. Now he slapped the stock of his rifle and stood straight. 'Come on,' he snapped.

They broke cover and tried to sprint up the gully, their rifles held high. Stones and ruts in the ground made them stumble and Hamilton grunted at a burning pain in his ankle as he felt tendons tear.

Ahead, to the base of the knoll, it was the longest fifty yards of his life. The enemy gun was still concentrating on the troops in the open ground. Hamilton could see three Turkish heads kept low within a large, spiky bush. Sandbags reinforced the front of the dugout. All he could concentrate on was the slim, black muzzle of the machine gun, because as long as he could still see it in profile they were safe.

It began to swing back towards them.

Nobody dived for cover. There was nowhere worthwhile anyway, and in the brief moments before charging, each man had resigned himself to reaching the gun, or to die trying. It wasn't a conscious effort at heroism or a grab for glory or medals. It was simply the quickest, if not the safest, solution to a problem. Like their landing on the beach and the helpless climbing of the cliffs while the Turks virtually sniped at their leisure, the soldiers were reacting to their training and gut instincts and trying to do the job they were given.

None of this stopped Hamilton's heart from freezing as the line of bullets moved towards them. His feet felt leaden and far, far too slow. With a dreadful, fatalistic certainty he could tell that none of their group would reach the dugout in time. The gunner knew this too, taking his time and lingering on the open ground and the other troops, making every round count, before turning to ensure his own survival by wiping out the small attacking force coming up the gully.

Then, just as the bullets began crashing off the rocks once more, the gunfire stopped.

There was still the intense firing all about them and the roar of the naval bombardment dominating everything, but the silent machine gun in front of them created an eerie silence for the four men striving to reach it, before it could open fire again.

Then they were at the dugout. Oakley burst through the shrub, kicking one of the Turks in the face and scattering the others as he landed on his feet behind the sprawled gunners. Moments later, McAllen and Hamilton arrived. Oakley loosed off a shot, killing the loader. At the same time, McAllen shot the gunner. There was only an officer left, who was wildly trying to unholster a pistol. In a mad moment of confusion neither Oakley nor McAllen worked the bolts of their weapons, fully expecting Hamilton to shoot the man before either could have the chance themselves. Hamilton automatically pointed his muzzle straight at the officer's chest and pulled the trigger, only to hear in utter horror a click as the firing pin fell on emptiness. He hadn't chambered a fresh round himself, since he'd reloaded.

'Jesus Christ!' he gasped, believing he was staring his own death in the face. The Turk had drawn his pistol and was swinging it up to kill Hamilton in a brave but useless gesture, because he would have no chance of beating all four Australians. Hamilton saw his only hope and acted instinctively, lunging forward and sinking his bayonet in the officer's chest.

Time stood still. Hamilton stared into the dying eyes of the Turk as the officer grasped weakly at the muzzle of the rifle pressed against his heart. He seemed to wear a pleading look with his last seconds of life, then the light faded from his eyes and he collapsed backwards, wrenching the gun from Hamilton's hands.

Shocked, for a long moment the Australians looked down at the dead officer.

'Fucking hell, Ben,' McAllen whispered finally. 'Bad luck,' he added with a strange sentiment.

Hamilton nodded dumbly and automatically reached to pull his rifle free. It wouldn't come, sticking in the man's chest with gruesome insistence.

'Ben, shoot off a round as you pull,' Oakley told him thickly.

Hamilton found he still couldn't speak, but he attempted to obey. It was awkward working the bolt with the weapon at such an unusual angle. It also wobbled horribly in the dead man's body. Hamilton couldn't wait to get it out. He tugged hard and squeezed the trigger at the same time. The rifle fired with a muffled sound and jerked free. Taken by surprise Hamilton sat down suddenly. He looked with dismay at the gore on the bayonet and the end of his rifle. Nobody said anything.

'Well done, fellows!' shouted an officer running past. He'd been leading the group taking casualties on the open ground and the survivors now rushed past, some throwing appreciative waves at the men in the dugout.

'Stupid bastard,' Oakley spat at the officer's departing shape.

It appeared their own action against the machine gun, combined with the Lighthorsemen's fierce fighting, had made the immediate area almost safe for the time being. Oakley took the opportunity to light a smoke, bending and inspecting the enemy weapon as he took an appreciative drag into his lungs. 'Jammed,' he announced, giving the gun a kick, then showing with the toe of his boot how the ammunition belt was kinked and twisted where the rounds fed into the chamber.

'Damn lucky, that,' McAllen nodded. 'I thought we were dead men.'

'Maybe.' Oakley blew a plume of smoke at the Turkish bodies.

'I reckon it was Ben's lucky charm.' Galther spoke for the first time since they charged.

'Shut up, Galth!' Hamilton snapped quickly, nervously. 'There's no such fucking thing as good luck charms.' His hand went automatically to his chest as he added quietly, 'I don't even know why I wear the bloody thing.'

Oakley looked at Galther quizzically. 'Where did you get to? I could've brewed a cuppa by the time you arrived. Can't you run?'

'Piss off, I was right behind you!' Galther denied hotly.

Oakley gave him a long, hard stare before shrugging, 'Yeah, I know. Just kidding.' Hamilton saw the doubtful glance he threw at McAllen, before hiding his expression by reaching down and removing some of the breech mechanism from the machine gun. 'Just in case they come back,' he explained, pocketing the parts.

'What do you think we should do now?' Hamilton asked him, purposely avoiding Galther's eyes and the hurt look in them.

'Keep going.' Oakley jerked a thumb inland, 'Find the next machine gun. We should be good at it by nightfall,' he joked.

Nobody found it very funny.

Later in the day the Australian troops, after infiltrating far and wide since landing, began retreating back to the beach through the sheer lack of knowing what else to do. The total failure of the attack planning, caused by their landing on the wrong beach, saw many units separated from the command structure. After hours of hard fighting, with little objective except to engage the enemy, most of the troops drifted back towards the beach in search of orders, ammunition and fresh rations.

At least, this way, the invading soldiers gradually coalesced into a definite bridgehead with a defendable perimeter, albeit a bridgehead much smaller and closer to the beach than the High Command had envisaged in their plans. In fact, it was probably much smaller than they could have established at the time, given more clear leadership, but poor lines of communication and high casualties among the officers took their own toll.

Given a clear target, the Turks were able to start shelling in earnest. The doubt was removed as to exactly who was where. The defenders rained down a torrent of shrapnel and anti-personnel fire from their artillery positioned perfectly in the hills surrounding the landing zone, a place soon to be known as Anzac Cove. The beach, especially, operated under the constant threat of vicious shrapnel shells, which burst in the air scattering metal balls. Snipers, too, made their presence felt and they were hunted down by the Australians with sometimes callous enthusiasm.

Hamilton and the rest of his group fought savagely, overcoming pockets of Turkish resistance or battering themselves to exhaustion against impregnable, fortified positions. Soon after leaving behind the first machine gun they met up with Nick Story, who looked grimy and exhausted, but cheerful. He lost his smile when they told him about Loel, but in turn cheered them up revealing Rogers had been temporarily drafted into stretcher-bearing and, at last report, was alive and well.

Their surviving the rest of the day was helped by both McAllen and Hamilton always being behind the pace, due to McAllen's wound and the latter's twisted ankle. Hamilton felt stupid, hindered by a mere sprain when there were men all around him soldiering on with real wounds. But there was no denying his ankle refused to take its full load, crippling him and slowing him down. Oakley would fuss around them like a concerned mother hen. Galther, on the other hand, seemed quite content to use the excuse to lag behind the main body of the attackers. Story forever leapt to the forefront of any action, like an eager puppy.

By the time the sun was sinking low in the western sky everyone was admitting that things hadn't gone to plan at all. The maps were wrong, the orders were senseless, and the casualties were high and seemingly pointless. Rather than surrender without a fight as they were supposed to, the Turks defended grimly and heroically against the increasing mass of khaki troops. With nightfall imminent the Anzacs began back-tracking to the beach, seeking orders and direction, and the Turks filled the gaps they left, sometimes negating advances and small victories recently gained at a high cost in lives. Australian casualties increased more as Turkish troops moved in under their own artillery and began to dig in around the bridgehead. The situation was becoming desperate for the invaders. Sheer courage and determination began to falter through exhaustion. The ugly, difficult terrain increased their troubles tenfold.

And it started to rain. Heavy clouds that had swept in during the day released their moisture into the air, uncaring of the human tragedy unfolding below.

When Hamilton called for a halt to dig in for the

night, they'd fallen back to the same point where the first machine gun battle took place. Oakley agreed and purposely led them back to the emplacement.

'It's as good a place as any,' he argued, dropping down. The others looked dubiously at the pile of Turkish bodies, a black huddle in the growing darkness.

'What about them?' Galther nodded at them.

'They won't hurt you. Not any more.'

'Shouldn't we bury them?'

'You can, if you want to, but I'm too buggered to bother digging a hole for one of the bloody enemy. The graves rego' blokes will take care of them in the morning, if we're still here.'

'Hey, what do you mean—if we're still here?' Story asked anxiously.

Hamilton answered. He'd been thinking along the same lines as Oakley.

'Face it, Nick. We must've landed on the wrong beach. We haven't achieved any of the objectives we were supposed to by now. At least, I don't think we have. Everybody's moving backwards to the beach, as far as I can tell. The Brass might decide to cut their losses and pull us out.'

This took a moment to sink in.

'But we've only just got here!' Story exploded. 'We can't give in now!'

Hamilton's wistful smile was hidden in the gloom. 'No, it doesn't seem right, does it?'

'You mean, they could be leaving now? Without us?' Galther broke in anxiously.

'I doubt it,' Hamilton shook his head. 'We would have heard about it somehow. But we should try and check,' he added.

'I don't reckon we're alone yet.' McAllen gestured wryly at the darkness around them. It was filled with sporadic bursts of rifle fire, interspersed with the sharp cracks they'd come to recognise as hand-thrown Turkish bombs.

'You think one of us should go back to the beach? Find an officer?' Oakley asked. He ignored McAllen's snort of derision aimed at officers.

'What about half of us?' Hamilton suggested. 'Then whoever goes can carry back some rations and a bit of ammo. I'm low on both.'

The others agreed, but Oakley pointed at Hamilton's foot. 'We should carry you down and get your ankle seen to.'

'Not bloody likely!' Hamilton snapped. 'There's blokes down there shot to pieces, no doubt. I'm buggered if I'm going to wander in with a twisted ankle! Besides, I've done it before and I know what to do myself. As long as I don't take my boot off I'll be right. It'll fix itself in a few days.'

'Fair enough,' Oakley nodded. 'But it rules you out of any walks to the beach. How about we leave you young Nick, the bleedin' hero here, to look after you? We can get a fresh dressing on Macca's wound, too. We should be back in an hour or so.'

'We should be right, Nick?' Hamilton asked.

'Never a problem,' Story replied confidently.

'Righty-ho.' Oakley raised himself up and peered

cautiously over the rim of the dugout. Bright muzzle flashes betrayed skirmishes all around, but nothing seemed to be happening close by. 'Come on then, you blokes. Let's leg it.' He scurried out into the night, quickly followed by McAllen. Galther hesitated, obviously torn between the safety of the dugout and the prospect of getting away from the corpses at the other end of the emplacement. Having no real choice, he finally scrambled out after McAllen.

'Now what do we do?' Story asked Hamilton.

'Take turns to get some rest. One sleeps, while the other keeps watch. I wouldn't want to have somebody fighting for this place again tomorrow. We were damned lucky today.' He went on to describe to Story the action of taking the machine gun. When he finished telling it, Hamilton realised he couldn't see Story's face anymore. The sun had dropped completely over the horizon, falling into the Aegean Sea.

'Used the bayonet, hey?' Story's voice was full of admiration.

'I didn't like it,' Hamilton told him flatly.

Story didn't comment on that. He raised himself cautiously to look out of the dugout. 'Look, maybe I should scout around and find some more men? Get some help, like?'

Hamilton almost said no straight away, but he quickly realised there were other factors to consider. The position was important. It shouldn't be allowed to fall back into Turkish hands and just the two of them would have trouble fighting off a determined attack. Plus it was a good, big dugout. There may be men only yards away, out in the open, who could use the cover.

He forced down a knot of fear at being left alone to say, 'All right then, but make it a quick one. I won't be able to hold off anyone on my own.'

Without another word, but with a grin flashing in the darkness, Story crawled over the lip of the emplacement and paused, appearing to test the air. Satisfied there was no rifle fire coming his way, he rose to his haunches, just as Hamilton called, 'And be bloody careful I don't shoot you when you come back!' He was answered by a bark of cheerful laughter.

Immediately, Hamilton began to feel dreadfully lonely, and found himself wishing that Story would return soon. Without realising, he pushed his hand between the top buttons of his shirt and began fingering the charm laying against his skin. Then other memories started edging into his mind, thoughts that had been driven away by the fury of the day. He remembered the mocking laughter and the whispering voice urging him to stand up when it would have meant his certain death. *It would have been suicide,* he thought. *Am I really going mad? Why do I keep seeing that poor bastard who fell from the pyramid? Did I catch some dreadful disease back in Egypt?* Syphilis, Hamilton knew, was rife among the girls in the Haret El Wasser, and one of the symptoms of the disease was hallucinations.

But he hadn't gone near any of the prostitutes. Naive in these matters, he wondered if there was any other way he might have caught it. Then, becoming even more confused with his fear, Hamilton tried to shut his mind to all of it.

To add to his miseries, it began to rain harder, the drizzle building into a steady downpour. A puddle began to form in the middle of the dugout. After a while he inched his way up the shallow incline of mud to look out across the open ground, watching for Story's return. The stabs of light from muzzles and explosions told him the fighting was still isolated and individual, not controlled as a co-ordinated counter-attack might appear. With a sigh he slid back down, resting on his back and ignoring the sticky dampness that instantly seeped through his clothing. Hunching over, using his body to hide the flare of a match, he lit a cigarette. He was careful to keep his hand cupped over the glowing end. Taking a long drag, he allowed himself the luxury of closing his aching eyes for a moment.

He heard a groan.

Hamilton's eyes snapped open and he stared at the dark bulk of the Turkish corpses. Nothing appeared to have changed, or moved.

'Don't be stupid,' he told himself shakily. 'They've been bloody dead all day.'

He crawled back up the slope again and looked yearningly out for Story. Then the skin on his back crawled at the sound of another groan. He twisted around violently, dropping with a splash to the floor of the dugout in the same movement. *Perhaps,* he thought wildly, *one of the Turks was only wounded and he's been lying, suffering all this time. We didn't notice, and now the rain's revived him.* Hamilton's heart felt like it might burst from his chest.

'Hello?' he called, and felt ridiculous. He knew he should go over and check the bodies, but something was stopping him.

One of the corpses began to move.

With painful, tortured movements a shape detached itself from the dark bulk of the piled-up dead men. It hauled itself dreadfully to its feet. Hamilton could hear a shocking, bubbling sound and with an icy shock of new fear he knew it was the Turkish officer trying to gasp air through his punctured lungs. The figure stood, silhouetted against the distant flash of explosions, wavering and facing Hamilton. The corpse's hands were clutched to his chest as if to stem the flow of air escaping from his ruined body.

'For God's sake, you're dead,' Hamilton whispered.

Gurgling blood and breathing wetly the figure began to stumble towards him, one hand now outstretched in a hopeless gesture of pleading. Hamilton snatched up his rifle and worked a round into the breech. Without thinking he squeezed off a shot. The advancing corpse staggered backwards momentarily with the impact, then recovered and kept coming. Hamilton, beginning to groan with terror, fired again. The figure stumbled, regained its balance and continued on. With a terrible purpose, Hamilton raised his rifle to his shoulder and deliberately put a bullet point-blank into the thing's face. It collapsed backwards with a strange sigh back onto the other bodies and writhed for a few seconds, before becoming still.

In the silence following Hamilton thought he heard someone laughing in the distance with a terrible, familiar laughter.

Story and two other men jumped noisily into the dugout, splashing heavily into the muddy water. 'What's going on, Ben?' he cried. 'What's happening?' They waved their weapons around menacingly.

'I don't fucking *know,*' Hamilton said desperately, dropping his rifle carelessly and burying his head in his hands, 'One of those Turks just tried to attack me. I had to shoot him again.'

'What Turks?' Story kept urgently scanning the darkness.

'One of the corpses.' Hamilton didn't care how it sounded.

'But they're dead!' Story said stupidly, after a moment of confusion.

'I know, for Christ's sake!'

'Take it easy, mate,' one of the new men said gently. He stepped closer and put a calming hand on Hamilton's shoulder. 'It must have been some bastard Turk who's been laying doggo in the bodies and comes back to life when there's a good target. Like a sniper,' he added knowledgably.

Hamilton didn't answer. He started to tremble. He watched as the other three went over to the corpses and, one by one, irreverently tossed them beyond the rim of the dugout. Hamilton felt he couldn't face any more questions or debating, so he kept silent and didn't mention that there were three bodies now—and there had only been three that morning, too. He hadn't shot any extra, hidden sniper.

The two new men introduced themselves, then the four of them settled into a rotating guard for several hours. But when it was his time to rest, Hamilton couldn't sleep. An hour after midnight, from somewhere in the open ground, he heard his name called softly. Story answered for him and McAllen, Galther and Rogers dropped into the emplacement. McAllen carried a box of ammunition, Galther a tin of water and Rogers a sack containing rations.

Before anyone could speak McAllen told them, his voice filled with grief, 'They got Annie. A fucking mortar killed him straight—the bastards!'

At first everyone was too shocked to reply, the two strangers keeping quiet through respect. Finally, one of them said, 'Sounds like we've all lost some good friends today.'

'Yeah! But not Annie! Oh fuck—you wait till tomorrow,' Story said, despairing and savage. 'If I get my hands on a Turk, I'll strangle the bastard. Shooting's too good, I reckon.'

Deeply dismayed at the news, Hamilton couldn't

think what to say to calm Story. Instead, he said quietly, 'What's the news, Macca? Are we pulling out, or do we keep going?'

McAllen replied, 'All the brass-hats on the beach are saying it's a right royal fuck-up, there's no doubt. We're miles from where we're supposed to have landed, for a start. But the Old Man says we gotta dig deep and keep our heads down. Stick it out and do our best. We're here to stay, for a while at least.'

'Good!' Story said. 'We'll run right over the bastards, you watch.'

'They tell us an Australian submarine has got through the straits and is shelling Constantinople,' Rogers said. 'That's very good news. The entire British fleet didn't manage that, some months ago.'

'Yeah, if you want the job done right, call for us,' Story said, using fierce pride to block out his grief over Oakley.

Hamilton smiled sadly at him in the darkness, then said to Rogers, 'Good to see you in one piece, Teach. How's it been?'

'They had me carrying stretchers most of the day. Kept me out of serious trouble, I reckon.' He sounded almost apologetic.

'Rubbish! That's dangerous business, going out into the open to fetch casualties. Rather you than me, that's for sure.'

'Actually, I don't think the Turks bothered much with stretcher-bearers and medics. They seemed to pretty much leave us alone, especially as we were picking up their wounded, too.' Rogers seemed to direct this at Story, but Story missed the point.

'What? Picking up their wounded? After you got all our blokes, I bloody hope!' he snapped.

'Well,' Rogers shrugged, 'I admit we were a little biased,' he offered. This appeared to satisfy Story.

'Hey, have you blokes got any food?' asked one of the strangers, deciding it was time to return to more practical matters.

'Any water?' added the other.

Forgetting their woes for a moment, everybody took a share of the provisions brought from the beach. The new men introduced themselves again and told their story of the day, while McAllen recited their own. After, they settled into a routine of watching for enemy counter-attacks, while others slept. The loss of Oakley weighed heavily on their minds.

In one way, Hamilton was glad of that. It stopped anyone mentioning the incident of the corpses. The newcomers would have repeated their theory of an enemy hiding amongst their own dead, but Hamilton knew in his gut that nothing of the sort had happened.

He knew he'd been attacked by a dead man.

10

By the time Brendan got home from Carl Netthold's, another towering, black storm was dominating the evening sky, making the atmosphere in the street still and expectant. A jagged line of lightning crawled down the face of the clouds, followed moments later by a long, low rumble vibrating the windows of the house.

He picked up the local newspaper from the front lawn, tucking it under his arm and, after needing to jiggle the front door key in the lock, let himself into the house. Muttering about the faulty lock, he kicked the door closed behind him and walked straight through the gloomy passageway into the kitchen. After dropping the paper onto the table he flicked on the overhead light and went to the fridge for a beer. His conscience told him alcohol wasn't going to help, but Brendan didn't care. He'd been on an emotional high for a short while since leaving Carl Netthold, but the mood hadn't lasted, as if his driving into the oppressing weather had taken away the brief flare of optimism the older man ignited. On the way home the urge to taste a strong drink became too much to ignore, so Brendan had stopped into a small bar, but a noisy crowd soon chased him back out into his car. Now he just wanted to have a quiet beer and read the paper to occupy his mind. He noticed there was a message waiting on the telephone answering machine, but Brendan couldn't be bothered replaying it just yet.

He was sitting down with the paper and the beer opened in front of him when he heard a car pulling into his driveway. The engine died and there came the squeak of a door opening.

'The last thing I feel like right now is company,' Brendan growled aloud, getting up again. Instead of going straight to the front door he detoured into the living room and twitched the front curtains aside. He was alarmed to see the fluorescent blue lettering of a police car. After hurrying back through the house Brendan put his hand on the front doorlock at the same time as it rattled to a determined knock.

Standing outside were two uniformed policemen and, behind them, a plain-clothes detective. They looked at him warily.

'Mr Brendan Craft?' asked one of the constables.

'That's right,' Brendan answered, easily. Stepping aside he gestured into the house. 'You want to come in? Looks like it might rain pretty soon.'

The offer took them aback and Brendan realised they were expecting a more hostile reception. 'Come into the kitchen,' he said, before they had a chance to refuse. Gesturing for them to follow him, Brendan used the short journey to puzzle hard over why he was getting a visit from the police. He offered them coffee over his shoulder, but they politely declined. At least, Brendan thought, suppressing a moment of panic, it couldn't be bad news about Gwen. They weren't putting out that sort of vibe—and it wouldn't be worth a detective, would it?

'I'm Senior Constable Coughlin,' the first policeman explained, waving at the others. 'And this is Constable Georges and Detective Kearne.'

'This sounds important,' Brendan said, smiling and trying to ease some of the tension.

Kearne stepped forward. He was young and very clean-cut looking. 'Have you had any bad news today, Mr Craft? Anything to upset you?' he asked carefully.

'No. Should I have?' Nodding towards the telephone, Brendan added, 'There's something on the answering machine. I guess that could be your bad news. I could play it back now, but I have a feeling you're going to tell me what it is, anyway.'

'Can I ask you what you did today?'

'Mostly research, actually.' Brendan was beginning to get annoyed at Kearne's abrupt, unfriendly manner. 'At the library, then at a colleague's. On the way home I had a few drinks at Rolley's Tavern.'

'And last night? What were you doing?'

'I was at home all night—look, what is this?'

But Kearne had caught a scent of something wrong. 'Alone? Last night?'

'Until about three in the morning. Then my girlfriend came home from a late shift. She's a nurse.'

Faltering for an instant, Kearne asked, 'You're in a de facto relationship? She lives here? Permanently?'

But Brendan had had enough. 'Yes, she does,' he snapped. 'Now, I'm not going to answer any more questions until you answer mine. What the hell is this all about?'

Kearne took out a notebook, consulting it. Brendan suspected it was more for show. 'Do you know a Jeneatte Mary Beason?'

A sudden dread hit Brendan. He knew it was going to be very bad news. 'Yes, of course I do. She works for me a lot, doing research and sometimes ghost-writing filler articles for me.'

'Mr Craft, Jeneatte Beason was found in the Lever Tributary around midday today. We estimate her body has been in the water at least twenty-four hours, maybe more. She was drowned, but there were other injuries inconsistent with a simple drowning,' Kearne explained flatly. 'Severe cuts and abrasions that haven't been identified as yet.'

Stunned, Brendan needed to sit down, quickly. Coughlin saw this, putting a guiding hand on Brendan's shoulder and steering him into one of the kitchen chairs. The constables exchanged a look, but Kearne began pressing for more information.

'Are you capable of proving you were home all night last night, Mr Craft? Any witnesses? Did someone telephone you, perhaps?'

'No, no,' Brendan shook his head absently, his mind in a turmoil. Immediately, he knew there was a connection between his own problems and Jeneatte's death. He didn't know where or how, he just knew, then a thought came to him. *She did look in the tin. She touched the charm.* He felt sickened.

'Did you say your girlfriend was a nurse?' Kearne was asking. 'Have you known her long?'

'Yes. She's—she's more than just a girlfriend—you already asked me that. Of course, I've known her for a while.'

'Mr Craft, when was the last time you saw Miss Beason?'

Brendan began to feel trapped, worrying his answer might get him into some trouble he didn't deserve. The conversation was moving too fast. He quickly calculated the last time he'd seen Jeneatte and realised that would put him exactly into the time-frame to be a suspect. He thought about lying, but common sense struggling through his confusion stopped him. 'Yesterday,' he said quietly. 'I left her here, doing some work for me. When I got home she was gone, but that's nothing unusual. Jeneatte has her own key and knows she can come and go as she pleases. We have a very loose arrangement.'

'What time did you leave her?'

'Just before lunch. About eleven, I guess.'

Coughlin spoke, his tone more matter-of-fact. 'Mr Craft, Jeneatte was wearing a jacket of yours. Is that usual, too? It had your name inked on the label, a sports jacket.'

Brendan looked at him, frowning and trying to understand. 'Not really, no. Hang on a moment, I know the jacket you mean.' He got up, walking towards the hallway. At a nod from Coughlin, the other constable quickly followed, but Brendan missed the significance. Going into the bedroom he saw his jacket was in fact missing from the back of the door where it usually hung. He wondered why he hadn't noticed it earlier. With Constable Georges watching, Brendan checked the wardrobes anyway, in case Gwen put it away somewhere else. He didn't find it, finally turning and shrugging wearily at the policeman. 'Ah—an imitation black leather one, right?'

'Mr Kearne has the details,' Georges said, shortly. 'We'll have to check with him.'

Feeling like a prisoner under guard now, Brendan led the way back downstairs to the other two waiting impatiently in the kitchen. He described the jacket and Kearne nodded, again consulting his notebook.

'That sounds like the one. Why do you think she had it?'

Emotions were crowding in on Brendan and he was finding it difficult to stay calm. He heard Kearne's questions as slightly ridiculous, the answers obvious. Snapping again, he flicked a hand at the window. It showed a sky filled by the storm.

'For Christ's sake, she was probably cold. There was a storm yesterday, too. Maybe she wanted to borrow the jacket to wear to the bus-stop, in case she got caught in the rain—I don't know. You tell me—why the hell else would she borrow a jacket?'

Kearne said belatedly, 'I'm sorry, Mr Craft. I understand this may all be something of a shock.' Outside, thunder grumbled and a rattle of rain struck the house. There was a silence while the detective considered his next move, watching beads of water forming on the window as he thought. Then flipping his notebook closed he said, 'Thanks for your help, Mr Craft. I think perhaps I might leave it there, but I'm afraid with your being home alone for most of last night with no real way to prove it, it'll mean you'll probably get a visit from the Homicide guys, too. Maybe tomorrow.' Kearne didn't look all that sorry.

Brendan was still in a daze as he realised they were waiting for him to show them back outside.

At the front door, Coughlin favoured Brendan with an apologetic shrug while the young detective's back was turned. Then the policemen were sprinting through the now pounding rain to the car. Brendan closed the door and went back to the kitchen table. Absently, he took a long drink of his beer. His hands were shaking badly and he was glad the police hadn't stayed around to see that. He felt for the chair behind him and sat down, then put his head in his hands.

He felt himself falling into a deep depression and he didn't do anything to stop it. Although the news of Jeneatte's death was distressing, the certain inner knowledge that he had something to do with it was hitting him even harder. His imagination began to tease him cruelly, accusations of his own guilt rising into his consciousness.

Perhaps if I'd stayed home yesterday, Jeneatte would be alive? Why didn't I hide that damned tin?

As his spirits sank further, Brendan closed his eyes and saw different scenes flicking through his mind. If he wished, he could have picked each of them out and seen them in a startling clarity, like he might choose photographs from a collection. A small voice was trying to warn him he was letting himself slip too far, but there was nothing he could do. Letting himself go was the easiest thing to do, and Brendan didn't feel like fighting any more.

The scenes in his head became mixtures of real memories of Jeneatte interwoven with flashes from his nightmares, until, suddenly and shockingly, he was seeing Jeneatte standing in the niche in the chamber wall, instead of the high priest. She stood absolutely still, staring sightlessly ahead. She wore the same things Brendan had last seen her in, plus his own jacket. He mentally jerked at the sight of bloody rents all over her clothes and a jagged gash at the base of her neck. Strangely, he realised he could see everything—the entire chamber. The place was lit by burning candles on the walls everywhere, but the air was so still the light was unwavering. A dark pool of blood spread itself across the centre of the stone floor. One rivulet found its way to a crevice and ran quickly away. Another stain, a mixture of yellowed urine and excreta, told him of the fear of the last unwilling visitor into the catacombs.

As the scene began to change, Brendan looked on helplessly. Like an addict locked into a drug-induced trip and unable to awaken, he was only allowed to move within the fantasy from one awful vision to the next. The candle-lit chamber faded to be replaced by another, but this was lit by a dull glow coming from somewhere indefinable, as if the walls themselves were providing the light. This place had a low ceiling and a soil floor and was crammed with dirty, blackened men and women dressed in rags, stooping below the cavern's roof. Brendan knew the floor was hot, heated to within a knife's edge of where human flesh would begin to burn. The greasy, sweating people wailed their anguish and jostled each other in vain attempts to get away from the heat. With a sickening feeling in his gut, Brendan knew he was looking at a form of hell.

The image wavered in his mind, distorting and altering to become a scene of two men on a wide, stone step in bright sunshine. One was the high priest, but it took Brendan a moment to recognise him, because of the unexpected broad daylight and the gentle, innocent weather. The second person was being held captive by the priest, who gripped the much smaller and darker man in his left hand with a tremendous strength, the arm outstretched, with a vice-like grip behind the neck which rendered the man paralysed. His feet actually dangled above the stone in a parody of some terrified performing puppet. The high priest, his face a mask of impartiality, reached across with his free hand. Brendan could see he held the knife. With a swift movement, the priest cut a long slice across the prisoner's stomach. The man screamed with such an intensity of pain and fear, Brendan let out a small cry of fear himself. The priest shook the prisoner hard and bloody entrails began to spill from the gaping wound to hang and sway with the movement.

Brendan didn't know whether it was the horror of the vision or an enormous clap of thunder shaking the house which snapped him back to the present. Dazed, he rediscovered himself sitting at the table, the newspaper crumpled in front of him. Rain now lashed viciously at the window. He could still hear the thunder rolling off to the distance. Brendan felt confused and disorientated. Either the storm had developed with astonishing speed or he'd lost a lot of time. Another huge explosion of thunder made him jump to his feet with alarm. The house jerked and reverberated as if a giant had slapped at it with an immense piece of wood. The single light in the kitchen flickered, tried gamely to recover, then died, throwing everything into blackness.

'Oh, Jesus, not *now*,' Brendan swore, very uncomfortable in the darkness. *Where were the candles? They hadn't used them in over a year. What about his torch?* It was one of those things that he always seemed to be shoving out of the way, but now for the life of him Brendan couldn't think where it was. The darkness seemed to be actually touching him, caressing him like a sly lover's stroking hand. An idea suddenly struck him. The old house boasted a gas stove. He would light a couple of the top burners and give himself some sort of illumination until he found the candles. Eagerly, he began to feel his way towards the large, white blob in the darkness he knew was the stove.

The shattering, blood-curdling howl of the black beast-dog shattered the air, the sound so loud it smothered Brendan's scream as he instinctively turned and backed away from the window. He stumbled over a chair and fell, twisting around again and fetching up painfully against the stove, driving the wind from his lungs. Fighting the pain, he whirled around to face the window, his breath coming in laboured gasps and his back pressing hard against the cool metal of the oven.

A strange, diffused light seemed to be dancing outside the window. Droplets of rain on the glass glimmered and sparkled like diamonds. From outside Brendan could hear the howl subsiding to a low, rattling growl, then it stopped completely. Fearfully, he pushed himself away from the stove and approached the window. He had no idea what he might see through the window—but he couldn't stop himself from looking when he got there. He had to press his face against the glass and peer between the splashes of rain. At first, he didn't believe he was seeing right.

The neighbourhood had vanished.

It was replaced by a flat, featureless expanse shimmering with the wind and rain. The unusual light came from a long line of weak lamps, stretched thinly apart, moving slowly to the horizon. Brendan briefly wondered if he were still dreaming, but the wind battering at the glass in front of his face and the rain driving and hammering with it were impossibly real, and he knew this was no dream.

It was a different world outside his front door now.

A flare of lightning revealed more. Brendan's heart leapt into his mouth. The line of lights were held by soldiers, trudging bowed under the force of the storm. They walked singly and in groups. The spaces between the lights were filled with other men walking in darkness. Something massive in the distance was hidden as the lightning dissipated, disappearing before Brendan could take his stunned eyes off the soldiers. Another jagged fork stabbed to the ground and he saw some of the soldiers flinch. He waited for another flash, but this time he concentrated on the object in the distance.

It was a pyramid, thrusting itself mockingly into the sky in defiance of the elements.

'It's Egypt! Egypt in—in 1915!' Brendan whispered to himself, shocked. With the next explosion of lightning he noticed something else—something that seemed alien to the scene around it. A small, white figure lay curled in the mud at the very edge of Brendan's vision. He couldn't decide if it had been there all the time, or had just appeared. He saw it was a human being, someone hurt or sick, lying in the mud and rain, but none of the soldiers walking close appeared to notice or care. Something made him think of Gwen and the distant, prone figure suddenly possessed a dreadful familiarity.

Without thinking, Brendan left the window and made his way quickly through the passageway and to the front door. Although he knew what to expect, the reality beyond the doorway still stopped him dead for a moment.

The desert, under siege from the storm, lay all about him.

Before his resolve failed, Brendan plunged out into the deluge. In a moment he was soaked to the skin and almost blinded by the downpour. He had to run in a wide circle around the house to reach the side the kitchen faced. After a few steps, he glanced over his shoulder to check he'd closed the front door against the rain.

Now his house had disappeared.

Brendan staggered to a halt and stood, staring at the empty space he knew his house should occupy. His mind reeled and he ignored the rain beating down on his head and shoulders. Dear God, what had he done? Where was he? Several metres away the soldiers still walked resolutely along the muddy track, some of them holding the lights. Brendan could hear them talking amongst themselves. Some, he realised, even sounded a little drunk.

'Where am I?' he called impulsively, the words shaking. 'What's happening?' His voice was almost smothered by the storm, but he knew the closest men would still hear him, if they could. Nobody took any notice. Another fear began to fill Brendan—that he'd done something enormous and irreversible the moment he stepped outside his door. Then, through his panic, he remembered why he'd done that in the first place.

Still, he hesitated, unwilling to move too far from where the house used to be, but a gut feeling told him it would be useless to wait. He turned around and fought to walk into the rain, trying to judge where he would find the slumped figure. A flash of lightning helped. He saw the crumpled form lying as it had before, about thirty metres in front of him, and, with his courage almost failing him, he continued to approach it. The figure was small—small enough to be a child or, at the least, a woman. Though it was impossible, it *could* be Gwen.

He knelt down in the gritty mud, the rain thrashing against his back. Gingerly he reached out and pushed away the hair plastered across the pale, dead face.

It was Jeneatte Beason.

Brendan drew in his breath with a sharp hiss and snatched his hand away. She was lying in a tight, foetal position, her young body looking thin, almost emaciated. She was naked apart from his jacket. Her skin was grey and bloodless, her eyelids and cheekbones just darkened sockets.

Unexpectedly, Brendan felt tears well up in his eyes as he gazed down, seeing what death had done to a vibrant teenage girl. After a moment he looked desperately about him, stupidly hoping with his rush of compassion he might see something he could use to cover her body. In the distance, the indistinct figures of the soldiers moved through the blackness, but he didn't call out. He knew it was pointless—they couldn't hear him, nor see him. He looked back down at her, his fingers toying with the buttons on the front of his shirt as he contemplated using it to cover her face.

'I'm sorry,' he whispered, the words lost among the noise of the storm. He knew why he was apologising—he was somehow responsible for her death.

Jeneatte's eyes snapped open.

With a shocked cry Brendan pushed himself away and sprawled backwards into the mud. Only one of her eyes could focus on him and it fixed him with a terrible, accusing glare. Brendan lay gaping at her. Slowly, painfully, she pushed herself up onto her elbows, never taking her eyes off Brendan. With awful grunting noises she struggled to her hands and knees and stayed that way for a moment, swaying weakly. She sank into the thick clay up to her wrists so it looked like her hands had been amputated.

Brendan couldn't move. She began to crawl towards him and his horror grew impossibly, but he couldn't work a single muscle to take him away from the advancing corpse. As she crawled his jacket hung open away from her naked body. Above them, another jagged fork of lightning spread itself across the sky creating, in an instant, an eternity of time for Brendan to see the ghastly extent of Jeneatte's wounds. The lips of the savage cuts all over her body were puckered and whitened from lack of blood and long immersion in the water. Mocking the tragedy of her ruined beauty, only her breasts were still unmarked, full and firm. Within his fear Brendan loathed himself for a moment of uncontrollable sexual yearning—not for the pitiful creature in front of him, but for the living Jeneatte Beason he'd known.

'You want me, don't you, Mr Craft?' she called above the storm. Her voice was thin and teasing. She kept moving closer.

'No!' Brendan shouted, horrified. His voice nearly broke into a scream. 'No, stay away from me!'

'But you've always wanted me,' she said. She stopped her crawling and slowly cupped one of her breasts with her hand. Brendan could see the flesh was a lifeless grey. The corpse caressed her nipple for a moment, then began pulling herself towards him again. *'Here I come,'* she said, in a playful, sing-song manner.

'Leave me alone! I *don't* want you!' Paralysed with fear, Brendan's body was locked where he lay. He could only watch in utter horror as the corpse put one hand on his ankle, then the other on his knee. She began climbing over his legs. The touch of the girl's hands was burning hot through the wet material of his jeans. A fetid smell of decomposition washed over Brendan as she pushed between his legs and placed a hand on each of his shoulders, holding her mutilated body above him and pushing him back down into the mud. Water dripped down onto Brendan, some of it colouring pink as it washed through her wounds. The corpse started to lower her face to his. Ghastly smears of mascara and lipstick mocked him. The breath from her open, excited mouth, stank of dried blood and rotting flesh. Brendan began to scream, a hoarse, adult sound. A new flare of lightning showed him every terrifying detail as the corpse embraced him.

This time the lightning didn't fade. Instead it lingered to taunt him with the sight of his decayed, rotting lover. The very fabric of the world around Brendan began to tear and spin like a whirlpool. As her lips touched his face everything else seemed to be pulling apart, disintegrating and leaving behind a blackness.

It was a night off for Gwen. She'd spent the day in town attending to a few personal matters and looking for a birthday present to buy her sister. Having had no idea what she might get, or how big it may be, she'd played it safe and taken her car. As usual she regretted it, finding herself caught in heavy rush-hour traffic. Making the situation worse the storm swept over the city and brought everything nearly to a standstill, stalling old cars and causing minor accidents at crucial intersections. As Gwen finally, wearily, drew closer to home she felt easier, even though the storm seemed to be intensifying. The heart of it, she noticed, might even be near the house.

The windscreen wipers flayed ineffectually at the water cascading down the glass. As the inside of the windows steamed up, Gwen turned the demister on full-blast to cope. She couldn't open any of the windows, because the merest crack let in a spray of rain. Gusts of wind rocked the car. She flinched as a spectacular web of lightning crackled across the sky in front of her.

With a sigh of relief she turned the car into their own street. She drove slowly, not wanting to drag the sheets of water lying on the road into the motor, stalling the car so close to home. Something seemed different in the street, and it took her a moment to realise the streetlights were out.

'*And* a damn power cut!' she grumbled aloud. She leaned forward in her seat to peer through the windscreen, looking for the white stone letterbox at the end of their driveway. When it shone dully up ahead she also saw the red reflection of tail lights. Brendan's car was still in the drive. He hadn't bothered to move it into the carport beneath the house. 'Lazy sod,' Gwen said, without rancour. She steered into the driveway. As the headlights swept across the front lawn she saw an incredible sight. It was so surprising she instinctively stomped hard on the brakes and jerked the car to a halt halfway into the drive, transfixing the scene in the white glare of the lights.

Brendan was sprawled on his back on the lawn. Someone lay on him, smothering him. To Gwen's stunned eyes it looked as though the figure on top was hugging him, or kissing him passionately—rather than attacking him, which was her first, instant reaction. The size of the person suggested it was a woman. So did the longish, straggly hair.

The shoulders lifted and the head turned towards

the car. The terrible gaze coming from the lifeless face made Gwen let out a small cry. A shudder of fear and revulsion ran down her spine.

Then the girl dissolved in a flicker of movement.

11

The plane tilted slightly to avoid more storms building up south of the city. Brendan looked out his window and watched a patchwork of farms slide beneath the wing. A single musical tone announced that seat belts could be loosened. Immediately, he reached above his head and pressed the call button. A stewardess in a forward compartment brushed aside a curtain and walked down the aisle, looking for the illuminated button.

'Can I have a beer, before you get too busy?' he asked.

She hesitated for a moment. The man had dark

rings of fatigue around his eyes and he was very pale. She decided he was simply tired, and probably not a drunkard. 'Certainly, sir,' she said, switching on a bright, professional smile. 'It's two dollars—do you have the correct change?' she added hopefully.

'Yes, sure.' Brendan raised himself up to get his fingers into his hip pocket, but she waved at him not to rush.

'You can pay for it when I get back,' she said, moving away.

The beer wasn't the coldest he'd ever drunk, but it helped him relax. Brendan reflected he was drinking rather a lot these days, but figured he had good reasons. He put his head back against the seat and closed his eyes, tasting the beer on his breath. His weariness took over and Brendan let his mind reflect on the last few days.

He hadn't coped well with the second visit from the police the morning before. The two detectives invited themselves into the house and began asking the same questions. Their manner softened when Gwen had appeared, bleary-eyed, from upstairs. *A man with an attractive lady,* Brendan thought wryly, *apparently rates less suspicion.* He'd been in no condition to field questions from alert policemen, especially first thing in the morning and following his experience of the night before with Jeneatte Beason's ghost. Brendan's fatigue had showed, too. He appeared ill and as if he hadn't slept for a week, like a man who had something on his mind bad enough to keep him awake all night. And, like before, when it became known he'd been at home on the night Jeneatte was killed, but with no one to support his alibi, the detectives from the Homicide division started closing in, sensing a kill. Under pressure, Brendan remained adamant and finally convinced them that, if nothing else, he wasn't about to change his story.

Then something happened as they were leaving that made Brendan nearly lose control.

'We'll probably have to come back,' the detective called Francis had said. The threat was thinly veiled. Brendan could hardly blame them.

'Just let me know,' Brendan had replied, feeling relieved. It was then his eyes fell on the green tin box, lying next to the stove. He'd faltered and pointed a shaking finger at it. 'Hey, did you guys bring that in with you?'

'What?' Francis followed his line of sight. 'The tin? No—is there something wrong?'

'No—no, of course not. I thought I threw it in the rubbish, that's all.' Brendan was obviously upset and Francis was about to go over and check out the contents of the box. He was stopped by Gwen, who reappeared after going to the bathroom.

'It was me,' she called, an edge of desperation barely concealed from her voice. 'I decided I couldn't bear to throw it out.'

Francis looked at them both for a long time, sensing the sudden, different tension in the air, then he reluctantly accepted this and left. Once they were safely gone Brendan looked at her.

'Did you bring it back in?'

'No,' she said huskily.

Brendan surprised her with a dry, humourless chuckle. He said quietly, 'You know, I didn't really think it was going to be that fucking easy to get rid of.' Picking the tin up, he took it back upstairs.

Gwen watched him leave, a worried look on her face.

On the plane, Brendan's thoughts turned to the telephone conversation he'd had with Netthold later that day.

'I can put you close to the pin, Brendan,' Netthold's age-roughened voice told him.

'How's that, Carl?'

Brendan almost heard the frown cross Netthold's face. 'Are you all right?'

'Yeah, I'm just very tired.' Then he remembered how much he'd already told the older man, so he added, 'Actually, things are getting pretty hairy around here.'

'Scary? Is that what you said? This connection's not good.'

'Well, yes—same thing. Anyway, did you have some luck?' Brendan had changed the subject quickly, not wanting to even think about the night before. Besides, he couldn't begin to imagine how he'd describe the events to anyone.

'Some, perhaps not as much as you'd wish for.' There was a rustling of pages. 'The coloured badges were issued to one of six possible battalions, all from this part of the country. The First through to the Sixth, inclusive. They sorted the soldiers out on board ship during the transportation from Australia to Egypt and used them quite regularly during the training period there, but the system was shot to hell once they landed at Gallipoli. Nobody would have bothered to remove the badges from the uniforms, though. Things got rather informal from that point on uniform-wise and it just didn't matter. Whoever did eventually take those badges off probably had no idea what they were for and kept them, in case they were some sort of decoration.'

'Well, that's something, I suppose.' Brendan had paused and bitten his lip, while he looked down at the telephone thoughtfully. 'I don't mean to sound ungrateful, but I just don't know what I should do next.'

'Your first idea was probably the best,' Netthold said. 'Go to the archives and look at all those who served in the battalions and see if any names ring a bell.' He made it sound simple.

'Isn't that rather a lot of names?'

'Yes, and no. You won't be able to get a separate listing of men who served in the Gallipoli campaign in particular, but you will be able to narrow that down by looking specifically at that period of time, understand? Only look at those men who served, say, between April 1915 and all of

December the same year. Next to each name will be a code denoting what happened to the soldier. Nothing marked at all usually means the man survived the war and that's that, or there might be a decoration such as the DSO or DCM. What you'll be looking for is KIA—Killed in Action—which will cut down the names you have to look at to around fifteen or twenty percent, roughly.'

'Right,' Brendan agreed, struggling to absorb it all. 'I suppose the archives are in the city?'

'The Australian War Memorial.'

'But that's in Canberra!'

'Where else?'

'Yes—where else?' Brendan repeated. 'Couldn't I ask them to send the information to me?'

A chuckle came over the phone before Netthold answered. 'You could, but they wouldn't do it themselves. The Memorial gets hundreds of enquiries each week, so for any research like that they suggest private researchers who they have listed. It's efficient, but God knows how long it might all take. Can you afford to wait?'

A vision of Jeneatte Beason's corpse, lowering itself onto his trapped body, swept through Brendan's mind. 'No,' he said hastily. 'I can't.'

'From the sound of your voice, I can tell that. Besides, it might help you to have a look around.'

'What do you mean?' At that moment Gwen had walked into the kitchen. He made cryptic signs at her to pour him a cup of coffee from a simmering kettle on the stove.

'There was a tremendous amount of material recorded on Gallipoli,' Netthold was saying. 'Private cameras, many men kept diaries—it wasn't an unusual thing to do, in those days—and the letters home, of course. There's a lot of that sort of stuff at the memorial. You might see something to jog your memory and narrow down your search.'

'I'd be surprised,' Brendan told him doubtfully. 'I don't think I could be so lucky.'

'Still, it's worth a look, while you're there. What about the archives? Who will you be looking for? Another Craft?'

Brendan hadn't given it any thought before. He was exhausted and tense, and it all seemed to be too much trouble. He frowned and admitted, 'I'm not sure about that, either. Now that you mention it, this house has come from my mother's side of the family. The Craft name probably means nothing.'

'Well, I suggest you work out exactly what you'll be looking for, before you go there. Otherwise, you'll waste most of your day doing just that, leaving too little time for your real research.'

'Okay,' Brendan nodded. He smiled tiredly at Gwen as she handed him the coffee. 'Carl, I'm very grateful for all this help and advice—really.' He knew Netthold was doing all the thinking for him, when Brendan's own mind was too clogged by confusion and fatigue to function properly. He probably would have gone straight down to Canberra and arrived without the slightest idea what he was looking for, and achieved nothing because of it. He asked, 'I don't suppose there's anything I can do for you, while I'm down there?'

'As a matter of fact, there is,' Netthold had laughed, making it sound as if he were the one who should feel indebted.

Brendan listened and took notes on the telephone pad as Netthold explained what he wanted. Brendan then thanked him again and promised to call as soon as he returned.

He had a quick flight change in Sydney. Brendan carried just an overnight bag, so there were no problems with transferring luggage. He planned to stay only one night in Canberra and fly back the following afternoon. Before leaving home he'd insisted Gwen stay away from the house that night, too. She was going to visit a friend, stay overnight and go straight to the hospital from there. Her shift finished at six o'clock the following morning. By the time she got home it would be daylight and, while there was no reason for Brendan to assume the worst could only happen at night, he felt easier with this arrangement. At first, Gwen refused to stay away from the house simply because he wasn't home, although her brief glimpse of Jeneatte Beason had shaken her badly. Finally, she'd grudgingly agreed not to spend any nights alone in the house—for the moment.

Canberra city was cold, the fresh air chilling his face as he stepped onto the tarmac. Brendan hurried into the airport terminal and after re-confirming his flight back he headed out to the taxi rank, stopping as he left the terminal and pulling a tracksuit top from his bag. Aside from this he was wearing a collared T-shirt, jeans and runners. He managed a grin as he compared himself to the flock of grey-suited businessmen and government employees who bustled all around him.

'Penguin city,' he muttered, smiling. He didn't genuinely smile often anymore.

Fifteen minutes later he was in the motel he'd picked from a guidebook. It was within walking distance of the memorial. The room was warm, the management having turned on the heater after the booking was phoned through. And the double bed looked very inviting, because the beers on the flights and the rush at the air terminals were combining to wear him down. But Brendan reminded himself he wasn't in Canberra to rest and it would be foolish to waste any of his available time having a nap. He looked at his watch. The memorial was still open for another two hours. He could use them to check out the place, find his bearings and in the morning go hard for all the information he could get. If he worked at it, he might even get Carl Netthold's questions answered that afternoon, leaving the whole of the next day for himself.

Thirty minutes after arriving at the memorial Brendan was amazed at what he'd achieved already. A few enquiries at the information desk got him access to the Research Centre and photocopies of all the documents Netthold needed. Now, he was sitting at a computer terminal, scrolling through the list of all men recruited by the Queensland 1st Battalion following its inception in December 1914 through to 11 November 1918. The lists had all been transferred to computer disk and the programming was quite comprehensive. Brendan could have called up only the KIA's—Killed in Action, but he decided to look at the bigger picture first. The entire list of serving men did, as Netthold had told him, show a suffix with each name denoting any exceptional circumstances. He scanned through the list, easily picking out the depressing KIA initials—there were many. None of the names, however, sounded remotely familiar, except for the three different 'Crafts' shown. For all he knew they may have been relatives of some kind, but he didn't hope. Brendan noted their serial numbers with the intention of getting copies, if he could, of their enlistment papers. He figured information on those might cross-relate to his family history somewhere.

By the time he arrived at the last two lists his eyes were tiring from the computer monitor. He concentrated hard to pick out only each KIA now and check the identity. If he'd kept searching the entire lists Brendan would have seen a name which might have stirred his memory cells—but he didn't.

Because he believed he was looking for somebody who died in the line of duty.

Finally he became aware of the memorial staff doing their last rounds before closing, so he punched in a request for hard-copy printouts of the six lists and made his way to the information desk where the printed material would appear. Brendan was feeling disappointed after having so easily accessed the files he wanted—he'd imagined it would be the hardest part of the job—only to have no success. He wasn't sure what, exactly, he'd expected, but secretly he admitted he'd been hoping for some sort of startling revelation to leap out at him from the pages of history, answering all his questions and solving his problems.

Tomorrow will be the day, he told himself, trying to boost his own confidence. *Tomorrow I'll take a long, hard look at the displays and maybe something will give me a clue.*

The next morning he was woken by a muted ringing handbell and the thud of his servery door being closed. It was six-thirty and his breakfast had arrived. Brendan hadn't taken any chances the night before and had swallowed a dose of his sleeping pills. As usual the tablets were unwilling to release their hold on his body and it was an effort to get his feet on the floor and force himself to start a new day. Throwing off the covers he rolled out of bed to stand groggily, digging his toes into the thick carpet while he reorientated himself in the unfamiliar surroundings. A grey light was managing to enter the room from around the edge of the drawn curtains.

'Shit,' he mumbled, realising it was very cold on the other side of the blankets. He'd set the heater to turn off at one in the morning. Still half-asleep, he struggled with the decision of having a hot shower, or getting dressed to eat his breakfast. *A hot shower means a cold breakfast,* he told himself, shaking his head at his inability to think clearly and cursing the sleeping pills. He flicked the timer-override switch on the heater, turning the thermostat up to full, then quickly pulled on his jeans and sweater.

Breakfast was a generous helping of bacon, eggs and fried tomatoes, and a small bottle of chilled tomato juice. Two pieces of toast had already succumbed to the cold, adopting the texture of cardboard, but the rest of the food tasted good. After, Brendan made himself a cup of coffee from the tiny pantry and sat down to flick through the newspaper delivered with breakfast. A second coffee followed while he finished the paper, then he looked up to see the light from outside was now rivalling the fluorescents in the room. He got up and opened the curtains fully, revealing an overcast, chilly day and an identical row of motel units opposite, separated from his by a narrow access road.

After a long, luxurious shower and a shave, Brendan stepped out of the bathroom to discover the heater had turned the room into an oven now. Brendan cursed, good-naturedly this time, about finding a happy medium and slid open one of the windows. A waft of icy air swept into the room and he hurriedly closed it again, deciding he would rather cope with the heat. He got dressed and sat at a small writing alcove, resisting the habitual urge for yet another coffee while he worked, and made notes on what he'd done the day before. He re-sorted the lists of battalions out of the mess he'd made searching them again the evening before. As he did, he experienced a wry stab of his earlier disappointment. When he'd finished, there was time to pack his things, settle the account at the reception and take a leisurely walk back down to the Memorial. The motel's management had already agreed to let him leave his overnight bag for the day.

The air outside was brittle like the day before as he strolled down the pavement. It was past the rush-hour, but the streets were busy with cars and buses trailing plumes of condensation along with their exhausts. It spoiled the freshness of the morning and Brendan was glad to get back inside.

The doors had only just been opened, but already camera-toting tourists were pressing through the foyer. Brendan followed the signs pointing to the First World War and Gallipoli displays. Through an archway he discovered an entire room especially devoted to the Gallipoli campaign. For the first few minutes it was an effort attuning his mind to begin absorbing the details. He planned, when he'd seen it all, to go to the cafeteria and have a coffee, maybe a bite to eat, and start all over again.

The first display was an array of maps showing

Europe and the Mediterranean. Colour-coding pointed out the various political alliances and all the different theatres where Australian troops fought. Next were sepia photographs of queues of men in London, volunteering to take part in the 'great adventure' and the 'war to end all wars'. Brendan looked at these pictures a long time, staring at the lines of men all dressed in dark, heavy clothes and wearing hats. *How eagerly they went,* he thought. *Totally oblivious to the utter carnage the new, industrialised war could inflict upon them.* More photographs, further up the wall, showed similar scenes in Australia, under the stirring cry of the time, 'To the last man and our last shilling.'

Other scattered displays began a series of uniforms and equipment used by the different armies. Small notices brought the reader's attention to different details in the design and application of the gear. Vintage rifles lay in a low glass cabinet and Brendan stared at everything, becoming totally fascinated.

More maps and detailed models explained the Gallipoli offensive itself. Like many before him, Brendan was surprised to see the Gallipoli campaign was, in no way, the exclusively Anzac operation that myth and legend led him to believe. The Australian landings at Anzac Cove were just one small part of a much larger offensive involving tens of thousands of British and French troops attacking all along the toe of the peninsula.

A jarring sense of *déjà vu* went through Brendan at the photographs of Australian troops training in Egypt. One showed a crouching soldier, wearing the distinctive slouch hat, feeding a small wallaby which had, according to the accompanying caption, been brought as a battalion mascot. Behind the soldier were rows of uniformed men clustered in lines around several white, teepee style tents. In the background, as if to mock the men at their puny attempts at an imitation, two pyramids dominated the skyline. Stacks of rifles were nearly hidden among a confusing bundle of stores. After staring at the photograph for a long time, Brendan closed his eyes and, for a moment, could feel the heat of the sun on his back and the grating, scratching touch of coarse sand beneath his boots. Murmured voices came into his mind, along with the distant snorting and whinnying of horses. The crack of rifles told him there was a firing range nearby. A fragrant odour of the warm sand and the close, fertile strip of land bordering the Nile filled his nostrils, mixed with smells of thousands of men and their animals. Brendan found himself taking a deep breath, tasting the odours on the back of his throat.

The feeling he was *there*, that if he opened his eyes he would be inside the photograph, was suddenly so strong that Brendan was afraid to look. Then the near-hallucination slammed Brendan into a memory of the nightmare he'd had that first night, where he'd been dragged beneath the sand by clasping, dead hands. He snapped his eyes open and concentrated on something—anything—directly in front of him to push away the image beginning to fill his mind like a re-run of the dream, threatening to take control. He was sweating slightly and his breath now came in short, sharp gasps. Brendan put a hand on a thick braided rope in front of him designed to keep visitors at a distance from the exhibits. He leaned on it for support, but it began to collapse under his weight and he struggled to stay on his feet. At least, the need to retain his balance and the small panic it brought pushed the hallucination away further.

'Jesus, I'm not in control of my own mind anymore,' he muttered, slowly fighting off the dizziness. He looked around the room, but he was still alone. Nobody had seen him in trouble. There was only a life-sized dummy wearing an authentic uniform of the time, standing directly in front of him. The blank sockets of the eyes stared impassively at Brendan, making him feel strangely uncomfortable. Still feeling unsteady, he struggled to read the small plaque. This was, it explained, the uniform of a private in the Australian 10th Light Horse Brigade, adding that few of the soldiers bothered with the disciplines of dress and it would have been unusual to find any member of the Australian forces wearing such a correct uniform only a week or so after the fighting on the peninsula began. Brendan stared at the khaki-coloured dress and again he felt a sense of having been there, a familiarity that went beyond just knowing his history.

At the same time, unexpectedly, he began to fill with an awe and respect, surrounded by the physical evidence of the magnitude of the war and the bravery of those men who fought it. Brendan willingly focused on this, concentrating on everything around him and using it to keep back the lingering hallucinations in the back of his mind.

Countless photographs adorned the walls and partitions and he was reminded of Carl Netthold's study. There were displays of more rifles, hand-guns, personal gear and maps, both official and hand-drawn, and some captured Turkish equipment. One case showed scraps of paper with scrawled, indecipherable foreign writing. There was an early Turkish hand-grenade, along with a wicked-looking bayonet. Brendan stared at it all, moved by an adventurous spirit it kindled within him, even though he knew, in reality, the campaign had been a horrific affair costing thousands of lives.

It was after ten o'clock when the first rumblings in his stomach announced it was time he took a break. He didn't really want to. He could have stayed and continued studying everything about him, ignoring his hunger nagging for attention, but he knew the value of resting his concentration and giving his mind time to recover. He looked at his watch and saw it was twenty minutes past ten. He would go through until ten-thirty, he decided, and go to the shop for a coffee and a sandwich.

A small individual display caught his eye and Brendan figured it was something he could devote ten minutes to, instead of beginning a whole new section elsewhere. He walked over and read the introductory poster.

The exhibit was devoted to a Colonel Nicholas Story, a legend in the ranks of the Australian Army. Story had fought at Gallipoli, landing with the first waves on 25 April. He'd survived the war, even fighting in France and Belgium. In fact, he'd gone on to serve with distinction as a major in the Second World War in the Western Desert and become one of the famous Rats of Tobruk. Impressed, Brendan pursed his lips and read on. Story was indeed a real legend. In the last years of his military career the man had even managed to go to Korea amongst the Australian contingent sent there. The poster added that, after retiring, Story spent his time collating his vast collection of personal memorabilia and had donated a significant part of it to the museum. He shunned any suggestions his lifetime had been anything extraordinary and refused to write publishable memoirs, or sanction any attempts at biographies.

When he finished reading Brendan let out a low whistle of admiration and looked at the picture of a stern, moustached man who looked every inch the fearless, devoted soldier.

Next to it another, older photograph reached out to Brendan like a slap in the face.

It showed seven men, smiling into the camera,

backed against a sandstone wall. Judging from the grainy quality of the picture and the uniforms of the soldiers, it was obviously from the First World War. The caption beneath confirmed this: 'Story and others at a bazaar in Cairo, 1915, prior to embarking for Gallipoli (Story seen second from right).'

Brendan's breath caught in his throat and a chilling shudder ran down his spine. It wasn't Story's image that affected him, but that of another soldier in the photograph. The man standing at the end of the line with his hand draped casually over his colleague's shoulder. All the men wore sardonic, confident smiles, except for one whose grin looked a little strained, but the man at the end held a cigarette cockily between his lips.

Without a doubt, it was the soldier Brendan had seen shot down in his own house.

The photograph wasn't clear enough to really permit an accurate identification, but it was something in the man's stance, the way he held himself, and definitely the way the cigarette jutted out from his lower lip, that told Brendan it was him. And despite the age of the photograph and its lack of detail, the facial features looked right, too. Brendan just knew it.

'My God,' he breathed aloud, staring at the picture. His voice whispered around the room. By now several other sightseers had drifted through, but at that moment he was alone.

'It's *you*,' he told the photograph. 'I know it's you.' He leaned as far over the barrier rope as he could and studied the photograph intently, but close scrutiny only enhanced the picture's age and lack of quality. Frustrated, Brendan cast his eye quickly over the rest of the display. There were other photographs of Gallipoli, one showing Story in a dugout, another of him assembling home-made bombs out of used food tins. But these were all individual shots. Nowhere else could he see a picture of the other man.

He decided there must be more. If, as the poster claimed, Story had been a prolific collector, then the man must have more photographs, ones deemed unsuitable for the exhibition, but still something that might identify his friends.

On a sudden impulse Brendan turned away from the exhibit and walked quickly back through the corridors to the main information desk. It was occupied by a pleasant, middle-aged woman who recognised him from the day before.

'Good morning, Mr Craft. How are you today?' she said, watching him approach.

'I'm fine, thank you.' Brendan replied shortly. He could hardly contain his excitement. 'Look, there's a display in the Gallipoli room devoted to one man, a fellow called Colonel Story. Do you know the one I mean?'

'Nicholas Story, yes, we've had that—'

'Is there any more?'

'I beg your pardon?' A small frown of annoyance crossed her face. Brendan took a breath to calm down.

Don't upset her, for God's sake, he told himself, firmly. *I might need a few favours here.*

'I'm sorry.' He gave her his nicest smile and saw her expression soften again. 'But there's a photograph in the display that I think has a relative of mine in it and I was hoping I might be able to identify him. There's nothing else on the display, but I thought there might be some other photos somewhere that might help.'

'You want to identify someone?' She looked confused. 'Then, how do you know he's a relative? I don't understand.'

Brendan realised he should have thought his approach through, rather than rush the woman. She looked like someone who took her job very seriously, and he knew she wouldn't let him near any other material, if she had any doubts at all he was genuine. He thought fast.

'I'm sorry, I should have explained myself, but we have a similar photograph. We've assumed, all these years, that's he's a relative of some kind, but we've never been able to confirm it. Now, all of a sudden, I see him here! I don't know why I've never thought of coming here before, but then you wouldn't expect to see another photo, would you? I'm amazed, to tell you the truth,' Brendan added, hoping the glib story was rolling smoothly off his tongue.

'Isn't that fascinating?' She seemed genuinely pleased for him, but he saw her smile drop away to disappointment. 'But I'm afraid that's all of the

Colonel's possessions we have here, at the moment.'

'Damn,' Brendan couldn't stop himself. He gave her an apologetic look, then he realised what she'd said. He asked, 'What did you mean—at the moment?'

'Old Nicholas died just over a year ago and donated his entire collection to the memorial, but his daughter is still putting it all together and making her own records of every item, before she sends them on.' The woman twisted her lips, apparently offended at the inference the memorial couldn't be trusted.

'I see.' Brendan said quietly, staring thoughtfully at a framed photograph behind her desk. It was a well-known picture of Australians advancing under fire in the Western Desert. 'Could I get in contact with his daughter? Could you give me an address?'

'No, not just like that,' she said, suddenly sounding officious. 'I'm afraid you'll have to go through the proper channels. It's all a matter of protection and copyright.' She smiled her own apology, then added, as if to console him, 'She lives up in Queensland, anyway. It's a bit far to go.'

'But I'm from Queensland,' Brendan explained, exasperated. 'I flew down here yesterday.'

'That's a shame,' she agreed, gesturing helplessly. 'But you'll still have to write a formal request to the director of the memorial explaining what you want and why. You shouldn't have any trouble. I'll speak to him myself, when your letter comes through. It just takes a little time—' she finished, shrugging.

'Couldn't you just write it down for me now?' Brendan tried a pleading expression, but it didn't work.

A glint of resolve flashed in her eye. 'I'm sorry, Mr Craft, but it's official policy.'

Silently admitting defeat, Brendan got the details of how to apply for the privileged information. Then he got the idea of approaching the director personally, there and then, and asked her if it was possible. The woman sighed, beginning to tire of his questions and wanting to get on with her other work, but she put a call through to the director's secretary. The answer was the director could see him, briefly, in the afternoon, but the timing was dangerously close to Brendan's flight time.

'Okay, I'll take it,' he decided. 'I might have to make a few phone calls and rearrange my flight schedule.'

She pointed him to a long-distance payphone inside the kiosk, but instead of making the calls he wandered back to the Gallipoli room to think things over, with all thoughts of coffee and food gone. Another idea came to him almost the moment he stood again in front of Story's exhibit, absently re-reading the poster and seeing 'Korea' again. He wondered why it hadn't occurred to him before.

Carl Netthold, he thought, eyeing the colonel's photograph triumphantly. *He was in Korea, too.*

Besides, he's a war historian. He probably knows more about this old bastard than these people do—including where he lived. Pleased with this solution, Brendan walked quickly back in the direction of the payphone.

Netthold greeted Brendan's call warmly. Remembering that he was on a payphone Brendan quickly explained the purpose of his call.

'Carl, there's a display here dedicated to one man, Colonel Nicholas Story. Have you heard of him?'

'Nick Story? Of course I have,' Netthold said. Brendan could almost hear him nodding. 'One of our unsung heroes. I did know him—he's dead now, though—but by the time I was seriously researching the military he was an old man and not too sure of what was going on around him. I met him several times, but I dealt mostly with his daughter, Glenness. She has a good knowledge of most of Nick's material anyway. She's made it a personal crusade of her own, if you know what I mean, getting it catalogued and preserved.'

'Do you know where he lived? Where I can contact her?'

'She lives in Evanborough, about three or four hours north of here. Can I ask why?'

Hope flared inside Brendan. 'There's a photograph in his exhibition. The guy I've seen—the one I told you about.' He paused, looking warily at the people in the kiosk, and lowered his voice. 'Carl, he's *in* the photograph.'

There was a silence from the other end of the line. Netthold finally said, 'I figured it was possible you might stumble across something that could help, but that's beyond my greatest expectations. Does it say who it is?'

'No, that's why I want to look at the rest of his stuff. He may have another photo that'll tell me. In the one here, they all look pretty chummy, so I guess he must have been a good friend of Story's. There may be another picture somewhere that identifies him.'

'Or a letter,' Netthold added. 'His mother kept everything he ever sent from the trenches. Nick understood quite early that he was one of the few men to land on April 25th and come out of the war in one piece four years later. He kept diaries during the Second World War, too. I've read some of them.'

'So he kept diaries during the First War? In Gallipoli?' Brendan asked. As he spoke, the digital readout of the phone began to flash, warning him he was about to be cut off. He hastily fed another two dollars into the slot.

'No, but he wrote a lot of letters,' Netthold was saying. 'Like I said, his mother kept them all and now Glenness has them. You may get lucky.'

'I've already had more than my fair share of luck, I think,' Brendan said. 'But I won't say no to a bit more. What's Glenness like? She can't be too young herself, I suppose.'

'She's a nice woman—look, I'll tell you what—

why don't you give me a call when you get back tonight? In the meantime I'll telephone her and sound her out about your going up to see her. She won't part with anything, you see. You'll have to go and visit her. I'll spin her your line about tracing a relative. There's no point in worrying her with any of your ghost stories. I suppose you can go up there?'

'Almost straight away,' Brendan assured him firmly.

He promised to call Netthold again in the early evening after he'd arrived home. Before he hung up he noticed there was still more than a dollar left on the readout and on a whim he fed an extra coin in and dialled his own house. Gwen, he knew, would be home from work at this time of the day, but she probably wouldn't be in bed yet. Brendan was bursting with the news about the photograph and wanted to tell her.

A long minute later he was frowning with surprise, which turned to concern as the telephone rang out without being answered. Normally, if she didn't want to be disturbed or was ducking out for a while, Gwen would have turned the call-tone down and switched on the answering machine. She was very reliable about it.

Disturbed, Brendan finally gave up and put the phone down.

12

Gwen was determined to find some answers for herself, too, but she didn't want to discuss with Brendan what she might do, in case he tried to veto any of her ideas. Quietly, she wasn't sure he could be trusted to judge anything any more. The world was going crazy for him, and Gwen seriously worried what that was doing to his sanity.

In fact, she wasn't coping all that well herself and needed to talk to someone—anyone—who would be sympathetic without questioning the facts. There was only one person that could be. Jodie Seager was Gwen's best friend and the one whom

Brendan wanted her to stay with, if things got too much. It would help, too, that Jodie had her own slightly crazy view of the world. She was always embracing some new fad or belief and Gwen was never quite certain what the latest one might be as she rejected and replaced them all so fast. At least, Gwen could be sure her friend would have an open mind to their troubles and might even be able to contribute a few good ideas. At one time Jodie had gone thoroughly into spiritualism and reincarnation, and it was one of the few basic tenets that had stuck, while she weaved other new, alternative beliefs around it.

In direct contrast to her private life Jodie was a survivor in the hard world of advertising. Her friendship with Gwen often suffered long periods where they didn't see each other, because of the odd hours of Gwen's career and the demands of Jodie's own work which involved long hours and frequent trips out of town. It was always hard for the two women to find time to spend together, so when they did, they usually made the most of it. Jodie was living in a renovated two-bedroom house on a large grassy block. The previous owners had kept several sheep, but now the grass was growing high, besieging the house. She'd been through a succession of housemates, some good, some bad, but at the moment she was attempting to live on her own.

It was almost dark when Jodie opened the front door, throwing a flood of light across the narrow verandah.

'You're psychic,' she laughed at Gwen, who was picking her way towards the house through the unkempt garden. 'I just put the kettle on.'

'No, just blessed with good timing,' Gwen said, stepping onto the porch. She gave her friend a hug, then walked past her into the lounge room. Jodie headed straight for the kitchen to make the coffee. In one corner of the lounge a television softly murmured a game show. Gwen watched it a moment, then heard Jodie yelling at her to turn it off and put on whatever music she liked.

Snapping the set off, Gwen twiddled with the stereo unit beside it until she got a rock FM station. As she stooped over the player a cool breeze blew through an open window, raising goose bumps on her arms. It was coming through an old casement window and the moisture-swollen wood and ancient fittings defied all of Gwen's attempts at closing it properly, the hinges squealing in protest with every centimetre she managed to move it. In the end she had to be satisfied with pulling it hard against the adjoining window, but not clasping it.

Jodie came in carrying the two coffees and saw Gwen's struggles. 'Don't fuss yourself,' she said. 'That window closes properly about three weeks in the year, when the weather's exactly right and the wood isn't too swollen.'

'There was a chilly breeze coming through,' Gwen explained, taking one of the coffees.

'I just did the same in the kitchen. The wind can go through this house as if it didn't have any damned walls. It turns the place into an icebox,' she complained, lowering herself into a cane chair and gesturing to Gwen to do the same. 'One of these days I'll get myself together and move somewhere better.'

'You shouldn't leave this place,' Gwen said fondly. 'It may be a little draughty and old, but it must be great not to have any neighbours close by. You can turn your music up as loud as you like.' She stopped, then shrugged with a wry expression on her face as she thought that, in her own home, she would take all the human company and close neighbours she could get right now. 'Anyway, I think it's great,' she added lamely.

Jodie took a sip of her drink, carefully regarding her guest over the rim of the cup. 'So, what's been happening?' she asked casually. 'Are you working pretty hard? You look like it.'

'I've been doing a stint in the Emergency Room,' Gwen said, knowing Jodie would be aware what that involved.

'Oh, the heavy blood-and-gore stuff. And where's Brendan?'

'Actually, he's gone on an over-nighter to Canberra, to do some research at the war museum.'

'Hey,' Jodie said, raising her eyebrows. 'We could have gone out on the town and really played up! He won't get home until late in the morning, surely?'

'He flies back in just before lunch, but I have to work, remember?'

'You could have called in a sickie.'

'Believe me,' Gwen smiled, 'There's nothing harder than trying to pretend you've been sick the day before, when you're surrounded by doctors and nurses all the time.'

'Okay, I guess it could be tricky,' Jodie agreed, laughing. She gave Gwen a sly look. 'So how's it going with Bren?'

'Good,' Gwen replied lightly. 'Just the same as ever. We roll along and take everything as it comes, no problems.'

'Yeah? Well, what *is* the problem then?'

'No, really—no problems.' It was an automatic response.

Jodie sighed, shaking her head sadly like a teacher disappointed by her best pupil. 'Come on, Gwen. You should know better than that. Speak up.'

Gwen gave her a look, before saying, 'Is it that obvious?'

'You have "problem" written all over your face.'

'Yeah, I guess that's why I'm here.' Gwen hesitated for a moment longer, because this was her last chance to keep her mouth shut. She knew she had come here to talk honestly about everything, but her resolve began to waver. Suddenly, it all seemed slightly ridiculous. In this other house, just sitting and drinking coffee and with Jodie's friendly face waiting to hear it all, her stories of soldier's ghosts and dead young girls would sound unbelievable. Jodie would think she were mad.

Gwen had said too much already—her friend knew there was something wrong and it was too late to pretend there wasn't. Suddenly she thought about making up one big lie right there and then, something more believable than the truth. Then she reminded herself she wasn't very good at lying. Besides, she finally reasoned quietly, aware that a silence was stretching out between them, she just might glean some new perspective on things herself, while she shared her woes with Jodie.

Gwen explained, as a beginning, 'Well, Brendan doesn't want me to be in the house alone after dark. In fact, I need to stay here tonight until I go to work, if that's okay. I'm only doing a short, four-hour catch-up shift and I don't start until late.'

'Sure, it's okay. But why? Have you got a prowler hanging around?' Jodie was quickly excited.

'I wish it were something so easy.' Gwen couldn't help the smallest nervous pause again, before adding, 'Actually, we think we've got a ghost.'

'A ghost!' Jodie was so surprised she jerked forward in her seat, nearly spilling her coffee in her lap. 'You're kidding me!'

'No, of course not. We've both seen a few things. Bren's put up with a lot more than me.'

'Hey! So, what are we doing here? Let's go to your place and check it out! I'll stay the night while you go to work,' she offered, without thinking.

'Uh-uh,' Gwen was shaking her head. 'This isn't some Casper the Friendly Ghost we're talking about here. Why do you think I can't sleep at home alone, at night?'

'Really?' Jodie's enthusiasm wasn't dampened. 'Tell me more.'

Gwen couldn't stop herself asking, 'You believe me? Just like that?'

'Of course! For Christ's sake, Gwen, I believe in the damned *tooth* fairy—you know that!' Jodie waved enthusiastically at the walls around them covered with the mystic charts. She added, 'Besides, would you make it up? To me?'

'No, I wouldn't do that,' Gwen said quietly. She had a drink of her coffee, using the moment to decide exactly how much she wanted to tell. 'All sorts of things have been happening, but the latest and the worst was a visit from Jeneatte Beason.'

'She's the girl who does research for Brendan, isn't she—now hang on a second.' Jodie was awed by her own train of thought. This took a moment to sink in, then she pointed an excited finger at Gwen. 'Now I know who you mean. Wasn't she the girl they found in the river? My God! The name didn't connect when I read it in the paper—' Jodie fell silent, looking stunned.

'Yeah,' Gwen said dryly. 'Except she came to visit us *after* she was dead.' Inwardly, Gwen was marvelling at how she could face the facts so calmly.

'You're kidding me!' Now Jodie was staring at her, the coffee in her hands forgotten.

'No, I came home from shopping—it was the night of those really bad storms, right—and as I pulled into the driveway there was Brendan, lying on the front lawn in the middle of this howling storm, with a girl on top of him.'

'You mean it *was* her? She was attacking him?' Jodie said, whispering like a schoolgirl sharing a delightful secret. 'Like in "Evil Dead"?'

'She wanted him to make love to her.'

'Now you *must* be kidding me.' But Jodie obviously thought nothing of the sort. Her face was glowing with excitement. 'What was Brendan trying to do? I guess he was scared stupid—I know I would be!' She took a breath, absorbing it all, then shook her head in disbelief.

'Brendan said she was—pretty cut up. The police don't really know why.'

Jodie put her hand to her mouth, her eyes still saucer-like and staring at her friend. 'So, what did Bren do?'

'He sort of blacked out, he says. Like his mind didn't want to cope. The next thing he remembered was me dragging him inside.'

'I don't blame him! But what are you going to do about it? Have you told anyone?'

'No. What are we going to say? Who are we going to tell?'

Jodie shrugged, finally calming down enough to give it some serious thought. 'A priest?'

'You've been watching too many movies.'

'Well, it makes sense to me. Who else? Anyway, how many ghosts have you seen? Lots?'

'Bren's been dreaming things, more than anything,

but I hadn't really seen anything until a couple of days ago,' Gwen admitted, then she took a deep breath before plunging into an account of the soldier appearing in their kitchen.

As she spoke she realised with a surge of feeling that it did feel good to talk to someone about it all.

By the time they'd each drunk another coffee, Gwen had explained everything she could think of. She felt much better and found herself examining her own story with a clearer, more analytical mind.

'So you think this charm belonged to some sort of distant relative?' Jodie asked. 'Someone who left it behind?'

'It's the best shot we've got,' Gwen replied. 'We're certainly hoping to find a connection with someone previously in the house, whether it's a relation or not.' She put down her coffee and Jodie jumped to her feet, picking up the cup and heading for the kitchen to refill it yet again.

'It's like some sort of detective story,' she called out, apparently unmoved by the more horrific details.

Gwen rolled her eyes. 'I suppose so.'

'Hey, I've got an idea. I have an appointment in the morning with a client over your way. I'd like to drop in for a cuppa and see the house, is that okay? Will you be awake?'

'What do you mean, see the house?' Gwen was smiling now at Jodie's irrepressible nature. 'You've seen it a million times before. What do you expect to see this time? But you're more than welcome, of course.'

Jodie came back in carrying the coffee. 'I don't know,' she shrugged. 'Maybe I'll pick up some sort of vibe you guys don't notice, because you're used to it. I wouldn't mind having a look at this charm thing.'

'Actually,' Gwen said, suddenly looking nervous, 'I've got it here with me. I was hoping to get somebody to have a look at it, on my way over here, but I left it too late and the place I had in mind was closed. They specialise in old coins and medals, so I figured they might have come across this sort of thing, too.' She shrugged, making up her mind. 'Brendan doesn't know I've got it. Most people wouldn't want to go near the thing after hearing what I've told you, but I suppose you can have a quick look, if you want—' Gwen stopped, already having second thoughts about showing her the charm.

Jodie said, smiling kindly, 'You really think this thing's got to Brendan in some way, don't you?'

Gwen was already shaking her head. 'No, I'm not totally convinced, but it's the only damned answer we've got right now, and a pretty improbable one at that. But I don't care that I'm going overboard in the playing-it-safe department. That's the way I'm going to do it, until I get a few more answers, at least.'

'Sounds fair enough to me.'

In the silence following, the telephone rang,

making them both jump. Jodie glanced an apology at Gwen, getting up. 'I won't be a second.' She disappeared into the kitchen, only to return moments later. 'It's the hospital—for you.'

'Sorry,' Gwen said. 'I gave them this number, in case they wanted me to come in early.'

'No problem.'

Gwen came back into the lounge a minute later and finished her coffee standing up, looking around for her things and explaining, 'Some accident's tied up half the staff in the operating theatre, so they're a bit short-staffed in the emergency room. I said I'd go in now. Sorry about this.'

'That's okay,' Jodie said, dismissing the apology with a wave. 'I'm getting used to it. Before you dash off, you'll have to at least show me this trinket that's causing all the hassles.'

Gwen looked troubled and felt a subtle, nagging fear, despite the new confidence that talking to Jodie had given her. 'We don't really have the time, now,' she said, knowing it sounded lame. 'I could show it to you in the morning.'

'Oh, come on Gwen! Just a quick look, before you go—' Jodie became thoughtful. 'Hey, where did you say you wanted someone to have a look at it?'

Gwen explained again about the curio store and before she finished Jodie was interrupting her.

'I've got a much better idea. Why don't you leave it with me and I'll get a guy I know to check it out in the morning? He works at the museum and I speak to him a lot, because he's who we deal with if we want to use some weird and wonderful artefact in one of our advertising campaigns. He's a bit too straight, but he's okay. I could do that and still be over at your place before my appointment at ten o'clock—how about that? Then I could tell you all about it. Will you be awake by then?'

Gwen felt trapped, finding it hard to refuse her friend without sounding distrustful or churlish. 'I really don't know, Jodie. It's not as simple as it sounds. I mean, you haven't been putting up with all this shit, like we have. It's damned scary.'

Jodie was sighing, exasperated. 'I'll be careful, don't worry. Do you want it checked out or not?'

Gwen did want the charm examined by somebody who might recognise it properly, and now she was being offered a much better opportunity than she could have arranged herself. Jodie was a responsible person she could trust more than anyone else. Still, it had never been in her plans to let the thing out of her sight. Gwen reluctantly put a hand in her shoulder bag and felt around, finding the paper bag she had put the charm in. She held the bag out to Jodie, who took it almost reverently.

'All right, then. But this is against my better judgement. Promise me you'll treat this thing like poison, okay?'

'Stop nagging me about it—I'll be a good girl.'

Gwen had a fleeting impression Jodie was being overly glib and not taking her seriously, but it was too late now. In a last attempt to impress the severity of the occasion on her, Gwen said, 'And don't let this guy tomorrow keep it. Bren doesn't know I've taken it and I don't want him to find out. I want to put it back straight away. I shouldn't even let it stay out overnight,' she added, realising belatedly this would have been a better excuse for not leaving the charm with Jodie. That chance was now gone, too.

Suddenly Gwen put a hand to her forehead. 'Oh damn! And I left the stupid tin on Bren's desk! I got so wrapped up trying to find that paper bag, then the damned phone rang—I forgot! How bloody stupid of me. I must remember to fix things up when I get home in the morning, before he gets back and goes into his office.' She swore again, annoyed at herself.

'Don't worry. I'll have it back to you first thing, before his plane's even due to land. And if I'm late and Bren's wandering around, I'll sneak it back to you, okay?'

'Normally I wake up after only an hour or two's sleep,' Gwen said, still fretting at her mistake. 'Which will be about eight-thirty or so. Why don't you give me a call, before you leave? I don't mind if you wake me up. That way you can remind me about the tin, and you'll be able to tell me if there's any change of plans.'

Jodie stood up again. 'Sure, if it'll make you feel better. I'll scribble a reminder on the whiteboard in the kitchen, just in case. Sometimes I fly around in the mornings in such a tizz, trying to get ready for work, that I forget half the things I'm supposed to do.' A moment later her voice was floating out of the kitchen again. 'You know, I left the iron on again the other day. One day I'm going to burn this place down.'

Gwen opened her mouth to reply, but stopped as she heard a voice coming from somewhere outside the house. She wasn't certain it was somebody close—close enough for them to be concerned, anyway. But she clearly heard what was said.

Someone had called out, *'Hey, Ben!'*

Unsure of what to do or say, she sat there for a moment, trying to decide. Was she getting too jumpy, for goodness sake? Jodie came back into the room and saw Gwen's worried frown.

'What's wrong? I suppose you've thought of another excuse.' Jodie mocked her, putting her hands on her hips.

'No—no, I thought I heard someone outside.'

'It's your place that's supposed to be haunted, not mine,' Jodie said easily. 'It's the trees you're hearing. A lot of them are rubbing up against the house. The slightest breeze and they make all sorts of strange screeching noises against the paint. You get used to it, after a while.'

'No, I'm sure this was voices. I heard someone call out, but they were pretty far away. It was probably your neighbours,' Gwen added, but not entirely convincing herself.

'They're old and crotchety,' Jodie nodded. 'And they yell at each other, because they're half deaf. On some nights you can hear them clear as anything.'

Gwen looked at her watch. 'It's time for me to make a move. I'll need half an hour to get into the hospital and park my car, and I told them I'd be in within three-quarters of an hour.' She smiled an apology. 'Sorry to be rushing off like this. Don't forget to call me in the morning, will you?'

'It's on the whiteboard, remember? I'd be lost without the bloody thing sometimes.'

Jodie followed her to the front door and stood there, waving and watching until Gwen was actually sitting in her car and the motor was running, the glare of the headlights washing over the house. Then she waved one last time as the car backed down the driveway and swung out into the road. There was an answering toot on the horn, before the red tail-lights disappeared up the street.

Jodie didn't notice, as she closed the door, that the night outside was as still as could be, undisturbed by any breeze that might make the trees rub against the house. And there was no noise coming from the neighbours either.

Jodie's first priority was to wash a few dishes. She hummed to herself, letting the kitchen sink fill with soapy water as she absently wiped down the benchtops. It was then Jodie realised she was a little nervous. The volume of the stereo in the next room was low and didn't really hide the silence of the house around her. The quiet, combined with Gwen's ghost stories, was putting her on edge like it never had before.

'Don't be silly,' she told herself, noticing a slight tremor in her voice. Shaking the suds from her hands and quickly drying them on a hand-towel she left the half-finished dishes to turn on the television again, making it loud. It felt better having the murmur of human voices filtering through the rooms. She returned to the kitchen and as she bent back over the sink a movement outside the house caught her eye. Seen through the window in front of her, but veiled by the reflection of the lights in the kitchen, she wasn't certain. Jodie stopped and looked out.

For a fleeting second she thought she saw a face staring in at her.

She let out a small scream and backed away from the sink, dragging a splash of water with her. She stood absolutely still in the middle of the kitchen, staring back at the window. *Had she really seen it? Or did she just imagine it?* With a flash of bravado Jodie reached out and flicked off the overhead fluorescent, throwing the kitchen into darkness. This didn't feel so good either, but at least it took the reflection off the glass and she could see outside better. Still, nothing appeared to be moving out there. Finding more courage, she went slowly toward the window until she was again pressed against the sink, her face close to the glass. Now Jodie could see outside quite clearly, picking out of the darkness the familiar trees and shrubs, and the distant lights of her neighbours. Nothing unusual, no strange shadows or figures, moved against the normal scene.

Christ, Jodie. You're letting Gwen's stories get to you, she told herself, trying to smile at her own nervousness. *Even if Gwen's house is haunted, it's on the other side of the damned city.*

'But the charm isn't. It's right here,' she said aloud, almost startling herself with the sound of her own voice. She let out a quiet groan and tapped herself on the forehead. 'God, now I'm talking to myself!'

With a sudden move Jodie snapped the curtains closed across the kitchen window.

She finished her cleaning, quickly rinsing the dishes and resisting the urge to glance at the closed curtains all the time, as if she might be able to see through them and check the yard again. Then she stood undecided in the middle of the room, finally telling herself again she *was* being silly and there was no reason why she should do things any different tonight to any other night. She would have a shower, take a book and the charm to bed and do a bit of reading until she felt too drowsy.

Jodie went to her bedroom to get a fresh towel out of her closet. While she was in there she drew the curtains here, too. Next, passing through the lounge, she did the same for all the casement windows and detoured past the front door to lock it properly.

The bathroom was an extension of the laundry, serving as a toilet as well. The bathroom was still, however, a separate area with a lockable door. Jodie felt safer as she pushed the bolt home, at the same time still silently deriding herself for her fears. She undressed, wrapping the towel around herself, then stood at the basin washing the day's make-up from her face. Directly above the sink was a louvred window looking out to the back yard, the sheets of glass closed tightly. She stopped herself from opening them and peeking out. Instead, she fixed her attention on the mirror beside the window. Satisfied her looks had survived another day, she reached out and twisted on the hot-water tap for the shower, returning to the basin to brush her teeth while the gas heating system built up some warmth. As she brushed, Jodie couldn't stop herself opening the glass slats with her free hand and looking nervously between the louvres at her neighbours' lights filtering through the trees. At that moment it struck her that the night was a very still one indeed, with no wind stirring the leaves and branches in front of the lights.

She remembered Gwen thought she'd heard someone outside.

'For Christ's sake,' Jodie told herself angrily, spitting out a mouthful of toothpaste. She cupped her hand under the running tap, rinsing her mouth out. After checking the temperature of the shower water and adding a little cold, she carelessly dropped the towel to the floor and stepped into the shower. Bowing to her fears slightly she didn't pull the shower curtain all the way across, instead leaving it agape at one end so she could still see the door. It was silly, she told herself, because the door was locked. But it made her feel better.

Jodie luxuriated in the shower longer than usual, then reluctantly turned the taps off and stepped out, picking up the towel and quickly drying off. Wrapping the towel around herself again and leaving her clothes where they were, she automatically unlocked the bathroom door without a moment's thought about her earlier fears.

But padding through the house in wet, bare feet she was stopped by the sound of a distant scream, making her heart suddenly race wildly. Another scream followed and Jodie felt fear build up inside her like a pressure in her chest, making her muscles turn watery. Then an impressive burst of momentous music made her realise it was only the television. With relief washing over her, she leaned weakly against the wall next to the bedroom door.

'I'm going bloody crazy,' she told herself, half-laughing. The television continued a racket of screams and discordant music. 'I'm not going to listen to any more of that shit!' Jodie said aloud, pushing herself off the wall and heading for the lounge room.

As she bent over the television set to change channels, exchanging the scenes of mayhem for a placid documentary on wildlife, a slight, cold breeze touched her shoulder.

'See?' she said to herself. 'There is a breeze out there moving the—' she stopped dead, her fear returning like cold fingers touching her spine. She looked up to see the window Gwen struggled so hard to close was still closed—in fact, she'd just drawn the curtains across, too. The whole house was closed up tight.

But it felt like a chill draught was sweeping through the house. At least, her bare skin was suddenly cold, raising goose bumps.

Jodie immediately glanced over her shoulder, although she knew she was alone in the room.

Come on, girl. Don't start getting spooked by a few ghost stories. Gwen and Brendan have been smoking too much dope, that's all. And even if they have a ghost, it's bloody miles away, remember? It's stupid to get scared, just because you've turned the damned television off.

But Jodie couldn't even lie to herself convincingly. She'd believed everything Gwen told her.

I know, I'll get a stiff drink and go to bed.

She turned the television off and went back to the kitchen, taking a bottle of bourbon from the top of the fridge and slopping a generous measure into a tumbler. After adding ice there was barely enough room for some cola—just enough to make it fizz.

In her bedroom, with the door firmly closed, Jodie felt safer again. For a moment her mind drifted to the telephone. But who could she ring? What about one of her men friends? Any one of them would get themselves over as fast as they could, like dashing white knights, if she told them she felt unsafe. But they would take too long, and she might be settled down before they arrived. Besides, they probably wouldn't understand she only wanted someone around tonight and would end up having an argument about sex, which was the last thing she felt like right now.

She considered the paper bag with its charm and told herself firmly it was time to take a look at what was causing all the problems. She took it to her dressing table. This had a big mirror backing it and Jodie looked at the towel wrapped around herself for a moment and thought about changing into the tracksuit she slept in when it was cold. Quickly, she decided that could wait for a few minutes. The chill had gone away and she was feeling warm from the shower now. Impatiently, Jodie deftly shuffled out the contents of the bag onto the dresser. The dog-shaped charm slid onto the wooden surface and Jodie tried to pick it up, but her long fingernails kept getting in the way. Finally, she held the charm by the leather and, with a sudden inspiration from remembering Gwen saying just looking at it might be dangerous, Jodie stared at the reflection in the mirror of herself and the swinging charm.

The metal figure twisted and turned on its leather, teasing whether it would stay still long enough for Jodie to get a good look. Annoyed, she gently tried catching its outer edges with her fingertips, but the reflection tricked her, so she tired of the small game and turned to look at the real thing, lightly capturing it between her thumb and index finger. She found herself staring directly at the charm.

And nothing's happening, she thought. *So what's the big deal?*

Jodie studied it closely. The dull gold metal felt heavy in her fingers. There were no markings on it at all, which disappointed her. Any sort of writing on it might have given her something to chase up. Only the green stone winked at her as it caught the light from above on the ceiling. On an impulse Jodie lifted it above her head, poised to drop the leather around her neck. But in that instant, a noise came from outside the house. It was a totally alien, yet recognisable sound.

The sound of a horse, snorting for breath, and the jingle of its harness.

Instantly, Jodie knew something was going wrong—very wrong.

Still holding the charm by its leather thonging she went slowly and with mounting fear to the window. She knew she didn't have to do this—pull the curtains aside and look out. It may even be safer to ignore what was going on outside her house now. She could just bury herself under her blankets right now and pray it would all go away.

With a shaking hand Jodie reached out and parted the curtains.

Instead of looking across her own small block, her bedroom window now showed a short, narrow valley with steep, rugged sides. Bright moonlight gave the scene a silvery, almost festive, appearance, but the valley was filled with grim-faced soldiers going about their business with rifles slung on their shoulders. Many of them led pack mules, moving to and from haphazard piles of supplies. On the ridge to Jodie's right could be seen the rapid sparkling of gunfire and frequent explosions. As she watched there came a much larger explosion which made her flinch and cry out. The glass in front of her shook.

'Dear God, what's happened?' Jodie whispered, asking her own reflection in the window. She looked at her pale image and her face shivered as the window trembled to another explosion. The soldiers kept moving through the moonlight, apparently unconcerned with the violence close by as they tended their work. And none of them seemed aware of the young woman staring out at them. Then Jodie saw the glass was reflecting somebody standing in the room with her. She screamed and whirled around.

But the bedroom was empty.

Seeing something out of the corner of her eye, Jodie turned to her reflection in the dressing table mirror.

The mirror showed someone was in the room with her. Standing near the door was the decaying corpse of a soldier. He used the mirror to stare dreadfully into her eyes.

Jodie screamed again, dropping the charm and turning away from the mirror so fast she nearly fell. The golden figure bounced off the bed and tumbled in a tangle of leather to the carpet. The furthest thing from Jodie's mind was picking it up again and putting it on—she had no way of knowing that it might save her life.

Even Gwen wouldn't have known that.

With her back turned to the reflection Jodie couldn't see anyone and her scream stopped, locking in her throat, but her skin was crawling in anticipation of a chill, ghostly touch. She remembered Gwen's words that she, too, could only see a reflection of Brendan's nightmare ghosts. Jodie didn't want to turn back to check the mirror and see if the apparition was still there. Panic was shrieking ever-louder in her mind.

Don't look. DON'T *look. There's nothing here, you can see that. If you can't see it with your own eyes—who cares about the fucking mirror—it's not there, right? So just walk out of here now. Only three steps to the door, open it, and get the hell out. Get out!*

Screwing down hard on her panic, Jodie took one faltering step towards the door. Nothing happened—though she didn't know what could happen. Ghostly hands coming out of the mirror to hold her?

She let out a low groan of fear. Her next step went unchallenged. A third, and she yanked the door open so hard it nearly rebounded back into her. Then she was out, down the hallway and in the lounge room, desperately ignoring a touch of freezing air on the bare skin of her shoulder.

Her first thought was stepping out the front door and running for her life to the nearest neighbours, screaming her lungs out. But Jodie remembered her neighbours weren't outside anymore. There was only a spectral valley filled with ghostly soldiers and no escape that way. Running outside might be the very worst thing she could do. She didn't dare waste time on the telephone, either. Nobody would believe her. Only Brendan, and he was a million miles away. Anyone else would send an ambulance and a straightjacket.

Jodie became acutely conscious of her near-nakedness and suddenly felt twice as vulnerable. She wildly berated herself for being a lazy fool, leaving her clothes in the bathroom. Fresh clothes were in the bedroom, but she sure as hell wasn't going back in there!

Her fear grew worse, gnawing at her belly. *Where the fuck was he?* WHAT *was he?* Her mind was silently screaming again and it took a big effort not to let the sound escape her lips, too. *What about the bedroom? Was he waiting in there still or not? Waiting for her to come to bed? Would he be behind the door? Had she closed it?* She couldn't remember.

She realised she'd just spent long moments standing uselessly in the lounge room.

Do something, Jodie!

Fighting through the mist of terror an idea dawned on her. She'd walked from the bathroom to here unscathed, hadn't she? Chances are, if he were waiting in the bedroom she could retrace her steps. Her dirty clothes were there. She could get dressed again and then make a run for it out the *back* door. Maybe the bastard wouldn't be expecting that, and it had to be a normal world somewhere. Maybe the valley with its soldiers was some sort of trick in the glass and if she opened the back door everything would be revealed to be the way it was supposed to be.

Jodie felt she might have a better chance of escaping, if she were at least properly clothed. It was about the only thing she could try.

Summoning up all her courage and strength, instinctively holding the towel tighter around her, she began walking slowly through the lounge room and into the small passageway outside her bedroom leading to the laundry. It took her past the open archway to the kitchen, too, and with a stab of horror she realised she'd never given the kitchen a thought. Was he in there now? Then she was past and into the hallway. Jodie's eyes locked on her bedroom door and saw it was open. She waited for the slightest movement heralding somebody stepping out. If they did, she would scream as loud as she could, turn around and run for the front door, for whatever that might be worth.

But she passed there too, using a tremendous willpower not to look through the doorway and into the dressing table mirror. With the hairs on the back of her neck prickling with fear, expecting to hear movement behind her, she stepped into the laundry. Then, with a gasp of relief, she rushed the last few steps into the bathroom.

Jodie snatched up her jeans from the floor. Fumbling in her haste she tried to shake them out—they'd reversed themselves as she'd pulled them off her legs. At the same time she tore the towel off and threw it aside.

From somewhere beyond the back door there came a terrifying howl, so loud it seemed to shake the house itself. Jodie screamed hard enough to rip at her throat and tears came to her eyes. She froze as she stood, the jeans held in front of her. She looked through the doorway at the back door, her eyes wide and staring like a cornered animal, but she couldn't tell if it was locked. It seemed impossibly far away and she was still stark naked. With a whimpering cry she dropped the jeans, jumped forward and slammed the bathroom door closed instead, ramming the locking bolt fiercely home. A small mocking voice reminded her that the door probably wouldn't make any difference, but she closed her mind to it. Her heart was beating painfully in her chest and she stared at the door's wooden panelling for what seemed like an eternity, waiting breathlessly for the first sound to come from the other side.

There came the scratching of claws on the painted concrete floor. She heard a low, throaty growl.

Jodie screamed again and shouted, 'Go away! Leave me alone!'

She burst into tears. For a minute there came strange sounds at the door. Laboured, painful breathing and muttered sentences in a foreign tongue. Jodie was sobbing now, scared and completely losing control. Her terror wouldn't let her think straight.

The noises from the other side of the door stopped, but Jodie didn't feel any safer. For the first time she thought of a weapon and looked around desperately, but there was nothing. The idea came to her to throw scalding water at whatever came through the door, but there was nothing to hold it, except for an ornate mug filled with toothbrushes and razors. The happy, smiling ceramic face on the cup mocked her. Instinctively, Jodie had backed away from the door until she could feel the coldness of the wash-basin pressing against the skin of her rump.

Then she remembered the bathroom had a mirror. A dreadful feeling told her to turn around and look. This time she couldn't stop herself.

A different soldier stood in the bathroom with her, his back to the door. He looked foreign. His eyes were the only thing with any sort of life, filled with a burning fever. The skin of his face was blackened and decaying. So were the hands, clutching at the rotting fabric of the uniform. With a painful, shuffling movement he came towards her. She could see a bubbling wound in his chest.

This time Jodie screamed so hard it felt like something broke in her chest. She didn't turn around to see if the ghost was really in the room with her, but flung herself at the louvred window next to the mirror, smashing at it with her fists. Without waiting for the glass to clear she put one knee on the wash-basin and tried to propel herself past the jagged edges of glass through the small opening. On her first attempt her knee slipped on the smooth porcelain surface and she nearly fell back all the way to the bathroom floor. Her limbs flailed to keep her purchase, her right hand grabbing a broken edge of louvre, slicing the skin cruelly. Her other hand inadvertently flung open the cabinet door, smashing the mirror. As the pieces cascaded to the floor the soldier's images disappeared, but Jodie was too terrified and panic-stricken to see. She kept trying to get out the window, believing it was the only escape from the dreadful thing in the room.

With her next attempt she got her head and shoulders outside the window, before her knee slipped on the porcelain again. This time, as she fell backwards, two pieces of glass in their metal louvre caught in her neck, dragging against her jawbone and cutting deeply. Arterial blood spurted out, splattering across the wall beside the window and into the cabinet. Jodie clutched with senseless fingers at the wound as she continued falling backwards. She hit the floor badly, her head jerking backwards and bashing onto the concrete surface, knocking herself unconscious. She lay there, blood running freely from the cuts on her hands, arms and fingers—but mostly from the deep wound in her neck. After a minute her eyes flickered open, but they only flared with life for a moment, then turned sightless. The red pool grew around her.

In the house next door Jodie's elderly neighbours were disturbed from their television-viewing by her last scream.

'That sounded like a scream,' the woman said, frowning at her husband.

'Probably the girl next door,' he grunted, with the disdain of someone who thinks young women bringing home different men within the space of six months deserve all they get.

'I mean, a real scream,' she insisted.

'Leave it alone. It's none of our business.' He didn't take his eyes from the set.

'Geoffrey,' she scolded, pushing her ageing, protesting body to its feet and moving to the window. She peered out at the night, trying to see through the trees. 'I can't see anything,' she reported. Nearly fifty metres separated the two houses.

'Whatever it is, it'll be in her bedroom,' he grunted again. His wife wasn't deterred and continued watching, being rewarded moments later by the sound of breaking glass.

'There!' she said, almost triumphant. 'Did you hear that?'

'She threw something at him,' he judged.

'Oh, she's not that bad a girl. You hardly ever

talk to her, so you wouldn't know.' She stood on her tip-toes at the window, as if this might give her a better view. 'It sounded like breaking glass to me.'

'Come away. Don't bother with it.'

She considered something before answering, 'No—no, I think I might telephone the police.'

'What? What on earth for?' Her husband was growing annoyed, shifting uncomfortably in his chair. There was no point in getting themselves involved. 'It's just some lovers' tiff probably, at an ungodly hour of the night, I might add!'

'It's still early, for young people. And it's better to be safe than sorry,' she replied, moving to the phone. Capping the argument, she added, 'Anyway, if it's nothing important, it will teach her a lesson to keep her private affairs private and not disturb us with them.' She was mildly surprised that her finger was trembling as she stabbed at the buttons on the telephone.

Fifteen minutes later a young constable walked cautiously to the front door of Jodie's house. A second policeman sat behind the wheel of their car, watching for the first signs of trouble. Their arrival and subsequent sitting in the driveway for nearly a minute hadn't prompted any response from the house. It was taken as a bad sign.

The constable knocked on the door and called out. There was still no response. He tried again and found himself with no choice but to try around the back. He signalled his intentions to his partner, who immediately radioed an update to their despatcher, who chose to send another unit on its way to assist.

Out the back, having walked down the opposite side of the house to the bathroom, the constable was regretting his bravado, because something felt wrong. Lights were on, but nobody was around. The door to the back laundry was unlocked, so he let himself cautiously in. Moving quickly through the small house he stood in the lounge room, noting the television and the closed windows. There were no signs of violence or forced entry—but then, he'd just let himself in easily. He went through the passageway, stopping for a searching look into the kitchen.

'Hello? Is anybody here?' he called again. 'Don't be alarmed, it's the police.'

No answer.

When he stepped back into the laundry, looking more carefully now, he saw the trickle of blood under the bathroom door.

'Oh shit,' he said grimly.

Making sure he didn't step in the blood, he tried the door. It was locked. He experimented with his weight against the panelling, feeling it bow easily under the strain. Gritting his teeth he leaned backwards, then swung his shoulder against the wood. The door burst open.

The smell of blood washed over him, nearly making him retch. Jodie lay where she had fallen.

Her flesh was almost translucent now, drained of her blood which was already congealing on the cold concrete. Within the redness, broken pieces of mirror glittered gaily up at him. The stench was so strong the constable failed to detect, underneath, an acrid smell of decomposition and the mustiness of old cloth.

Ashen-faced and shaking, he belatedly fumbled his weapon from his holster and held it ready. Then he realised he'd got too far already. If someone dangerous was still in the house, he'd have known it by now. He couldn't tell what killed the woman—only that she seemed to have tried escaping out the window.

He took a moment to wonder what had been so terrifying that it made her try such a desperate escape route, before he ran out of the house.

13

Gwen smiled at Brendan. She was standing next to the bedroom window where the only light was coming from, a faint gleam of the street lamps sneaking through the small cracks between and around the closed curtains. Still, in the dim light he recognised the smile. It was a special look she kept for close, intimate moments. Excitement began to fill his chest and loins as she started to slowly unbutton the flannel shirt, the only thing she wore. Moving sensually, knowing his anticipation would be growing, she climbed onto the bed and sat next to him, tucking her legs underneath her.

He reached forward as she came close and pulled the shirt down off her shoulders, making it fall in a tangle around her waist. Gwen's breasts were firm and her nipples were jutting forward, hardened with her own arousal. Brendan ran both his hands over them, squeezing gently and flicking at the nipples with his fingers. She closed her eyes and let out a small moan of pleasure. After a few minutes Brendan pulled himself forward and started kissing her, using his tongue instead of his fingers. Without opening her eyes, Gwen gently lifted one leg over his body, straddling him, and moved herself against his erection.

Now Brendan closed his eyes and fell back against the pillows, letting himself simply enjoy the ripples of intense pleasure spreading out from his groin. When the feeling grew almost to a release he suddenly decided he wanted to be selfish this time. He wanted to orgasm inside Gwen now, even though that normally signalled the end of their love-making and meant Gwen probably wouldn't climax herself. He stilled her movements with a touch on her shoulder, then pushed his hand under her, searching for her clitoris, but really hoping to find she would be wet enough to let him inside. Gwen understood and without complaint lifted herself slightly, reaching down and guiding him. With a single push he went deep, then grasped her shoulders and pulled her hard down on top of him so her breasts were crushed against his chest and her cheek nestled into his neck. They began moving again with low, slow thrusts, Gwen's breath coming in timed, warm hisses of pleasure against his ear.

He came suddenly, pumping into her with a surprising rush, but with such an intensity it felt like his heart might stop. When it was finished they lay silently with Brendan catching his breath and Gwen waiting for him to make the first move. Finally, in a game they played often he felt around for her braid, intending to tug it. His hand searched her back, feeling a sheen of sweat there although it was only a mild night and the sex hadn't lasted long enough to make himself perspire. He realised Gwen was sweating profusely and Brendan dimly wondered if she was all right. The thick cord of her hair was proving hard to grasp, so he put his hand to the nape of her neck to find its beginnings.

It wasn't there. Brendan's fingers touched shorter, styled hair.

Someone else's hair.

Puzzled and becoming frightened, he dropped his hand away and went to grip Gwen's shoulders, so he could push her away and see her face. Again he felt the slick of perspiration on her skin. He smelled something unusual and it took him a moment to recognise it. Fear burst fully inside him, filling his chest as he realised it was blood he could smell.

Gwen was covered in blood, not sweat.

With a cry of revulsion he pushed her further away. She sat upright, still straddling him.

It was Jodie Seager on top of him now, grinning down at his terror with a savage delight. Her neck was a mess of jagged cuts, bleeding profusely with red rivulets of blood running down her chest and between her breasts.

'*Come again, Brendan,*' she said, with a soft giggle. '*See if you can come again.*' She moved herself against him, but his shrivelled penis had fallen out.

With another strangled noise, Brendan tried to shove her off him. But Jodie's image vanished the moment his hands touched her.

He found himself sitting up in the bed, the sheets tangled around his knees.

His terror slowly subsided, but the nightmare lingered in his mind, making him tremble, and he took several deep breaths to calm himself. He looked down at Gwen, who was still soundly asleep next to him, and for the first time in her life she'd taken a heavy dose of sedatives. The news of Jodie's death sent her into a mild state of shock. At least his latest nightmare hadn't disturbed her, Brendan thought.

He realised there was a dampness in his groin and on the sheets and he groaned. The nightmares could evoke such intense emotions in him—stark terror, and now even make him orgasm too.

'Jesus Christ, I have to beat this thing,' he whispered desperately to the dark bedroom around him. 'I have to, before it kills me.'

*

The outskirts of the city turned into an impressive freeway leading to the holiday coasts to the north. Brendan kept the station wagon on a steady 120 kilometres an hour—twenty over the limit. Still, some drivers weaved their way around him, blasting along at even greater speeds.

Gwen sat beside him holding her hands tightly in her lap. Her face was drawn and pale, her eyes not seeing the lush, green countryside speeding past. The hospital hadn't hesitated to give her time off, especially as Brendan had called in and explained, in blunt terms, exactly what had happened. Since Jodie's death Gwen had spoken little, mutely accepting Brendan's comfort, but relying mainly on her own inner strength to cope with the shock. He reached over and took her hand.

'I know it sounds a stupid thing to say, but try to take your mind off it for a while.' He winced inwardly at the inane saying.

'I'm trying to,' she said quietly. 'That's why I came along on this trip, remember? But it's not easy.' There was an edge of accusation in her voice. It hurt Brendan, but he didn't know how to deal with that yet, so he tried a less touchy, but relevant, subject.

'I don't think the police like me very much at the moment. I had to call them and let them know we were doing this. The guy who answered wasn't happy about me leaving town,' he said, with a humourless smile.

She cocked an eyebrow at him. 'The coincidence

is a bit much to swallow, you have to agree.'

He didn't answer, concentrating instead on swinging the car around a caravan being towed by a small car. It was lumbering along at half the speed limit. Then he said, 'I was in town when Jeneatte was probably killed, although I can't prove I stayed at home all that following night, because you weren't there. But I *was* in Canberra when Jodie was murdered, and I can prove that.'

'Can you?' Gwen gave him a strange look.

Brendan was surprised. 'Of course I can! What about the flight tickets?'

'You could have got your seat allocation and simply walked out of the terminal.'

Brendan was disturbed at Gwen's sudden lack of faith, but he tried not to show it. 'What about the return ticket?' he asked, hiding a frown.

'All they ever do is scrawl on the ticket. You could have done that yourself. Nobody's bothered to look that close.'

'I called Carl from Canberra, he'll vouch for that.'

'You can drive for thirty minutes out of town and get a long-distance tone on the telephone. You don't have to go all the way to Canberra for that.'

'So, what about this wild goose chase today?' She gave him another look and he added quickly, 'Well, no—it's not a wild goose chase. You know what I mean. How did I find out about Nicholas Story, if I didn't go to Canberra?'

She thought for a moment. 'Maybe you've had

this information all along from Carl Netthold.'

Brendan smiled grimly as he capped his argument. 'And how did I manage to get my signature on the motel's registration form? How did they get my signature on a credit card slip twelve hours later, when I paid the bill?'

'Okay, you could have flown back to Brisbane, killed Jodie, then gone back to Canberra for the morning,' Gwen tried lamely, running out of options. 'Anyway, why didn't you tell the police that?'

'I did, actually. You were on the phone at the time. You know, you'd think the boys in blue would've been quite happy to eliminate one of their prime suspects, but in fact I think they were rather annoyed I had a cast-iron alibi. Hey—' he added, getting suddenly angry. 'I didn't damn well kill anyone, all right? What the hell are you trying to do to me? I *need* you now, Gwen. Don't do this to me.'

Gwen put her head back against the headrest and let out a long sigh, then her own anger came out in a rush. 'I don't know—I'm just feeling so bloody confused and crazy. God, I'm going to *miss* Jodie. I wish I'd spent more time with her—' Her voice trailed off for a moment, then she snapped, 'So what the hell *is* happening, Bren? Was it a coincidence? Were their deaths something to do with your damned ghosts, your nightmares? Is that possible, for God's sake? Is it *your* fault?' she added, almost cruelly.

Brendan took a long time to answer. 'No, I don't think it's impossible anymore and it may even be my fault in some way.' He threw a glance at her, seeing Gwen's distressed look. 'I don't know what is happening, but the odds against the two killings being coincidences are pretty high, which is why the police aren't buying it, either. The only thing I can guess is that *something* killed those two girls, and it seems that same something is the cause of what is happening to me—whatever the hell it is,' he added, convincing himself at the same time. 'Somehow, our ghost is a killer, which means it's not just a ghost from the past. It's something else, something more.' Mentally he added, *It's the priest—I just know it.* But he was keeping that thought to himself.

'For God's sake, are you trying to tell me something from your nightmares killed Jeneatte and Jodie?'

Brendan let go of her hand and made a gesture meant to convey how difficult he found understanding his own thoughts, without the added difficulty of explaining them to someone else. 'Gwen, I know it's hard to believe, but something is happening to me and we've decided it's caused by some outside influence, right? That soldier's ghost was there in the kitchen and you saw it, too. Now I'm saying that same outside influence, the ghost or whatever, is somehow the cause of those two killings, too. The coincidences are just too strong, don't you see?'

Gwen quickly argued back, 'Okay, I thought we'd agreed you were being haunted in the house or by something within the house, in particular the soldier. Now you're suggesting a much, much *worse* thing that goes beyond our house.' She, too, struggled for words that worked. 'I mean, I imagined we'd be dealing with things that happened to you or around you, not happening to somebody else who's miles away from you, while you're in another city!' She paused and added, fearfully, 'You're suggesting some larger, greater evil—something terrible.'

Brendan took one hand off the steering wheel to rub wearily at his eyes and forehead. 'I don't know what I'm suggesting. The trouble is, every time I begin to think of some possible explanations, they all sound like something out of a horror movie. They're just too out of this world to be given serious consideration, even though what we've already accepted is pretty fucking crazy.'

After this, they drove on in silence for a while, each deep in thought.

'Okay, so give me an example,' Gwen asked eventually, when her anger had drained away.

'An example? Of what?'

'One of these way-out theories of yours. The ones that sound like horror movies.'

'Oh, well—' Brendan narrowed his eyes, remembering. 'Okay, how about this one? I'm being haunted by a soldier, right? This soldier went to Gallipoli and trained in Egypt on the way. While he was in Egypt he picked up the charm and got himself a healthy Egyptian curse of some kind, or maybe he just caught a really bad disease, one that affected his mind and gave him hallucinations, but he was killed in the war before anyone noticed he was ill. So we're haunted by the ghost of a mentally deranged soldier.'

'The charm,' Gwen nodded slowly. 'I still don't see how or why something kills two innocent girls because they got close to that charm.'

'Jeneatte must have found it while she was sorting out the cupboard, but God knows what happened to her after that,' Brendan nodded, although he sounded strangely uncertain now.

'The same thing that happened to Jodie,' Gwen said sadly. Now she ran a weary hand through her hair and tipped her head back against the seat, closing her eyes. 'Have you thought about telling all this to the police?'

'And get thrown in the padded cell? No thanks,' he smiled grimly. 'So, at the moment I have no choice. In the end I can only believe in what we're doing now, taking one step at a time. Let's see if we can identify this poor bastard of a soldier, find out why he was never put to rest, and maybe we'll get some clues about other stuff.'

She looked at him quizzically. 'Never put to rest? Do you think he's been around for a while and isn't something we've just started?'

'I think we stirred him up, *woke* him up maybe, when we found his stuff in the tin. But in one form or another I believe he's been floating around since the day he was killed. *Why* he's a ghost is the real mystery we have to solve.'

After a moment Gwen said quietly, 'And what if somebody else gets hurt in the meantime? Before we find any answers. What are we going to do?'

'God knows.' Brendan took his eyes off the road long enough to look pointedly at her. 'To be very callous and selfish, we can only hope it happens while we are both out of town with a hundred witnesses to prove it. At least that might get the police off my back.'

'And the charm?'

'What about it?'

'What shall we do about it? Are we still going to try and identify it?'

'Yes, of course,' Brendan said after a moment. 'It could be the only way we'll ever get rid of it.'

Gwen sneaked a glance at him, seeing him watching the road ahead. Despite his words, Brendan hadn't sounded like he really wanted to lose the charm at all. What worried her more was his calm acceptance of the charm reappearing in its green tin once more—and that Brendan had instinctively known of its return.

Evanborough was an old town full of majestic homes built in the first half of the century. It wasn't a big place, so Brendan had little difficulty finding Glenness Parson's home.

'Wow,' Gwen said half-heartedly, as the car

pulled to a halt out the front. It was the first cheerful thing she'd said. 'I want it!'

It was a beautiful old house, raised slightly on short wooden stumps, and surrounded by immaculate lawns and garden beds. As they walked through the gate a man who looked to be in his late sixties called from where he tended a flowering shrub.

'Hello there! Are you after Glenness?' His voice was gruff, but friendly. 'Just go on up the stairs and knock. She'll hear you.' He waved at the house.

They called back their thanks and did as he said. The door was answered by a short, overweight woman who filled the hallway with her bulk. She had a boyish haircut, dyed a silver blonde that couldn't have been far from her natural colour. She was about the same age as the man they assumed was her husband.

'Glenness Parson?' Brendan asked politely.

'You must be Brendan Craft,' she replied, opening the flyscreen door and beckoning them to enter. 'And you've brought a young lady with you.' She smiled a sweet, elderly smile full of genuine pleasure at meeting new people.

'This is Gwen—Gwen Chisholm,' Brendan explained. The two women shook hands, then the visitors followed Glenness into her house.

They were led into a large kitchen where a long pine table dominated the centre of the room. On it, spread across a colourful cloth, were all the ingredients for a light lunch. Glenness bade them sit and began fussing around a simmering kettle. Obviously, Brendan and Gwen weren't going to be given the opportunity to refuse her hospitality.

After discussing, over her shoulder, the merits of the journey north Glenness became more business-like. 'What exactly are you hoping to find, Mr Craft?' She came over and began pouring hot water into a teapot.

'Please, call me Brendan—'

'And Gwen,' said Gwen quickly.

'I saw a photograph in your father's display in Canberra,' Brendan began, not totally sure he had her undivided attention as she continued to busy herself with sandwiches, biscuits and serving plates. 'And it showed six men standing against a wall in Cairo, just before they embarked for Gallipoli. Do you know the one I mean?'

'Of course,' she said confidently. 'It was the first photograph my father ever had taken of himself. It quite impressed him.'

'Really?' Brendan was taken aback for a moment.

'My father lived in this part of the country all of his life, before the war. Photographs were not unknown, of course. Back then, there used to be travelling photographers who called into the towns and did twelve months' trade in a week, then moved on. But my father never had a call for his own photograph before then.'

'Well, there's someone in that photograph I want to identify. One of the soldier's names might solve a lot of questions for us. Is there any chance we can do that? Are there other photographs with explanations of who's who?'

'None like that,' she shook her head. 'All the other pictures from that time are taken at Gallipoli itself, but there're no group photos. My father decided he quite liked having his picture taken, but he rarely noted who else was in the pictures with him,' she added with a sad but fond smile. 'He used to say he remembered them all, but of course in his later years his mind began to fail and it was too late, really.'

'I see.' Brendan hid his disappointment. 'Is there any other way?'

'His letters. All of his letters mention friends and acquaintances. Perhaps if I were to let you see the first dozen or so, you could get some names to track down?'

'It's as good a place to start as any,' Brendan nodded eagerly.

But Glenness forestalled him by saying, 'Well, I'll call my husband John inside for a bite to eat and a cup of tea, then we'll have a look after lunch. I don't like having any of Father's papers out when there's drinks or food around.'

Gwen shot an amused look at Brendan, knowing he would be impatient. 'No, I imagine they must be quite valuable by now,' she agreed for the both of them, not trusting Brendan to remain polite. He pulled a face back at her, but he was secretly glad to see a flash of her old self.

Over lunch they talked of Gwen's work more than of Brendan's and discussed the joys of retirement. Glenness told them her husband could happily spend all day in their garden, while she often busied herself with her father's papers and kept shop a few hours a week at a nearby delicatessen. It was only after the visitors refused, several times, more offers of food and drink that their hostess began to clear the table completely. John Parson excused himself and went back out into the sunshine to tend his beloved garden. Glenness finished her chores by carefully wiping the table clean with a damp cloth, then drying it with a tea-towel. She disappeared from the room and returned a few moments later with a plain cardboard shoebox with its lid fastened by an elastic band. She put this in the middle of the table and tugged off the band.

'These are all my father's letters from the first year of the war,' she announced, almost reverently. 'They start at the training camp at Enoggera, go through the transport to Egypt and into the campaign, of course. They're fairly simple things, mostly. You have to remember my father was only seventeen at the time. He lied about his age to get into the army, and by all accounts they didn't look too hard anyway. He wasn't a well-educated man either, by today's standards.' She dropped a pile of frayed and fragile papers on the table from the box and untied the ribbon holding them together. She began to rummage through the pile, discarding the top dozen or so. 'I doubt whether the men you saw in the photograph would be anyone in these first letters. Nicholas Story chose his friends carefully and over time. I'd say any names you came across in the earliest letters may mislead you. So perhaps if we go straight to the camp at Mena, in the days before they re-embarked for the Gallipoli offensive, you might have more of a chance. That was, after all, the period when the picture was taken.'

Brendan watched her as she looked at each letter intently, deciding if it would be of some use or not. It occurred to him that, after working with her father's own history for so long, she was probably quite an expert on Australian military history as a whole.

'Try these six,' she offered, holding them out. Then she hesitated and said, 'You'll forgive me if I ask you to be very careful with them?'

'Of course.' Brendan took them, handling them like fine crystal. When he looked at the top letter he blinked in surprise.

Glenness was obviously expecting his reaction. 'They're all censored,' she explained, reaching and tapping the top letter with her finger to point out the thick, black lines drawn through some of the words. 'Any indication of where they were, or what they were doing, was crossed out.'

'I see,' Brendan said. He began to pick his way through the first letter. The handwriting was large and child-like. Some of the spelling was phonetic in its errors and he was amused to see 'finx' got past the discerning eye of the censor, while another word, which looked like it might have been 'piramids', had earned for itself a condemning black line. While he read, Glenness stood and went to a nearby drawer. She produced a blank writing pad and a pen and put them next to Brendan's elbow.

'If there's anything you don't understand, just note where it is and I'll help you when you've finished. Otherwise, you can use it for your own notes.' Glenness turned to Gwen. 'Are you going to help him? Or would you like to see John's garden?'

'I'd love to see the house, as well,' Gwen asked, standing. 'We were admiring it when we stopped outside.'

'It is a grand old house, even if I say so myself. It's been in the family for some time, of course. John's worked very hard to keep it the way it is.'

Brendan watched gratefully as the two women drifted away. He then immersed himself in the first letter. It wasn't very long and spoke of endless sand, hot days and training exercises. Brendan thought it wouldn't have taken very much thought by any would-be spy to figure out where Nicholas Story was shipped. Then again, he had the benefit of hindsight, after all. Aside from this, the letter told him nothing. It made a passing reference to some 'mates', but didn't mention any names. The second letter was much the same, as was the third, and Brendan started to realise the letters were probably the product of a guilty conscience, written in haste—the young son, away on the adventure of his life, making an effort to stay in contact with his parents.

It was the fourth letter, dated February 1915, that gave Brendan the break he was looking for. The letter told of a race between some men up a 'piramid' (this time the word got past the censor) and how one 'had fallen and—'. The rest of the sentence was censored. Story and a man called Ben hadn't bothered to wager, but others had, in particular a 'fellow called Galther. Everyone else gets called by their first names or their nicknames, but we all call Galther by his last name. Sometimes we call him Galth. He's not a bad bloke, really, but he is not the sort of mate I'd have in peace-time. He still collected his money from the bookie.'

Galther.

It was a name Brendan knew from his childhood, but he couldn't remember why. He closed his eyes and concentrated. Nothing came.

He knew better than to try and force the memory out. These things came unbidden and more quickly of their own free will. He wrote down the name on the writing pad and read the rest of the letter. He peeled another half-dozen papers from the pile next to the box and continued reading. Three more letters later he came across another name, 'Annie', followed quickly by the explanation—Oakley. Then again, just as Gwen and Glenness walked back into the kitchen, he read in another letter written soon after the landing at Anzac Cove that

Oakley had been killed on the first day. Brendan's hopes surged and deflated in the space of a few words as Story went on to say Oakley had been 'bowled by a mortar'.

'Any luck?' Gwen asked. Predictably, Glenness went straight to the kettle. Brendan pushed the notepad with its solitary name towards Gwen.

'Galther who?'

'It's his surname,' Brendan said.

'Oh,' Gwen looked at the pad again and silently mouthed the spelling. 'Who is he?'

Brendan tapped his head with one finger. 'He's up here. He's a long-ago memory I can't quite grasp, but the name means something, I know.' He turned to Glenness, 'Do you know the name?'

'I remember it cropping up in those earlier letters,' she nodded, without taken her attention from replenishing the teapot. 'But I don't think it comes up again. Actually, not many names come up at all, as the time goes on. I think it was just his way of not letting on about casualties. It would probably get censored anyway.'

Brendan looked doubtfully at the remaining letters. Glenness saw his expression. 'Oh, I'm not saying don't look any further. I'm only saying your chances of finding a name from the Mena Camp period will get smaller, the further you go, because there were so many casualties. Anyway, I have got quite a few photographs, mostly of my father, like I said, but would you like to see them as well? They might help.'

'Sure.' Brendan fingered the pile of letters again. 'But I might just read the next few of these first, then look at the pictures, if that's not too much trouble. I'd certainly like to see the photos. You never know what you might see in the background,' he added.

Glenness put a mug of tea on the sink drainer. 'I'll leave this here for you, all right? We'll drink ours out in the garden with John and I'll fetch the photos when we come back inside.'

She turned out to be correct. Brendan found nothing more of any interest, although he knew he wasn't looking too hard. In his gut he felt he'd already found the significant name he needed. Later on, browsing through the collection of twenty or so photographs, he struck out again. He did, however, gain a moving impression of what life must have been like for the troops in those times. The men all looked thin and exhausted, even though they never appeared unhappy or demoralised. The pictures were of everyday things, such as washing, eating and trying to get some sleep in the trenches. There were no stirring images of soldiers charging into the arms of a dreadful foe—only fading photographs of normal men trying to survive terrible conditions and avoid a bullet from the enemy.

Brendan and Gwen left to return home soon after that. He thanked Glenness and John for all their help and promised to let them know if he had any success or, in particular, if he came across any further information that they might add to their records, too. On the trip back Gwen fell asleep within minutes of their striking the main highway, leaving Brendan to search his memory for the long-forgotten name.

Galther.

He could almost see it in some particular context. After worrying at the thought, like trying to undo a tight knot with his fingers he realised with a burst of recognition that he was looking at it from the wrong angle. In fact, he could recall seeing the name *written*. It meant there was a good chance he might find something in the family documents. He knew, in the house somewhere, there was a collection of yellowing paperwork that, until now, had hardly been considered worth keeping. Excited, Brendan nearly turned to announce this news to Gwen, but she was so fast asleep he left her alone.

About an hour outside of the city they stopped at a large, modern service-station for coffee and burgers. Gwen blinked owlishly in the late afternoon sun and offered to drive. Brendan accepted gratefully and went back to the counter to order another cup of coffee to take away. He didn't sleep for the last part of the drive. Instead, after he'd explained his hopes that he might find the name Galther in the family files, he and Gwen talked easily about the Parsons and how nice it would be to move to a country town and take the pace out of their lives.

'I'd have to work, still,' Gwen said. 'I couldn't just sit around, washing your dirty dishes and clothes, while you write your latest masterpiece.'

'You could try gardening—like John.'

'I keep *people* alive a damned sight better than plants, believe me.'

'Well, one day, anyhow,' he sighed hopefully. However, the conversation had held a false tone.

The future had become such a great unknown.

Gwen couldn't help a slight hesitation as she pulled into their driveway. This time the headlights swept over an empty lawn and a dark house.

'I wish we'd remembered to leave a light on,' Gwen said.

'It'll be all right,' Brendan assured her, but his voice was uneasy.

'I'll never forget that sight as long as I live,' she said softly, remembering Jeneatte Beason's white face turned towards her and striking Gwen cold like a chill wind.

Brendan said, 'I think I was so confused and terrified my mind threw up these defences, maybe to keep my sanity in one piece. Otherwise, my mind could have snapped. I feel a little sick, just remembering it now.'

'I don't want to talk about it,' Gwen said pleadingly. 'Not now, in the dark and without any lights in the house.'

'Okay.' Brendan squeezed her hand, then gestured for the car-keys, meaning he would go first.

He let himself out of the car and waited for Gwen to catch up. He walked confidently to the front door, resisting the urge to twist his head around and search every shadow with his eyes. Gwen reached for his hand and followed close behind. The city murmured around them, but it was no comfort. Close by, from a neighbour's house, the tinny scratching of a loud television drifted across the fence. Brendan fumbled as he inserted the key. Rather than let go of Gwen's hand he shoved the door open with his foot. He put his hand around the jamb and flicked on the light switch, before taking a step inside the house.

The hallway was empty. The light flooded out onto the pathway.

'This is crazy,' Brendan said. 'I'm scared, but I'm not going to tip-toe around our own house the rest of my life.' He began to walk boldly through the door, but Gwen stopped him with a hand on his arm.

'What if we moved, Bren? Went to another house? What would happen?'

He studied her, again tempted to tell her something that might be a comfort, but it was no time for lies. 'The chances are, this thing has come from halfway around the world. I'm sorry, but I don't think a move of a couple of suburbs is going to make any difference.'

They went inside. Brendan still took the precaution of turning on lights where he could, before entering a room. The house, as far as they could see, appeared to be empty. Ten minutes later they were both sipping a hot chocolate drink, sitting in the kitchen.

'Early bed tonight,' Gwen said, dark rings under her eyes, despite the sleep she had on the drive home.

'Sounds good to me.' Brendan suppressed a yawn.

'You're not going to try and find those papers you told me about?'

'Not tonight,' he shook his head. 'As much as I want to, I know I wouldn't achieve much, or think straight if I did find them. It can wait until morning.'

'Tablets?' Gwen automatically began to rise.

'No, I don't think so,' he surprised her.

'No?'

'I'm so buggered I think I'll just crash. I won't need the tablets.'

'What about the nightmares?' She couldn't believe he was serious.

'I'll chance my luck,' he shrugged. 'I can always get up and pop some pills, if I want.'

She gave him a sideways look before saying, 'Okay, but I'll get some out and put them on the bedside table, just in case.'

Brendan was feeling too tired to explain that he thought the time for nightmares might soon be over. Before, somebody or something had been just playing with his mind, taunting him. Now, after wrestling with Jeneatte Beason's ghost in the rain and, more importantly, the killing of Jodie Seager, things were getting more than serious, if that were possible. Nightmares or not, Brendan didn't want to spend eight hours of every night so drugged that he was incapable of any action—not unless he absolutely had to.

He was scared things were really going to start to happen.

Brendan heard his name spoken. It came from somewhere within the bedroom. He awoke from a dreamless sleep and sat bolt upright in bed, instantly alert. The voice still rang in his head like someone had pressed their mouth close and whispered in his ear. He looked down at Gwen, but she was curled into a tight ball, her mouth open slightly as she snored with quiet grace. Brendan watched her for a moment and waited, thinking she might have spoken in her sleep, but she lay unmoving and silent.

He twisted forward to look at the clock-radio on Gwen's side of the bed. The glowing green figures told him it was five-thirty in the morning. He became aware of a faint light outside the window as the sun tried to climb above the horizon.

Who had called his name?

He climbed gently out of bed, trying not to disturb Gwen. A nervous roiling in his stomach warned him he was going to see, or do, something he might regret. Nevertheless, he reached across to a rack and pulled a robe down, wrapping it around himself as he went to the window. Worried about waking Gwen by flooding the room with grey light, he slipped his body between the curtain and the window, pressing his face against the cool glass. Outside, the street lamps were beginning to lose the fight against the increasing glow in the east. The lawn, the shrubs, even the roof of the station wagon, wore a silver coating of frost. The whole street had the washed, born-again freshness of a new morning. Above the suburban roofs with their countless spidery television aerials, the scattered clouds began to glow soft shades of pink and orange.

And then he saw the girl standing at the end of the driveway.

Even from that distance and in the uncertain light Brendan recognised the jacket. Her fair hair, dishevelled and filthy, tried to shine a golden colour with the growing light in the sky. Her feet were bare, two pale smudges against the grey of the concrete.

Jeneatte Beason beckoned to him, slowly raising her arm and twirling her fingers.

Brendan was scared, but he also realised with a panic that if he didn't go down and confront the spirit outside, she would come into the house and into the bedroom. He didn't want Gwen to witness Jeneatte's tortured spirit again. An icy calm overtook him, born of necessity, freezing all his other emotions and helping him to clamp down on a rising well of horror and fear building in his chest. As quietly and quickly as he could he discarded the robe and pulled on a tracksuit top and bottom. He searched under the bed, finding his runners and tugging them impatiently onto his feet. He glanced at Gwen several times, making sure he wasn't disturbing her. She hadn't moved. Brendan let himself quietly out of the bedroom and kept to one side of the stairway as he went down in case the steps creaked. At the bottom he was faced by the front door and whatever lay beyond it.

He swung the door open, letting in the damp, cold air of the morning. He saw that Jeneatte Beason's spectre had crossed to the centre of the lawn, directly opposite the front door. Her feet left no tracks in the thick frost. She was staring expectantly, directly at him. Brendan stepped out the door and moved beyond the flagstone path that meandered across the lawn. He walked in a straight line, his own feet quickly soaking in the chill frost, until he stopped a few metres short of the girl. He stared at her.

The jacket was moulding and disintegrating now. What flesh he could see was parched and discoloured, stretched over her bones like the skin of an old drum. Her hair was lank and lifeless—a dead white, he realised, instead of the fair golden colour he'd imagined he'd seen from the upstairs window. Only the corpse's eyes reflected any vestige of life. But it wasn't a trace of human life, Brendan saw. Something burned within the body, using the girl's decomposing remains as a garment to drape across itself, like a cloak thrown around the shoulders. He felt his self-control begin to slip as he looked into the insane, feverish eyes of the corpse, his hands and arms starting to tremble. The shaking threatened to spread to his entire body and cause him to sink to the ground.

He rasped, before he lost all his courage, 'What the hell do you want?' It seemed such an incredible thing, to be talking to this ravaged ghost.

There was a silence, broken only by the muted sound of distant traffic and for a moment he thought the spirit wouldn't answer. Then it spoke with a harsh, coughing voice.

'You must take your own life, Mr Craft, to end this. Take your own life—but it must be by your own hand.'

Brendan's senses reeled at the awful voice and it took a moment for him to comprehend the words. Worse still, he could hear the old Jeneatte—the living one, in the way she echoed that Mr Craft. The same way she always had trouble bringing herself to call him by his Christian name. The memory left him gripped by an awful sadness and pity, and he had to drag himself mentally back.

'What? What are you saying? End what?'

The corpse swayed, as if weary, and Brendan took an involuntary step backwards, but it came no closer.

'Kill yourself and the Setris *will let us rest, Mr Craft. He's chosen you, not us.'*

'Who's us?' Brendan asked, although he could

guess. The sun was getting stronger below the horizon and Jeneatte Beason's image was fading with the increasing light. Brendan made an effort to look beyond her and thought he could see another wavering form. He couldn't make out any details, but instinctively he knew it would be Jodie Seager. It made him all the more glad Gwen wasn't awake to witness this—*if she could see it,* he reminded himself.

'Kill yourself, Mr Craft.' This time the corpse's voice was pleading. *'Set us free.'*

'Why don't you go to hell and leave me alone?' Brendan suddenly snapped, anger pushing through his fear. Stupidly, a part of his mind registered that, although he was talking to the girl's spirit now, he still couldn't bring himself to use stronger language.

She moved unexpectedly, bringing her face close to his. A stench of rotting flesh and decay washed over him. *'I am in hell!'* she hissed, frustration and anger twisting her ruined features. As Brendan held up a hand to keep her away the corpse straightened and let out a cry of anguish. When she spoke next her voice had changed, becoming firmer and more guttural.

'Next time, you may be seeing this,' she said.

The corpse's form flickered and moved, changing itself. Suddenly Brendan was looking, not at Jeneatte Beason, but an image of Gwen in the spirit's place. She wore her nurse's uniform and her long hair was bundled up on top of her head, exactly as if she were at work. But the front of her dress was torn and savaged, as if an enraged animal had attacked her. It was totally soaked in bright red blood, such a mess of gore it was impossible to tell what was material and what was her flesh beneath. Only her face was unmarked. Her expression was an alien, cruel leer, filled with amusement at Brendan's shocked reaction.

He cried out, throwing his hands up again and at the same time shutting his eyes and twisting his head away from the sight. He took two steps backwards and began to fall.

He tumbled only a few metres. He was so surprised and taken unawares he didn't try to save himself. The air was punched out of his lungs as he struck a sandy floor and for the first few seconds Brendan could only press his face against a dirt wall and whoop to get his breath back. Finally it came, in laboured, painful gasps. Then he managed to roll onto his back, supporting his weight on his elbows and look around him in total confusion to see what had happened.

He was in a trench, surrounded by soldiers. Brendan's newly regained breath caught in his throat and he stared in amazement. The trench was packed with men, all staring anxiously up at the lip as the sun began to climb into the sky. Brendan couldn't understand how he hadn't struck one of the soldiers as he'd fallen. As it was, he was almost entangled among their booted feet. He reached out tentatively and touched a nearby boot—and he was shocked to find he could. But when he struggled to his feet, jostling against the others, the men seemed to acknowledge a presence, without recognising or reacting to the fact that one of their number was dressed in a bright blue tracksuit of seventy years in the future.

God, they must see me as one of them, Brendan thought vaguely. *I* am *one of them.*

Above the noise of scuffing feet, murmured conversation and jingling equipment Brendan noted sporadic rifle-fire in the distance. It took until this moment for the truth of where he was to sweep over him.

'Jesus Christ,' Brendan whispered. He leaned backwards and rested on the rear wall of the trench. He was in Gallipoli, or more correctly, on Gallipoli—the Gallipoli Peninsula.

These were Australian soldiers and he was in the front line.

His mind raced into a panicked madness and came close to breaking. Was it real? Or was it all another illusion, like the night of the storm and the lines of plodding soldiers he'd seen then? But had that been an illusion? Was he doing some sort of impossible time-travelling? Brendan kicked out with his foot. His running shoe buried its toe into the sand wall opposite, causing a minor cascade of dirt to pour to the floor of the trench. The soldiers around him were real enough, too. He'd touched one of them.

Brendan's self-questioning was brought to an abrupt halt. The sounds of bugles from outside the trench caused the soldiers to brace themselves, bringing their weapons to the ready. There was an extended rattling as hundreds of rifles had their breeches worked. A couple of the men called out encouraging words to everyone in general. Then an order passed rapidly down the trench—*fix bayonets*. The soldiers obeyed quickly. Another command immediately followed. The men stepped onto the narrow fire-step and sighted their weapons out into the open. A high-pitched scream floated through the air, taken up by a score of other voices. Among the shrill yelling Brendan could hear cries of '*Allah!*' The rifle shots from the other side increased to a continuous roar. At the same time the defending troops opened fire, causing a deafening noise and startling Brendan. Terrified, and yet amazed and curious too, he climbed up on the fire-step and took a cautious look over the top.

Over the ground in front of them came other men dressed in the baggy uniforms of Turkish soldiers, weaving and running towards the Australian trenches. As Brendan watched, many began to fall, leaving gaps in the attacking wave. The defending fire was thick and furious and the attack lasted less than thirty seconds. The Australians were laying down a withering barrage and reducing the oncoming wave of Turks to a dreadful few who, belatedly, realised their failure and attempted to regain their own trenches. Most of them were cut down as they tried.

Brendan wasn't sure exactly what happened next. Either some of the Australians were so elated by their success they acted of their own accord, causing a chain-reaction to flow along the trench, or an official order was passed to carry out the same. Either way, with their own style of yelling and screaming, the Australians launched themselves at the parapet and clambered out in pursuit of the enemy. At the same time a second wave of Turks rose out of their own trenches and advanced too. The opposing sides shot at each other as they ran, then the two lines clashed in the middle of no-man's-land. Vicious hand-to-hand fighting ensued. Some of the Australians broke through and ran on to attack the Turkish trenches. At the same time, several Turks burst out of the mêlée and rushed on towards the Australian defences.

Brendan was startled to see one of them heading straight for him.

The Turk was a huge man, looking indestructible as he trotted unharmed towards the Australian positions. As Brendan watched he was startled by a soldier tumbling into the trench beside him, having come from somewhere behind. The man was only young and he fumbled with his weapon to ready it, concentrating on it too much and oblivious to the approaching Turk. Realising what was about to happen, Brendan yelled a warning, but the youth didn't hear. Either he was deaf to Brendan's voice, or he didn't pick out the words in the din of the battle. The soldier looked up, fear suddenly written all over his face, as the shadow of the Turk fell over him and he tried desperately to raise his rifle. The Turk fired from the hip. His breech hand was a blur of action as he pumped three bullets into the young soldier. Brendan saw the first round punch the man to the ground. The next two hit him in the chest, spraying blood and shreds of khaki. Mercifully, the boy was already dead.

Brendan was too stunned to move. He stared down at the body, unable to believe these things were happening before his very eyes. He realised the Turk, standing boldly on the edge of the parapet, was now looking at him, a malevolent gleam in his eyes as he slowly worked the breech again.

'Hey—how . . . *why*—' Brendan couldn't get a grasp on what was happening. It was impossible that this man was going to kill him. Brendan wasn't at Gallipoli—he was really at home, wasn't he? On his own front lawn!

The Turk's trigger-finger whitened at the knuckle.

At the moment of truth, when Brendan believed he was going to feel his own body ripped open by a bullet, a wild burst of machine-gun fire struck the Turk from behind. The man's chest exploded outwards and he was shoved, as if by a giant hand, off the parapet to crumple into the trench. Brendan jerked backwards with a yell of horror as some of the bloody stuff spattered onto him and he stumbled and fell onto his rump. The Turk crashed down in front of him, his body striking the wall of the trench and causing a landslide of dirt. He lay still, his open eyes now uncaring of the grit falling into them as they stared accusingly at Brendan.

Brendan's panic grew and he told himself he had to get away. Run. Anywhere—or at least away from the dangers of the front line, until he could work out how to get out of his nightmare. Now other soldiers were dropping into the trench from both sides, some reinforcing from the rear, others pulling back from the mad advance. The Turkish machine gun regularly traversed the top of the trench, ripping at the soil and spraying clods of earth down. Apparently, the gunners had decided to disregard the danger to their own kind still fighting in the open ground and had begun firing on the Australians. Numbly, Brendan realised that to retreat now towards the rear over the open ground between the trenches was suicide. He had to work his way along the lines until he found a communication trench heading in the right direction.

He threaded his way through the soldiers, some tending their wounds or the injuries of others. Brendan stepped over many who simply lay or sat on the trench floor recovering their breath, counting their blessings on still being alive. He had no idea how long he walked this way, avoiding other men, pressing himself against the trench wall to make room for stretcher-bearers and ammunition-carriers. Eventually Brendan figured he'd entered a sector of the line where the fighting was only sporadic. The men here were listening casually to the sounds of the distant battle, occasionally looking over the parapet and firing off the odd shot towards the enemy. Dawn, it seemed, had passed uneventfully in this section. The trench had a sentry post just before a sharp bend. The two soldiers manning it looked curious, but unalarmed, by Brendan's passing. As he turned around the corner the trench turned into a natural gully between steep, rocky outcrops.

From here the gunfire was more distant and at first Brendan was confident he was working his way towards the Anzacs' rear area. But the gully twisted and turned, devoid of any soldiers at all and this began to worry him after a while. Uncomfortable, but with few choices, he decided to press on.

After rounding a large boulder, the sight beyond stopped him.

The gully widened out, flattening across the floor with the angles of the sides becoming less steep. The entire area of the gully was filled with dead soldiers. Men lay contorted and tangled within each other's limbs. The corpses were jammed together and piled atop of one another, like they were all part of a crowd struck down by one terrible sweep of God's hand. The place reeked of dried blood and human waste. Brendan's arrival caused a thick blanket of flies to rise from the corpses and hover uncertainly above them, but they quickly settled again to their feast. All the dead were Turkish, Brendan saw—the result of another suicidally stupid attack, he guessed. He gagged as a stench washed over him and he went to turn and retrace his steps, when a realisation made him pause in fear and brought his heart into his mouth.

So he couldn't be behind the Australian lines, could he? He must have wandered onto another part of the battlefield. In fact, he had to be in some part of no-man's-land.

Brendan hastily turned to rejoin the Australian lines, but before he took a single step foreign voices brought him to a halt. They came echoing from the trench he had just walked through, the strange words bouncing off the walls of the gully and clearly above the noise of the distant, isolated gunfire. They were Turks, and they were coming his way.

This dream had already been too real for him. Brendan wasn't about to wait and see if they would notice him or even register his presence. He'd looked down the barrel of one rifle once that morning and he didn't want to do it again. He had to hide or get away. Looking over the mass of bodies, he knew instantly there was no place to conceal himself there. If he tried to make himself appear as one of them he would surely be found, and he couldn't have brought himself to do it anyway. A glance at the sides of the gully gave no hope either. Although they weren't so steep here, there was little in the way of cover and the shale surface would cascade down below him, giving him away. And the higher he climbed the sooner he would reveal himself to anyone approaching from the gully. That left only one way for him to go.

Across the pack of corpses until he found somewhere else to hide.

Without giving himself time to think, Brendan took his first step. He tried to put his foot down in a clear space between two bodies, but it was hard to pick a spot. As he did so the flies rose up once again in a choking cloud. Brendan cursed savagely as they flew up his nostrils and into his mouth. He flapped at them angrily and without effect as he tried to see where he could place his second step. He ended up straddling two bodies, his legs splayed, like he was playing a child's game. He was moving too slowly. At this rate the Turks, who would arrive at any moment, would catch him cold.

With his next step Brendan deliberately put his foot down on a corpse's back. The soft feel underneath was probably no different to if the man had been alive, but Brendan felt revolted. Fear and self-preservation drove him on. He used the bodies as stepping stones, making his way towards the other side of the mass, about fifty metres away. Some of the bodies made protesting noises as his weight came down and for a moment Brendan was appalled that he might be treading on wounded men, then he realised it was just bodily gases escaping under the pressure. He knew he must still be going too slowly. The Turks would come around the corner, see him, and shoot without questions.

If they can see me, he thought with a weak hope, his mind a desperate whirl of fear and confusion. Perhaps he would simply hear a shout, before he heard the bark of a rifle and feel a bullet ripping into his back. Brendan was halfway across the corpses when he felt someone grip his ankle. Horrified, he looked down.

One of the bodies had reached out and grabbed his leg as he passed. A thick-fingered hand, covered in dry blood, circled his ankle. Brendan tried to pull his leg free, but couldn't. As he tugged desperately, another hand grasped his other leg. Brendan felt himself toppling. With a cry he fell face-down amongst the reeking corpses. Immediately he tried to push himself up again, forcing his hand between the bloody limbs and torsos to get a solid purchase on the ground beneath. His horror grew when he discovered, instead, his arm was trapped. Then his other arm was gripped too. He was spread-eagled on his stomach and being pulled down hard on the stinking dead bodies. For the first time, as he struggled, Brendan became aware of an insistent whisper coming from the dead.

'Join us . . . join us . . . join us.' Spectral voices filled his mind, at once both urging and mocking him.

'No!' Brendan half-screamed, trying to wrench himself free.

A weight pressed itself down against his legs,

then another on the small of his back. Something landed across the top of his shoulders, forcing Brendan's face into the back of the corpse below him. The cloth of the uniform smelled rancid and bloody. More weight fell upon him and Brendan realised with a terror that scraped at his very sanity what was happening. He was being buried alive under the corpses. They were crawling, piling themselves on top of him, smothering him. He tried to cry out, but the effort only gave the growing press of bodies the moment to push the air from his lungs. Brendan couldn't draw in fresh air and after only a few seconds he started to lose consciousness. Small, dazzling pin-pricks of light flooded his vision as the pain in his chest increased.

'Join us . . . join us . . . join us.'

His lungs felt like they were about to burst. A vicious, intense pain lanced through his skull and Brendan mercifully blacked out.

Gwen awoke because of an intuitive sense of alarm. She stretched her hand out to Brendan's side of the bed and became doubly concerned—though not surprised—when she found it empty. She pulled herself across to his side and blearily inspected the floor next to the bed. His tracksuit, usually lying close by in case he needed to get dressed quickly, was missing. She couldn't see his shoes either, although they tended to be thrown anywhere about the house.

Quickly becoming fully awake, Gwen got to her

feet and padded across the carpet to the window. Sweeping the curtain aside revealed the rising sun, blinding her for a moment. She had to turn her head away, blinking, before she looked out again. With a shock she saw Brendan lying on his back on the front lawn. His head looked to be on one of the flagstones and he was writhing uncontrollably.

She grabbed her robe and, trying to force her arms through the sleeves as she went, ran down the stairs so fast she almost fell. She just managed to wrap the robe around herself as she went through the open front door and out onto the lawn, dropping to her knees next to Brendan. Gwen didn't think for a moment of her own safety or that Brendan may have been being attacked and she was putting herself in danger, too. A horrid, gurgling sound came from him and she understood he'd swallowed his tongue. Straddling his body to counter his thrashing and gripping his jaw with her natural right hand, she pinched the points of the joint, forcing his mouth open wide. Aware he might overcome her hold and snap his teeth shut at any moment, she reached into his mouth with the fingers of her left hand and pulled his tongue free of his throat. His contortions immediately changed to huge relieved gasps as he sucked in lungfuls of air. His fluttering eyes opened for a moment, not focusing on anything, then they closed gratefully.

Soon Gwen was able to get him on his feet and back inside the house. While he sat, slightly concussed and largely unaware, she inspected the abrasion on the back of his head, presumably where he'd hit it on the flagstone. The wound looked bad enough to prompt a trip to her hospital for X-rays.

It wasn't until early that afternoon when they had returned home from the hospital, where his X-rays had showed no serious injuries, that Brendan was able to explain, clearly but in a halting, shocked whisper, what had happened to him.

And what Jeneatte Beason's ghost had said to him.

14

Warden Anthony's mother had a strong faith in names and the importance of choosing the right name for the right person. It was why she'd christened her son Warden. She'd believed if she called her son something she considered 'common', like Jack or Bob, her boy would undoubtedly grow up without ever aspiring to greatness. He would end up a bricklayer or a truck driver, rather than a leader of men or a famous achiever. As soon as Warden arrived in the world and she knew she had given birth to a baby boy, his mother scoured books of all types for something scholarly to name him, because she was determined her son was to be an expert in something—anything, as a matter of fact—and she believed this would be more easily achieved if he bore a distinguished name. No one told Warden about this idea. He grew up to become adept at some quite ordinary things, such as football, weightlifting and archery. He did well in school, but nothing that would rank him a genius.

It wasn't until he was twenty-five years old that things changed. He started work as a sales assistant in an electronics business. The store sold computers and Warden Anthony discovered he had an uncanny understanding of how they worked. It wasn't long before he owned his own machine and he was spending many hours investigating the innards of different programs—'hacking' into them, as it was known, and changing and improving them.

In three years he'd established a comfortable one-man business writing computer software for regular customers who, in tacit agreement, never mentioned to Warden his talents might be worth a damned sight more money to one of the bigger, multi-national companies. What they didn't understand was that Warden wasn't interested anyway. Involving himself in something that might demand more of his time simply wasn't attractive, regardless of the remuneration, because Warden had another interest which needed a lot of time, too.

Ghosts.

Ghosts, spirits and poltergeists—and anything else supernatural. But particularly ghosts, because he'd seen one.

It all started a year after he got the job. The store he worked in was sited in a down-market part of the city. By day the area was an acceptable business sector, but by night nearby hotels, bars and nightclubs made the streets unsafe for the unwary. For the same reasons a small park near the store, a place for pleasant, summertime lunches with its benches, shady trees and a sadly unkempt war memorial became, in the evenings, a haven for vagrants, small-time muggers and the occasional drug deal. Warden walked across this park to and from work every day, except for Thursday nights. Thursdays was late-night shopping day and he didn't finish until after nine o'clock in the evening. Then he would walk around the park, keeping to the street-lit footpaths and trying his best to mind his own business. It took extra time, but it was safer.

There came a night when every second counted and Warden decided to swallow his fears and rush across the park. There was a young lady waiting for him in a bar downtown and that was reason enough to take the risk. Besides, Warden reminded himself, he was a large, well-built man, which was true, and not a likely target for a mugger. He was fit, too, and figured he could out-run most threatening things. True love, such as he imagined was awaiting him, was a strong incentive to be courageous.

With the stars above him winking encouragingly,

he set off across the park, stumbling occasionally on tree roots forcing their way through the narrow bitumen paths. At first he immediately regretted the idea, finding himself peering nervously into the shadows for any ominous signs, but his night vision slowly improved and he began to relax, feeling certain he would see anything unwelcome coming for him.

It remained only for him to stay on the right track and not get lost in the darkness or step into any mud or mess. The familiar outline of a bench assured him he was heading in the right direction. Next was a crooked rubbish bin—more confirmation. He knew the memorial to the First World War should be coming up on his right, and it was, but as Warden drew closer he became at first confused, then puzzled, thinking there was something different about it at night. He could see a faint glow coming from the stone. It was so unusual, Warden was curious—it didn't occur to him to be frightened—and intrigued enough to leave the path and walk in a wide circle so he could observe, without disturbing anyone who might not appreciate the intrusion, what was going on. The light seemed to be coming from behind the memorial. Detouring from his route, Warden walked in the direction of the strange light. He saw a young woman standing in front of the monument, gazing up at the line of engraved names. It was, Warden thought, a rather strange time for someone to be paying their respects. Then it occurred to him she might be about to deface it, or perhaps make a spray-can statement about women and war.

Then a stunning realisation shocked him to the core.

The woman carried no torch or light of any kind. It was the woman *herself* who was glowing with an inner radiance.

Warden had to take three deep breaths and calm himself. He knew, instinctively, what he was looking at. It had to be some sort of spirit, a visitation—whatever was the right term. Still more fascinated than scared, he began to move gently forward. The woman didn't seem to pose any threat. He could see now, more because he was looking for it, that she was dressed in an old-fashioned style. Her long skirt touched the ground, high waisted and matched by a tight-fitting blouse buttoned to her neck. She was young and pretty, but her looks were marred by an aura of tragedy. Warden didn't realise how close he'd moved towards her until she turned and spoke to him.

'Has he come back?' she asked. Her voice resonated decades of sorrow and disappointment. Warden was suddenly, deeply touched and felt he might start to cry, because of her voice and the look of sheer, desperate grief on her lovely face.

'Who?' he asked shakily, unable to think of anything else. The spirit looked again at the monument.

'He shouldn't be there. He doesn't belong there,' she said.

Warden looked at the stone too, trying to decipher which name she meant. A car's headlights from the nearby street swept across the face of the monument and, at the same time, appeared to extinguish the ghostly glow from the woman.

When Warden turned back to ask her which name she was referring to, she was gone.

He didn't make his date that night. Instead, he went home in a mild state of shock. The next day, and for several days afterwards, he pursued the story of the woman's spirit with a tenacity which surprised himself. He didn't really know why, only that the experience and possibilities fascinated him. As he walked to work, he tried talking to old people who lived nearby. In his lunch hours he searched the library for local legends and researched the history of the park itself. In the end, it was from an old soldier living in pathetic squalor, who regularly graced the park's benches during the day, that Warden found the most likely answer.

The woman, he told Warden, was the spirit of a girl who never accepted that her sweetheart was killed in France. She waited every day until well after the war, convinced he would return someday. Then, when they erected the monument to the fallen, she protested loudly at his name being engraved with the rest, but to no avail. A madness that was always suppressed within her began to strengthen and she took to waiting for his return at the monument itself, explaining to any passers-by who would listen that her fiancé's name shouldn't be on the memorial.

For several years she kept her vigil, surviving on hand-outs and welfare. With the world collapsing into the Great Depression, she wasn't an unusual figure. Many other tragic human lives were living and sleeping in the park with her. Her health deteriorated with every passing day. She slept the nights in a lonely hovel, returning first thing in the mornings to take her station. Sometimes she stayed far into the night.

One winter's night she didn't leave at all. They found her body huddled against the cold stone. The overnight moisture had hardened in the predawn chill, freezing her dead cheek to the mortar.

Some said, the old soldier told Warden gravely, she still kept her vigil.

It launched Warden into an interest of psychic research. Disappointingly, although he traced ghosts, spirits and poltergeists in all manner of places, he never witnessed any of the phenomena claimed to exist and certainly never saw anything to rival his own experience in the park. Still, he ended each investigation always undaunted and eagerly awaiting the next one, always hoping each new opportunity would show him something fantastic. He even took holidays in Europe, making sure he visited every famous haunted house, but he found most of them crassly over-commercialised. After one such trip, returning home to Australia he began researching the oldest of ghosts, the Dreamtime inhabitants of the Aborigines. Here, at least, he found an originality that was refreshing and it led him to make comparisons to other ancient myths and legends.

He also began to investigate another avenue of thought concerning ghosts and the supernatural. The possibility that such paranormal activities and strange sightings might be the product of the observer's mind or an unconscious extension of the human imagination. It was an idea which, one day, brought him into contact with David Mooreson, the head-injury specialist at Gwen's hospital.

And eventually led to his name and phone number being scribbled on a piece of paper and tucked absently into the pocket of her uniform.

Sitting in the lounge room of Brendan's house, Warden listened patiently and without reaction to their story. He spoke little until they finished, occasionally just asking them to clarify something. Brendan told him most of it, speaking in a flat, weary voice.

Then, without preamble, Warden told them his views. He sounded authoritative and confident, despite the unusual subject. Now just over thirty years old, Warden still looked like a contender for the front row of the national football team. He was a solid, well-muscled man totally devoid of any flab. His size obviously gave him physical confidence, while he feared nobody's opinion of his intelligence or ability. He had short, curly hair framing a square block of a face. His nose was slightly flattened, courtesy of a stray elbow during his schooldays playing football. His large hands and thick fingers seemed unsuited to punching the keys of a computer.

After quickly dismissing any suspicions of trickery he became more serious.

'Folks, I gotta tell you, this is an awful lot to take in, in one lump, but I'm trying,' he said, spreading his hands in a plea for understanding. Sitting on the sofa, he spoke in a pleasant, melodious voice which rumbled from his wide chest. 'I'll admit, I'm more used to dealing with the odd dinner plate falling off the dish-rack, or footsteps on the stairs and heavy breathing in the dark, that sort of thing. You two sound like you've got ghosts moving into the spare room and using up all the hot water!' He smiled, so they wouldn't think he was mocking them. 'The idea takes a lot of getting used to, if you don't mind my saying.'

Gwen sighed, rose from the opposite sofa where she sat next to Brendan and picked up the now-cold cup of coffee beside Warden. 'I'll run this through the microwave for you, or would you rather have a beer?' She waited in the doorway. Warden grinned at her. It was a friendly, confident grin and Gwen decided she liked it.

'I can never say no to an afternoon beer,' he said. 'Especially when I'm listening to a good ghost story.'

Gwen caught an agreeing nod from Brendan and turned on her heel, saying, 'I only wish it were just a good ghost story, Warden.'

Warden ducked his head and called after her. 'Oh, don't get me wrong. I believe in ghosts. I've seen one—spoke to it, as a matter of fact.'

Gwen reappeared instantly in the doorway, the coffee cup still in her hand. 'What?' But Warden gave her a cheeky look and she glanced down at the cup in her hand. She said, 'Oh, right. I'll be back in a second.' She disappeared into the kitchen.

'It's all so hard to accept,' Brendan said, while she was gone. He was pale and quiet, suffering from a slight, but persistent headache.

'I wouldn't give a pinch of salt to any of it—and I mean *any* of it—' Warden waved a hand to encompass every ghost story ever told '—if it wasn't for my own experience. I'm a practical sort of bloke, which is good sometimes, because it gives me a different slant on these things.' He flashed his grin again. It affected Brendan the same way it had Gwen. 'Like, when the furniture starts shifting around the joint and everyone's screaming "poltergeist", I get out a spirit-level and check to see if the floor's got a slope,' he shrugged. 'Know what I mean?'

'Sounds fair to me,' Brendan nodded. 'So, now we've told you our story. What's yours?' he asked, accepting a beer from Gwen. She gave one to Warden and held a white wine for herself. Warden looked at Brendan's drink.

'Are you going to be all right?' he tapped his own head.

'I've tried panadol, aspirin, codeine and anything else you care to name,' Brendan looked wry, 'And I've still got a headache. It's about time I tried a bit of medication from the brewery.' He ripped off the top of the beer.

'Wisely said,' Warden agreed and did the same. He went into a detailed account of his meeting the ghostly girl at the monument. Gwen and Brendan listened in rapt silence.

'Wow,' Gwen said, when he'd finished. 'So you believe in ghosts and you've been chasing them for fun ever since.'

'I can't see much fun in it,' Brendan muttered, pulling a face.

'Well yes, I believe in them, in certain forms,' Warden nodded. 'And I've been looking for them, as a sort of hobby, since that night. But I've yet to see anything rivalling what I saw in the park. In fact, I have never since seen a single apparition, strange light or any physical evidence of anything paranormal, but I keep looking. How's that for stubborn?'

'Why do you keep trying?' Brendan asked.

Warden laughed. 'Why does a golfer keep trying to lower his score? Why does anybody do anything for fun? It's just my hobby, like photography or painting. I agree, it's a bit weird. You meet some interesting characters, too.'

'I'll bet,' Gwen said. Then she asked, after the smallest hesitation, 'So, what do you think of our troubles?'

'Fucking amazing, actually,' Warden said with a wide smile, then broke into a moment of laughter. When he stopped, he paused long enough to draw a deep breath. 'But okay, let's look at it from a clinical point of view. Now, if everything you tell me is correct,' he paused again and held up a hand, along with an apologetic look, 'then you've got yourselves a regular little haunted house here. So, let's begin with the basics. For starters, we have things like poltergeists, right?' He didn't wait for an answer. 'They're generally just a pain in the arse, moving furniture and stealing your beers, bullshit like that. Occasionally, they're malicious, but we haven't had anything like that so, simply, we can probably forget poltergeists as they are recognised in their most common form.' Warden put his can of beer on the table and began to gesture animatedly with his hands. 'After that we've basically got two types of ghosts and you lucky people seem to have both.' He hesitated, choosing his words, then used it as an excuse to have a long pull on his drink.

It gave Brendan the opportunity to slip in, 'Two types of ghost?'

'Sure. First, you have the type that you and I both seem to have seen. It's a spirit, or a figure of a person who used to be alive. The ghost appears to occupy the same time and space as us, they are aware of our presence and they even respond to questions, although my own story has a shade of doubt in this area,' he added easily.

'Why?' Gwen asked, her glass at her lips.

'Because the woman I saw at the monument may have said exactly the same thing, no matter what I said—or who said it to her, which would put her in the other category of ghosts.'

'Okay,' Brendan smiled tiredly. 'So what's the other type of ghost?'

'It involves a lot of rubbish about different dimensions,' Warden painted a big picture with his hands. 'But I can try to simplify. It's just another school of thought, really. The idea is, when somebody dies or is killed in a particularly dramatic way—an unexpected way, perhaps—the trauma of that occasion or of that event is so strong it becomes imprinted on the fabric of our dimension, much like an unexposed film records the image of a picture through the camera lens. What we see, when we witness ghostly forms re-enacting certain events over and over again, is really only a re-run of the occasion. The spirit of that person or what many religions call the soul, if you like, is not there. That's gone to—to wherever,' he finished with a vague gesture in the air.

'You mean, like the ride of Paul Revere in America?' Gwen asked frowning. 'They say, on the anniversary of his ride, you can see his ghost riding through the streets warning that the British are coming.'

'Exactly!' Warden was pleased with her.

'But he wasn't killed,' said Brendan, causing Gwen to frown.

'Right again.' Warden pointed an enthusiastic finger at him. 'Which is why, under this particular theory, the existence of such a ghost is regarded as unlikely. But if he *had* been killed during his famous ride, then he would be a prime candidate, understand? His ride, by all accounts, was a high-powered, high-energy, traumatic thing, so he would have left that imprint-business behind.'

'Fascinating,' Brendan said, his headache forgotten. He was surprised to see he'd drunk his beer. 'Hang on a minute. Don't say anymore until I get back.' He scooped up his empty beer can, grabbed Gwen's glass to refill and went into the kitchen. He came back a moment later with two fresh beers, one of which he lobbed at Warden, and Gwen's wine. As he sat down, he continued his questions. 'But what about battlefields? Surely there's a good case of thousands of people dying under traumatic circumstances? Where are their imprints?'

'Two arguments,' Warden replied crisply. 'One is that soldiers are mostly resigned to the element of danger and accept the possibility of a violent death as an everyday fact of life. Thus, you remove a majority of the trauma factor. The second argument is that there have been, in fact, witnessed re-enactments of major battles. Entire ghostly armies fighting each other for eternity.'

'My God,' Gwen whispered sadly. 'Wouldn't that be awful?'

'Well, like I said,' Warden shrugged, 'in theory we're not talking about the souls of these poor men, but a picture hung on the fabric of a dimension in time and somehow that picture becomes visible in our dimension or time.' Warden screwed his face up, 'It's very difficult, because the more you think about it, the more confusing the whole thing can get, and it is only one theory amongst many—although a popular one, I might add.'

'And you're saying,' Brendan ventured slowly, 'that the ghost of Jeneatte Beason is one of the first kind, but the soldier we saw being shot is one of the second?'

'Ah, yes,' Warden said, but he looked uncomfortable. His expression was comic enough for Gwen to let out a small laugh.

'After all that, you're going to tell us there's a snag, aren't you?' she said.

'Well yes, there is a snag,' Warden admitted, with a wry smile. 'He's in the wrong place.'

'I'm sorry?' It was Brendan's turn to frown.

'I think I get it,' Gwen said, but let Warden explain.

'The ghost of Paul Revere you would expect to see somewhere along the route of his ride. They say Anne Boleyn wanders around the Tower of London with her head under her arm, get the idea? Your soldier might have all the ingredients to be a ghost, but not here. On the Gallipoli Peninsula, maybe, but not on the other side of the world to where he was killed.'

'Okay, I can see that.' Brendan thought a moment. 'So, where does that leave us?'

'Well, don't we have some idea who this ghost of yours is?' Warden asked.

'A good idea, actually.' Brendan got up again. 'I'll go and get all the junk and let's see what we can find out.'

As he went through the doorway into the passage, Gwen called out, 'And bring down that damned charm and let Warden have a look at it.'

'Ah, the charm,' Warden said, almost rubbing his hands together. 'It sounds like an interesting little critter.'

'Do you really believe it could be the cause of everything?' Gwen asked, moving to the edge of her seat.

'Well, it comes under the same great big paradox as all paranormal phenomena.' Warden grinned at the mouthful of words. 'Meaning it's all supposed to be nonsense, but there's an overwhelming amount of evidence, both good and bad, that these supernatural things exist. I mean, think about it, Gwen. In the same way, there have been charms, amulets, written symbols, death masks—there's a million of 'em—which are supposed to have exhibited some sort of mystical power. For thousands of years, some of them, ranging from just an ordinary old number seven, or unlucky number thirteen for that matter, to our own Christian cross. Nowadays, our solid, twentieth-century cynicism normally refuses to believe an inanimate object can do anything.' He lowered his voice, 'But the evidence is still there, if you look for it.

You told me yourself on the phone, it somehow came back into the house on its own. That's pretty damned incredible.'

'I just don't know what to believe anymore,' Gwen shook her head tiredly. Watching, Warden realised she was under a great amount of strain and doing a good job of hiding it. She went on, 'And I don't know how the bloody thing came back, that's for sure. It was suddenly *there* and Brendan knew it. God knows how.'

'Gwen, I'll tell you this. You can *believe* probably about less than five percent of what you hear.' Warden surprised her, coming up with such an assessment. 'And even that amount still contains a liberal dosing of information described as "unexplained", which means there's still a good chance for a perfectly rational, non-paranormal reason as to why the events occurred. They just haven't worked it out yet.'

They heard Brendan stomping back down the stairs and waited in silence for him to return. He came back into the room carrying the tin containing the charm, an ancient, cobwebbed expander-file and the computer print-outs given to him by the War Memorial in Canberra. The latter were threatening to spill out of his arms. Brendan sat and dumped everything on the floor. He picked up and opened the print-out first.

'Okay, we're looking for the name Galther. When I gave it a bit of thought, it rang a bell in my brain, but I didn't know why. Then I got a feeling

I'd find it in these papers,' he nodded down at the expander-file. 'But first, let me show you something in these lists. It shouldn't take a minute. They're in alphabetical order.'

The only sound in the room for a while was the rustle of pages as Brendan flicked awkwardly through the sheets balanced on his knees. Then he let out a murmur.

'Here he is, in the Fifth Queensland battalion—' He stopped short and held the list so Warden could see for himself. 'But according to this, he came out in one piece. He wasn't killed. There's only this—W.I.A.?' He gave it a moment's thought and quickly came up with the answer at the same time as Warden.

'Wounded in Action,' they said together.

'But that could mean anything, I suppose,' Warden said. 'It could mean he got a nick on the end of his finger, or he lost both arms and a leg. Still, I guess, as you say, the point is he came out alive.'

'What about if he died in hospital, on the way home?' asked Gwen.

'Same thing, I think,' Warden shrugged. 'Basically, if you're killed in action you rate the KIA letters. Anything else, like dying of wounds at a later date, is regarded as something else.'

'The man we saw was definitely shot in the head,' Brendan said. 'I can't believe he could have survived that and died later on in hospital.'

Warden's shrug suggested that they shouldn't get

too involved with the idea at the moment. 'Who do you think he is, anyway?' he nodded at the old file. 'A relative who lived in this house?'

'Right.' Brendan dropped the computer lists and took up the expander-file. 'Let's see if we can find out. I'm certain we'll find something written in this lot.'

For the next five minutes they worked methodically from the front to the back, pulling out dusty, deteriorating papers on Brendan's family. There were old birth certificates, medical records, school report cards and legal letters, which were dumped on the floor after being shared around the three of them to be examined closely for the name. It was surprising, therefore, when the answer came quite blatantly in the form of a large buff envelope. It had the name *Adrian Gordon Galther* written in impressive, florid handwriting on the front. Brendan stared at it for a moment, suddenly almost afraid to open it.

'Well, you said you'd seen it written,' Gwen breathed, just as apprehensive.

Brendan nodded. 'But not like this,' he said. With a shrug he flipped open the end and peered inside. After a pause he leaned forward, tipping the entire contents of the envelope into a clear space on the floor. Gwen and Warden moved closer, while Brendan pushed the other papers well clear. Then he picked up a smaller envelope, one of several.

'See this?' he held it up. It had Galther's name on the front above the address of the house. One corner displayed an old, but common, stamp partially obliterated by the post office's mark. 'Now I know where I saw the name. We were always getting mail in his name. I would have collected it from the mailbox as a kid, though I don't remember getting this much.'

'Can I look at one?' Warden asked, picking up a similar letter.

'Sure.' Brendan carefully slit his thumbnail under the flap, where the years had resealed the glue. He pulled out two sheets of paper and unfolded them, then tried reading the contents. Warden did the same, discovering the contents of his letter were almost identical. Gwen began thoughtfully sorting through the other papers for something different.

'What is it?' Brendan twisted the paper this way and that, squinting at the small, precise writing.

'Look at the heading,' Warden told him.

'Williamdale Veterans' Home,' Brendan read aloud. 'Is this what I think it is?'

Warden nodded. 'It's a routine medical report on the condition of our Mr Galther. Look at the dates—mine's September 1959.'

'This one's June 1960,' Brendan told them, dismayed. 'This guy lived a long time after the war. He *can't* be the one.'

'Don't be so quick to dismiss him.' Warden was pensive and began to pick through the papers on the floor with more purpose.

Gwen surprised them by announcing, 'Look, he was your grandmother's brother.' She showed them an official-looking letter. Gwen went on more soberly, 'It's a letter from some sort of senior clerk, addressed to your grandmother. It confirms for her that, after her death, if she is survived by her brother, then her daughter—your mother, Brendan—is allowed to be custodian of Galther's affairs and would receive all of these.' She waved at the papers scattered around them.

Brendan looked both puzzled and disappointed. 'I can't understand why my mother never really let me in on all this.'

'Even *our* mothers were of a generation that preferred to leave some things unsaid,' Warden said quietly, looking at another medical report. 'You know, considering that these things appear to be quarterly, then there must be nearly a hundred of these things somewhere. This one's dated 1942.'

Gwen plucked the paper from Brendan's hand and looked at it. 'It's fairly normal and routine,' she judged. 'It mentions his height, weight and diet, all that sort of stuff, and has a space for any special comments. I would say you'd probably throw most of these away, after reading them.'

'There's only a dozen or so here,' Warden guessed. 'So nobody was really bothered about keeping them.'

'Perhaps just these ones have something special?' Gwen said, but when she looked up at Warden she saw a glint in his eye. He'd discovered something.

'1942,' he repeated, shaking the paper. 'Even if Galther lied about his age when he joined the army, he still couldn't have been younger than sixteen or seventeen years old, the same as the century.' Warden raised his eyebrows, 'What's a forty-year-old man doing in a Veterans' Home?'

There was a silence, until Brendan said, 'He could have been a much older man.'

'But that would mean he was in his nineties, say, in 1960,' Warden said. 'In the same way, I can't believe a man who reaches ninety needs to be in a Home when he's sixty, see what I mean? Besides, did any of the men in that photograph look that old?'

After a moment Brendan said, 'Hard to be sure, but I don't think so.'

'Right. So, my guess is there was something seriously wrong with Galther. That's why he was in a home so long. Over twenty years, just according to what we have here. Over *forty* years, if he was invalided straight from his war injuries into the home and your family got these regular reports.'

'Did he ever live here? Why are the letters addressed to him, if he was always living in a home?' Brendan asked. Gwen answered that.

'Just an old-fashioned thing,' she explained. 'I've come across it before. It's fallen out of practice now, of course.'

'So, was he an invalid?' Brendan suggested. 'Is that the sort of home it is?'

'It's the most obvious conclusion,' Warden nodded. 'But can we find out? Does this place still exist?'

'Yes,' Gwen stopped and considered. 'I haven't

seen it, but I've read advertisements for jobs there. They get posted up on the bulletin board at work.'

'Then they should still have records available. I say the next useful thing we can do is go out there and ask,' Warden said.

Three more drinks came out of the fridge as a minor celebration of their progress. Then Brendan handed over the green tin to Warden. 'Next,' he said, with a nervous smile.

Warden popped off the lid without any trouble. Brendan had the badges and hatpin in a separate place now, so only the charm rattled around the metal box. Warden let out a soft whistle of appreciation as he lifted it out by its leather thong.

'You should see it in the flesh,' Brendan said uneasily. 'It's the biggest, nastiest bastard of a dog you'll ever see.'

'It's not a dog,' Warden replied absently. 'It's a jackal, a very popular symbol of the ancient Egyptians.'

Gwen groaned and rolled her eyes at Brendan. 'Of course! How stupid are we?'

Brendan didn't answer.

Warden suddenly jerked his head to one side and thrust the charm out to arm's length, 'Shit!' he half-laughed, getting very excited. 'I've read about such things, but now I've seen it! That's incredible.'

'Seen what?' Gwen was alarmed.

'I reckon this thing just tried to get me—*reach out* in some way. I'm not sure, because I didn't want to stick around to find out. It was like somebody trying to get inside my head and touch my mind. Have you seen it?' His casual, almost bantering tone belied the real effect it had on Warden. He was stunned by the moment, brief though it was, and it instantly promised a new chapter to his long search. He didn't care that it defied all logical and scientific reasoning. Gwen was shaking her head, but not denying his words.

'No. That thing gives me the utter creeps for some reason. I refuse to even touch it and I don't like to look at it.'

Bright-eyed, Warden was fascinated by her response. 'Really? That's interesting. Maybe it's an intuitive thing warning you off?' he said, a hundred possibilities running through his head. He turned to Brendan. 'Hey, what about you, Brendan?'

'No, I've no idea what you're talking about,' Brendan replied blankly.

There was a short silence. Gwen, frowning with concentration, said, 'Just a minute. What about the day we found it? Remember we were in the spare room and you took a strange turn? You went all dizzy?'

'No,' Brendan looked straight at her.

'What?' Gwen started to laugh, 'But you must—' she stopped when she caught an unexpected, warning look from Warden. 'Well, maybe you don't,' she finished lamely.

'Maybe it only affects certain people,' Warden said, his tone killing the subject, while he flicked a glance at Gwen. He looked thoughtful as he made a show of sealing the charm back in the tin, tapping the lid with a finality. 'Brendan, when you saw Jeneatte Beason's ghost on the front lawn—the second time, I mean—what did she say to you again?'

'She told me to take my own life. It was something about leaving her in peace, or that somebody would leave her alone.' Brendan suddenly sounded very tired again.

'Who was it exactly, can you remember?'

Brendan screwed his face up as he tried to recall. 'The Setee, I think it was—no, it was *Setris*, that's it. The *Setris* would leave her in peace. Does it mean anything to you? I've never heard of them.'

Warden murmured the word several times and finally sighed, 'No, it stirs a few memory cells, but nothing more.'

'Let's see if it gets a mention over here,' Gwen offered, standing and going to a nearby bookcase. She chose a concise encyclopaedia, then sat back down and balanced it on her knees as she thumbed through the pages. After a minute she said, 'There's no *Setris*, but we've got a Set, which is—' her voice trailed off as she read, until she announced unhappily, 'Ah-hah, I seem to have struck something.'

'Well, come on. Don't leave us in suspense,' Warden said lightly, as she took a sip of her wine, before explaining more. She stabbed her finger at the page and gave a brief account of what she'd read.

'Set was an ancient Egyptian god. He was murdered by his brother, Osiris, and the Great God, Ra, punished Osiris by making him—guess what?'

'God of the Dead,' Warden was nodding grimly. 'And now that I think of it, Osiris is usually depicted in ancient paintings and hieroglyphics as a man with the head of a jackal.'

They all looked at each other. Gwen said, 'What the hell have we got ourselves into?'

Nobody wanted to venture an answer.

Instead, Warden came up with a plan where he would dig deeper into the Egyptian lore and see if he could find more specific references to the *Setris*. He said he knew an expert in Kent, England, who had several rare books on such things, primarily for his own research into Druids and other ancient European cultures. Warden thought he might also have material on Egypt. Otherwise, he would do some reading at the city library.

Gwen and Brendan gave themselves the job of visiting Williamdale Veterans' Home and trying to discover more about Adrian Gordon Galther. Gwen still didn't have to work for a few days and she was keen to do it as soon as possible. Warden, too, was plainly excited to be on the trail and his enthusiasm was infectious. Brendan could only gratefully agree and blustered about paying Warden for his time or thanking him in some way, but Warden simply grinned his friendly smile.

'You've got to be kidding. This could be the best fun I've had in years,' he told them. 'I can't wait to get my teeth stuck into some searching for you guys. This could be a good one. I'll probably tackle the library tonight and by the time it's closed, it'll only be a few hours until a good time to call the UK. When will you go out to the Veterans' Home? Tomorrow?' Warden was surprised to see Brendan and Gwen exchange an unhappy look.

'Tomorrow is Jodie's funeral,' Gwen said, quietly. 'We'll see how we feel after that, but I don't think I'll be up to much. I hate funerals at the best of times and Jodie's is going to be a bad one for me.'

Warden looked at Brendan and seemed about to say something. Gwen guessed he was going to suggest Brendan not go to the service, but he apparently changed his mind about saying anything and only offered them a sympathetic shrug.

15

The funeral was in the late afternoon, beginning first with a service held in a small, run-down church in her neighbourhood. The eulogy brought tears to Gwen's eyes with unexpected force, because the presiding priest, Father Trent, chose his words carefully, displaying a personal acquaintance with Jodie that Gwen was unaware of and surprised about. She hadn't known Jodie attended church regularly. Brendan sat next to Gwen stoically and fought off his own tears by feeling, instead, the misery of Jodie's parents who sat in the pew in front, their slumped shoulders and bowed heads echoing the depth of their despair. He allowed himself a moment of self-pity, thinking he would have to do this again with a service for Jeneatte Beason. The police still hadn't released her remains, much to the distress of the girl's relatives.

If the police want any details cleared up, I could just ask her for them, Brendan thought with a mixture of wry humour and a touch of the hysteria which often seemed to be lingering on the edge of his consciousness now. He clamped down hard on his wandering mind by concentrating on the words of a prayer echoing around the inside of the church.

At the conclusion of the service Brendan was one of the pallbearers, shouldering the casket and moving slowly down the narrow aisle and into a watery sunlight. As they approached the open tailgate of the hearse a distant peal of thunder made the wood of the coffin, touching his cheek, tremble slightly. It was as if the corpse inside had moved. Brendan closed his eyes and tried to shut out a mental picture of Jodie waking out of death and screaming, finding herself in a silken blackness. They carefully slid the coffin into the vehicle and stood back as attendants arranged wreaths of flowers around the casket and checked those affixed to the roof. Other mourners were walking slowly through the church grounds to their cars for the journey to the cemetery. Many of them cast their eyes uneasily at the sky, which was darkening with yet another seasonal storm.

Gwen and Brendan moved to the station-wagon. He drove, switching on his headlights and needing to bull his way into a line of uncaring traffic that had slipped in behind the hearse.

'Damn,' Gwen muttered, her eyes still damp. 'Nobody thought about the bloody rush-hour building up at this time of day. Doesn't anybody work until five o'clock anymore?'

'God knows, but it doesn't look like it,' Brendan replied. 'It seems to start earlier every day. No one considered these damned storms either,' he added ruefully, bending forward to look up through the windscreen at the sky. 'We might get wet.'

'Oh well, too bad.' Gwen shrugged, then turned around and checked the line of cars behind. It wasn't nearly dark enough for headlights to be normally turned on, so a trail of glaring, twin lights indicated the funeral cortège among the regular traffic. 'At least quite a few people came to the service,' she said. 'I always feel terribly sad whenever I see a funeral hearse with no attending cars.'

Brendan glanced in the rear-view mirror. 'I don't think the concrete truck's part of the procession,' he said, with a thin smile.

Gwen managed a dry laugh. 'Jodie would love it.'

The procession threaded its way through the growing traffic. The cemetery was off the main arterial roads and they managed to avoid the worst of the peak-hour jamming, arriving at the graveyard with the train of mourners' cars virtually intact. The bulk of the approaching storm appeared to be kindly veering off to the east too, though a thick arm of heavy rain cloud looked fated to sweep over the cemetery before the service was finished. As if in warning, a chill wind came through the open window of Brendan's car.

Only the hearse and the attending black sedan containing Jodie's parents could drive into the cemetery grounds. Everyone else had to park outside. Brendan nosed the car close to a low stone wall and switched off the ignition. He got out and opened the rear door, reaching in and taking two thick, padded jackets off the back seat. One was a light brown in colour, while the other was dark blue. As he shrugged into one he saw Gwen standing on the opposite side of the car, looking at him doubtfully. He looked down at himself and realised the jacket struck a jarring note with his black jeans, boots and black windcheater.

'She wouldn't mind,' he said softly. 'It's going to rain, for Christ's sake. I'm sure she wouldn't mind. In fact, she'd insist. Here—' He held out the other jacket for Gwen to put her arms in. After a moment she nodded easily and walked around the car, but instead of donning the jacket properly she draped it across her shoulders.

'If it really starts to rain,' she explained, 'I can pull it over my head.'

Brendan was the last of the pallbearers to return to the hearse where the others were waiting patiently. They pulled the coffin out and walked it carefully across to the fresh hole cut into the ground. Brendan looked at the dark soil and found himself thinking that the smell of freshly-turned earth usually meant the welcome start of something new. Here, at a funeral, the aroma was like the stench of blood, the neat, square hole in the ground a wound in the flesh of the world.

The pallbearers stepped warily along the edge of the grave, forced to take a narrow path between the hole and the mounds of discarded earth either side. Each pile was covered with a blatantly false length of synthetic turf. The bearers' footsteps dislodged small clods of dirt to fall softly into the grave. Two shining chrome bars supported the casket above the grave while the burial service was to be read. Next to them were the canvas straps for lowering the coffin into the ground. Father Trent waited silently for all the mourners to gather around and the funeral parlour attendants to transfer all the wreaths to the gravesite.

He looked almost apologetically at the sky, saying, 'I don't like to rush funeral services just because of inclement weather,' he explained. 'Unless it gets dangerous, of course,' he added.

If anyone disagreed, they didn't say. The Father opened his Bible and began to read. Out of the corner of his eye, Brendan saw the wind picking up. Small pieces of paper, food wrappers and leaves lifted themselves off the ground and whirled between the headstones. Flowers left in jam-jars of stagnating water bent their heads towards the ground before the growing breeze and a distant howl built up in nearby powerlines, causing Father Trent to pause just the slightest moment for another glance at the clouds. Thunder rolled from the heart of the storm and the mourners huddled closer together, hunching their shoulders against the wind. Brendan was glad he'd grabbed the jackets. The temperature was dropping rapidly.

From somewhere close by came a loud clinking noise, followed by a ceramic rattling, as a flower-filled vase toppled over on a neighbouring grave. Brendan couldn't help taking his eyes from the casket to look around, seeking the source of the noise. When he brought his attention back he glanced across the coffin to the opposite side of the grave to see if Jodie's parents were disturbed.

What he saw then made his heart come into his mouth and he actually felt the blood drain from his face, leaving his skin chilled and clammy in the cold wind.

Jodie Seager was standing directly behind her parents. The other mourners were gathered so close, moving in around the Seagers and the spectral image of the girl that Brendan was sure they must all have been touching one another. He couldn't understand how no one else noticed the ghost was there. All he could really see among the press of black clothing was her pale, lifeless face above her father's shoulder and a wasted, white arm protruding from behind the bulk of his dark coat. A flash of colour nearer the ground told him she was wearing an evening gown Gwen herself had chosen as her burial raiment.

Jodie was looking directly at Brendan.

Brendan was holding Gwen's hand and he squeezed it hard with his shock. She jerked at him for his attention and, eyes wide, silently mouthed, '*What is the matter?*' Brendan dragged his eyes away from the spectre and looked at Gwen. He decided she was suffering enough on this day of grief without being told the ghost of her best friend was attending her own funeral. He gave her a quick shake of his head and looked back at the ghost, who suddenly spoke to him as their eyes met again.

'You must take your own life, Brendan.'

Brendan started so violently at her speaking that it warranted another questioning glare from Gwen. He glanced around desperately, but no one else appeared to have heard. Father Trent droned on, his pace quickened a little despite his earlier words of not acquiescing to the worsening weather. The spirit's voice had carried clearly above the priest's, unaffected by the wind. And it wasn't Jodie's voice, but the guttural alien voice Brendan heard Jeneatte Beason speak, just before he'd fallen into the trenches of his nightmare.

'Take your own life, Brendan.'

Keeping her eyes fixed to his, the ghost stepped to one side, moving away from the crowd to reveal her entire body. The wind made the thin material of the evening gown cling to her body. As Brendan watched in horror he saw a narrow, red stain begin to grow from beneath her breasts and down to her abdomen. Her face split into a mocking, humourless grin at his reaction.

'Be a God, as I am a God, Brendan and control your own destiny. I can fill every moment of your life with a suffering and torment beyond your worst dreams, unless you become your own God and leave this world. Take your own life and live forever with me, where you will find peace. This life holds only grief and fear for you, now.'

'What the hell are you?' Brendan whispered hoarsely, causing a few people close by to look at him strangely. Gwen frowned and tightened her grip on his hand without turning her head.

The girl's spirit casually raised a hand and seemed to place it on her father's shoulder in a friendly, comforting gesture. For a moment nothing happened, then Frank Seager let out a sob and collapsed down to his knees beside the grave. The priest faltered a moment in his reading, then forged on as he saw the man's wife put out a calming hand.

'No, leave him!' Brendan half-called aloud, unconsciously reaching out himself, but his cry only brought him more looks from the other mourners, some compassionate, others disapproving.

Frank Seager pitched forward onto the mound of synthetic turf, clutching his chest and making no effort to stop his face striking the ground. His wife stepped backwards with an uttered croak of alarm, her handkerchief held to her mouth. Father Trent stopped his recitation with a small 'Oh', and gazed down at the stricken man uselessly. Only Gwen reacted with any purpose, hissing out an oath and making to step across to the fallen man. The grave was between them, so she hastily back-tracked and ran around the open grave and the group of people. She tried to shoulder her way through the small crowd, who had recovered from their initial shock quickly and were pressing forward to look.

'Get out of the way! He's having an attack,' she grated, shoving people back with her elbows. 'Let me get to him, for God's sake!' She kneeled down next to Frank Seager, grabbing his shoulder and attempting to flip him over onto his back. He was too heavy. 'Somebody help me!' Gwen naturally looked for Brendan and was surprised to see him backing away from the gravesite, his face anxious and fearful. As she watched he turned and almost ran towards a distant part of the cemetery. Gwen had no chance to call or even worry, for Father Trent heeded her call, leaning forward to help.

Something had told Brendan to get away. If he left the scene, maybe he would draw away the terrible spirit that just struck down an old man with the touch of a spectral hand. As Frank Seager had fallen forward, nearly tumbling into his daughter's grave, the ghost of his own little girl looked down at him dispassionately. Then she'd turned her white, ruined face with its blackened eye sockets back to Brendan.

'The Setris will leave—if you take your own life,' she explained simply, in her own voice now. In Jodie Seager's voice.

Brendan didn't answer, but staggered backwards awkwardly until his heels struck the cement border of the adjacent grave. He turned and trotted blindly towards a wrought-iron gate some distance away. At first he thought it was the gate which he and Gwen used to enter, but when he realised his mistake he didn't stop, thinking instead he could walk around the outer perimeter of the cemetery and back to the car.

In a sudden flurry the black clouds opened and poured heavy rain drops onto his back. He threw a glance back towards the gravesite. He heard cries of dismay and some people began scuttling quickly away towards their cars without waiting for the end of the service. Most stayed though, crouching protectively over the prone body of Frank Seager. Like mushrooms responding to the weather, several umbrellas popped into life. One of the departing figures shouted they would use their carphone to call an ambulance.

Brendan reached the gate and discovered it was heavily padlocked. He looked up at the imposing structure hopelessly. Even if he threw his dignity aside, he couldn't climb it. He called himself several kinds of fool for not seeing that the wall, too, was nearly two metres high, instead of the low construction he'd parked his car behind.

He turned around, but indecision dogged him.

To make his way to the correct path leading to his station wagon meant he would have to retrace his steps towards the funeral. He didn't want to do that. He was scared of what might happen if he got close. The ghost of Jodie Seager might choose to display her deadly talents again. Brendan looked to his left and judged the wisdom of picking his way through the graves. There was, of course, enough room to walk between them all, but something forbidding held him back.

As he looked, the compacted dirt on one of the graves cracked and moved.

Sucking in his breath with a hiss, Brendan stepped backwards again, his eyes riveted to the stirring soil. Like a miniature earthquake within the bounds of the stone edging, the dirt began to heave and writhe. The headstone slowly tilted backward as if it were tired of its long vigil over the grave.

Brendan took another step back.

Behind him came an explosive whoof and the sound of cascading earth and rocks. Before he could move, something gripped his ankle with a ferocious strength. Brendan cried out and fell forward, twisting around to see his attacker as he struck the ground.

Bursting out of the ground, scattering dirt and debris in a wide circle, a skeletal figure had lunged at Brendan and caught his ankle with one decaying hand. The grotesque corpse was hip-deep in its own grave. No flesh remained on the skull. The rain was bouncing spectacularly off the round, white bone. Ragged strips of rotting matter hung from the limbs. Pieces were around its neck too and stuck to the rib-cage and pelvic area in a parody of attempted decency. A fetid stink of putrefying meat washed out of the grave over Brendan, making him gag. The skeleton clawed at the loose dirt and slippery mud with its free hand, either trying to climb out of the grave or find enough purchase to drag Brendan in with it. The concave sockets of the skull seemed to stare imploringly at its captive.

'Join us. Join us and all will be as it should.'

Brendan heard the whispered words inside his head.

'No!' He screamed and kicked out with his free foot. His boot caught the skull a heavy blow, knocking it askew. He lashed out again and this time the skull separated from the spine completely, lobbing neatly off to fall back into the grave. Brendan's instant of elation evaporated when he realised it made no difference. In fact, the corpse's other hand stopped trying to grip the ground and began groping blindly for Brendan. In a moment of total clarity Brendan saw past the stinking skeleton to the headstone lying at the top of the grave. 'R. L. Jones, Private A.I.F. Died of Wounds, 18 April 1917.' He realised within the same fraction of time some of the decaying stuff hanging from the corpse was the remains of a khaki material. The man had been buried in his uniform.

Brendan couldn't pull his foot out of the corpse's grip, but he could move his leg from side to side, taking the skeletal limb with it. For the moment he managed to avoid the second hand trying to find a hold on his leg, but it was only a matter of time. Coming to a sudden and sickening decision Brendan jackknifed forward and grasped the arm holding him just above the wrist. Grunting with one big effort he wrenched as hard as he could, feeling the hand separate from the arm with a terrible, splintering crack. In his head Brendan heard a howl of anguish. He ignored the hand still gripped around his ankle and scrambled to his feet, meaning to run back towards the others regardless of the consequences. He only took a few steps before pulling again to a halt.

Now Jodie Seager stood between him and the distant funeral, blocking his way.

'You must kill yourself,' she told him, reverting to the same guttural voice. *'Kill yourself and all will be well.'*

Brendan stared at the image of a girl he'd known so well. She still possessed the figure, although the visible flesh was sagging and turning grey. The blonde hair, plastered down around her face, was dead and lifeless like Jodie herself. The red bloodstain down the front of the gown was wider now and smudged to pink by the falling rain. He'd seen Gwen choose the gown and remembered Jodie wearing it on several occasions. In all respects Brendan was looking at Jodie Seager returned from the dead.

Except for the eyes. The ghost's eyes burned with an inner malevolent purpose which was definitely not Jodie.

Brendan darted sideways, stumbled over a grave, then without looking back ran through the graves themselves in an awkward, dodging run, leaping over some of the smaller graves and swerving around the taller headstones. He didn't look back. He imagined at any moment more long-dead figures would burst from the earth and try to grapple him, but nothing happened. Racing through the gate, he kept going until he fell against the car with enough force to make it rock on its springs.

Panting for breath Brendan folded his arms on the roof and cradled his head, oblivious to the rain noisily hammering the thin metal. He didn't know if he was safe outside the cemetery. He was almost too shocked and exhausted to care, but he knew he couldn't go back inside for the end of the funeral.

Gwen was ripping open Frank Seager's coat and loosening his tie. She then pulled the coat from around her shoulders and rolled it into a ball, putting it behind his head. Shutting her mind to the commotion around her she calmly felt for a pulse at his wrist, but could find nothing. She pressed her fingers to his neck and found a fluttering which seemed to die at that very moment beneath her fingertips.

'Does anybody know their artificial breath?' she asked urgently. At the collective uncomprehending stares she snapped, 'Can someone give him mouth-to-mouth?'

Father Trent, now kneeling beside her, said, 'I've been taught how, but it was a long time ago.'

'Well, give it your best, Father, because I'm going to keep his heart going,' Gwen told him grimly.

They bent to their tasks, the rain dripping off their foreheads unheeded onto the patient. Someone yelled they would call an ambulance on their carphone. The rest of the funeral party milled about in the rain, uncertain of what to do. Once, Gwen stole a moment to look for Brendan, squinting her eyes against the downpour and seeing him at the far end of the cemetery. At that moment she saw him fall and thrash about on the ground. Even at that distance she could tell something was wrong and she paused to look helplessly down at Frank Seager. Gritting her teeth she decided to massage his heart for a full minute at least, then she might have to abandon him to help Brendan.

But the next time she looked he was sprinting awkwardly through the cemetery.

The rain eased to a drizzle, the heavy cloud passing over to assault the suburbs to the north. Brendan watched the ambulance splash its way through the gate and into the cemetery. The flashing red lights on the cabin glittered with drops of water and reflected off the wet metal roof. One of the ambulance men gave Brendan a strange look as they passed.

He could see Frank Seager's face was uncovered as they put the stretcher into the ambulance. Somebody, probably Gwen, he realised, had kept him alive. It raised a few questions in his mind, but he was too exhausted to search for any answers. Some of the mourners used the departure of the ambulance as an excuse to leave themselves, trailing in the wake of the vehicle as they had followed Jodie Seager's remains into the cemetery. Brendan stayed where he was, observing from a distance Father Trent stubbornly finishing the funeral service for a much depleted congregation. Somebody took Brendan's place at the canvas straps and the gleaming casket was finally lowered into the ground. Everybody hastily tossed a handful of mud down into the grave, before thankfully turning away and hurrying towards their cars. Only Gwen stayed longer, watched by Father Trent. She stood and gazed down into the grave, a forlorn figure silhouetted against the darkening pre-dusk sky. She scooped up some soil and let it trickle through her fingers as best she could. The priest put a consoling hand on her arm as they turned away. The instant they stepped onto the pathway between the headstones an engine growled into life from behind a shed and a mini front-end loader scurried out to fill the grave before dark. Some overcoated workers followed on foot, shovels and rakes slung over their shoulders.

'What happened?' Gwen asked Brendan bleakly, when she reached the car. She felt numb, stunned by the day and its events. She wasn't angry with Brendan at all, she realised, and she was too exhausted to really care what had gone wrong, anyway.

'Later,' he replied, nearly pleading.

Gwen nodded, then said, 'Why didn't you get in the car? Out of the rain?'

'I don't know. It just felt—better, I suppose. Out in the open, I mean. Can you drive?'

'Me? Sure—I guess. Why?'

To answer Brendan held up one of his hands. It trembled violently.

Once they were on the move, Brendan slid down in his seat until the back of his head touched the headrest. He closed his eyes, then a thought made them open again.

'Is he going to be all right?'

'Frank? I think so. He looked in pretty good shape when he went into the ambulance, but you never can tell. You know what these things are like. Sometimes the most impossible cases pull through, while the minor ones who should be going home in the morning can die in the minute your back's turned.'

Brendan nodded. He closed his eyes again. 'You know, it's important if he dies or not,' he murmured, puzzling her. Dully, he was thinking the ghost may have known somehow the attack was coming and used the moment, rather than caused it.

'Of course it is.' Gwen frowned, misunderstanding him.

'No, I mean—' He stopped and waved a weary hand. His eyelids felt like they were made of stone.

'Later, too?' she said.

'Yeah,' he nodded slowly.

Gwen drove for a while without speaking. Glancing at Brendan, she thought he might already have fallen asleep. Absently she adjusted the rear-view mirror.

The mirror showed her Jodie Seager sitting in the back seat.

Gwen felt chilled all over, while her heartbeat leapt into high gear. It took immense courage not to stomp her foot on the brake pedal. Instead, she slowly turned around and looked over her shoulder into the back seat. It was empty, but twisting back to face the front, the mirror still showed Jodie sitting there. Gwen had expected that. She saw that her friend still wore the evening gown she'd chosen and that Jodie, too, was sodden by the rain. That struck Gwen as strange. Worst of all, a large bloodstain softened by water covered her front. The spirit sat upright, eyes closed and completely still.

The eyes snapped open and regarded Gwen in the mirror with such an utter sadness Gwen almost burst into spontaneous tears. Jodie's voice filled her mind. It was her friend's own voice, not the harsh guttural words Brendan had heard.

'Brendan is to kill himself. He must take his own life, not by your hand or anyone else's. Only then the Setris *will leave us all in peace. You will be left in peace, too. It's only Brendan he must have.'*

Gwen's eyes were filled with tears now, blurring the image in the mirror. 'But why, Jodie?' she whispered wretchedly. 'Please tell me, what's happening?'

But the ghost vanished without another word.

Gwen braked hard and swung off the road, getting a few angry honks from nearby cars. Brendan was startled awake and watched in surprise as Gwen grabbed handfuls of tissues out of the console and buried her face in them. She was crying hard.

Brendan waited patiently for some time, before asking gently, 'Later, Gwen?'

Gwen didn't raise her face, but nodded slowly.

16

'I think you should leave the house,' Warden said. He was stalking up and down the lounge room, waving his arms and talking loudly. As he moved, his image was reflected in two full-length mirrors he'd recently brought into the house. Brendan watched him wearily, but without any resentment at Warden's mood. Gwen sat next to him, toying with a cup of coffee.

Brendan said, 'I don't think it would make any difference. In fact, what happened at the funeral proves it. I don't have to be in the house to experience any of this shit. It can happen to me wherever

I'm living, or working—no matter where I am.'

'But it all started in this house. Maybe you should try moving away. You never know.'

Gwen raised her eyebrows thoughtfully and asked, 'Did you have any troubles when you went to the war museum? Any nightmares?' Warden shot her a grateful look for her support.

'No,' Brendan admitted, then changed his mind. 'Hang on a second. I did have a funny turn at one point. It was like an hallucination. One of the photos really struck me and I remember I could feel the sun and the ground beneath my feet. I heard voices too, and animal noises.'

'What did you do?' Warden asked.

'I sort of snapped myself out of it when I realised something weird was happening. I didn't feel threatened, but it was still pretty scary.'

'Amazing,' Warden shook his head. 'The strength of this thing—the power it seems to have.'

'Look, I don't want to run away from it anyway,' Brendan said, before Warden could start again. 'Even if moving out of the house did improve things, it wouldn't be the real answer. I'm not saying I want to be some sort of hero or anything, but believe me, if I honestly thought I could escape by simply moving away, I would. I'd certainly give it a lot of serious consideration.' He shrugged and sighed. 'But I know inside myself, I think, that things are all linked together and I can't run away. The dreams, the charm—I mean, look at the damned charm! We know we can't get rid of that.

When I tried to put it in the rubbish, the bloody thing came back into the house all on its own somehow! It's obviously impossible to lose—'

'Well, we haven't seriously tried,' Gwen interrupted him. 'You only put it in the rubbish bin.'

'No,' he agreed, after a pause. 'But look at it this way. What would happen if we tried something serious? Like melting it down? Or cutting it into little pieces with a bolt cutter? How do we know we won't start something much worse, that we can't stop?'

Warden agreed. 'It would be a risk, I suppose. And something we couldn't reverse if things did start to go crazy. Maybe we'll find out more in a minute,' he added, looking at his watch. He was going to make an overseas call to his colleague in Kent, England.

Gwen said carefully, 'Let's not forget something else. It looks like it could be getting all the more—well, more dangerous.' She couldn't help glancing at Brendan.

It was a warm evening. He was dressed in shorts and a baggy, faded T-shirt. His feet were bare. One ankle showed clearly the angry dark bruising patterned like that of a human hand, the markings of the fingers quite clear.

It still wasn't certain for them what happened to Brendan at the funeral. He insisted to them, without changing his story, that the rotting corpse of the soldier attacked him. But there were no signs of disturbed earth or wrecked graves when Warden went back to check the next morning. The skeletal hand that had gripped Brendan's leg and tried to drag him into the grave had been, in some way, real. The finger-shaped bruise on his ankle was proof of that, but there was no evidence of anything else.

'That's what I feel too,' Warden said grimly. 'I can't help thinking it's all getting closer, if you know what I mean.'

'Closer?' Gwen looked alarmed.

'Well, it's hard to put a finger on it, but to my way of thinking there's been a sort of progression here.' Warden paused and tried sitting on the couch, his hands clasped in front of him. 'First you had the dreams, then you saw things out of your dreams in your daily life. Next you have visitations from people you know—dead people, I mean. Now we've got something—something more,' he ended, screwing his face up.

'Aggression,' Gwen said.

'Aggression—you've got it.' Warden pointed at her. 'This was an actual attack on your person.'

'During the storm Jeneatte attacked me,' Brendan reminded him.

'No, she didn't. She wanted to make love to you,' Warden corrected, aware of how incongruous that sounded. 'At least, it didn't have this aggression we're talking about now.'

'Okay, but this *aggression*—as you call it—is all the more reason to try and get to the bottom of everything, not run away,' Brendan said stubbornly.

'But we don't even know where to start,' Gwen groaned, rubbing her forehead. 'I mean, what's a damned *Setris*?'

'Hopefully Gerard can tell us,' Warden said, looking at his watch again. 'It's only a few minutes early. I might as well give it a go, what do you think?'

'Why not?' Brendan nodded at the telephone. 'Do you want us to leave the room?'

'Hell, no,' Warden smiled. 'There's nothing secretive or underhand about this. I've known Gerard for several years and I'm not going to ask him to reveal anything he doesn't want to. I doubt if he even knows anything like that at all. Anyway, I'd better do it now, in case that storm comes in.' In the distance, yet another wet-season storm was rumbling on the edge of the city.

'Dial away,' Brendan said. Gwen picked her feet up off the floor and snuggled in closer to him. They both watched as Warden punched in an extensive overseas telephone number. He tipped them a wink as he waited for the connection, then his face became animated as he greeted a familiar voice.

Brendan and Gwen tried to glean something out of the one-sided conversation, but Warden disappointed them by lapsing into monosyllabic grunts and words, or asking questions that made little sense to them. At one stage his face lit up with some sort of understanding and he looked sideways at the couple with a raised eyebrow. In all, the call took over ten minutes.

'Wow,' Warden said, fingering his ear as he hung up. 'That was like a crash-course in the supernatural.'

'Who the hell is he, anyway?' Gwen asked.

'I was going to explain that, before I tell you what he just told me,' Warden said. 'Otherwise, you might think he's just a crazy.'

'Great,' Brendan muttered. 'The guy needs explaining.' Gwen gave him a nudge to shut him up.

'Gerard specialises in ancient cultures,' Warden began, settling back down on the couch.

'You mean the Greeks, or the Romans?' Gwen asked.

'Nothing so straightforward—comparatively, I mean. No, Gerard specialises in people like the Druids, the Incas and a few African tribes as well. Mainly, they're people or races who based their tenets on forms of magic, witchcraft or sorcery.'

'Didn't they all?'

'No, not really.' Warden scratched his nose thoughtfully for a moment. 'If you look at the Greeks and Romans, you could say they were pretty big on gods and goddesses, right? They built entire cities devoted to a particular god or simply had thousands of statues all over the place—but,' he held up a finger, 'they weren't very interested in talking to the gods directly. Oh, they were always sacrificing something-or-other to somebody,' Warden waved a hand. 'But they usually didn't try and converse with the gods, or in particular manipulate them the same way some of the African sub-cultures tried spells and incantations to get the gods to do what *they* wanted, see the difference?'

'Sure,' Brendan shrugged. 'So now, you're going to tell us this Gerard guy is some sort of a witch, right?'

'Hardly,' Warden laughed. 'He's in his seventies now, so I can't see him dancing naked around a bonfire in the middle of the Kent countryside.'

'So what's he do?'

'Not *do*,' Warden corrected him. 'It's more a case of what he's got, which happens to be books, as far as we're concerned.'

'Books?'

Warden nodded. 'Some of the oldest books in the world—known books, anyway—on subjects like ancient cultures, beliefs and such.'

'But we're already sure there's some sort of connection to Egypt and the ancient Egyptians, because that's where the Australian army diggers trained. Not the Druids or anyone like that,' Gwen said.

'True,' Warden said. 'But a lot of his books spill over into that field, because the Roman empire, for example, spread itself across the entire globe. Mind you, when I say books, we're not talking about your basic Encyclopaedia Britannica here.'

Something in his voice prompted Brendan to ask, 'What do you mean?'

'Well, some of them are quite dangerous in a

way. Some of the spells work, if you do them right.' The approaching storm punctuated this with a rolling peal of thunder.

Brendan and Gwen glanced at each other, as if to confirm they were hearing Warden right, then Brendan burst out, 'You've got to be kidding! You mean, turning people into frogs, that sort of thing?'

'No,' Warden replied calmly. 'But Gerard did once arrange an experiment with a friend. He made him ill with a mild spell, then removed it just as quickly.'

'Incredible,' Gwen whispered.

Brendan leaned back with a sigh, saying, 'Okay, so the guy seems to know what he's talking about. Did he tell you what a *Setris* is?'

'Yeah, and it's bad news, I'm afraid,' Warden said. He gave them a look which promised a lengthy explanation. 'Okay. Now, Egyptian folklore or mythology changed many times during its long life. Different gods came and went or changed from human form to animal, then back to human again over the space of the centuries, and even decades, in some cases. Many of the changes can be attributed to the various Pharaohs who ruled at the time imposing their own personal beliefs on the population. But there was always a basic core to their religious tenet that remained virtually unchanged, in particular the belief that after death your soul left the surface of the world and went underground to the Afterworld to be judged.'

Warden made a settling motion with his hands. 'This is where things start to vary again, but at some stages of history they believed that judgement would affect where you spent Eternity. For instance, it could mean in the comfort of some form of Heaven, or burning to a crisp on the bottom floor, okay? You only had one mortal life and then an eternal existence afterwards.'

Brendan said nothing, but Gwen nodded, smiling at Warden's glib interpretation of Hell.

He went on, 'At other times that same judgement would decide your fate by way of reincarnation. How good you were, or how worthy, would affect what you would return to Earth *as*, in other words. That judgement was called Ma'at and just to make things confusing, Ma'at was at different times an Egyptian princess, a minor god, a variety of animals and—last and most often—a state of mind.'

This took a moment to sink in, with Gwen twisting her lips and saying, 'Tricky.'

Brendan had a better grasp at it. 'So, you mean the dead were judged according to their Ma'at or state of mind, much like our Christian beliefs, but at some periods of time they believed they were actually judged *by* Ma'at, who was some sort of god.'

'Or even both,' Warden added for him.

'Okay, I can absorb all that—I think,' Gwen said. 'Where does it take us?'

'The *Setris*. Gerard told me what a *Setris* is, and from what he said it confirms that's what we're up against.'

Brendan drew in his breath with a hiss. 'Okay, what is it?'

'First of all, Gerard says that what we're discussing here is a borderline case in the credibility department. There's been scant evidence of the *Setris* existing for a long, long time—though there's a possible reason for that. And anyway, he says chances are the *Setris* was always an Egyptian fairytale, rather than an entity that actually existed or was recognised at some point in ancient history. There is only one semi-documented case he could find which referred to the *Setris* by name, and that was an archaeologist late last century called Edmond Drummer. Unfortunately, no one at the time apparently took Drummer's claims seriously and he was dead before his story was known in England, where he might have found a more sympathetic hearing. Apart from Drummer, there's nothing else documented about any *Setris*. So, Gerard was more than surprised I was asking about them.'

'We might have a few more pleasant surprises for Gerard,' Brendan said wryly.

'Well, he was rather excited by the prospect,' Warden nodded. 'Anyway, we have to go back to the Ma'at theology, okay? The system works something like this. A soul is judged by its Ma'at by way of the heart being weighed. What concerns us the most is that the worst sin in the eyes of Ma'at is to take your own life.' Warden paused for a significant look at Brendan, so he didn't miss another brief exchange of glances between the couple. 'If you commit suicide your soul is taken to the lowest station of the Underworld for eternal torment. The *Setris* are the guardians, or demons, of this place.'

'There's more than one?' Gwen asked.

'Yes, but in dwindling numbers, if the mythology is accurate,' Warden replied. 'You see, in times past the *Setris* used to roam the earth in search of souls to capture. They would try and entice their victims into killing themselves, purely to populate their part of the Underworld. Gerard's books even tell of the *Setris* using a lure of some kind, which allows them to possess a living human until that person dies.'

'The charm,' Gwen said quietly, getting a nod from Warden.

'There is a plus side, of kinds. When these demons get their hands on somebody, the two of them—the *Setris* and its captive—are inextricably bound until the victim dies. So, in a way, the *Setris* is forced to protect the other too, because if the victim does die from natural or other causes, the *Setris* is left in a sort of limbo.'

Brendan ventured, 'Which apparently happens seeing, as you say, that they're around in dwindling numbers.'

'That's the idea,' Warden nodded. 'Now, they *are* protective, that's without question, but their abilities are fairly limited. Like, they couldn't protect someone from the sort of military violence we can cook up against ourselves these days. Not indefinitely, anyway. So, presumably there's been a rate of attrition amongst the *Setris*. It's interesting that some of the ancient Egyptians, and later the Arabs, used other spells to actually control the *Setris*. In other words, the Arabs used to let themselves be possessed, then use the protective side of the demon's possession to keep them in good health. They had a certain knowledge which allowed them to prevent the spirit to get the better of them, see?'

Gwen sighed. 'This is all becoming a bit much.'

'I can boil it down,' Warden offered. He took a deep breath. 'I think Brendan is being—' He stopped again and tried to come up with an appropriate term, '—haunted, for want of a better word, by one of these *Setris*. . .'

'Hang on a second!' Brendan got to his feet, suddenly angry, 'Are you saying I'm possessed, or something? That I don't know what I'm doing or— or I'm under somebody else's control?'

Warden looked at him a long time, before he said, 'Not possessed like you're thinking, Brendan. We're not talking about turning your head 360 degrees and throwing up everywhere. But this *Setris* thing has got some sort of hold over you. Don't you realise? It's controlling your mind by filling it with any image it wants. You don't know anymore which ghosts are real, and which are imagined, or where your nightmares end. Don't you agree there are times when you've got no control?'

'No, I don't! I know my own mind, for God's sake.'

Carefully, Gwen said, 'Brendan, where is the charm now?'

He didn't answer, but got up and walked over to the window. He stared moodily out. The others silently watched him.

Outside, the street promised a peaceful world. Nothing moved in their quiet suburb. Most houses displayed lit windows and the spectral, reflected flickering of a television.

Did he still have complete control of his own thoughts? Could someone—or something—else be manipulating him. What about the charm? How did he feel about it? There was one dreadful answer there. He had to screw up his courage to tell them.

'I'm wearing it,' he said softly.

Just as quietly, Gwen asked, 'Did you really think I wouldn't notice? Why are you wearing it, Bren?'

He thought about trying to explain the complex turmoil of emotions the charm prompted, but it felt impossible. He hated it, yet he wanted it, too. The idea of wearing it had burst into his mind like an answer to all his problems and when he had lowered the leather thonging over his head he'd felt an aura of relief wash over him. That sensation didn't last, but strangely Brendan didn't consider for a moment taking the charm off again. Instead, trying to recapture that feeling of relief, he kept touching the gold through the fabric of his shirt, pressing the charm against his chest and feeling the chill of metal against his skin. He knew, too, he was being almost childish and perhaps even dangerously foolish. But like an alcoholic who loathes his sickened mornings and foolish, drunken behaviour, but can't resist that first nip of the bottle every day, he continued to finger the charm.

Perhaps now, Brendan realised in a moment of desperate honesty, *it might be worth the risk to do something drastic, while his thoughts and rationale could give him the strength.* He remembered he had a pair of heavy metal cutters in the shed. *He could get Warden to cut the bloody thing up into tiny pieces—things couldn't get worse, could they?*

But instead of suggesting this, Brendan turned around and heard himself say, 'It's the safest place for the charm to be. While I'm wearing it, no one else can get hurt. You probably think this is just another way—'

He suddenly realised there was another ghost in the room.

Brendan had stopped in shock and gaped at the sight of a muddied, bloody soldier sitting next to Gwen. The soldier was sitting absolutely still, calmly composed with his hands in his lap, looking straight ahead at nothing.

Aware that Gwen and Warden were staring at him, Brendan slowly raised a hand and pointed. 'There's a soldier sitting on the couch next to Gwen,' he whispered, shakily.

'What?' Gwen said, instantly frightened and confused by Brendan's change. Warden reacted faster, rushing over to one of the mirrors and turning it until Gwen and the couch were in its reflection.

And the soldier.

'Jesus fucking Christ,' he breathed, staring mesmerised into the mirror. 'Who is he?'

'I don't know,' Brendan answered flatly. He hadn't moved from the window. 'We haven't seen him before.'

Gwen was feeling panicked. Now she could see the image in the mirror too and her first impulse was to move away from the glass. Then she realised the spectre was actually sitting right next to her and with a small cry she sprang up and moved closer to Brendan, who put a protective arm around her shoulders.

'What's he doing?' she asked, although she could still see the ghost herself in Warden's mirror.

'Nothing,' Warden said in an awed voice.

The soldier was bare-headed, his matted fair hair falling in a lank lock over his forehead. His khaki uniform was caked with dirt and torn in several places. He wore long-legged, baggy shorts and a short-sleeved shirt. Three shocking red flowers of blood were stitched across his chest. He was hardly more than a youth.

The soldier turned his head and looked directly at Brendan. His eyes burned with desperation and an intensity of feeling, like an overwhelming grief. Staring back, Brendan felt he was fixed in that gaze for an age. Then the ghost spoke, his voice husky and broken.

'It's mine,' he said, sounding saddened as if burdened with guilt.

Brendan felt Gwen start nervously beside him and it stunned him further to know she'd heard the voice, too.

Warden muttered a low 'Shit.'

'What's yours?' Brendan asked the spirit, his own voice barely above a whisper.

Without warning the soldier jerked violently as if he was being struck again by the bullets. He let out an anguished cry which echoed in their minds and arched his back in agony. Before their horrified eyes his body began to disintegrate and decay. His skin yellowed and fell away from the bones. Hair dropped from his scalp in a tumbling cascade. The burning eyes collapsed inwards to make blackened sockets. Seeing this, Gwen finally cried out in horror, burying her head into Brendan's shoulder. Now maggots appeared, crawling down the soldier's ruined cheeks. His limbs wasted to nothing and the tattered shirt deflated as his body decomposed within it. In seconds only a skeleton occupied a rotting uniform. The process slowed, the bones greying and crumbling. In the end, the remains of the soldier simply faded to nothing, disappearing completely.

Another voice—a different voice—broke into Brendan's mind. It was low and menacing, demanding attention.

'He is dead. He has no voice.'

The three of them stood shocked and speechless for a long moment, then Brendan gently led Gwen to another chair and sat her down. Warden, his own expression glazed, watched as Brendan walked, almost stumbling, out of the room towards the stairs. He went to call out after Brendan but the words stuck in his throat.

Brendan mounted the steps one by one, his shoulder bouncing off the wall as he went. At the top he turned left and let himself into the bathroom, locking the door behind him. Unexpectedly, nausea washed over him and he knelt urgently at the toilet bowl and began vomiting with great, heaving motions. A stream of bile, laced with blood, splattered the clean ceramic. Brendan looked at this with horror, but he couldn't stop himself retching until he fell back totally exhausted. He sat with his back against the wall, spittle running unchecked down his chin. Eyes closed, he stayed there so long he almost succumbed to his exhaustion, drifting into a kind of doze. When he finally opened them again he found himself staring at the long, deep bath beside him.

Brendan saw himself lying in the bath, which was full to the brim with gently steaming water. He was naked, his body floating easily. His eyes were staring sightlessly at the ceiling. The water was bright pink. More redness oozed out of two vertical cuts on each of his wrists.

Instead of being frightened Brendan was

swamped by a numbing apathy. He stared at his own corpse almost listlessly, beyond reacting. A thought surfaced in his mind—that he nearly envied the dead Brendan Craft's serenity. There were many advantages to dying, he realised.

But I don't have to die like that, he told himself. *There was an easier way.*

He tipped his head to one side and looked back into the toilet bowl. Vomit still coated the sides and scummed the water, but the blood was no longer there. Gathering himself for the effort, Brendan put one hand on the bowl and levered himself painfully to his feet. He stood swaying in front of the mirror. A man with black-rimmed eyes, pale skin and a haggard expression looked back at him. Glancing to his right, he noticed the bath was empty again.

Something outside caught his attention.

Through the window he could look down at a large mango tree in the back yard. Flickering lightning bounced off the clouds in the distance. From next door a floodlight in the neighbour's yard bathed the tree and the ground beneath it in a revealing golden light. A form, hanging in an awkward pose, swayed from a rope tied to one of the largest branches. On the ground an up-ended chair threw angular shadows. As Brendan watched, the figure slowly twisted around. Again he was confronted with his own corpse, now with a contorted face, the rope biting cruelly into his left cheek. Despite the distance and the poor light Brendan could see every detail of his own hanging. He recognised the chair from the kitchen. The tow-rope came from the car.

But he told himself he didn't have to do it that way, either.

He reached out uncertainly and opened the medicine cabinet. Lately, Gwen had been more trusting with his sleeping tablets and no longer hid them. The squat brown bottle with its warning label was in front of the other medicines. Brendan twisted off the top and tipped the entire contents into his cupped hand. Over a dozen pills nestled in his palm. From the window sill he picked up a china cup shaped with a smiling face and emptied the toothbrushes, razors and toothpaste it held into the sink. They clattered noisily as they struck the hard surface. Awkwardly using the free fingers of his hand holding the pills he turned on the tap and filled the cup. Next he opened his jaw wide and took all the pills into his mouth. Immediately a bitter taste assaulted his tongue and he sucked a quantity of water from the cup. It needed several mouthfuls before he managed to swallow all the tablets. Tipping the rest of the water down the sink Brendan looked at the smiling face on the cup. On an impulse, with a wistful, sad smile of his own, he tossed the cup out the open window. He heard it smash on the ground below.

Downstairs Gwen and Warden were regarding each other with a strange kind of wariness. It was Gwen who dared to ask first.

'We did see it—him—didn't we?'

Warden nodded, relieved. 'You bet. That was the most amazing fucking thing I ever saw.'

'But did we both see the same thing?'

'Well, what did you see?'

'A soldier. A young one, and he was sitting on the couch. He was covered in dirt and blood and he looked like he'd been shot in the chest several times. Then he said something to Bren. Something like, "It's mine".' Gwen stopped, unwilling to describe what happened next.

'I heard that, too,' Warden agreed. 'Then he started decomposing right before our very eyes, right?'

'Right,' she grimaced. 'That was horrid. I couldn't watch.'

'It was pretty bad. Looks like Brendan didn't cope with it at all. Sounds like it, too,' he added, gesturing at the ceiling. The sounds of retching came through.

'I should go up.' Gwen moved towards the stairs.

'Wait.' Warden held up a hand. 'Can we just talk about this thing quickly? We might not get another chance.'

Gwen gave the stairs an anxious glance, then agreed. 'Sure.' She moved back and sat nervously on the edge of the couch. 'For a minute.'

Warden looked at her hard. 'I can see Brendan having a severe nervous breakdown very soon, especially if he sees something like that again and he's on his own. God knows he's been seeing them for too long already. Now we know what we're up against, we've got to remember—' he paused to make his point. 'The *Setris* is trying to drive him insane or so damned crazy and scared he'll act without thinking. Brendan might *just* kill himself, if no one's around to stop him. It wouldn't be his fault. He's losing control.'

'So, you really do believe in this *Setris*?' Gwen asked, her voice tinged with sadness. 'It sounds so fantastic.'

'There's no doubt anymore about everything else that has been happening. None of this is a product of Brendan's own mind.' Warden spread his hands in a helpless gesture. 'We just saw the ghost of a World War I digger in this very lounge room. We've got no choice but to assume the rest is real, too. It's the only theory we've got,' he ended, his voice tight.

Gwen rested her elbow on her knee, covering her face with a hand. She stayed like that for a while. Warden didn't speak. 'What about the charm?' she asked finally. 'Can't we destroy it?'

'I doubt it,' Warden shook his head. 'It's been around for more than two thousand years, maybe longer. I don't think it will be that easy to get rid of.'

'So, what the hell are we going to do?'

Warden picked up a sheet of paper from the coffee table. It was one of the medical report forms from Adrian Galther's file. 'All we know at the moment is that Adrian Gordon Galther somehow survived this shit for over sixty years. We should try and find out how he did it.'

'In a damned padded cell,' Gwen muttered tiredly.

'I'm afraid that's exactly what we're going to find out,' Warden agreed grimly.

The sound of something smashing outside startled them both. Warden jumped to his feet and headed for the front door, but Gwen stopped him.

'No. I think that's Brendan,' she said, her intuition coming to the fore again. It didn't make sense to Warden and he looked confused, glancing towards the door. 'I just know!' she cried, running for the stairs. Warden rushed after her.

Brendan sat on the floor again facing the bath. His other dead form was back, floating in the steaming, pink water. Except now the corpse's head was turned towards him and smiling. Brendan vaguely registered another peal of distant thunder. Closer, he thought he heard the howl of a large dog.

His peace was shattered by the rattle of the door handle, followed by furious pounding on the wooden panels.

'Brendan? Brendan! Open the door! Open it now!' Gwen's voice came from the other side.

Brendan felt twinges of panic, and he felt guilt and a strange longing, too. The corpse in the bath vanished, leaving a few tendrils of steam vaporising. Something told him it was too late, anyway. Troubled, he decided to ignore the calls at the door, which were followed by muted, urgent conferring.

Next, the bathroom door suffered a tremendous

blow making it bow inwards and creak in protest, but it didn't give way. A second assault saw the door burst inwards with a shower of wooden splinters from the jamb. Warden came through with it, shoulder-first. He stopped dead and stared down at Brendan.

'Brendan, what have you done?' he asked carefully. 'What's up?'

Brendan looked up at him fearfully and scrambled to his feet, backing away against the wash-basin. He couldn't speak, suddenly consumed by fear at the sight of his own friends. Gwen stepped around Warden.

'Are you all right, Bren?' she asked, a cool professional tone in her voice. 'Is something wrong?' Brendan silently watched her, his eyes wide. His feet shuffled uselessly as he unconsciously tried to back away further against the immovable basin. 'Oh, shit,' Gwen grated through her teeth, nodding at the empty pill bottle on the sink. 'He's overdosed on his sleeping tablets,' she told Warden.

He looked at her helplessly. 'What do we do about it? Call an ambulance?'

Gwen shook her head. 'We've got to get them back out of him again,' she said grimly. 'I need to get him into the kitchen right now.'

'Okay,' Warden said shakily. 'I think I can do that.' He walked towards Brendan, his hand held out placatingly. 'Take it easy, Bren,' he said soothingly. 'We're just going to give you a hand.' Like a startled animal, Brendan watched him approach. Without warning, Warden struck fast, punching Brendan in the solar plexus, bringing the wind out of him with a whoosh and felling him to his knees. Effortlessly, Warden picked Brendan up and slung him over his shoulder. 'Let's do it,' he said to Gwen, who had watched with wide eyes.

Less than a minute later, Brendan was seated in a kitchen chair. He wasn't struggling, but all the same Warden kneeled behind him and circled his chest with one strong arm. With the other he cupped Brendan's chin, holding his head up, using his fingers as Gwen instructed to pinch Brendan's jaw open. She stepped closer, a large mug filled with very salty warm water in her hand. She tipped it into Brendan's mouth, using her free hand to stroke his throat.

He alternatively gagged then swallowed until, at a signal from Gwen, Warden clamped his hand over Brendan's mouth, while she kept stroking.

'Here it comes,' she warned after a moment, stepping back.

Warden released his hands and Brendan jerked forward with an explosive cough, followed by a stream of gut-wrenching vomiting. Gwen watched anxiously, uncaring of the mess falling to the floor. Warden felt his own stomach churning rebelliously at the sight. She nodded with wry satisfaction at the sight of a collection of white tablets, hardly digested, swimming amongst the regurgitated water and bile on the linoleum.

As Brendan vomited the blank idiocy left his

eyes, too. When he eventually coughed the last spittle from his mouth and looked wretchedly up at Gwen, she thought she could see the suicidal madness was gone.

'What in God's name did I do?' he croaked feebly.

'You took all your sleeping tablets,' Gwen told him, her voice hard. Sympathy had no place here, she knew. Many a would-be suicide coerced their rescuers into leaving the room by evoking sympathy, giving them a second chance.

Warden squatted down next to him, pinching Brendan's shoulder with a fierce grip. 'You've got to understand, that's what he *wants* you to do—kill yourself,' he said fiercely. 'But it's not a way out. It's the way to something much, much worse and it lasts forever. Fucking *forever*, do you understand?'

'Yeah, I know,' Brendan was nodding feebly, hanging his head. He looked up and tried to look Warden in the eye. 'Honest I do. I don't know what went wrong then.'

Warden looked across at Gwen, who shrugged back.

'I believe him,' she said tiredly. 'I don't think he knew what he was doing. But you're right—I guess we're going to have to watch him like a baby from now on.'

'Until we get some more answers,' Warden agreed.

17

The nights at Gallipoli were a cruel contradiction. Above the peninsula a canopy of gentle stars inspired thoughts of home, love and a world without gunfire and sudden violent death. But other stars could be seen, too. Flashing, winking pinpricks of light spat out from the dark mass of the land, betraying enemy positions keeping up a steady rate of harassing rifle fire into the Australian trenches. The invading troops answered in kind, firing away from the sea, where Ben Hamilton floated on a supply boat, the muzzle flashes closer to the water. The flat cracking of the shooting was heard by everyone. Occasionally the night was lit by the brighter flare of an exploding bomb or falling shell from the Turkish artillery.

Tonight Hamilton thought himself lucky. Troops were often pulled from the trenches in rotation to help carry fresh ammunition up to the front line, but it was unusually fortunate to score the job of riding the lighter out to the unloading ship. It was, he suddenly realised, the first time he'd been safely outside the Turks' range of fire since the morning they'd landed. He should have felt elated or at least safe.

Instead, without needing to keep his undivided attention on simple survival, Hamilton found himself analysing his inner thoughts and feelings. There was no elation or safety waiting for him in his own mind.

So many men around him appeared to thrive on the war. Even when they looked certain to go over the top to their deaths, there was still a gut feeling they would live and grow from the moment. 'Camaraderie' was not a word that would occur to most of the soldiers. It was beyond the education of most. But mateship and the code of thinking of others, rather than yourself, was something they'd understand. They would sneer or laugh, however, if it were suggested they were a party to such a thing. Each man considered he was doing a job and nothing else.

Hamilton benefited from all this, and his friends, and he enjoyed the mateship of the trenches as much as the next man, but the war was eating away at his insides. Instead of feeling elated at their triumphs, angry at the defeats and always determined to win no matter what, Hamilton often just felt desperately tired. Lack of sleep was one thing. Another was his inability to relax even when he was in the comparatively safer rear areas doing things like tonight—carrying ammunition.

When he wasn't busy fighting the enemy he saw other things, dreadful things, that the others didn't. He no longer knew or cared if they came from his own head. Except for the voices, which had to be in his own mind, because no one else heard them. These were urgent, whispering voices telling him it was only a matter of time. Wouldn't it be quicker and easier, they asked, to take his own life cleanly? Why wait for the dreaded stomach wound or the shattered legs that would see him die of thirst in no-man's-land?

One night he awoke to the loud popping of an enemy flare. He looked down the length of his body, washed in the wavering magnesium glare. He'd screamed when he saw both his legs cruelly broken below the knees, white shards of bone protruding from torn, bloodstained trousers. His booted feet were at unnatural angles to his legs.

The hallucination vanished with the flare hissing to extinction on the ground. Rogers had come running up to see if Hamilton were wounded. After seeing the horrified expression on the younger man's face, but nothing else, he'd given Hamilton a reassuring hug and pat on the shoulder without saying a word. Lots of soldiers were having nightmares. Rogers wasn't to know Hamilton's were any different.

Over the weeks Hamilton constantly saw gruesome hallucinations where either himself or his friends were savagely mauled by the enemy. Never killed, but only wounded or incapacitated in the most dreadful, sickening ways. Sometimes it took all his efforts not to try and run out to them in some pointless, saving gesture. He could only wait until the image vanished.

Of course, sometimes he wasn't imagining things. It was real. But he couldn't tell the difference.

Hamilton stumbled slightly as the lighter blundered into the wash of another, baulking at the small wave and turning the bow slightly.

'Steady,' came the soft voice of the sailor casually leaning on the tiller, a cigarette between his lips. Next to him, sprawled at his feet, another sailor occasionally reached up to accept a puff. The shore was closer and in the starlight Hamilton could make out the moving forms of men waiting on the makeshift pier, preparing to unload the precious cargo of shells and food.

He knew, within himself, where the root of all his problems lay. It hung around his neck on a thong of broken bootlace. Hamilton had no idea how he knew. Also, he understood he wasn't *supposed* to know. His addiction to the charm was an incredible thing—senseless and self-destructive. Yet, that the charm protected him from harm was beyond doubt. Hamilton knew he wasn't exactly immortal while he wore the golden jackal. If he were to stand exposed on a parapet in the front lines he would be gunned down like anybody else. But the instances of enemy soldiers turning their attention away from him, or of thrown bombs not exploding were too much to consider sheer fate anymore. What hurt Hamilton most were the times when other men appeared to take the bullet destined for him.

The young soldier was possessed by something else, too. A personal conviction, born from his simple Christian upbringing and combined with his parents' gentle teaching on what was right and fair. He knew it was wrong for him to have the charm working for him so. Other men took their chances with nothing except their own courage on their side. Compared to them, he felt smaller and ashamed.

Now, standing under the starlight on a gentle ocean, that shame still felt strong, while his instincts for self-preservation were diminished by his distance from the shore—a distance quickly getting smaller. He could, he realised, just give the charm away—Galther regarded it with the hunger of a starving child looking at a morsel of food—but to do that, Hamilton would have to wait until he was back in the trenches and with a pang of shame he doubted he could do that once he was again amongst the falling shells.

He reached through the collar of his shirt and fingered the charm. The metal was warm from his skin. It felt like it belonged there. Closing his eyes and pulling on his resolve, Hamilton slipped the leather cord over his head and held the charm before his face. Light from phosphorescent waves pushed by the lighter glittered on the golden surface. In the distance, blurred as his eyes focused on the charm, the pier was coming closer. Hamilton held the thonging by his fingers and reached out over the side of the boat. The charm swung lazily in the wind of the lighter's passage. He willed himself to let go, but couldn't. His fingers were frozen in a grip. Closing his eyes again, he almost begged his hand to release its hold.

But it couldn't.

A hand slapped his shoulder. 'You don't want to be standing there when we come into the pier, mate. We won't hit none too gentle, because of the chop from all these other bastards. You might pitch straight over the bow and get y'self crushed against the buffers.'

It was the sailor. He'd moved forward to deliver the warning. The touch on Hamilton's shoulder was so unexpected it had startled him badly. The charm had flown from his fingers and plopped into the water. A faint ripple on the surface passed quickly astern.

'Drop something?' The sailor frowned at the water. It took Hamilton a moment to answer.

'No—no, I was just feeling the breeze,' he

stuttered, feeling appalled. The sailor couldn't see his expression and nodded, understanding, and moved back to the stern.

After an initial shock and a deep stab of regret, Hamilton was surprised his sense of loss faded quickly. In fact, he didn't think anything had changed at all and he unconsciously put his fingers to his throat often to check he no longer wore the charm. Soon the lighter nosed into the pier and there was a bustle of activity as everyone laboured to get the ammunition to the shelter of the base of the cliffs. Several Turkish shells landed in the cove, for the enemy knew supplies were nearly always landed at night. As usual, none came close.

Since Hamilton was involved in loading to and from the lighters, he was excused from having to carry any supplies up the cliff-face to the lines. However he shouldered a box of .303 shells and started to plod steadily up the sandy, narrow pathway. While he climbed, his mind played on the charm and what its loss might mean. Strangely, he still couldn't think of himself as being without it. Finally he dropped the ammunition off at a deep dugout, informed an NCO he'd brought it and made his way towards the slit trench where his unit waited as first reserve. Like everyone else, he no longer noticed the desultory fire zipping over his head from the Turkish lines, the passing bullets humming and hissing like angry insects. When he got back to his section he discovered all his friends had been moved forward to plug a gap in the front line caused by a patrol towards the Turks. Hamilton shrugged and lay down in one of the vacant bunk-holes cut into the back wall of the trench. He pulled a torn blanket across the hole to block out any more flares and soon dropped into an exhausted sleep—something he hadn't done for months.

The dream came quickly. At first Hamilton smiled in his sleep, recognising the familiar vista of his family's property in Queensland. It was summer, he thought, noting the dry grass and hard-baked earth. All the colours of the land were faded under a hot sun, waiting for the first rains of the wet season. Then the dream started to sour. He saw it was more than just a summer dryness. The cracks in the earth were wide, the grass brittle and almost white. The garden around the homestead, always carefully tended by his mother, was dead and ugly. A shimmering heat-haze obscured the horizon. From the haze a large shape staggered into view, followed by another. They were cattle, some of his father's prime stock. But now the animals were wasted, their skin hanging from their bony frames like ill-fitting garments. Their legs trembled from the effort to keep themselves erect, while they stared mournfully at the homestead.

A creaking sound brought Hamilton's vision back to the house. His father had walked through the open front door onto the porch. Hamilton's sleeping, frowning face lightened again at the sight of his dad, but the worry returned when he saw what a changed man his father had become. Now his features were gaunt and desperate. His face was thin and bitter under a dusty bushman's hat. In one hand he carried a length of coiled rope. In the other, supported by the crook of his arm, was a kitchen chair.

Hamilton's attention was drawn briefly to the open door of the homestead. Despite the shade thrown by the porch he could see something protruding from the doorway. It was a foot, wearing one of his mother's favourite slippers. It lay at an odd angle. Flies buzzed around the open doorway.

The dream moved back to his father, who was striding purposefully across the yard to a large, dying tree. Small puffs of dust rose from his boots as he walked across what was once a beautiful lawn.

Belatedly, as his father threw one end of the rope across a stout bough, Hamilton realised what he was witnessing.

He cried out for his father to stop.

In reality it came out as a low, restless moan. Something his fellow soldiers had long before learned to ignore.

His father was an expert with a rope. It took him less than a minute to secure the length to the tree then, standing on the chair, fashion a noose at the other end. Satisfied, he hesitated for a moment, then turned and looked into the omnipresent eyes of his son.

'It's the easiest way, Ben,' he said quietly. His

voice held that complete confidence with which he'd always tutored his son. Hamilton's father had to stand on tip-toe slightly to get his neck firmly in the noose, then he awkwardly kicked away the chair.

The hanging man lost all his dignity, thrashing and straining against the rope around his throat, while his legs kicked uselessly above the fallen chair. Slowly, his efforts dwindled until he stopped completely, his face blue, a swollen tongue protruding from his lips.

Ben Hamilton awoke gasping for his own breath and clawing at his throat. His fingertips caught on something—a cord. There was a familiar feeling of something bouncing against his chest beneath his shirt.

He was wearing the charm again.

With a groan, he rolled out from behind the blanket to land on his knees on the trench floor. He realised it was still night, though now a late, full moon flooded the peninsula with a silvery, revealing light. The small stretch of trench was empty. Hamilton turned his head to one side as he fought to get his breath back and become fully awake.

On the trench wall before his eyes the sand stirred, causing a trickle to fall to the floor. A face started to appear, formed from the dirt. Hamilton froze, fascinated and frightened at the same time. Men had been buried by collapsing trenches since the beginning of the campaign and it wasn't unusual to use the enemy's dead to bulk up battlements—it was easier than filling sandbags. But this was different. The face was forming itself—cheekbones, nose, forehead and a strong chin moulding out of the sand. The eyes were closed as if the face were in a peaceful sleep, then they flickered open and stared straight at Hamilton. They were devoid of any expression. At the same time Hamilton recognised who it was.

'Join me,' Oakley whispered, the moving lips dislodging more sand to cascade to the trench floor. *'Join me and the dreams will be over.'*

'Annie,' Hamilton groaned, a tear coming to his cheek. It was all he could do.

Without warning, an arm broke out of the trench wall and reached with groping fingers towards Hamilton. He backed away, shuffling awkwardly on his hands and knees. A second arm burst from the dirt, showering sand.

'Join me,' Oakley's voice grated again. This time there was a hard edge to it.

'No,' Hamilton said, scrambling to his feet. With horror he could see all along the short section of trench the faces and limbs of long-dead soldiers breaking out of the trench walls. All of the stilted, waving arms and clutching hands seemed to be reaching for him. A whisper filled his ears.

'Join us, join us . . .'

'No!' Hamilton cried again, trying to back away, but finding himself encircled by the dead faces and grasping hands.

Seeing his only chance he put his hands on top of

the parapet and one foot on the firing step, vaulting himself out of the trench. He felt hands clutching at his ankles momentarily, but he easily broke free. Then he was lying breathlessly on the hard sand, totally exposed by the bright moonlight.

It was well past midnight. During those hours, except while major offensives were being mounted, no one from either side was particularly interested in shooting anyone. But there were always those vigilant few who couldn't sleep and there were always the snipers. Hamilton was in a very dangerous position. Yet he couldn't bring himself to drop into another trench. He feared the whole terrible scene would be waiting for him again. Instead, he stood crouched over and leapt across the trench he'd just left, looking down as he passed to see it still filled with feebly groping, dead limbs. He heard the first shout go up. It sounded Turkish. There was the crack of a rifle and a bullet hissed past his head. Hamilton zig-zagged and jumped another trench. More firing and more bullets passed close to him. Something tugged at his flapping shirt, but he ignored it. Now some of the Australian troops were sleepily responding to the Turkish fire and shouldering their own weapons. As he leapt another trench, still running erratically, he heard someone grumble, 'What the fuck's he think he's doin'?'

Hamilton rounded a small hillock and fell gasping to the sand. The exchange of gunfire had turned into a minor battle, with the entire section of the front line now trading shots.

Hamilton lay on his back and concentrated on getting his breath back. The moon shone down, painting the landscape with a clarity unsuitable for wars. It took a moment before he realised he wasn't alone.

Standing several yards from where he lay was the unmistakable figure of the old Arab who sold him the charm. The old man wore the flowing robes of his people. A deep hood was pulled over his head, obscuring his face. His hands and feet were bare. Both his skin and his clothes were bleached a dull white by the moonlight. Hamilton couldn't find the strength or even the fear to get up and run.

'I don't care any more,' Hamilton whispered hoarsely, not really sure of what he was saying.

The ghost of the Arab waited some time before replying. Its voice was harsh and broken. '*You do not need to care. You need to know.*'

'I don't know, either,' Hamilton said, wretchedly.

There was a silence, then came a soft sound as one of the spectre's hands separated from his wrist leaving behind a ragged tear of skin. As the hand fell to the ground, a thin rivulet of dust poured from the wound.

'*With knowledge,* the ghost uttered, '*the* Setris *is a legacy of protection. Like a beast on a leash and with its claws blunted. Without that knowledge the* Setris *is a legacy of a demon who will taunt and torment you until you take your own life, as it is destined to do.'*

'The *Setris*?' Hamilton groaned. 'I don't know what you're talking about.'

The body within the robe continued to disintegrate to dust and the ghost suddenly fell to its knees. Its voice became more pained and laboured.

'It is the charm you wear as good luck. You own the Setris, *yet it owns you, until you take your own life.'*

Hamilton began to laugh, a broken cracked sound. 'You want me to kill myself? I can get killed any day of the week! Any time of the damned day!'

But the Arab had crumpled to nothing and faded away without saying anything more, leaving Hamilton to suddenly doubt it had ever existed. He didn't trust anything his senses told him anymore.

After some time he carefully made his way to a nearby communications trench and, after identifying himself to a startled guard, rolled into it. He spent the rest of the night in the rear areas, moving back to his unit's position just before first light.

The next morning Hamilton found Galther, Rogers and McAllen huddled around a tiny fire waiting for a billy of tea to boil. They looked at him warily.

'What happened?' Rogers asked, being the only one who probably could.

'A nightmare,' Hamilton explained, shaking his head tiredly. He knew he couldn't get into trouble. It would be a hard man who would accuse him of deserting. Besides, there was nowhere to desert to, as everyone knew. 'I just woke up and started running. I had no idea what I was doing until I fell into a rear trench.'

'You nearly got yourself killed, the way I hear it. Someone recognised you as you ran past. The whole front line started shooting.'

Hamilton didn't reply, but rummaged in his nearby kit for a mug. When he came back to the group Galther looked at him with a strange yearning.

'There's going to be that big push today, Ben.'

Hamilton nodded. 'I know. Something about keeping Johnny Turk busy while somebody lands somewhere else.'

'It's going to be a slaughter, they reckon. We won't have a hope going against them machine guns.'

'They always say that and what happens? We end up taking the position. A few blokes get bowled over, of course. You have to take your chances.'

'When your number's up, your number's up,' McAllen murmured, sipping his tea.

'Bullshit,' Galther suddenly spat. 'Not if you've got luck like Ben here.' He looked pointedly at Hamilton's chest.

'I may be lucky,' Hamilton said with a bitterness they didn't understand. 'But I'd rather not have it. I'll tell you what, Galth. If I get knocked, you can have the damned thing.' The charm nestled beneath his shirt, out of sight, but they both knew what he was talking about.

'Don't talk like that,' Galther said, uncomfortable.

They lapsed into a silence. McAllen filled it by carefully taking out the makings and rolling himself a cigarette. He patted his pockets forgetfully for a match. Eventually, he asked, 'Anybody got a light?'

'Next to the firing slit,' Hamilton told him. Most of the prepared firing holes had boxes of matches nearby to cater for the home-made jam-tin bombs the Australians used to counter the Turk's own hand bomb. McAllen stepped backwards and found the box. He struck a match and touched the flaring end to his cigarette. After taking a deep drag he looked ruminative.

'You know what I reckon?' he asked, obscurely.

'What?' said Rogers, forever indulgent.

McAllen didn't get the chance to reply. The sniper's bullet took him high in the right temple and exited just below his left ear, spraying blood and brains over the wall of the trench. It was, in fact, an excellent shot through the narrow firing slit—obviously one the sniper had waited for patiently.

'Macca!' Hamilton cried, dropping to his knees next to the body.

'Bastards,' Galther mouthed, turning away. Rogers looked on for a moment, passing his hand wearily across his face, before walking off to find a stretcher-bearer.

Hamilton found himself alone with the corpse. A wave of weariness washed over him and he felt a hundred years old. The whole war suddenly seemed so impossible, yet it also felt so necessary to do something and make all the death and waste worthwhile, too. The confusion created its own pain. 'Don't worry,' he whispered to the bloodied, ruined head of his friend. 'I'll get them instead. I'll get them for you—I promise.'

The forward trenches tried to keep up the illusion that the day was like any other and business was as usual. Periscope rifles sniped at the Turks at regular intervals. Patrols were sent out in attempts to find weaknesses in the defences. Only a few bombs were thrown, however, because a like response from the Turks would have caused havoc. The front-line trenches of the Australians were packed with men waiting for the word to attack in strength.

The attack was timed for ten o'clock in the morning. It was hoped that by then the Turks would have dismissed the idea of an assault for the day, having waited for it since sunrise. Hamilton and Galther waited nervously, cramped together by the mass of men.

'Bloody Nick's got the luck of the devil,' Galther complained. 'I'd rather be sniping, than going over the top any day.'

When Hamilton answered, his eyes were expressionless. His body kept up the pretence of conversation, but his mind was elsewhere. 'I don't call that luck, sitting out in the open and annoying the fuck out of the Turks. You know the way we go after their snipers.'

'Still,' Galther grumbled, trying to sound calm, but unable to stop his nervous darting eyes. 'Sniping's not a frontal assault, is it?'

'We're third wave,' Hamilton said. 'We probably won't even have to go, unless it's to secure the new line. Don't worry too much.'

However, Hamilton *was* sweating nervously. The press of waiting soldiers played on his mind, reminding him of the groping, reaching hands of the dead he'd seen in the night. He was determined to do well in this attack and almost hoped the assault would need a third wave. Something *inside* of him needed defeating, too, he sensed. Unbidden, a phrase from the Bible came into his mind. He was going to make it a day of reckoning.

Non-commissioned officers began pushing their way down the trench, patting men on the back and quietly getting them ready.

'First wave, on the whistle,' one NCO said, passing by.

'Teach is in the first wave,' Galther said. 'He said he was going to wish us luck, but he must be caught up.'

'He'll be okay,' Hamilton replied absently.

Suddenly it was happening. A whistle blew from the far end of the trench and was repeated by several junior officers along the line. With wild yells the first human wave of soldiers launched themselves over the parapet, many getting helpful leg-ups from those staying for the next attack. The Turkish response was slow, a rattle of rifle fire followed by one, then another, machine gun. In the space of ten seconds the whole line opened up and the remaining Australians waited tensely for some indication as to what was going on. The shooting began to abate. Someone tugged at the sleeve of an officer who was using a periscope.

'Are they in?'

The officer stepped down and looked at the expectant faces. His own face was deathly pale. 'No. A few got there, but they couldn't break into the trenches. The rest were cut down by the machine guns. They'll send the second wave, no doubt.'

This had a sobering effect. The second wave wouldn't have the advantage of surprise—as useless as it had proved to be. The Turkish gunners would be waiting for them to rise out of the trench.

The NCOs made their way down the line again, readying the second wave. Some men shook their mates' hands in case it proved a final farewell. Letters were exchanged with brief promises to send them on, if the worst happened.

The whistles blew again and the troops threw themselves at the parapet. Predictably, some men only got to expose their bodies above ground level before the machine-gunners cut them down, toppling them back into the trench. Those that got out barely advanced ten yards. The Turks were well aware of what the whistles meant and were more than ready.

'They won't do it, will they, Ben?' Galther asked in the awful silence, his voice hoarse and shaking.

'I think they will,' Hamilton said blankly. 'We're supposed to be keeping them busy.'

'But it's pointless! We're getting cut to pieces!'

Hamilton didn't answer. His head was filled with a buzzing sound, beneath which he thought were voices calling for his attention. It was taking all his willpower to ignore them.

Galther jumped violently when a passing NCO touched him on the shoulder.

'Wait for the whistle, mate.'

'Ben! I'm going to stick close to you,' Galther said desperately.

Hamilton gave him a strange look. 'That's fine, Galth. Whatever you reckon.'

The whistles blew a third time.

Again, the Turks were slow to respond. Perhaps they didn't expect the assault to continue. More likely, they were ordered to wait until the attacking line was fully exposed.

Hamilton managed to scramble unharmed over the parapet. Staying crouched, he began to run towards the Turkish lines, but was almost checked immediately when he found himself faced with the task of trying not to step on any of the dead and wounded. He ended up running with awkward hopping motions, placing his feet on patches of clear ground. Unwittingly, he was making it hard for Galther, who was trying to keep himself shadowed from the Turkish lines by Hamilton's body. The rifle fire grew in strength, then the machine guns opened up in earnest. Hamilton squeezed off a shot as he ran, then slowed a little as he tried to work the bolt action. He wasn't thinking about anything except the task of reaching the Turkish lines and fighting.

Three machine gun bullets tore into his chest in a diagonal pattern, the first smashing his heart and the life out of him in an instant, but the impact holding him upright long enough for the other bullets to strike, before he dropped to the ground. The same sweep of fire hit Galther in the left thigh and the right kneecap. He actually stumbled forward a few more steps before pitching to the dirt, falling right beside Hamilton.

Through a haze of pain, Galther understood what had happened. He lay, with his face pressed into the sand, staring at the gored chest of his friend. Hamilton's blank, open eyes said it all. From the ragged, bloodstained remains of his shirt something golden glittered in the morning sun. Galther used his last strength to reach out and grasp the charm, pulling it roughly over Hamilton's head. Only seconds later the firing eased to nothing again, leaving only sporadic sniping and the buzzing of flies over the battlefield.

That night stretcher-bearers risked their own lives to creep into no-man's-land and answer the cries of the wounded. If the Turks were aware, they didn't open fire. One of the stretcher parties stooped next to Hamilton, flipping him over and peering closely at his face.

'No,' one said, shortly. The other made to do the same with Galther, who responded with a groan at the man's touch.

'In the legs here. Lost a lot of blood, but we'd better take him. He's lasted all day,' the other said, after a brief inspection.

They rolled him onto the stretcher and struggled back to the forward line.

18

Gwen didn't realise Brendan was leaving the house until he was out the door. Her mind sleepily registered him rising from the bed, but she didn't know he had a light jacket and a pair of running shoes downstairs, otherwise his getting dressed might have alerted her. Next, she heard the front door click. After dozing for a few minutes more, Gwen suddenly realised what she had heard and leapt out of bed. Dizziness hit her and she had to stand still for a moment, before she could move to the window.

She looked out just in time to see Brendan round

the corner at the end of the street and disappear from view.

He didn't know where he was going. He awoke with an urge to walk—anywhere. Get out of the house and put some space around him.

Brendan's suicide attempt the night before had affected him deeply. He realised he was no longer in full control of his mind in many ways and that he had to be on his guard constantly. The excuse was there for him to use, but it wasn't any comfort. It would be easy to say he hadn't tried to kill himself and that it had been the demon inside of him—the *Setris*—manipulating and tormenting him, trying to drive him into an insanity where taking his own life would make perfect sense. That meant Brendan was a victim, not someone weak or ill.

But still, it was difficult to accept that he *had* allowed himself to be taken to the brink of killing himself. In fact, taken *over* the brink, because Gwen and Warden had saved his life. He had willingly allowed himself to be led into an action that defied his common sense and logic. Now, he was asking himself if he should doubt his every thought, every move and each word that he spoke. Who would be speaking? Himself, or the *Setris*? Was he truly possessed? Brendan's hand went to the charm hanging around his neck and he fingered the metal through the material of his shirt. He couldn't remember putting the thing on. It was like someone who got uncontrollably drunk during the night and couldn't remember the next morning what they had done. No matter how hard he tried he couldn't recall going into his office, taking the green tin down from the shelf, opening it and placing the charm over his head. He knew it must have happened some time after Jodie's funeral or Gwen would have seen it sooner. And the funeral had only been the day before last. Why couldn't he remember?

And why couldn't he take it off?

Brendan was walking down a main street now, unknowingly retracing Jeneatte Beason's footsteps to her death at the bridge. Early morning traffic sped past him, sometimes alarmingly close to the path, as the drivers tried to squeeze an extra second's advantage in the daily race to their workplace. Brendan hardly registered the constant stream of cars until a truck came thundering past with one of its rear-vision mirrors sweeping dangerously over the footpath. He ducked instinctively away, too late, but unharmed. It made Brendan stop, turn and stare after the truck. What if the truck had hit him? What if, completely by accident, the truck had mounted the kerb and run Brendan down? The *Setris* was supposed to be protecting him too, according to Warden's friend in England. But how does an ancient spirit from thousands of years before deal with an eight-tonne truck rolling out of control?

Standing and gazing after the truck, although it had since been swallowed by the distance, Brendan had a creeping sensation, between his shoulder blades, that someone was watching him. He spun around on his heel.

That part of the highway was bordered by old suburban brick-and-tile houses that, when they were built sixty years before, had never been expected to contend with a main road running past their doors. As the years passed and the road became wider to accommodate more lanes, the front gardens of these houses were slowly reclaimed until they were tiny splashes of lawn and flowering shrubs, cowering behind neat wooden fences and tended, mainly, by a generation of old-age pensioners struggling to keep their houses as real homes against the city getting larger and louder around them.

Brendan found himself in front of one of the houses. The brickwork was clean and the window sills and eaves freshly painted. The lawn was immaculately trimmed, edged by rose bushes and other plants in bright flower. Standing behind a low timber and wire fence was an old woman staring fixedly at him. She was dressed in a pleated frock, stockings and good shoes, and she clutched a matching handbag to her waist. Her face was heavily made up, powdered white with a touch of rouge on the cheeks, while her lips were a slash of red.

She continued to stare almost angrily at Brendan and he felt compelled to say something.

'Is there something wrong?' he called over the

noise of the passing traffic. Her reply was waspish, her reddened lips turning down at the corners.

'What business have you here?' she demanded in a high, thin voice.

'Business?' Brendan was puzzled, and confused by her anger. 'What do you mean? I'm just walking past.'

'I mean, what business have you with me?' she snapped impatiently.

'I'm sorry, I don't understand.'

'You have no right to be here!'

'Here? Where? What are you trying to say?' Brendan began to suspect the woman wasn't completely normal or perhaps suffering from senility. He was torn between moving away—because he was feeling too burdened already with his own problems to cope with someone else's—and humouring her to the point where he could leave without being too rude. He glanced at the house behind, expecting someone to come through the front door and take control of the situation. It was then Brendan noticed the house was tightly closed up and had an unmistakable unoccupied look about it. Looking further along the fence he also saw a 'For Sale' sign almost obscured by the colourful flowering shrubs surrounding it.

He began to feel something was wrong and his nerves reacted, bringing the hairs on the back of his neck alive. 'Do you live here?' he asked her carefully.

'Of course I do,' she said. 'I've lived here for over

forty years.' There was something about her which bewildered Brendan. Although the woman spoke to him, he saw she didn't follow him with her eyes and she didn't actually move herself. She stood immobile, frozen in her posture like a wax character. 'You have no place here,' she added with finality.

Brendan moved closer to the fence. 'What are you doing?' He didn't expect her to answer.

'Waiting for my husband.'

'Have you been waiting long?'

'Does it matter? I'm just waiting.'

He took a few steps to one side, looking at her from a different angle and uncaring what she might think of that. Before he could say anything more Brendan became aware of two youths roller-skating down the footpath towards them. He pressed himself back against the fence to give them room and watched them carefully as they passed. In turn, they stared at Brendan as they went by, uneasy with his examining them. He noticed neither of the boys even glanced at the old woman.

On an impulse he called to their retreating backs, 'Hey, do either of you guys know this lady?'

They twisted around without stopping, their skates clattering noisily on the gaps between the paving slabs. Both of them looked at him with puzzled, slightly frightened expressions. One called back, half-heartedly, something unintelligible, the words lost in the traffic. They didn't halt, but kept rolling away from Brendan down the footpath. Confused, he turned back to the woman.

'They couldn't see you,' he told her accusingly.

'What are you doing here?' she replied, as if she hadn't heard him.

Brendan realised with a shock he was talking to a ghost. She was the spirit of a woman who died while she was waiting for her husband to return and now was doomed to stand impatiently in her front yard for eternity. Fearfully, he started backing away from the fence.

'What's happening here?' he whispered to himself. 'What the hell's going on? Why can I see you?'

'What business is it of yours?' she snapped again, but this time he couldn't be sure she was even talking to him.

Brendan turned and hurried away, almost breaking into a run. He heard her call after him.

'You shouldn't be here!'

He didn't turn around to answer. Instead, he kept moving at a fast walk, his head down and watching the pavement at his feet. He didn't want to look around him anymore in case he saw more ghosts. More tormented spirits.

Then he nearly walked straight into one.

He stopped just in time, pulling up short as he was about to bump into someone. He looked up, alarmed, and stared into the tragic eyes of a young girl. She was thin and wasted, her skin pale and unhealthy-looking. Dark hair hung lifelessly from her scalp. As he drew in a sharp breath, startled and scared by her gaze, Brendan realised that her image shimmered slightly.

'I see your mind's been opened,' she told him sympathetically. 'Don't be surprised if you don't like what you can see. And don't let any of us play with you. You won't like it.'

'Who the fuck are you?' Brendan snarled, twisting away and earning odd looks from several people close by. The girl's ghost let out a giggle of delight and waved him goodbye as he moved quickly on.

Brendan kept moving, his thoughts in turmoil as he worried over what she had said—that his mind had been 'opened'. Who had opened it? There was an obvious answer to that. The *Setris* had found a new way to torment him. Understanding this, Brendan struggled to keep calm. He walked past the ghost of a small boy who sat disconsolately on the kerb, his chin in his hands, as he stared with eternal longing through the traffic at something he must have wanted very badly. Brendan wondered how many times the tiny spectre had attempted to cross the road only to be crushed again and again under the uncaring tyres. And what about the drivers of those cars? Did they feel anything as their vehicle unknowingly smashed through the ghostly child? Did they experience a moment of doubt or end up having a bad day, as if they'd walked under a ladder or chanced across a black cat?

Brendan was passing a small park with playground equipment designed, he guessed, to keep children entertained while someone attended to the shopping in the centre. The park was built on a grassy knoll and he was stunned to see a corpse hanging from a tree crowning the highest point of the playground. Frightened, but perversely attracted, Brendan moved closer to see, walking with an effort up the slight rise. The hanging corpse was a man, his hands bound behind his back, but his legs were free. The clothing on the figure was old-fashioned, the pants and shirt ill-fitting and roughly made like the dirty leather vest he wore. The tree, from its size, must have been hundreds of years old and Brendan realised the executed man must come from a bygone era, too. He went close enough to stand looking directly up at the body. The corpse's feet swung level with Brendan's face.

Someone said, in a strangled, pained voice, 'Cut me down.'

Brendan felt a shock of fresh fear and he took a step backwards away from the corpse. Staring up into the bloated face, above where the rope bit cruelly into the man's neck, he saw the man's eyes were open. He was glaring down at Brendan with an odd mixture of anger and pleading.

'Cut me down,' he repeated in the same, dreadful voice. 'Cut me down and take my place. They said, if I could find someone to take my place, they would hang them instead. It's the law.'

'Dear God,' Brendan groaned. He could almost feel the rope catching under his own throat, choking him and the pain of asphyxiation exploding with bright, agonising stars inside the blackness of his mind. As if to tease him or drive him to sympathy the corpse began to kick its legs, re-enacting his final death-throes.

'Stop! Stop that,' Brendan shouted frantically. 'I can't help you. I'm alive.'

'That's why you can take my place,' the corpse told him, the tortured words punctuated by his frantic struggles against the noose.

Brendan turned and fled, running from the park back towards the road. He misjudged the slope and when he reached the pavement he was going too fast and nearly ran on into the traffic. He stopped and teetered dangerously on the kerbing, windmilling his arms for balance. Several cars honked their horns angrily at him as they swerved away. Recovering, but still feeling shaken, Brendan stood, out of breath and undecided. He glanced back at the tree and saw the corpse was still kicking its legs futilely, as if aware Brendan would look again and give him one more chance at life. A panic rose in Brendan's chest and, worse, he feared it was going to get the better of him. He was losing control. Desperately, he looked from side to side, trying to work out what he should do to escape the madness.

With a screech of tyres a car pulled up directly in front of him, causing more havoc and anger on the busy road. It was Gwen, and she leaned over to the passenger side and shoved the door open.

'Get in, Brendan,' she called. 'Quickly, before we cause a bloody accident.'

He was so dazed and confused it took a moment for him to recognise her and understand what was happening. To the accompaniment of more passing drivers leaning on their horn buttons and yelling shouted curses Brendan tumbled into the seat and pulled the door closed after him. Before he had a chance to fasten the safety belt, Gwen had the car accelerating hard back into the traffic stream.

'I woke up this morning and you'd disappeared. What were you doing wandering the streets at this time of day?' she asked lightly, trying not to make it sound as if she was reprimanding him or that she'd had a fright. Actually, Gwen had been alarmed at the sight of Brendan standing at the edge of the road, looking as if he was going to step out in front of the next large vehicle.

'I needed a walk—a breath of fresh air,' he answered dully.

'Are you okay?'

'Not really.'

'Why? What's wrong?'

'I—I can see things. People, their ghosts,' he ended, shaking his head.

'I know that, Brendan. We're trying to help you, you know that. But if you walk out of the house without—'

'No, I mean now. All the time. I can see these ghosts all the time.'

Gwen took her eyes off the road long enough to give him a searching look. 'Give me a second,' she said. At the next corner Gwen turned the car into a short, quiet sidestreet and parked at the first available space in front of a house. After setting the handbrake, she twisted in her seat so she could look directly at Brendan.

'What do you mean?' she said firmly. 'Brendan, I want you to tell me exactly what's happening.'

To answer her Brendan sighed shakily and made a point of slowly searching the suburban landscape around. He pointed through the windscreen. 'See that woman standing at the top of her stairs?'

Gwen's gaze followed where he was pointing. 'In the blue dress? Sure, what about her?'

'Okay,' he nodded and kept looking. 'What about that kid sitting under the tree in that yard? He's got a schoolbag or something between his legs.'

'Yes, I can see him, too,' Gwen told him patiently.

Coming up the footpath towards them there was an elderly man dressed in a very old-fashioned suit. Several rows of military ribbons were on his breast. He walked in as soldierly a manner as his ageing body would allow him, his head held proudly high and his arms swinging, but he moved slowly and stiffly, too. Brendan wasn't going to mention him, because the old man seemed so real and *there*, but while he searched the streets more for other people he said, 'You can see the old fellow marching up the road, can't you?'

Brendan expected Gwen to say 'yes', but there was a pause before she asked cautiously, 'Where?'

'There, in front of that house with the white porch . . .' Brendan's voice trailed away, because as he spoke the old soldier vanished. In the same instant, catching his eye, another figure appeared at the very end of the street and began walking towards them. Brendan immediately recognised the walk. It was a marching gait and the dark suit was unmistakable. 'My God,' he uttered quietly. 'The poor old bastard just walks the street, forever and ever. He must have died on his way to a memorial service. Maybe he even died on Remembrance Day.'

'What?' Gwen asked, frustrated. 'Who are you taking about?'

'He's down at the end of the street now. An old man—he must be an old soldier, because he's wearing a chestful of ribbons. He's walking up the footpath towards us on the right-hand side.'

'Brendan, I can't see anyone like that.' Gwen pointed at the footpath. 'That side of the street?' When he nodded she added, 'It's empty, as far as I can see.'

'See what I mean?' Brendan's momentary fascination with the old soldier's spirit faded and his expression returned to reflect his own torment as he remembered instead the hanging corpse in the tree. 'How the hell am I going to put up with this all the time?'

She didn't answer. He watched as Gwen reached under his feet for her handbag. She produced a small hand-mirror and attempted to angle it so she could see the section of street Brendan was talking about. He tried to guide her until the old man's ghost vanished once more and reappeared at the end of the street. Gwen shook her head.

'I didn't see him.'

'I—I think this is different. These are just ghosts, I mean normal ghosts.' Brendan paused and shrugged helplessly at the incongruity of this. 'Nothing to do with the *Setris*. At least, not directly.'

'How come? What's causing it?'

'I don't really know, except some of them talked to me. There was a corpse hanging in a tree—' Brendan grimaced. He didn't want to explain it. 'And there was a girl. She looked in pretty bad shape. I think she might have been a drug addict. She said my mind had been opened and I might not like what I can see. I just ran after that, and I could hear her laughing at me. God, Gwen, they're everywhere. Everywhere I look.' He looked at her and Gwen could see he was near to breaking.

She started the car and said calmly, 'Okay, then we'd better get you home. I'll call Warden and tell him to come over as soon as he can. He was coming for lunch anyway. He'll want to know about this.'

'I don't know if that's a good idea,' Brendan said, almost in a whisper. 'Going home, I mean.'

'Why?'

He was remembering one of his own thoughts from a day that seemed a long time ago now, when they began clearing out the spare room for his office and he'd decided his house would be full of the ghosts his mother claimed she could talk to and hear. Now, Brendan was thinking his home might be the worst place he could run to, if he wanted to escape the Dead.

'No, forget it. I—I'm not thinking straight,' he said, suddenly deciding to keep his thoughts to himself. There was nowhere he could run, if that was the case. He would have to face his own house sooner or later and with a fatalistic despair he wanted to get it over and done with.

'Don't worry too much, Bren, there must be something we can do,' Gwen said. But she didn't sound convinced.

Predictably, it was Warden who arrived with an answer.

'This is Doctor Robert Lawson,' he announced, ushering through the front door a thin, bespectacled man who looked to be in his late forties. Lawson nodded a nervous greeting to Gwen, who couldn't stop herself from showing surprise that Warden wasn't alone. The doctor peered past her into the hallway.

'Does he know?' Gwen asked Warden, pointedly. She wasn't sure if she should be annoyed or not. Things were difficult enough as it was.

'He knows everything—and don't worry. Robert's not a sceptic who's here to tell us we're all going crazy. He might be able to really help Brendan. Where is he?'

'In the lounge. He hasn't moved since I got him home. He doesn't want to go into any other part of the house yet, in case he sees something he doesn't want to see.'

Warden lowered his voice. 'How is he feeling?'

'Not good. He's very depressed at the moment.'

'I can understand that,' Warden said grimly.

Gwen led the way into the lounge room. Brendan was sitting in a single chair, holding his head in his hands and staring down at the carpet between his feet. He looked up as everyone came into the room, but he didn't register any surprise at the newcomer. He listlessly shook Lawson's hand after Warden introduced them.

'A doctor?' Brendan said wearily. 'Have you come to take me away in a straightjacket?'

Lawson regarded him for a moment. 'Actually, I am a psychiatrist, Brendan. Warden didn't ask me here because of that, though.'

Warden quickly explained, 'Robert's regarded as one of the leading experts in the country for using hypnosis in medicine.'

There was a silence. Lawson smiled sadly and said, 'They say I'm one of the best quacks around.'

Brendan seemed almost disinterested, while Gwen looked alarmed. 'Warden, I don't know about this—' she began, but he cut her off.

'Robert might not try anything at all, but I figured it was a good idea for us to have the option. I would have called you, but Robert's clinic isn't far out of the way and I took a punt and dropped in. He hasn't got very long, before he has to get back. We're lucky it's still early in the morning.'

'What do you think you can do?' Gwen asked Lawson.

'It's actually Warden's idea,' he admitted, moving closer to Brendan and squatting down so he could look directly into his eyes. 'He told me you had said Brendan's mind has been "opened", is that correct?' He glanced over his shoulder to see Gwen nod, then he turned his attention back to Brendan, who returned his stare resignedly. Lawson directed his comments towards him now. 'And that's basically what I do, Brendan. When I hypnotise people, in certain cases anyway, I open their stronger, subconscious mind to a suggestion and quite often it sticks. Of course, sometimes it doesn't,' he added meaningfully.

Gwen was doubtful. 'You think Brendan's only been hypnotised?'

Still looking deep into Brendan's eyes Lawson let out a small chuckle, letting Gwen know he understood her doubts about him. 'No, after everything I've heard from Warden in the last thirty minutes, I doubt very much whether your problems stem from something so simple. You're lucky that I've known Warden for some time. Otherwise, I certainly wouldn't be here. Your story is just too incredible,' he added matter-of-factly.

'You should see it from my side,' Brendan said dryly, showing some animation for the first time since he had arrived home.

Gesturing at Lawson, Warden told them, 'There's a theory that some supernatural phenomena might be a psychic projection of the victim's own mind. That Brendan would be creating the ghosts himself from his own imagination. We know that's not the case here. It's just how I know Robert. He's been good enough to discuss the theory a lot with me.'

Lawson wore a small smile. 'If I charged you for the time, I could afford to retire.'

The banter between the two men helped ease some of the tension created by having a newcomer in their midst. Only Brendan was still uncomfortable, nearly squirming under the doctor's constant appraising stare.

Gwen asked, 'So, what do you think you might be able to do?'

'Well, like I said, I don't think Brendan's suffering from something so simple as being hypnotised. But while the cause of his problems might be quite beyond our understanding, the effect could be very similar.'

'You might be able to hypnotise him, so the *Setris* can't get to him?'

Lawson finally dragged his gaze from Brendan, who visibly relaxed. The doctor stayed crouched down, but twisted around so he was speaking to all of them. He was obviously troubled with discussing plainly such an incredible subject. 'Look, I can't really comprehend what you're dealing with here. It's totally beyond anything I've experienced before, short of horror books and scary movies.

But if I understand it right, this thing that's—that's haunting you, as you say, is practically capable of walking into the room now, just like we have. I can't hypnotise Brendan into a state where he won't recognise somebody or some *thing* has walked into the room. That's the stuff of circuses and stage show quacks. I'm only hoping I can deal with today's problem, by trying accepted methods of hypnosis that have been used in medicine for some years now. Warden explained to me that Brendan was told "his mind had been opened", which was what prompted him to think of me in the first place. I'm simply hoping to close again that "openness" and basically bring Brendan back to the same level as we are.'

Gwen was frowning. 'Alternatively, you could hypnotise us to the same level as Brendan. That we could see the same ghosts as he does?'

'Possibly,' Lawson nodded slowly. 'But only someone like yourself perhaps, because of what you've been subjected to lately. The theory is, it's what Brendan's experienced recently that's allowed his mind to *be* opened. It's a matter of acceptance. A normal person wouldn't usually accept the notion that we're constantly surrounded by unhappy spirits of the Dead, therefore I couldn't put them into a state where they can always see them. It's like the fanciful idea that a good hypnotist might coerce someone into being their slave or sexual partner, but the reality is people won't allow themselves, through hypnosis, to adopt something they wouldn't normally accept, understand? On the other hand an ability to, say, quit smoking is readily acceptable and therefore hypnosis is often tried.'

'Because of what's been happening lately, Brendan believes now that we are surrounded by ghosts and unhappy spirits of the Dead, therefore he was open to the suggestion he should see them?'

'Exactly! However, his acceptance of that probably didn't come easily—'

'He thought he was going crazy,' Gwen interrupted.

Lawson nodded, 'Right, so it's a door in his mind that's been almost forced open. With a bit of help from me, Brendan's subconscious is probably more than willing to close it again.'

Warden was nervously waiting for a chance to ask something. 'Robert, are you saying Brendan can actually see these ghosts? That they exist, but normally we don't want to recognise them?'

'As always, it's a matter of what you choose to believe, Warden,' Lawson said carefully. 'It's possible his mind has been opened to something —perhaps another dimension—that we can't normally perceive, but whether that dimension actually exists or is a product of Brendan's or someone else's imagination, we still can't answer.'

Warden laughed. 'There's still the element of doubt that sceptics like you will hide behind.'

'It helps me sleep at night.'

Warden looked at his watch. 'I'd like to keep you

here all day, Robert. But if you still want to get to your clinic on time, we'd better try something now, if that's what we want to do.'

Lawson became very serious and turned to Brendan. 'I'd like this to be your decision, Brendan. I can try and put you into a state of hypnosis, ask you some questions and with your answers attempt to suggest that your ability to see these ghosts be suppressed. That's a little simplified, but basically what I *can* do. Do you want us to try?'

Brendan shrugged without hesitating. 'What have I got to lose? I doubt you'll be able to put me under, anyway,' he said, looking away distractedly.

Lawson spoke firmly, making sure Brendan was still listening. 'I can see one potential problem. In certain cases of schizophrenia, for example, that I've treated, where the patient has a second, suppressed personality the hypnotic state has allowed that other person to emerge hot and strong. It can cause some—unexpected—developments.'

Gwen understood him first. 'You mean the *Setris* might take over his body?'

'Only his personality, Gwen. And only superficially during the hypnotic state—' Lawson stopped and shook his head. 'I don't know. I'm sorry, but I don't really know. This is all beyond my experience. I just thought I'd better warn you of this, in case it happened.'

'It could be dangerous,' Warden said quietly. 'We think this thing has already caused two deaths.'

By the way Lawson looked at Warden, this was obviously something he hadn't bargained for, but before he could comment Brendan spoke in a low, desperate voice.

'Look, we've got to try it anyway. This morning was a walking, living fucking nightmare that's going to get worse. I won't be able to live with it for very long at all. I'll try anything to get some of my damned sanity back.'

After a moment Lawson said, 'That's important. He really wants to shut this thing out of his mind and get back to normal. It might even be easier than I thought.'

'Can we stop at any time?' Gwen asked. 'If it gets out of control, can we just stop?'

'Of course we can. In fact, most patients wake themselves out of hypnosis at the first discomfort of any kind.'

Gwen looked at the two of them in turn. Lawson sounded confident and Warden seemed to have faith in his friend. She didn't know enough to argue anymore.

So she nodded her agreement at the doctor.

Brendan stayed seated where he was, while Warden moved another lounge chair directly in front of him for Lawson to be comfortable, too. Now the doctor regarded Brendan's face with a deep, penetrating gaze and he began to speak in a low, melodic voice.

'Brendan, I want you to relax. Don't worry about what I'm trying to do here, don't let yourself fight me and don't try to help me either. Just listen to what I tell you and let yourself relax. Think of yourself as listening to some of your favourite music. You're taking it easy and there's nothing to worry about.'

Lawson's voice droned on, insistent, yet with a soothing quality that Gwen marvelled at. Warden, who had seen it before, caught her eye and tipped her a wink. It wasn't long before Brendan's head began to nod downwards involuntarily. Lawson invited him to keep his eyes closed and let himself sleep. A minute later Brendan seemed to do just that—fall into a deep sleep with his head lolling on his chest.

The doctor held his breath a moment and waited. Brendan didn't stir. Lawson whispered over his shoulder, 'That was quick. He was very responsive. Usually on the first time they fight like hell and I can barely get them under. This guy's well and truly gone. Has he been hypnotised before? That's what it comes across like.'

'I don't think so,' Gwen whispered back. 'I'm sure I would have heard about it.'

'Hmm,' Lawson put a finger on his lips as he thought. 'Well, we'll be thankful for small mercies.' He leaned closer to Brendan and spoke slowly and clearly.

'Brendan, can you hear me? It's Robert Lawson, remember? You can call me Robert.'

Brendan stirred in his sleep and mumbled. A frown creased his forehead and he tried again. 'Yes,' he said, his voice thick.

'Okay, Brendan. I'm going to ask you a few questions and you answer them any way you please. Take as much time as you like. Let's start with this morning. Why did you leave the house?'

Brendan's replies came in a sleepy voice that needed patience to listen to. 'I—I couldn't sleep. I needed to get out of the house, get some fresh air.'

'Why?' Gwen asked. 'Why couldn't he sleep?'

Lawson told her quietly over his shoulder, 'Don't expect revelations with every question, Gwen. A lot of his life is still quite normal in many ways, don't forget. Not sleeping and needing fresh air is probably all that happened.' He turned his attention back to Brendan. 'Where did you go? Where did you *want* to go?'

'Nowhere—anywhere,' Brendan shrugged in his sleep, looking slightly comical and a little childish.

'All right, so you went down the road. What did you see? What do you remember most?'

Brendan frowned again. 'A woman. I met a woman.'

'Did you talk to her?'

'Yes.'

'What about?'

'She said—she said I had no business being there.'

'Why? What were you doing wrong?'

'She was dead, and I wasn't. It upset her, I think.'

Lawson drew in his breath with a sharp hiss. He glanced at Gwen and Warden in turn.

Warden muttered, 'I'll bet he's only just starting.'

'I've never heard anyone lie or even exaggerate under hypnosis,' Lawson said wonderingly. 'He must be mistaken.'

'Did you think I was making all this up?' Warden prodded him gently.

'Of course not. I wouldn't be here, remember?' Lawson pressed his lips together. 'Brendan, why do you say she was dead? What do you mean?'

Now an expression of frustration flickered across Brendan's' face. 'She was dead—a ghost. I could see it, after a while. And no one else could see her, anyhow. Two kids went past and they didn't even look her way.'

'What did you do then?'

'I got scared and ran away. I just left her. I didn't know what else to do.'

'Why didn't you come home?'

'I wasn't thinking straight. I didn't know what I was doing. I left her, that's all.' Brendan looked guilty.

'That's okay, Brendan. You didn't do anything wrong, don't worry,' Lawson said easily. 'So, what did you do next?'

'There was a young girl. I—I nearly ran straight into her. She told me my mind was opened and I wouldn't like what I might see. She—she laughed about that as I turned away from her. Then I saw a child, a small boy. He must have been killed trying to cross the road. He was sitting on the kerb and watching the traffic. I think he would try and cross the road again. I mean again and again, and get killed every time. Then I saw the man hanging in the tree.'

'Hanging from a tree?'

'Like, he was hanged. With a noose. But he was still alive and he asked me to take his place. He started kicking and dying all over again and telling me I could take his place, because I was still alive and he wasn't—' Brendan's hand went involuntarily to his neck. Behind Lawson, Gwen let out a sigh of sympathy.

'Take it easy for a moment, Brendan,' Lawson commanded. 'Let yourself relax some more. Have a few deep breaths.' When Brendan was visibly more at ease Lawson looked to Warden. 'What do you think? This is more your area of expertise than mine. I just got him talking.'

'It sounds pretty bad, but it's the sort of thing we've come to expect,' Warden said grimly. 'Even damned corpses hanging from trees. Can you help him?'

Lawson thought for a moment. 'This is all pretty wild stuff. I can hardly believe I'm here listening to this, but the same theory still applies. Let's give it a try and see what happens.' Again, he moved forward closer to Brendan.

'Brendan, listen to me carefully now. What you have seen this morning is not *right*, do you understand? It is not normal and you are being forced to accept these things against your will. You have been told to believe these ghosts and spirits are with us, but it is not your choice to believe this.

You can go back to making your own choices now, Brendan. You can be strong enough to recognise these things cannot be so and you do not want them to *be* so. You can't see ghosts, Brendan. Nobody can see them. Tell yourself you can't see them.'

As Lawson spoke, Brendan's face was twitching with emotions. Sometimes he pulled away from the doctor, pushing himself back in his seat in an effort to get away. Then, in the silence with Lawson waiting for an answer, he suddenly leaned forward and whispered harshly, his face contorted with pain.

'The dead are everywhere. They *have* to be. Countless millions of displaced souls are trapped here. We *should* see them. We should see them in a *crowd*.'

Lawson answered him calmly. 'No, until this morning you couldn't see them, Brendan. *That's* the way it should be. That's the way it will be, when you awaken.' Brendan reacted to this with more agitated movements in his seat, his face moving through different pained expressions like a child who is trying to swallow a bitter medicine. Again Lawson spoke over his shoulder to the two watchers. 'That was too soon to make a suggestion,' he said, annoyed with himself. 'I needed to gain his confidence a little more, but I'm a bit thrown by this whole situation.'

'What if it worked?' Gwen asked. 'Is that it? It's finished? He won't see ghosts anymore, when he wakes up?'

'Hopefully, but post-hypnotic suggestion usually has a shelf-life, if you like. He'll have to come and see me several times and we'll repeat the process. It will only be more firmly embedded in his mind that way.'

His eyes closed, Brendan said clearly, 'It would be easier if I joined them.'

'No, Brendan—' Gwen began to say, her voice rising with concern, but Lawson stopped her by holding up his hand.

'Brendan, killing yourself is not the answer,' he said, raising his own voice. 'There is no peace of mind for you that way. You mustn't think of suicide.'

When Brendan spoke next it was with a different voice. It was harsh and guttural, laced with a strange accent, shocking them.

'I am destined to be one of the dead. I hear a calling and I have to answer.'

'Who the hell was that?' Gwen whispered.

'I'll give you one guess,' Warden told her nervously. 'Brendan! You don't even have to listen to these voices—this calling. Make your own choice,' he added, taking a cue from the doctor.

'I have no choice. I have no life of my own. I belong to Set and he has sent his servant to guide me down.'

'Robert, I don't like this,' Gwen said urgently. 'Something's not right. I think you'd better bring him out of it.'

Lawson was already nodding. 'I was just about

to say that.' He held a hand in front of Brendan's face and clicked his fingers several times.

'Brendan, listen to me now. Only listen to me, nobody else. I want you to wake up and when you do, your mind will be closed to any spirits or ghosts you could see before. Remember how we talked about that? Your mind will close the door that was opened against your better judgement. You will make that choice for yourself.' He clicked his fingers again. 'Come on now, Brendan. You can wake up and talk to us.'

Brendan didn't open his eyes, but continued to squirm uncomfortably with awful expressions crossing his face. Lawson looked at Warden and Gwen.

'Don't worry,' he said quickly. 'Sometimes they need several invitations to wake up. Especially the ones that go under easily. I threw in repeating that suggestion about not seeing his ghosts for good luck, more than anything. I haven't really had a chance to work on that and I was too quick before—'

Lawson was cut off by Gwen letting out a short scream and suddenly lunging past him. Warden's face had gone a deathly pale. Lawson spun back around to see what was happening.

Brendan was sitting absolutely still, his eyes wide open.

He wasn't breathing.

19

'Dear God, is he dead?' Lawson asked stupidly.

'He will be if we don't move fast!' Gwen snapped, her voice trembling all the same. 'Warden, help me get him on the floor.'

Lawson rose from his seat slowly, his legs unsteady, and spread his arms while he stared at them handling Brendan to the carpet. 'This isn't me, Gwen. I've got nothing to do with this. How the hell could I make someone die? It's just hypnosis, for God's sake!' he finished, croaking as the words stuck in his throat.

Gwen was ripping open the front of Brendan's

shirt and pleading to Warden. 'Tell me you know what's going on! Why has he stopped breathing?'

He stared back at her, distress written plainly all over his face. 'I don't know, Gwen,' he said hoarsely. 'This is supposed to be the last thing the *Setris* wants. I'm sorry, but I just don't know.'

Gwen had her ear to Brendan's chest. 'Shit, his heart's *stopped*.' She straightened and pressed her hands against Brendan's sternum. 'I've got to do cardiac massage. Warden, you'll have to give him mouth-to-mouth. Do you know how?'

He nodded jerkily and moved closer to Brendan's head.

Lawson said shakily, 'I'll call an ambulance.'

At his words a strange instinct came into Gwen's mind—a feeling that any more outside interference would only make things worse. She almost shouted, 'No! I'll get him back myself, or not at all. *Don't* call an ambulance. Not yet, anyway.'

Lawson faltered. 'But I'm a doctor, Gwen. I have to do what's best.'

'Then get the hell out of here. Forget you ever *came* here.' She didn't waste any more time or words on Lawson, concentrating on her task with Brendan. Warden was bending down to breathe into Brendan's open mouth and didn't spare Lawson a glance.

The doctor hesitated, then came to a decision. He backed nervously out the door.

Brendan was falling.

He knew he was falling, because the blackness

around him seemed to tumble past in splotches of dark colour. Without this, it would have been like being suspended impossibly in mid-air, because there was no sensation of the air rushing past his body or pulling at his clothes. He flailed his limbs uselessly, striking out at the emptiness. Fear began to fill him about what would happen when he hit the bottom of this abyss—if there was a bottom. Brendan was in such a state of shock and disbelief he hadn't yet found time to be frightened about exactly what was happening to him. Only that he might be hurt when he reached the end of it.

The falling ended abruptly. He didn't feel any pain. He didn't even feel any sense of stopping, or if there was, it was hidden by a sudden transition from the blackness to a blinding white light. With a yell of surprise and distress for his hurting eyes Brendan threw a hand up in front of his face, attempting to squint through his fingers. Despite this, he still couldn't open his eyes to try, the light was so intense. He vaguely realised there was no heat in it. He also understood something else—any fears he held were gone. He had no idea what was happening, where he was or how he got there. But he understood this was not a place to be frightened. Fear didn't belong here.

Then he became aware of other presences within the light near him and a soft murmuring of many voices. He tried again to see, cracking his eyelids open a fraction, but they were forced painfully shut by the glaring light.

'Where am I?' he called, without thinking. 'Can somebody tell me? Help me?'

The voices around him changed and he knew his call had caused some sort of confusion. It wasn't so much what he heard, but rather what he felt, like an atmosphere in the place that he was closely attuned to. Brendan couldn't understand it. He didn't have the courage to attempt searching around to find the answers. The brilliant light rendered him as good as blind and he was worried what might happen if he tried moving.

Someone called his name, startling him. There was something instantly recognisable about the caller, but at the same time something different or odd, which stopped Brendan putting a name to the voice.

'Brendan?' the caller came again. It was a woman. 'Is that you? What are you doing here?'

'Who's that?' he asked loudly. 'Where are you? I can't see you for all this light.'

There was a puzzled pause. 'Brendan, do you know where you are?' Something in the question brought a nervousness crawling into Brendan's stomach.

'No, of course not. I don't even know how I got here—' Memories flooded back to him about Robert Lawson and the hypnosis session, but the last real thing Brendan could remember was a feeling of overwhelming tiredness.

'Am I asleep? Is this what happens when you're hypnotised?' he asked, though he knew the questions were most likely ridiculous, but he had to ask something, just to keep contact with the reassuring voice.

'No, you're not asleep.' Again, there was a confusion in the woman's words and an indefinable quality that nagged at Brendan for recognition.

'Who are you?' he asked.

There was another moment of silence.

'I'm your mother, Brendan.'

The reply stunned him.

'What?' he burst out finally. But before the woman said anything more, Brendan knew it was the truth. It all made sense—the long, strange falling to the brilliant light with its feeling of safety. The lack of fear, despite the totally alien surroundings. It all fitted with the many accounts of near-death experiences he'd read and heard about. And he'd failed to recognise his own mother's voice, because she sounded much younger and stronger, not like the ailing, ageing woman he last saw when she was alive.

'Where are you?' Brendan said, trying vainly once more to see something in the surrounding white glare. His mind and emotions were reeling now.

Instead of answering, his mother said, 'Why are you here, Brendan? You're not supposed to be here yet. I know that.'

'I—I don't know.'

'You must go back.'

'Go back? How can I? I don't know how I got here!' Brendan felt his panic begin to rise again.

With every passing moment he was understanding more about where he was and what was happening to him. With one wrong move he would be here forever and an instinct deep inside him told Brendan he wasn't ready for that, yet.

It wasn't his time.

Through his eyelids he detected a shadow, a darkness as complete as the light, moving around him. With the same instinctive understanding, Brendan knew this darkness was something to be feared and that it no more belonged here than he did. He could feel the alarm and confusion it was suddenly causing among the others with him in the light-filled world. The shadow was an unprecedented intrusion that no one knew how to deal with.

The awful truth came to Brendan in a rush. This whole thing was a mistake. An error in judgement. Something had gone badly wrong for him—and for the *Setris*. For everyone.

'Brendan, what are you doing here?' his mother called, with a touch of desperation that also didn't belong. It seemed a desecration in this place. 'What have you brought with you? What have you done?'

'It's not me! I don't know what's happening,' he cried. He felt so helpless, completely blinded by the light and unwilling to take a single step in any direction in case it brought disaster. Summoning up his courage, screwing up every ounce, he asked, 'Am I dead? Is that what's happened?'

'I told you, you're not supposed to be here yet.

It's not your time,' she added, echoing his own belief.

The ominous darkness was skittering around the edge of Brendan's awareness. It made him think of an animal that has suddenly found itself released, but doesn't know what to do with the unexpected freedom and space around it.

It's the Setris, *and he doesn't know what the hell's going on either—he doesn't know where he is,* Brendan told himself, a moment of grim satisfaction breaking through all his other thoughts and emotions. *It must have been the hypnosis. It's thrown everything out of control.*

'You have to leave,' his mother said, her voice suddenly close to his face. Brendan thought he caught the scent of her favourite perfume and knew that would be for his benefit. She added from somewhere nearby, 'You have to leave and take the evil with you.'

On an impulse he reached out towards her voice, but he couldn't grasp anything. 'I can't! I don't know how!'

'What have you done, my son?' she asked sadly. It hurt him to think she blamed him.

Something new brought another change in the air. Though he was still unable to open his eyes Brendan detected a different shifting in the brilliant light and felt a sense of some momentous event that was about to take place. It both exhilarated and frightened him, and he tensed himself to expect anything.

'What's happening?' he called aloud.

No one answered.

'Mum, can you hear me? Tell me what's happening?'

Again, there was no answer and Brendan realised with a touch of deep sadness it was too late. His mother was gone and he was alone. Except—he saw with growing panic—for the shifting, frightening patch of darkness that still moved within the light.

And something else. Something that was immense and getting closer with every breath. The darkness sensed it too, its movements becoming skittish and jerky.

The white light surrounding him flared to an impossible brightness that burned through Brendan's eyelids and left him seeing only splotches of colour against a black background.

And he was falling again.

20

Gwen felt tears stinging her eyes and she took a deep breath, forcing herself to stay calm. *This was no time for any of them to lose control.* She had been doing the cardiac massage for over two minutes and Brendan hadn't responded. She caught Warden's eye and they exchanged despairing expressions. Gwen opened her mouth to say something—anything to encourage them both, when she felt Brendan give a small jerk under her hands. With a cry of triumph she put her ear once more to his chest.

'It's beating again on its own! Thank God!' She

listened further and felt his chest rise against his face. 'He's breathing, too. The heart's still unsteady, but quite strong.' A relief swept over her and she started to tremble with relief. Watching her from where he squatted on the floor, Warden appeared just as stressed.

'Will he be all right?' he asked hoarsely.

Gwen took a moment to reply, then she nodded weakly. 'I think so.'

There was a tense silence as she checked Brendan's pulse and breathing. Warden slowly got up and walked through the house to the back door and out into the yard. The morning sunlight made him squint. He had no idea what he was doing, except answering a need to get back in touch with the normal world again. It didn't make much sense and he felt guilty about leaving Gwen, but it helped to breathe the fresh air. Immediately, his mind began to work furiously to understand what had happened and what they could do about it.

What the hell were we going to do if he didn't come back? How were we going to explain that he's died of some demonic possession? Maybe I should be getting the hell out of this crazy set-up, before I end up in serious trouble?

Warden shook his head irritably—he mustn't think like that. Brendan and Gwen needed his help.

He moved slowly around the outside of the house until he came onto the front lawn. A car drove past, its driver looking at Warden curiously. Warden had a curious sense of being strange or attracting attention, so he bent down to pick up a morning newspaper in an effort to maintain an appearance of normality. Absently he slit his thumbnail through the binding tape, opened the newspaper out and scanned the front page. He didn't read the words. Instead, beyond the newspaper he scanned the street and neighbouring houses for anyone watching him. He was unexpectedly nervous too, but the garden and everything surrounding it was as peaceful and innocent as it could be in the bright early sunshine. From the upper floor of the house he heard a door open and figured it was Gwen getting something medicinal from the bathroom. He decided he really should be back in the house helping her.

Warden returned through the back door. In the kitchen he realised the newspaper was still in his hand. He went to throw it onto the dining table, but that was covered by all the old family papers they'd been searching through the night before. Someone must have made an effort to bring them in from the lounge and spent time trying to sort them out.

A notion flashed through his mind that simply disturbing the old documents might have triggered Brendan's 'visions'. After all, the mere act of discovering the *Setris'* charm started everything else. Warden tossed the newspaper on top of the stove instead, just in case there was a clue among the papers that might be hidden, if he rearranged anything now. At the bottom of the stairs he met

Gwen who was coming down with a bottle of pain killers.

'You okay?' he asked softly.

She nodded and whispered wearily, 'He'll have a hell of a headache. Not surprising, of course. God, I hope we did the right thing. Do you think Lawson will tell anyone what happened?'

'I doubt it. He'll only damage his own reputation. I'd better give him a call and tell him Bren's okay, though. He *is* okay, isn't he?'

'As far as I can tell.'

There was an awkward pause, then Warden said, 'Jesus, Gwen, he nearly *died*.'

She gave him a strange look, then pushed past him towards the lounge, saying as she went, 'Maybe we should have let him.'

At Gwen's touch Brendan groaned, opened his eyes again for a moment and moved slightly. He was still lying where they left him.

'We'd better get him upstairs and onto the bed,' Warden said, dropping with Gwen down beside Brendan.

She shook her head. 'Let's just put him on the chair first. If he suddenly goes crazy while we're all trying to carry him up the stairs, God knows what could happen.'

They man-handled Brendan back onto the lounge chair. Warden shoved the second seat close so they could put his feet up as well, then went into the kitchen for a damp cloth, which Gwen took with a nod of thanks and began patting Brendan's face. His eyes flickered a few times, then remained half-open and unfocused.

'Brendan, are you all right?' Gwen said softly.

He ran his tongue over his lips and nodded slowly, without saying anything.

Warden said lightly, 'Hey, pal. Where the hell have you been? You had us half scared to death, pulling a stunt like that.'

Brendan turned his head slightly so he could look at Warden. His eyes were still glazed. When he answered his voice was a painful whisper, 'I'm not sure.'

Warden squatted next to Brendan's chair. Gwen perched herself on the armrest on the opposite side. 'How are you feeling, pal? Any better?' Warden asked him.

Brendan was quickly becoming more alert and awake. He nodded wearily. 'Yeah, I'm starting to come together. Has the good doctor made a run for it?'

'I doubt whether he'll ever do a house call again,' Warden said, with a thin smile.

'I don't blame him.'

After a glance at Gwen to make sure it was okay, Warden said, 'So what happened, do you know?'

'What happened *here*, first?'

'You died,' Warden said flatly. 'You stopped breathing and your heart quit, too.'

'Jesus Christ,' Brendan whispered, taking a second to accept this. 'So, it wasn't only in my head?'

'I nearly died with shock when it happened,' Gwen said, putting her hand on his arm.

Brendan surprised them with a small smile. 'It was the most incredible thing,' he said, pausing to regain his strength for a long explanation.

'I was falling through this blackness, a darkness so complete that I wasn't even sure I was falling. When I hit the bottom it didn't hurt. I just sort of landed, but I can't remember the exact moment I stopped falling. Then it was different, because there was such a blinding white light that I couldn't open my eyes at all. I couldn't even squint or look through my fingers. One of the funny things was, I realised I wasn't frightened. I wasn't scared at all. I was just lost inside this fantastic, blinding light.' Brendan paused, hearing Warden beside him suck in his breath with surprise and he knew that Warden, too, would be thinking about instances of near-death he would have heard about. 'It was like being blind, except it was from too much light, instead of darkness. After a minute maybe—I don't know how long—I heard voices, then someone called out my name.'

Brendan stopped again, twisting his fingers through Gwen's and including Warden with a glance. 'It was my mother. My mother was in that light with me and she started talking to me. She asked me what I was doing there and said I wasn't supposed to be there. It wasn't my time.'

'Hey, I'm not quite sure I understand this,' Gwen said carefully.

It was Warden who explained, giving Brendan a chance to catch his breath.

'I've read a lot of reports about people who die—or nearly die,' he said with awe, watching Brendan close his eyes again to rest. 'When they're revived they tell stories of being drawn towards a brilliant white light and hearing deceased friends or relatives encouraging them to step into it. But the theory says, if you do go into it, that's the end. You've stepped over the threshold into Eternity. I've never heard of anyone actually being *inside* the light and returning to tell the tale.'

'I wasn't supposed to be there,' Brendan repeated, without opening his eyes. 'I could feel the distress, almost like a panic, that I was causing by being there. It really felt bad. Then I'm pretty sure our friend arrived and that really upset things even more.'

'The *Setris*?' Warden asked, leaning closer. 'You saw him?'

'I couldn't see anything, remember? But there was this shadow I could pick out, moving through the light, that put out such a sense of wrong—' Brendan stopped, recalling something else. 'My mother asked me what I'd brought with me. She told me I had to leave and—and take the evil with me.'

'But that goes against just about every religious doctrine there is,' Warden said disbelievingly. 'He shouldn't have been able to go near that place.'

'Well, he was there, and maybe you're right,

because that bad feeling got a lot worse. It's impossible to describe. Then something else happened, which I can't even begin to explain and the next thing I knew was hearing your voices and feeling the carpet on my face.'

'Try and tell what that other thing was,' Warden said. 'You should try and remember as much as you can now, while it's still fresh in your mind. There must be something you can tell us.'

'I—I can't, really,' Brendan said, but he frowned in concentration. 'It was like knowing the most important thing in your life was about to happen, even though you don't actually know what that is—' He gave up with a shake of his head. 'Maybe I'll be able to write it down one day. I can't tell you now. The words aren't there in my head.'

Warden was disappointed. 'Did you actually see anything, or sense anything?'

'No, not really.'

'The whole thing was the *Setris* trying to give us a message,' Gwen said, surprising them. 'I'm sure of it. He was telling us not to play games like hypnosis or any of our own mumbo-jumbo. He was showing us he is in control, even to the point of killing Brendan.'

'But that's the last thing he can do,' Warden frowned at her.

'But he knew I was here and could bring Brendan back.'

'I have to say it sounds unlikely, Gwen.'

'I know, but I got a strong feeling about it. That's

why I stopped Lawson calling an ambulance. The *Setris* wouldn't have liked that, either.'

'What do you think, Bren? Does that make any sense to you?'

Brendan closed his eyes again and thought hard. They were disturbed by the sound of something heavy falling to the floor from the coffee table nearby. Everyone turned to see what had happened. It was a flower vase, filled with a dry arrangement, which now lay on its side on the carpet. The brittle stems were spread in disarray with some of the dead leaves and petals broken off.

There was a nervous silence, until Gwen said, 'How do you think that happened?'

Warden gave Brendan a sharp look. 'Are we alone?' The question startled Gwen, when she realised what he meant.

'I can't see anyone,' he said, getting alarmed.

Warden went to one of the mirrors and began twisting it around, using it to search every corner of the room. 'I can't see anything either,' he announced after a while.

'Maybe we're getting too jumpy,' Gwen said doubtfully.

'Well, we've got good reason to—'

This time it was a framed print which sprang from the wall, falling and smashing softly on the carpet. Frightened, Gwen moved closer to Brendan, nearly sitting in his lap. Warden went back to frantically moving one of the mirrors as he tried to look in every corner of the room at once.

He snapped, 'Maybe Robert did too good a job on you, Brendan. You might not be able to see anyone, but I think we've got someone in here with us anyway. I'm damned if I can find them, though.'

The wedding photograph of Brendan's parents slid from the mantelpiece. Another picture leapt off its hook. Gwen couldn't help a scream as it flew horizontally across the room to shatter against the opposite wall. Then an ashtray launched itself from the coffee table and hurtled into the curtains, becoming trapped like a netted insect. It narrowly missed Warden and he ducked away with a yell.

'This is getting bloody serious!' he cried, tensely waiting for the next missile. 'Are you sure you can't see anything, Bren?'

'I can't see a fucking thing!' Brendan almost shouted. Books on a nearby shelf began to topple to the floor. Some of them swept through the air like escaping birds, their pages rippling and tearing. A paperback struck Gwen on the shoulder, making her cry out again. The drapes around all the curtains began to billow outwards, as if they were being struck by a strong wind.

'We'd better get out of the room,' Warden called, crouching to avoid the flying books and moving towards Brendan to help him get up. But Brendan surprised them by pushing Gwen away, then holding his arms out, keeping them both at a distance.

'No, wait! Just wait!' he said urgently. Shocked, Warden and Gwen stood frozen, staring at him. Brendan stayed in that pose. Books that were still in the air dropped suddenly to the floor and the others stopped tumbling from the shelves. The curtains collapsed back into their place. Within a few seconds an unreal calm filled the room. Brendan kept himself absolutely still, barely moving his lips as he spoke.

'It's me,' he said, very quietly. 'I think it's me, doing this.'

Gwen stared at him as if he'd gone mad. 'What the hell do you mean, *you're* doing it?'

'I think so,' Brendan whispered, nodding with exaggerated care. 'I—I don't know how it started, but I remember thinking when the picture flew off the wall that I hoped my favourite painting didn't do that. As soon as I thought about it, it happened. Then I began to panic and imagined all sorts of things happening, like the books, the ashtray, and they happened. That's when I realised it was me and I had to calm myself down. Right now I'm trying to keep my mind clear, or concentrate on one thing like talking to you two. It's not easy. I keep wanting to think about the books flying through the air and stuff. I'm afraid it will start again if I do.'

'You mean, if you stay exactly like that and keep thinking of nothing, we'll be safe?' Gwen said, shocked. 'You can't just stay like that!'

'I've *got* to stay calm,' he told her, an edge of desperation creeping into his voice. A single book fell from the shelf.

'Hey, you can do it, too. I know you can,'

Warden said quickly, moving closer and putting a comforting hand on his friend's shoulder. Brendan jumped like a startled animal and the overhead lights flickered on and off several times. They could hear the switch near the door snapping up and down.

Gwen exchanged a look of anguish with Warden, then she said carefully, 'Brendan, I've got something here that will help you stay calm. It's a sedative and I'll have to inject it, but I've got some needles, too. Do you want me to?'

Brendan lowered his arms to rest on the sides of the chair, but he kept his eyes closed and was keeping himself very still. 'I don't know if I should let anything fuck with my mind—drugs, I mean. God knows what could happen.'

'It's only something that can help you relax and make you feel a little drowsy. I know you think you've got yourself under control, but I can see you're really wound up tight. You won't be able to keep it up, Brendan. A sedative will help you relax until we can figure some damned thing out.' An edge was creeping into her voice now.

'I agree,' Warden said, with a worried glance at her. 'I think it might help you.'

Brendan didn't say anything for a moment and Warden wasn't sure he was going to answer at all, then he slowly nodded his head. 'Okay, let's try it.'

Gwen quickly left the room and went into the kitchen. She found the plastic container of drugs and syringes where she'd left it at the back of the refrigerator. Taking the whole box she hurried back to the lounge room.

'How long have you had this stuff in the house?' Brendan asked her, as she knelt beside his chair.

'Not long,' she replied, concentrating on tearing the packaging away from the syringe. 'I thought it might be a good idea, but I knew you'd probably get upset with me, so I didn't tell you.' She kept her voice level, not wanting to provoke him into an argument. With deft, professional movements she unwrapped a small bottle of clear liquid, inserted the needle through the seal and carefully filled the plunger to a measurement mark. Next she inverted the syringe and bled out all the air until a droplet of liquid appeared at the needle's tip. 'Hold that,' she instructed Warden, handing it to him. He gingerly took the syringe between the tips of his fingers. Gwen took another small bottle—this time of disinfectant—from the container and used a cotton swab to clean an area of Brendan's forearm. He watched her blankly, still trying to keep his mind clear. Without preamble, she plucked the syringe back out of Warden's fingers, checked it once more for air bubbles, then touched it against Brendan's skin. The point disappeared beneath his flesh. Gwen pressed the plunger slightly, then retracted it again. She was rewarded with a wisp of red being drawn into the needle. Satisfied she'd found the vein, Gwen slowly pumped all the sedative through the needle, then withdrew it and held the cotton swab over the puncture wound as she did.

'How long?' Brendan asked her, quietly.

'Three or four minutes at the most, before you start feeling some sort of effect,' she said, glancing at her watch. 'It might be an idea if we made a move immediately to get you upstairs and onto the bed. Otherwise, we'll have to carry you up the stairs.'

'The bed? I thought this was only going to be a sedative? Something to slow me down?' Brendan said, frowning.

'Some people react to it more than others,' Gwen told him quickly. 'You might get drowsy enough to lie down for half an hour or so, until your body adjusts.' He looked stubborn, so she added, 'Come on, trust me. I want to clean this room up too, so I don't want you lying around here.' Gwen tried to sound as if it were a perfectly normal thing to do, even after the events they'd just witnessed.

'Okay, let's move upstairs,' Warden said, offering a hand. Brendan didn't bother to take it, but when he stood he swayed alarmingly and Warden grabbed his upper arm to steady him.

'Hell, this stuff works fast,' Brendan muttered, putting a hand to his forehead.

'I don't think it's the sedative yet,' Gwen said, moving to his other side to support him.

As they guided Brendan from the room, making sure he didn't step on any of the clutter strewn across the floor, both Gwen and Warden glanced around uneasily, expecting at any moment for something else to take on a life of its own and move. It was difficult to know if the shifting of the curtains was natural or not and at the last moment another book fell from the shelf, but that might have been normal, too. What remained of the orderly lines of volumes were a jumbled mess, some of them balanced precariously.

Brendan was stumbling by the time they lowered him onto the bed. Gwen removed his shoes, then busied herself closing the curtains tightly so no light at all showed between them. She turned back to the bed as Warden appeared from the bathroom carrying a glass of water.

'In case he wakes up with the dry horrors,' he explained, putting the glass on the bedside table where Brendan would be sure to see it. 'Is he asleep already?'

Gwen placed her hand on Brendan's forehead. 'Bren? Are you still awake?' He didn't stir and his breathing had fallen into a deep, slow rhythm. 'Out like a light,' she said, relieved. 'This will be the best sleep he's had for weeks. I hope it was the right thing to do.'

'How long do you think he'll sleep?'

'About twelve hours. By then it'll be in the middle of the night and into his normal sleep cycle, for what that's been worth lately. Still, it means he should sleep right on through to tomorrow morning.'

'What?' Warden was worried. 'You've knocked him out for twelve hours? Do you think that's wise?'

'I didn't have the chance to discuss it with you and I know Brendan would have refused, but it was the only thing I could think of! It might give his mind a chance to sort itself out—I don't know.' Gwen wearily rubbed a hand across her eyes. 'I found myself thinking that this—' she stopped, uncertain.

'It's a form of telekinesis,' Warden helped her gently. 'A damned extreme case, but that's what I'd call it.' He tried to sound casual, but in fact he had been staggered by what he'd seen.

'Okay—whatever. The hypnosis may be triggering that, but Robert said the treatment would probably need further sessions to take hold. I don't think I *want* it to take hold now. Maybe it'll wear off, while Brendan's zonked out.' Gwen looked at Warden and shrugged helplessly. 'That's what I was thinking, anyway.'

It didn't need to be said that Brendan returning to his previous state might not be desirable either. He could awaken and again be seeing dead spirits at every turn. Warden gave her an encouraging smile across the dim room. 'Hey, that's a better idea than mine. I didn't even have one,' he told her.

Gwen left the bedroom, gesturing for him to follow. As they went down the stairs together she asked, 'What are you going to do now?'

'If it's okay with you, I might stick around here for an hour or so and make sure nothing else crazy is going to happen. Then, if it seems everything's going to stay calm, I think someone should still go out to that veterans' home and check the records about Adrian Galther. You never know, there might be some sort of clue there about what we can do. I could do that this afternoon, as long as you feel safe about being on your own for a while.'

Gwen gave him a grateful look. 'Thanks. I'd appreciate the company for a little while. But you're right. If Bren doesn't stir and nothing happens after an hour or two, I'd say everything will be okay. It only remains to be seen what will happen when he wakes up. We still need some answers, too. I only wish I could come out to the home with you. With my training I might understand something more from any records out there.'

'If I come across anything that seems remotely important that I don't understand, I'll ask them to photocopy it and I'll bring it here.'

'Will you stay the night here? There's a spare room with a single bed.'

Gwen looked so pleading that Warden didn't hesitate to reply, 'Sure. But I think I'll camp on those chairs in the lounge. I'll sleep better there, rather than a strange room. Besides, I want to be in the middle of where everything's been happening.'

'Then maybe you'd better sleep with Brendan, and I'll camp on the couch,' Gwen suggested, joking weakly.

Warden managed a chuckle, glad to see Gwen pulling herself together.

21

Williamdale Veterans' Home turned out to be a collection of white, low-level brick buildings scattered among flowering gardens. The buildings were old, but well maintained. Warden drove very slowly, negotiating the speed bumps and keeping his eye on the arrows pointing towards the administration building. This turned out to be a more modern building attached to what seemed to be the original offices. He parked his Ford in a space reserved for visitors.

More gardens of bright flowers guarded the entrance to the reception area. He pulled open the door and went inside, hearing it hiss closed behind him as he crossed a small foyer to an information desk. The air was tainted with disinfectant. Behind the counter stood a neat, efficient-looking woman in a white uniform. Warden wished her a friendly good morning, before introducing himself.

'I'm looking for the records of a former resident of the Home,' he explained smoothly.

The woman looked at him carefully, measuring his credibility. 'I see. Medical records? You'd need to see the doctor assigned for that.'

'Not necessarily medical records,' Warden said, trying to disarm her with his nicest smile. 'Any records, really.'

But her professional guard had already started to come up. 'May I ask why?'

'It's a legal matter, actually.' The lie came smoothly. Warden had concocted the story in the car as he drove there. 'Apparently, the gentleman I'm looking for signed papers involving some property.' Warden lowered his voice. 'To be honest, we're not convinced he was in any condition to sign anything, at that time.'

She didn't look too convinced, but offered, 'There may be a few things I can show you, but certainly not very much that isn't confidential. It will be very general and I doubt it will help you.' She paused. 'I'm not sure I'm even allowed to do this,' she added uncertainly.

'I am here on behalf of a surviving relative, who's empowered me to see any records I want, but I'm sure I don't need to see anything too confidential,' Warden added encouragingly. Then he frowned and looked annoyed at himself. 'I should have had a letter drawn up, I suppose. Something I could show you.' He watched for her answer, aware that he'd also given her the excuse to refuse him. She could tell him to come back another time with the proof of authorisation.

She gave a slight shrug and seemed to decide upon helping Warden, rather than avoiding the issue. 'I don't suppose there's any point in making you go to all that trouble, at this stage. Let's see what we can find first. Is this ex-patient deceased?'

Warden nodded. 'His name was Galther—Adrian Gordon Galther. As far as we can tell he died in the mid-seventies, but we're not sure exactly when,' he added apologetically. Now he was genuinely annoyed with himself. He could have got the exact date from the paperwork at Brendan's house.

The counter clerk seemed happier with this. 'Mid-seventies. That's almost ancient history these days, so I guess there's not too much damage can be done—especially if he's deceased. I'll have to go to the old microfilm files next door to find the paperwork.'

'He was here for a very long time,' Warden offered helpfully. 'He was a Gallipoli veteran.'

Turning to another woman, similarly dressed and sitting at a nearby typewriter, she said, 'Sister Green, would you mind the counter for me, while I find a file for this gentleman?'

Sister Green was obviously her senior. She offered a curt nod of approval and the woman bustled off after waving Warden towards a pair of hard plastic seats. He sat down and looked for something to read, but there was nothing, so he turned and stared out at the garden.

He had to wait over twenty minutes. Sister Green began to cast a few annoyed glances at her wristwatch. The counter clerk eventually returned carrying a thick file, but before handing it over she regarded Warden with a renewed suspicious eye.

'What were you saying about a signature, Mr Anthony?'

'Is there something wrong?' Warden asked, sensing trouble.

She waved the file at him. 'According to these, Mr Galther would have been troubled to put his name on anything from the very first day he came here.'

'Oh dear,' Warden looked crestfallen while he thought hard. 'That means I might be looking at someone falsifying his signature. This could be getting more serious.' Silently, he congratulated himself.

'Oh, I see,' the counter clerk said, surprised and unconsciously handing over the file. 'That is quite serious. Shouldn't this be a police matter?'

'I'll certainly be speaking to them, if that's the way things are,' Warden agreed. 'I don't suppose I can take this away?' he added hopefully.

'No, of course not,' she said firmly, back on familiar ground. 'There's a photocopier in the next room, if there's anything you want copied. Twenty cents per page.'

Warden thanked her and retreated back to the plastic chairs. He balanced the thick file on his knees. After leafing through the pages for some minutes he gave up, wishing Gwen had been able to come with him. With a frustrated sigh Warden went back to the counter.

'Could someone please explain what all this means? It's rather confusing.'

The clerk began to return to the front desk, but Sister Green stopped her with a look, pushed her chair back from the typewriter and came over herself. Taking the file from him, she opened it and rifled through the first few pages.

'What is it, exactly, that you'd like to know?' she asked in a firm, no-nonsense manner.

'Well, I suppose I'm trying to work out what condition he was in normally.' Warden looked helpless for a moment. 'Like, how sick was he?'

'You don't have to be sick to be a resident in this home,' she said, throwing him a sharp glance. 'Why do you think he was sick?'

'I've got some idea of the problems involved,' Warden replied, immediately losing hope that he might break through the sister's cool professionalism. 'That's what has brought me here.'

Sister Green murmured something non-committal and continued to scan through the pages in front of her. Warden was surprised to see a glimmer of interest suddenly show on her face.

'Now I understand something,' she said obscurely. 'Look.' She put her finger on a hand-written report. Warden twisted his head to read it upside-down, then shook his head. She explained, 'This fellow was considered unstable from the day he came here. In those days I suppose it wasn't anything unusual. Shell-shock, post-battle trauma, that sort of thing was quite common. But they didn't regard it, back then, the way we do now. Real psychiatry was in its infancy at that time, don't forget,' she added absently, reading again. 'What's obvious here is that your Mr Galther didn't get better. In fact, he got worse.' She flipped through some more pages. Warden had to stop himself from leaning too close with his excitement as he tried to read the file with her. 'He tried to commit suicide when he first came in, then again in 1917,' she announced, raising her eyebrows. 'That's when they got serious about watching him.' She read for a moment more. 'In fact, they put him in the equivalent of a padded cell.'

'What did you mean, when you said before you understood something now?' Warden asked.

'We do have a room here that can be converted into a special place, but I thought we'd never used it. There are studs on the walls where mattresses can be attached, that sort of thing. Now I'm thinking Mr Galther was the first and last resident to have used it.'

'What you're saying,' Warden asked carefully, touching the papers in front of them, 'is that Adrian Galther was quite insane, right?'

'Suicidally so,' she nodded and glanced down at another page. 'Here's a note about somebody called Hamilton. Apparently Mr Galther was obsessed with the idea he'd stolen something from someone called Hamilton. There's no cross-reference to any other residents named that, so it wasn't anyone here. Back in those days, it could have been a Christian name, but there should still be some sort of indication, if it was another patient.'

'Poor old bugger,' Warden said. 'So, how did he die in the end? Old age, I suppose.'

Sister Green flicked to the end of the file. Here the forms were more modern, the reports typed. She paled at what she read.

'Actually, it says here he finally managed to do it,' she said quietly.

'What? Kill himself?' Warden held his breath.

'He cut his wrists with a screwdriver left by a maintenance man.'

'A screwdriver?' Warden felt a little sickened. He could imagine how difficult and painful that would have been—and more importantly, how desperate Galther must have been.

'That's what it says here. I doubt if there's a mistake.'

Warden looked at the sister and sighed resignedly. 'Well, that tells me something, I suppose. More than I expected really, thanks to you. He was crazy enough to kill himself like that. God, it must have been agonising.' He paused, and the sister agreed with a wry nod. He said, 'I wish these forms and reports weren't so impersonal.'

She tapped the top of the counter with her fingernail while she considered something. 'You could go and ask Mr Turner if he remembers anything about him.' At Warden's questioning look she explained, 'He's another long-term resident here—but don't worry, he's not crazy. He's just very old now. He's a World War II veteran who lost both his legs and gets around in a wheelchair. He's been here since the day he came back. Says he never wanted to be anywhere else, although he's so self-sufficient he could live anywhere.' Looking wistful, she added, 'In the beginning, he just didn't have anyone else to look after him. Anyway, he's a nice old man who'll probably appreciate the visit, even from a stranger.'

Warden realised that the sister was extracting a service from him in return for her help, so he agreed it might a good idea, too. 'Sure, I'll go and have a chat with him. He might be able to tell me something.'

After the sister gave him careful directions Warden left the reception and began weaving his way through the gardens in search of Turner's home. Five minutes later he found the right place.

Turner answered the door of his flat and gladly offered to talk with Warden, but outside, he suggested, because it was such a nice day. Turner was a wizened old man with strong arms from propelling his wheelchair for nearly half a century. The rest of his body was wasting away with his age. Above the thin, chequered blanket covering his stumps a shirt bagged from his narrow shoulders. He had a habit of occasionally running a calloused hand across his pate, which held onto a few grey wisps of hair. Warden sat on a grassy patch outside the front door to bring himself down to Turner's level.

'Do you remember a resident here called Galther?' Warden asked, squinting in the sun.

'Adrian! Of course I do.'

'You must be the only person left who was here when Galther was.'

This made the old man think and he turned rueful. 'I guess that'd be true. Must be nearly twenty years ago since he did away with himself.'

'Did you know him well?'

'I used to open his windows for him, then have a bit of a talk. His windows operated from the outside, see? Beyond the wire, so he couldn't smash them and cut himself with a bit of glass. He was dead set on killing himself for as long as I can remember.' Turner shook his head and pursed his lips, waiting for the memories to come. 'Mind you, he quietened down in the last few years. His age, most probably. That's why they let a tradesman in to fix something, I suppose. They wouldn't have done that a couple of years earlier. They would have taken Adrian away somewhere first.'

'How—how mad was he?' Warden asked carefully.

'Oh, as a hatter!' Turner chuckled to himself for a moment. 'He came back from Gallipoli with a couple of leg wounds and went crazy before he recovered. He was already well on the way, on the boat back, they reckon.' He bent closer to Warden and lowered his voice. 'He shouldn't have been here, really. I don't know why they kept him, instead of putting him in a hospital—if you know what I mean. They built a special flat where he couldn't hurt himself and that's where he stayed for over sixty years.' He leaned back and raised his voice again. 'I used to talk to him through the window,' he repeated. 'He used to tell me there was someone else in the room with him, giving him hell—or that his mates were there. Used to yell that his mates from the war had come to visit him. You know, he can't have been a very popular man.' Turner tipped Warden a slow wink. 'He never did sound too pleased to see 'em.'

'What about the name Hamilton?' Warden tried. 'The records in the office here mention he used to say that name a lot.'

'Ben,' the old man nodded. 'Ben Hamilton. That was a name he used to yell a lot—I remember it well. And Macca. But you know, everybody was called Macca or Lofty or Smithy, in those days. Macca could've been anybody. But Hamilton, Ben Hamilton, I'd say must've been someone special.'

'What about him? Did you know him?'

Turner smiled. 'If old Adrian spoke to him, you can bet he was a dead man. One of the boys killed on Gallipoli, no doubt. Adrian rarely spoke to anyone alive.'

'So, he was mad as can be,' Warden said, with a grim finality.

'Maybe,' Turner said, obviously relishing the chance to be dramatic. A different, wary tone came into his voice. 'They all said he was mad for nearly sixty years. Normally, I'd tell you myself he was mad as buggery, rather than start an argument. But what do *you* know? Do you think he was mad? You must know something, or you wouldn't be here today gossiping to an old man like me.' He gave his visitor a hard look.

'I'm not sure of any of the facts,' Warden said, being deliberately vague. 'I know some people get senile when they get old,' he shrugged. 'But like you said, he was supposed to be off his rocker since he came back from the war.' He had a feeling something important was coming from the old veteran, but he knew better than to spoil Turner's fun by rushing him.

Turner sighed and looked distant. 'You know, I don't sleep much,' he said, then he paused. Warden didn't question the change of subject. 'There isn't much I can do, so there's not much to tire me out, right? I often just get around at night, taking my time and looking at the stars and smelling the garden. It smells different at night. I still do it now, but not so much. When Adrian was here I was up every night, wheeling myself here and there. It was safer back then, too.' He hesitated again, before going on. 'Sometimes I'd find myself going past Adrian's place. The lights would be on, and Adrian would be in there, swearing and cursing at all sorts of folks. Don't get me wrong, though.' Turner pointed a crooked finger at Warden, who was already fascinated. 'The man was scared right out of what little mind he had left, you could tell. I say he was swearing and cursing like a man filled with anger, but he was scared, too. Damn well terrified, the poor bastard.'

This time Turner paused as if to give himself courage to go on. 'Well, sometimes he'd have the lights on just so, and you could see reflections on the windows, like they were mirrors. And some nights I'd swear, too, he wasn't alone in that flat, even though it couldn't have been any other way, according to the folks who make the rules around here—and how they treated him, anyway. Sometimes I'd creep closer and have a peek through the glass, but you couldn't see anything that way. Adrian would be in there, raving quietly to himself. He never made much noise or they gave him a needle to settle him down and he hated that even more. When I'd back away, taking my chair down the path, I could see those damned reflections again. You'd have to be in just the right spot and you'd see reflections in the glass that looked like someone was in there with him. Strangest thing I ever saw, I reckon.' Turner leaned back and relaxed again. 'Maybe that's what was keeping him crazy. I couldn't tell anyone about it, though.' He chuckled for a moment. 'I figured they might put me in a room just like his, if I did.' He finished by giving his visitor a challenging look, daring him to disbelieve him.

There was a silence, which Warden broke by saying, 'Well, between you and me, Mr Turner, I think I know what you saw.'

Turner nodded wisely. 'That's what I figured, as soon as you started asking about Adrian Galther.'

Warden didn't think he needed to know more from the Home, but just in case he ever needed to return and ask for more favours, he popped his head back into the reception area and thanked Sister Green and the counter clerk again.

'What about the signature?' the clerk called, before he could retreat back out the door.

'Signature?' Warden was momentarily confused and left hanging through the doorway. He hadn't been aware he was supposed to sign anything.

'You said you were trying to find out if Mr Galther really signed some papers or not. Have you decided?'

'Oh—' Warden recovered his composure. 'Ah, no. I can't see him having signed anything, to be honest. The poor man was quite mad, I'd say.' He tried to back out the door.

'So, should I keep the file out, in case the police want to see it?'

Warden was regretting returning to the office. The two women had been so helpful and he didn't want to lie to them any more than he had to. 'Perhaps you can keep it available for a week or so,' he said uncertainly. 'If you haven't heard from anyone by then, I'd say it can be put away.'

'Julia, I'd say you can file it away now,' Sister Green said knowingly, eyeing Warden from her desk.

'Yes, probably,' Warden agreed with a wave and a shaky smile. He ducked away back out into the sunshine, before he had to answer any more questions.

Driving along the freeway heading back into the city, Warden had time to consider what he'd found out.

Galther lived for sixty years with what's haunting Brendan. They thought they were doing the right thing, keeping him locked away like that, but they trapped him in a padded cell with some sort of a monster. Warden shook his head and decided he was unable to even come close to imagining how horrifying that would be. How someone could endure such mental torment for so long. *But he didn't,* he reminded himself. *Galther was trying to kill himself from the very beginning.* Then Warden swore softly, annoyed that he didn't even think of having a look at the room Galther was kept in. But it might also have been pushing his luck with the formidable Sister Green, he realised, grinning to himself. Besides, after twenty years there would be very little, if anything, that would be the same as when Galther was living there.

Galther's personal possessions must have been

passed on to Brendan's mother, including the charm, which was sealed in the green tin. The demon was within the charm, waiting to pounce on its next victim. Why wasn't someone at the Veterans' Home affected, while they were handling it? Warden turned that one over in his mind with no luck, until he remembered Gwen sensed the charm's threat almost immediately and had refused to have anything to do with it. Perhaps that was what had happened at the Veterans' Home, when Galther's belongings were being packed away. Someone there experienced the same feeling of finding the charm ugly, or distasteful, and quickly put it away before anything could happen.

Logically, that meant certain people could be the same. Why should one person be trapped into the charm's spell, while others hated the thing? Warden reminded himself they were dealing with an ancient thing. Who knew what was real and what wasn't anymore? *It might be something so simple as a birthsign,* he mentally shrugged. *Anything's possible now—astrology, birthstones, God knows what. But where to start looking?* With his mind whirling, Warden stared out the windscreen at the three-lane traffic all around him, but in reality he was far away in the mysteries of Egypt, delving into the mythology which, for so long before today, had just been fantastic stories, but now could be true in every word.

He didn't see the accident happening, until it was too late.

The truck ahead of him in the lane adjacent had an untidy load of debris from a demolition site. Chunks of brick and mortar on top of a pile of dirt were being used to weigh down twisted sheets of roofing and gutters. Without warning the wind of the truck's passage got under one of the metal sheets and flipped it from the load, spraying the dirt and stones with it. With a grace belying its size and weight, the piece of roofing fluttered apparently weightless above the road in the wake of the vehicle, then it suddenly dropped to the ground with a clanging of steel. Cars everywhere were reacting with squealing tyres and barking horns. The sedan next to Warden's on the left, facing a direct collision with the debris, cut violently into Warden's lane as he braked the Ford hard.

'You fucking idiot!' he snarled, wrenching the wheel to the right. The two cars clashed with a ripping of metal. Still braking, he left the other car behind, but found himself heading for the collision barrier in the centre of the freeway. Warden overcompensated to the left, realising too late he couldn't control the car as well as he should—a front tyre must have blown. Miraculously, he speared through the traffic that was scattering in all directions and dropped off the edge of the road. The embankment was steep and the Ford wanted to run parallel to the road now. The speed had hardly slackened and Warden didn't want to try braking again with a flat tyre. He was fighting to make the car stay off the road now, bouncing along with the world at a crazy angle, the freeway above him on the right and a deep ditch at the bottom of the embankment to his left. Just when Warden thought he was going to get away with it, the car tilted over slowly and began to roll sideways down the embankment.

There were long seconds of Warden tumbling over and over, alternatively bashing his head and shoulders against the roof of the car, the driver's side door, then getting thrown into the empty space of the passenger seat. The windscreen changed to crazed, splintering glass in front of his face and he threw an instinctive, protecting hand up. He had no idea how many times the car rolled.

When it stopped, he was suspended upside down by his seat-belt, the back of his neck and shoulders resting painfully on the upholstered roof beneath him. The motor had stopped, creating a comparative, almost eerie, silence. There was only the ticking of hot metal beginning to cool and the occasional creak as the car settled into its unaccustomed position.

'Fuck,' Warden muttered, then managed a grunt of laughter. Swearing was the natural thing to do, but for once the word seemed rather inadequate for the moment. He slowly turned his head to the left, towards the road, but beyond the far-side window he could only see long grass pressing up against the car. The movement let him feel broken glass rubbing against his shoulders where he lay on it and Warden immediately told himself to keep still. It was unnaturally quiet and he worried about how far he was from the road. Was it possible he'd rolled so far that the Ford was obscured by the long grass and no one would see it? He might be trapped here for hours.

'Don't be bloody stupid,' he told himself. Those sorts of fears would only grow in his mind out of proportion, until he panicked and did something foolish. He realised, after a few seconds' logical thought, that it was quiet because the accident would have brought all the traffic to a standstill.

He heard a commotion coming from somewhere nearby. Suddenly a pair of boots appeared at his window, followed by an anxious, pale face. Clearly, it was somebody who expected to see something much worse inside the wreck than Warden's conscious figure.

'Shit, are you all right?' the face asked in a trembling voice. It was a young man.

'I've been better,' Warden replied calmly, feeling a surge of relief.

'Can you get out?'

'I'm not sure. Maybe, if you give me a hand.'

The car rocked alarmingly as the man tugged at the driver's door. It refused to open.

'Hang on, and I'll go around the other side.'

His saviour disappeared, then returned at the passenger side of the car. Again the car moved as he attempted to open the door, but it wouldn't budge. A moment later he dropped to the ground, lay on his side and reached in, careful to avoid the broken glass. Warden could see now that he was a tradesman of some kind.

'Okay, big fella, we'll try something different. Try and turn yourself sideways and I'll catch your legs and take some of the weight. Leave your seat-belt fastened as long as you can. I think it's doing some good at the moment.'

For a man of Warden's size it would have been difficult enough to draw his legs out from under the steering wheel and put them sideways across the car. Doing it while hanging upside down with the cabin partly crushed was twice as bad. It took some time and Warden had to ignore twinges of pain in his neck and back. Finally, panting with exertion, he lay curled on the ceiling across the width of the Ford.

'Now, can you come through the window?' the man asked doubtfully.

'I don't think I'd fit normally,' Warden said wearily. 'And now it's smaller than it should be.'

'What about the windscreen? Can you kick the rest of it out?'

'Okay, I'll try.'

The first few kicks, with no room to swing hard enough, made little impact. Warden decided to try one last time and unexpectedly the opaque glass burst out of the frame to land on the grass. However, the windscreen had been supporting the roof to some extent and the weight of the vehicle above suddenly sagged further, crushing the pillars.

'Jesus!' Warden cried, then held his breath waiting for the cabin to be flattened entirely. Again, there was some metallic creaking and groaning as the car settled into its new place, but the passenger space wasn't crushed any further. 'Get me the hell out of here,' Warden said, reaching out for a helping hand.

'No, wait a minute,' the man replied. Warden could tell by the sound of his voice that he was moving away.

'Hey! Hey, come back! Get me out of here!'

A command to stay still floated back from the distance. Warden groaned and closed his eyes. The urge to try and escape unassisted was strong, but he forced himself to wait. He must have actually passed out for some seconds, because he was startled back to reality by boots scuffling in the broken glass in front of the car. There was a harsh, rustling noise and Warden saw the man was laying a heavy tarpaulin down on the ground, covering the thousands of sharp glass slivers.

'*Now* we can get you out.'

There was a second helper now and by both of them grabbing Warden's outstretched hands they dragged him easily, on his back, out of the wreck. After lifting him to his feet they helped him to walk a few steps away from the Ford, but it was too much to get up the embankment for the moment. Shaking, he sat on the long grass, put his arms across his knees and rested his head.

Behind him now, from the roadway, he could hear the sounds of panicked shouting and the crashing of breaking glass.

*

Warden leaned against the side of the ambulance. He knew, once he got inside, he wouldn't have any say in the matter. There was a light blanket across his shoulders, but Warden didn't feel he wanted it.

'I don't want to stay in overnight,' he told the ambulance officer.

'That's not my decision, sir. Let's leave it up to the doctors, hey?'

'I'm not getting into this thing, until you promise you won't keep me overnight. This is not a good time for me to spend twenty-four hours in a hospital bed.'

The ambulance officer got frustrated. 'The sooner we get there, the sooner you can sort that out for yourself.'

Warden opened his mouth to argue further, then gave in and nodded tiredly. He was about to step into the back of the ambulance when something caught his eye. Much to the annoyance of the officer Warden changed direction and moved out of the man's reach. 'I'll be back in a second, okay?' he called, hurrying away.

The road was a scene of carnage. Three ambulances, their flashing lights revolving, were parked haphazardly with their rear doors open. Four police cars were in attendance, their own rooftop lights flickering in the sunlight. Broken glass lay everywhere. One lane of the freeway had been kept open, a line of bright, orange marker cones separating the accident area. A stream of traffic went slowly by, the wide-eyed occupants staring out as they passed. Apart from Warden's own Ford there had been three other cars involved in the accident. Two of them were serious write-offs and the reason for the ambulances. The third wasn't too damaged, but enough to render it undriveable. It was for this vehicle that Warden now headed, limping slightly because of a pain in his back. Next to the wrecked car stood a man in a smart business suit. His face was drawn and worried as he spoke urgently into a mobile telephone. He finished the call as Warden came close.

'Can I use your phone? It's urgent,' he asked without preamble.

'What isn't urgent?' the man replied tiredly, but handed the phone over unhesitatingly. 'Just dial the number and press "send".'

'Thanks—thanks a lot.'

Warden's fingers trembled as he punched in the number. The receiver to his ear, he heard several seconds of garbled noise, then a phone ringing. It was answered quickly. Gwen's voice sounded slightly more electronic than usual.

'Hello?'

'Hi, it's only me.'

'Where are you? What's happened?'

She sounded alarmed. Warden allowed himself a moment of wry humour. *Women's intuition is a fact, too,* he thought.

'I've had a slight accident.'

'Are you okay?'

'Sure, I'm okay. A bit shaken up, that's all.' He

went on to explain what had happened, keeping it as brief as he could. Then he told her about going to the hospital. 'I've already told them I'm not going to stay in overnight. I'll be back there as soon as I can.'

'If they want to keep you in for observation, you should stay,' Gwen told him, though she obviously wasn't happy about losing him for the night.

'No, I'm okay. I know I am. I'll let them go through the motions and check me out, then I'll be out of there.'

There was a pause. 'I won't be able to come and see you. I can't leave Brendan.'

'I don't want you to. The last thing I want is for you to be wandering around a hospital looking for me, while I'm outside trying to get to your place. Just stay put there with Brendan and I'll be back soon.'

'Which hospital will they take you to?'

Warden glanced back at the ambulance, where the officer was watching him impatiently. It was too far to shout the question. 'I don't know and it's a bit hard to find out,' he told her.

'I'll call work and ask them to keep an eye out for you anyway. You might go there.'

'Good. Anything that gets me back out on the street faster will be a help.'

They exchanged goodbyes and Warden handed the phone back with his thanks. He walked quickly back to the ambulance and said, as he got close, 'Okay, now you've got me—' He reached out urgently towards the ambulance officer as everything suddenly went blurry.

He heard someone say, as if from a great distance, 'I think you'd better lie down for the trip into town.'

22

Gwen put the phone down and stood for a moment, thoughtfully regarding the instrument. She told herself that things weren't as bad as they seemed, but the truth was she was shaken at the idea of suddenly having to face the immediate future without Warden's support. Warden sounded okay and it was most likely he would be able to discharge himself from any hospital after the usual thorough check-up. The last thing any medical centre wanted these days was a perfectly healthy person occupying one of their hospital beds. He would probably get back to the house soon after nightfall, and in the meantime Brendan would stay heavily sedated. All she had to do was wait.

She picked up the phone again and put a call through to her own hospital. It took her a while to locate someone she knew well in the emergency section. She asked for Warden to be processed through the system as quickly as possible. Arranging that was the easy part, but it came with some bad news. The hospital hadn't been informed of any incoming road-accident victims, which probably meant Warden was most likely being taken to some other hospital where Gwen had no influence. Depending on circumstances, Warden could be held up in waiting rooms or even admitted and given a bed for hours, until someone declared him fit to go home.

Increasingly worried about the way things were turning out, Gwen went to the kitchen to make herself a coffee and something to eat. But seeing the table still littered with Brendan's family papers and the stove covered by the newspaper was enough to turn Gwen towards a rack of wine glasses and the refrigerator.

It's the middle of the afternoon, isn't it? Oh, why the hell not? she thought, not needing much convincing. Stooping in the open door of the refrigerator she filled the glass to its brim from a cask of white wine on the top shelf. She ignored seeing the liquid trembling slightly in her grasp. There was a half-finished block of chocolate too, so she grabbed it, gently shoved the door closed with her foot and retreated to the lounge room. She turned on the television and moved to the couch. A remote control revealed that an American talk-show appeared to be the best viewing on offer. Grimacing at her poor lot, Gwen sipped her wine, nibbled on the chocolate and settled down to wait things out. The television chattered merrily at her, but Gwen got little comfort from it. Her eyes kept sliding to the clock on the mantelpiece. If it wasn't for the muted ticking she could hear when she listened, Gwen might have believed it had stopped. The hands seemed to be hardly moving at all, or at least they circled the dial much more slowly than they usually did.

If I was waiting for something bad, time would be flying, she thought.

When her wine needed refilling, Gwen left her empty glass on the bottom balustrade of the stairs and went up to check on Brendan. She tip-toed along the short hallway and eased herself through the bedroom door. Her caution proved unnecessary. Brendan was still sound asleep as he should have been. He was lying so still Gwen watched anxiously for a moment, until she saw his chest rise in a long, deep breath. More out of habit she crossed to the bed and put a hand on his forehead. His temperature seemed fine, too.

Satisfied, but still feeling oddly inadequate and that she should be doing more under the circumstances, Gwen left the bedroom and returned downstairs. She thought briefly about staying beside the bed to watch him, but decided she could drive herself crazy, staring at him and waiting for the slightest sign of something going wrong, when she should have more faith in the sedatives and use this time to get some rest herself. Gwen didn't want to sleep, but hoped the television could take her mind off things for a while. However, back in the lounge she saw the talk-back show was finished and the station was switching to children's programs. A quick search of the other channels showed her more of the same. Disappointed, she turned the set off with a slap of her hand.

There was a book she had been in the middle of reading, but she wasn't confident she could concentrate enough to read. But with no other option, Gwen made a second, quick trip upstairs to retrieve the novel from beside the bed. Returning to the lounge and choosing the couch, she tucked her legs underneath her and tried to get absorbed in the story.

The afternoon dragged on into the evening, then finally the daylight disappeared altogether. Gwen stayed in the lounge room the whole time, forcing herself to read the novel and seeing every page turned as more time passed. The only occasions she got up from the couch were to refill her wine glass—aware that she was drinking too much, but shutting out her conscience—and once to call her hospital again to check if Warden had been admitted. They told her his name wasn't on the register. He must definitely have been taken to another hospital. Gwen didn't try to track him down. With only minor injuries, he might have been taken to any one of many medical facilities.

She welcomed the gloom of nightfall as another sign that the time was going by, even if it was at a crawling pace. She was finally getting properly hungry, but Gwen was also feeling lethargic from the alcohol and the long lack of activity throughout the afternoon. The stress was taking its toll too, but she didn't recognise that. In a rare moment of indulgence she phone-ordered a small pizza for herself, even though she knew she wouldn't be able to eat much of it. She had to accept some unnecessary extras to make the minimum delivery amount.

It took some time to arrive, but at least by that time Gwen was starving. The television was back to adult viewing, so she sat on the floor in front of it with the pizza and another glass of wine spread around her. A movie came on that she wanted to watch and that helped to make more time pass. Gwen realised, at one stage, that it was getting late for Warden and he should have returned by now. She made a conscious effort not to fret about this. Warden, she knew, would be trying his hardest to get back to them as soon as he could.

Every hour Gwen went upstairs to check on Brendan. Each time he was the same, sleeping deeply and apparently dreamlessly, if his peacefulness was any indication. By the time the movie finished, just before eleven o'clock, Gwen was facing a small dilemma. She was very tired herself now, having struggled to keep her eyes open for the last half-hour of the film. She had no idea why Warden hadn't returned yet, other than the frightening prospect that he'd been hurt more than he had wanted to tell her and now he was trapped, admitted into a hospital. Still, she was sure he would come back to the house no matter the hour, as long as he could get away. It meant she would have to leave the house unlocked or leave a key somewhere he would find it, if she wished to go to bed—something she now desperately wanted to do. It was the effects of the wine, she admitted guiltily. Having a drink had seemed like a good idea at the time. Now she was paying for it.

In the end Gwen had to be content with leaving the front door unlocked and slightly ajar, so the deadlock wouldn't catch. It was risky, she knew. While most of the things she'd been frightened of lately wouldn't be deterred by locked doors or even solid walls, it would be tragic to fall victim to human intruders at this time. *Then again,* she thought, deliberately leaving the lower hallway light turned on, *maybe the ghosts will scare the damned burglars away.* Gwen mounted the stairs, climbing them wearily and unsteadily, recognising again she was more than a little drunk.

If she had stayed in the lounge room a few minutes longer, Gwen would have seen the curtains start to billow inwards again, away from the closed windows.

In the bedroom she was surprised by Brendan

letting out a single, soft snore and rolling over onto his side. Gwen worried for a moment that his breathing was slightly shallower now, then she told herself to stop being so panicky all the time. Her patient was doing exactly as she'd planned, changing from the drug-induced unconsciousness into a more natural sleeping state. Gwen got undressed and climbed into bed beside him. She lay on her back and stared up at the blackness above, dimly seeing the whirling ceiling fan. The whole room spun a little, thanks to the wine she'd drunk, but Gwen wasn't feeling ill. Experimenting, Gwen closed her eyes and could tell the urge to sleep was much stronger than any desire to be sick.

Minutes later a thin paperback novel toppled from a shelf downstairs to land almost noiselessly on the carpet—but by this time Gwen had fallen into a deep sleep.

Warden had been waiting for a long time—and not for the first time—in the sterile confines of one of the hospital's special departments. His dizzy spell back at the accident scene had prompted fears of concussion and maybe a skull fracture, so one of the examining doctors had ordered X-rays. However, from that moment, all urgency about Warden's condition appeared to evaporate as he was taken from one room to another and commanded to wait, then finally told to undress in a small cubicle and stay there until someone fetched him—another long delay. Next, he lay on the X-ray table so long he lost track of time completely and feared they had somehow forgotten all about him. When it finally happened, the X-ray process took an age, too, and Warden suspected a medical student was being taught at the expense of his, Warden's, time. Eventually he was told to put his clothes back on and wait in yet another room for one of the doctors to study the X-rays and form an opinion. This was where Warden sat now, tapping his feet on the worn linoleum and glancing at his watch repeatedly. Incredibly, it showed after ten o'clock at night. Warden figured the freeway accident occurred close to three in the afternoon. It had taken seven hours to get to this point and Warden was giving serious consideration to simply walking out. He kept telling himself that another five minutes would most likely bring him the X-ray results and he could leave legitimately, but the minutes kept passing without any such thing happening. Another thing stopping him from walking out was that Warden wasn't at all sure which way to go and getting caught wandering the corridors of the hospital, looking for a way to escape, when you were suspected of having a head injury, was probably one certain way to be kept in overnight and put under observation instead.

Just as the frustration and indecision were building to breaking point a white-coated technician, someone Warden recognised as one of the operators from the X-ray theatre, swept into the room with his eyes searching.

'Mr Anthony? Would you follow me, please.' He continued walking, apparently fully expecting Warden to leap to his feet and keep pace, which he did with a silent curse. There was no opportunity to ask for any results as they dodged through the corridors, sidling past wheeled stretchers and bustling medical staff. Finally, after passing through, what seemed to Warden to be every other section of the hospital, they arrived at an imposing pair of grey swinging doors. Instead of pushing through, the technician slipped into a small office just before them. He beckoned Warden to follow. Inside, an elderly nursing sister sat at a cramped desk.

'This is Mr Anthony,' the technician explained, handing her a slim manilla file. With a curt nod to Warden he pushed back past him and disappeared back into the corridor. The sister opened the file and scanned the two pages it contained.

'Have you any valuables you'd like us to keep here?' she asked, without lifting her eyes from the file. Remembering Sister Green at the Veterans' Home Warden was tempted to ask if it was a special trait expected of nurses that they should read files and carry on a conversation at the same time. But his confusion over her question kept him civil.

'I'm sorry?'

'Would you like us to store your wallet or watch in the safe here, rather than have them with you in the ward?'

'For how long?' he asked, feeling stupid.

'All night, of course. The duty sister in the morning will return them to you when you're released.'

'Released? You're keeping me in overnight?'

'That's the doctor's recommendation,' she said, tapping the file.

'But why?'

'The X-rays were clear, but the attending ambulance officer noted signs of severe concussion and possible internal head injuries. Just in case, we want to keep you in here overnight for observation. You can leave very early in the morning, if that's what you'd like.'

Warden opened his mouth to argue, but at the last moment remembered he was up against a system which was going to be impossible to talk his way out of—the sister wouldn't be empowered to release him. Instead, an idea formed in his mind. 'Okay, but look,' he said, trying to sound as if he accepted his fate, 'I really need to make a phone call, if that's the case.' He pointedly looked at the telephone on her desk and hoped he'd judged her correctly. The sister glanced nervously at it, too, as if it were something precious he might steal away.

'But hasn't a relative already been contacted for you by now?'

'I made a call earlier, but I didn't know I was going to be staying here overnight. It makes things different and it's very important I make just one call. It's long-distance, though,' he added, knowing that would make it worse.

'Then I'm sorry, but you can't use my phone,' she said, glad of the excuse to refuse him. 'I don't have access to long-distance calls from this extension.'

'But I must let this person know what's happening.'

The sister looked sympathetic and unsure of what to say. At that moment a young nurse put her head through the doorway. After an obvious appraising stare at Warden, who suddenly found himself wishing he *could* stay overnight, she said, 'Sister, could we have you in the ward for a minute?'

The sister nodded immediately and stood up. She said to Warden, 'There is a payphone at the visitors' reception desk on the ward. Go back down the corridor and take the first turn to your right. When you've finished please return here and we'll finish processing you into the ward for the night.'

'Thank you,' Warden said, backing out of the office. 'I'll be back as soon as I can.'

Trying not to appear in too much of a hurry he walked casually down the corridor, but when he turned the corner and was out of sight from the sister's office he doubled his pace. He strode straight past the reception desk, giving the girl there a friendly smile and a wave. She was on the phone and gave him a smile back without breaking her conversation. Warden discovered he was still in the heart of the hospital, but because it was an area designed for visitors there were exit signs on every corner guiding him outside. With every step Warden expected to hear someone call out his name or stop him and ask where he thought he was going. He breathed a huge sigh of relief when he finally pushed his way through some tinted-glass doors that let him out into the night air. It took him a moment to understand exactly where he was and which city street the exit opened onto. After working it out, Warden knew there was a taxi-stand around the corner to his left. He hurried on, hoping there would still be a cab this late at night after official visiting hours were over. Glancing at his watch, under a streetlight, he saw that it was nearly eleven o'clock now.

There was one cab. Warden surprised the driver as he climbed into the back seat. The cabbie put down his newspaper and looked through the security glass at his passenger.

'Where to?' he asked in a heavily accented, Slavic voice. Warden gave him the address and the driver grunted with satisfaction. It would be a large fare to Brendan's house from there. The cab pulled away from the kerb. After they had travelled only a few blocks Warden patted the bulge of his wallet, suddenly aware he didn't have that much cash.

'Do you take credit cards?' he asked, looking around the cab for the right sticker.

'Not this late at night,' the driver replied.

'What? Why not?'

'Because every time I've been ripped off, it's been by some guy who wants to use his credit card late at night. So I don't take 'em after ten anymore. Haven't you got cash?' he asked ominously.

'Probably not enough,' Warden muttered, thinking. 'Look, you'd better take a detour past a National Australia bank that's got an automatic teller machine. Do you know of one nearby?'

'Over this way.' The cabbie waved a finger at the windscreen. 'But it'll be out of our way—cost you more.'

'I don't care about that, as long as it's quick.'

The driver grunted again, not sounding very happy now.

When Warden got to the teller machine, he saw the 'Out of Service' message flashing across the screen. Swearing, he ran back to the cab, got in before the driver could take things into his own hands and leave him behind, then told him what was wrong.

'Now what?' the cabbie asked, plainly displeased at the chain of events.

'Well, where's another one?'

The cabbie reluctantly thought for a moment. 'There's a big one at the Andergrove Shopping Centre. It's got three machines. They can't all be out of order, but the trip will cost you even more,' he added meaningfully.

'Don't keep panicking about the fucking money,' Warden snapped, slamming his door closed. 'Just get going.'

With a theatrical sigh the driver put the taxi into gear.

23

Only weeks earlier, if Gwen had awoken in the middle of the night, she would have felt safe and secure in the familiar surroundings and with Brendan by her side. Tonight the bedroom looked the same. It was comfortably dark, the gloom broken only by slivers of faint streetlight sneaking in, as always, between the drawn curtains. The mirror on the wardrobe looked silvery, like a pool of mercury.

Gwen was sleeping soundly, despite all the stress and fear of the day. The alcohol helped, as did the fatigue and mental exhaustion. She was lying on her stomach and, in her sleep, pulled a pillow into her chest and snuggled against it. She went absolutely still, breathing deeply. Next to her Brendan began to stir, muttering softly without waking and rolling over again, taking a tangle of sheets with him. He was sweating and his own breathing was shallow and disturbed. A breeze suddenly swirled in the room, billowing the curtains away from the window which, in turn, washed everything with reflected streetlight, but neither of the sleepers were disturbed enough to awaken.

For a fleeting moment, something seémed to be moving in the mirror.

In Brendan's office next door the keys on the computer keyboard began to rapidly depress on their own, as if invisible hands were typing. The blank screen snapped back to life automatically and displayed an empty page for a second, then words started to march across the surface.

Brendan muttered something through his gritted teeth and began kicking the sheets away from him. Expressions of anger, fear and pain crossed his sweating face, but he was still deeply asleep.

Things were moving in the lounge room again, but not with the gathering violence of before. Now the books fell haphazardly to the floor and the ornaments dropped from the shelves as if dislodged by a gentle breeze or an errant child's hand as it walked past. The curtains here, too, continued to lift and sway, sometimes whipping with a soft cracking sound, although the swirling air wasn't strong enough to warrant it and the windows were still closed. The lights started to flicker on and off, with the switch on the wall rocking madly. In the lower hallway, the front door latched gently closed.

The ghostly chaos moved through the house and into the kitchen. There, a tap twirled open all the way. It was the hot water, with comparatively weak pressure, so rather than gush out and awaken someone upstairs with the noise, it gurgled softly down the drain. After a few seconds it began to steam with heat. The air began to shift and eddy strongly in the smaller, confined space, tearing the steam away from the sink. The scattered papers on the table suddenly, dramatically lifted and spun in a mini-vortex in the middle of the room. The newspaper that Warden left on the stove fluttered, as if it wanted to join in, but it was too heavy to be drawn upwards. A line of cooking utensils hanging nearby jangled musically together. The light switch began to snap up and down like its counterpart in the lounge, but here the fixture was a fluorescent and it wasn't powered long enough to start a glow. A square of light was provided by the microwave, the oven coming to life with its bell pinging and the hum of the carousel rotating.

The knobs on the gas stove turned smoothly all the way. With all four of the top burners on full, the hiss of flowing gas could be heard above the running water. The igniting switch depressed itself and stayed there, making a continuous clicking sound. In the gloom, the tiny blue electrical sparks could be seen jumping across the elements and, one by one, the gas burners burst into flame—including the one directly underneath the newspaper.

The newspaper burned with a different flame. It was a hungry, dancing yellow flame that grew large, climbing high and wide in the swirling air and reaching out to touch the brittle, dry documents that were Brendan Craft's family history. These caught fire immediately, still suspended above the table and now roaring softly as only a moving flame can do, as they continued to spin in mid-air. The curtains above the sink were the next to join the fire, wafting away from the glass far enough to be licked by the flames several times, singeing to black, then edging themselves with glowing red until these too became a living flame.

Finally, the wall closest to the stove caught fire. The house was old, the walls made of untreated timber and in need of new paint for many years. Here, the flames found a willing friend and took hold quickly. In less than two minutes the kitchen resembled the inside of a furnace with hot flames climbing the walls on every side and crawling across the ceiling. The burning papers had been completely consumed. In mockery, the hot water continued to flow uselessly down the sink.

The entire house was timber and the flames moved fast.

*

At first, Gwen thought the sound she heard was hard rain falling on the roof. It was a heavy, roaring noise that was unusual enough to drag her out of her alcohol-affected sleep and make her sit up groggily and listen. She took a moment to curse whatever it was that had disturbed her—she needed all the sleep she could get. Next she looked down at Brendan, who was curled into a tight ball with his back to her. He'd never slept in that way before, for as long as she had known him, and Gwen wondered if he was, in fact, asleep. She reached out to touch his shoulder, then drew back in alarm as Brendan suddenly shouted a nonsensical noise and jerked, as if kicked.

'Bren, are you okay?' she asked quietly, then stopped, becoming aware that something wasn't right.

It was hot—very hot. With the tropical storms it could stay warm, but normally with the rain starting to fall the temperature did, too. Gwen quickly got up from the bed and moved towards the window. She had to stop still for a second and wait for a dizzy spell to subside, then she swept the curtains aside. The glass of the window was dry and beyond it, there were no falling sheets of heavy rain. From somewhere in the house a strange orange glow was spilling out onto the front lawn. The roaring noise was already louder.

And she could smell smoke. She wondered why it had taken her so long to notice it.

'Jesus Christ,' she whispered fearfully, the

dreadful realisation dawning on her. Gwen rushed back to the bed and shook Brendan hard. 'Bren! Bren! You've got to wake up. There's a fire downstairs,' she snapped, trying to keep calm. 'We've got to get out of here.'

Brendan groaned and stirred, but went quiet again. Gwen took a few steps away so she could turn on the main light, slapping at it with her palm. The sudden light blinded her for a moment. Standing closer to the doorway allowed her to feel the warmth rising from the lower levels of the house and coming through the timber panelling. Fearing what she was going to see, she cracked open the door and peered through the gap. The hallway was brightly lit by a shifting orange glow. Shc pulled the door wider and leaned out, now feeling the fire as a real heat on the skin of her face. Looking towards the head of the stairs, Gwen could see tongues of flame climbing the stairs themselves. 'Oh God, no,' she said, seeing their line of retreat was being cut off. She had an urge to slam the door closed, as if it might make everything go away. Instead, she used precious seconds to force herself to be more calm and keep a cool head. Looking over her shoulder back into the bedroom Gwen saw Brendan was still lying on the bed. He had apparently fallen back to sleep. *Unconscious, is more like it,* she told herself, bitterly remembering her decision to use the sedative. *Come on, Gwen. Think!*

There was no sense in trying to drag Brendan to

the stairs, only to discover they were impassable. She had to find out for sure, first. Gwen hated the feeling of leaving the comparative safety of the bedroom, but she stepped out into the hallway and walked cautiously towards the stairs. The heat pushed at her and she put a hand up in front of her face. The noise of the flames out in the hallway was a loud, angry crackling. *Surely someone's noticed? The fire brigade must be on their way. We should wait until they get here, and we'll be able to escape out the bedroom window.* This appeared to be the only option, because the closer Gwen got to the stairway, the more obvious it became to her that it wasn't going to be an escape route. The fire had taken hold of the railing and the steps themselves. It was impossible to try and descend without having to pass through some significant flame. At the bottom of the stairs the front door beckoned with its promise of safety—but it was unreachable. She stared, mesmerised, at the fire and wondered if she were looking at her own death. She ignored the smell of her own eyebrows beginning to singe. The dancing flames were at once frightening, and yet fascinating.

Then a figure began to form in the fire. Gwen opened her mouth to scream, thinking it was someone trapped in the fire and burning to death, but a sudden terror for a different reason stopped her. There was nothing particularly shocking in appearance about the thing in the flames. There was little she could see—nothing horrid or dreadful. But the inhumanness of it, that it had to be something not of her world existing in the fire and a part of Brendan's living nightmare, told Gwen it was something to be greatly feared.

It looked like a man, standing calmly in the very heart of the worst flame and looking towards her.

Gwen turned and fled back to the bedroom. Brendan hadn't moved. She rolled him onto his back and began slapping his face. The flames were now making so much noise in the room that she had to raise her voice. 'Brendan, wake up! You've got to wake up! Come on, for God's sake. You can't still be drugged!' He responded by opening his eyes and looking up at her glassily. 'That's it,' she shouted encouragingly, immediately moving off him, but taking him with her, hauling Brendan into a sitting position with his legs over the side of the bed. 'The house is on fire, do you understand? We have to get out the window.'

Gwen could have cried or cheered—or both—when a semblance of understanding came into Brendan's expression. It quickly turned to fear. 'What the hell's happening?' he asked thickly, looking around and blinking in confusion. Focusing back on Gwen, he saw she was sweating profusely with the heat now. He noticed a redness where her skin had started to burn and he was going to say something, when the overhead light suddenly died, the electrical cabling burned away. The room was well lit with the flames beyond the open door.

'The house is on fire,' she repeated urgently, rubbing his face repeatedly to quicken his recovery. 'Listen to me. There's no way we can use the stairs to get out. There's too much on fire. We'll have to go out the window.'

'What the hell—' he got unsteadily from the bed and pushed past her to lean on the open doorway as he stared out along the hall. Gwen heard him call a curse. He came back to her. 'You're—you're right, that looks too dangerous,' he said breathlessly. He shook his head, trying to think clearly. He uttered a string of curses.

Gwen was hurriedly pulling on some clothes. Buttoning up her shirt with one hand she bent down to the floor and picked up Brendan's jeans, throwing them at him. 'Get dressed, for God's sake. And don't forget to put on some shoes.'

He nodded dumbly and started dragging the jeans over his legs. He didn't bother with a shirt and slipped on his runners without socks. Then he stood uncertainly in the middle of the room. Gwen was fully dressed.

'The *window*, Bren.'

'Yeah, right,' he nodded vaguely and went over to look. He reached up to the curtain rod, lifted it off the supports and threw the whole thing aside as Gwen joined him.

Outside, people were gathering on the front lawn as close as they dared to the flames, staring up towards the house. Three men had the presence of mind to run garden hoses over, one from the neighbours on each side and Brendan's own, and were directing the thin streams of water into the lower windows, but with little effect. There was still no sign of the fire brigade, except Gwen thought she heard the faint wail of a siren in the distance.

The window was a dual-casement style, the opposing frames hinged at the top and bottom to swing out from the house and, when closed, meet in the middle to lock together. With both of them pushed outwards to the limits, there was easily enough room for a person to go through and drop themselves the short distance to the lower roof outside. From there, Gwen and Brendan should have been able to jump onto the lawn without being hurt. But as Brendan shoved hard at the windows, trying to widen them as far as they could go, he looked down at the roof beneath.

'Shit,' he said softly, pulling back and blinking at the heat that had come up at him. At least, it had served to push away most of the dullness still inside his head. 'I don't think we can do it.'

'What? Why?' Gwen asked, glancing back towards the bedroom doorway, where the flames were plainly brighter. She imagined the fire had an evil mind of its own and was coming to get them, or the burning man would walk through the door. 'It's not too long a drop, is it?'

'It's not that. The roof below us has nearly burned through. It looks bad. If we try to stand on it, we might break through into the room below.' He didn't have to explain what that would mean.

Gwen could see for herself the tall flames licking out of the lower windows.

'What the hell are we going to do, then?'

'We'll have to wait for the fire brigade,' Brendan said unhappily.

'But we could fall through this floor at any moment too, right? We haven't got time to wait for the fire brigade.'

'We haven't got much choice, either.'

'There must be *something* we can do. What about the bathroom window?'

'It's too small—though I suppose you might get through it.'

'No—we'll find a way together, Brendan.'

They were shouting now and the heat building in the room was making them gasp for breath and bathing them in sweat. Brendan drew her close. 'Don't worry,' he said, knowing it sounded ridiculous. 'The fire brigade will be here soon and we'll walk out of here down a ladder, just you see—' He stopped and suddenly stared at her with wide, frightened eyes. 'Where's Warden?' he snapped.

For a second Gwen panicked too, thinking Warden should have been asleep in the lounge room, then she remembered. 'He went out,' she said, shaking her head. 'And he didn't come back. He—he wrecked his car, but he's okay,' she added quickly, seeing the concern appear on Brendan's face.

Before he could ask any more, there was a splintering crash from somewhere in the house and a spectacular shower of sparks came through the bedroom door, filling the room. Both of them yelled in fright and ducked, feeling the hot ashes burn their exposed skin. When the moment of immediate danger had passed, they looked at each other, very frightened.

'They'd better hurry up,' Brendan said quietly, pulling her close again.

There was another loud noise, this one an incredible howling sound as if a tremendous wind were ripping through the house. Brendan instinctively turned away from the open door again, taking Gwen with him, but the expected assault of heat and sparks didn't happen. Instead, when he lifted his head to look, the fire beyond the door appeared to have lessened a great deal. There were still flying sparks, smoke and the shimmering yellow glow, but the intensity of the fire had undoubtedly declined.

'What the hell?' he said, moving to see. He suddenly hoped the fire brigade had surprised them, attacking the fire from the rear of the house. Brendan stopped at the doorway, trying to look out, but there was nothing to see from that angle. Tentatively he walked out into the hallway, testing the floor with his weight with every step. The walls of the hallway were blackened and scorched, with tendrils of grey smoke drifting up to the ceiling. When Brendan looked towards the stairway he saw an amazing sight.

At the bottom of the stairs, standing back and

half in the doorway to the lounge room, stood the figure of a man. He was totally engulfed by flames, burning with a white-hot heat. It was impossible to see any details—who it could be. But then Brendan knew it could only be one person.

The *Setris* slowly lifted an arm and beckoned Brendan to come down the stairs.

The fire on the stairs, too, had been extinguished leaving behind smoking timber and charred railings. The steps were still intact, although how safe they were he couldn't guess. Brendan stared at the demon below and knew the *Setris* had somehow absorbed the fire from the timber.

Of course! Brendan thought dazedly. *The last thing that bastard wants is for me to die in the fire.*

He felt Gwen come close behind him. He reached backwards and found her hand. 'Come on,' he called over his shoulder. 'We're going down the stairs.'

'What?' she yelled back, then he heard her gasp as she came through the doorway and saw what had happened. 'No, Brendan!' she cried, pulling him back. 'Don't go near him!'

'It's our only chance! He can't let me die in the fire, remember? He's supposed to protect me.'

Gwen groaned aloud with fear, but let Brendan lead her along the hallway. The floorboards creaked alarmingly, weakened by the fire. The closer they got to the head of the stairs, the more heat they could feel rising from the lower sections of the house. The smoke was much thicker, biting at the backs of their throats and filling their nostrils. The *Setris* faced them, but was unmoving. The flames from his body were burning a hole on the timber ceiling above his head. With Brendan's first step onto the stairs themselves, there came a cracking sound of timbers breaking and he quickly pulled back. He cursed himself for not concentrating and when he tried again he placed his foot close to the wall. The step supported his weight, so he turned around and gestured to Gwen to show what he was doing, pointing down with his spare hand. She nodded desperately back, her face blackened by the smoke. Keeping their backs to the wall, despite feeling the heat of the fire which had just been burning there, they crabbed sideways down the stairs. Near the bottom Brendan realised they'd have to contend with the intense heat coming from the demon itself. He could feel it already. With only a few steps to go he looked directly at the burning figure.

He could see the awful, familiar face within the flames now, but in the moment Brendan looked, the skin began to blacken and peel shockingly from the *Setris'* cheeks and forehead. It was as if his face was melting with the heat. Still, his lips were drawn back in an ugly grin. Portions of his skull started to show as the flesh dripped off in burning gobs. Brendan tore his eyes away to glance at Gwen, hoping she couldn't see this, but by the horrified expression on her face he knew she could. Desperately, he lunged the final distance to the front door past the burning figure, dragging Gwen with him so that she nearly fell. He grabbed for the handle with his other hand. The hot metal of the doorknob seared his fingers and palm, but Brendan held on and frantically twisted it, wrenching at the door. It pulled open, bringing part of the frame with it in another shower of sparks. He didn't wait for them to abate, but ran through the falling curtain of red embers.

The outside air felt like a splash of chilled water on their faces and Brendan was temporarily blinded, running away from the bright flames into the relative darkness. There were urgent voices all around and he felt hands grip him on the upper arms. Suddenly feeling completely exhausted, he let himself be lowered to the cool lawn and saw that Gwen had done the same beside him. The first thing he noticed fully was the flashing red lights on top of the fire brigade vehicles. There was a fine mist of moisture in the air from the canvas hoses jetting water at the house, but it was too late for these by now. The house was utterly destroyed.

He rolled over and propped himself on his elbows so he could watch. He could see now that the lower sections were burning intensely and it was a small miracle that the upstairs rooms hadn't fallen through before now. The flames were climbing high into the air and clouds of sparks leapt upwards with them in a brilliant display. Brendan was too shocked to feel anything—any emotional pain at seeing his own home being razed to the ground. He just lay there and stared at the fire. Recovering beside him, Gwen reached over and grabbed his hand, but he hardly noticed. Then someone was yelling in his ear and he turned to see the smoke-grimed face of one of the fire-fighters trying to ask him something.

'Is there anyone else in there?' he shouted above the noise of the fire.

Brendan dumbly shook his head. The fire-fighter patted him on the shoulder for a moment then hurried away.

A double explosion ripped through the house, making all the watchers flinch and some cry out in fear. The blast tore out the little support left under the house and the whole upper structure tipped quietly over, like a sinking ship, and collapsed into the inferno beneath causing a secondary plume of sparks and burning embers.

'What the hell was that?' Gwen croaked beside him.

'The gas tanks,' he told her, his voice dead. There was a fresh commotion among the spectators and the firemen started calling to each other urgently. Some people were pointing at the flames and Brendan tried to see what they were looking at. 'Dear God,' he breathed, when he saw what it was.

The *Setris* stood in the very centre of the inferno. The outline of his body was still clearly evident by the white-hot flames. Brendan realised that was what everyone *else* could see. He didn't believe anyone could see the demon within the flames. The fire-fighters and the watching neighbours thought they were looking at someone trapped in the fire. The fireman who had questioned Brendan ran past, pausing only a moment to snarl something about how the house was supposed to be empty. Brendan didn't bother to answer him. Several hoses immediately directed their streams towards the blazing figure, but the water had no effect except to create billowing clouds of steam that were quickly dissipated by the fire's heat again. Like before, the demon wasn't moving, but appeared to be staring out from the flames and searching for something—or someone. Only Brendan knew who the demon was looking for. Only he felt the *Setris'* eyes locate him in the darkness.

Incredibly, the demon swept his hand towards him and bent forward in a low, mocking bow. Then it disappeared with a final, hissing flurry of flame.

An hour later, working under some blazing arc-lights running from a generator, the fire brigade was damping down the remaining embers of the blaze. Brendan and Gwen still sat in the same spot. There had been no reason to move. Ambulance people had come over and treated the superficial burns, draped blankets over their shoulders and eventually left after Gwen convinced them they were going to be okay. Warden had arrived, looking both frantic and exhausted himself, soon after the *Setris* vanished. But he had to wait for a chance when the three of them were left alone, before Gwen could reveal what had happened. Warden got angry at himself for not being there when they needed him, then realised the futility of feeling this way and fell quiet. As soon as he had a chance he told them what had happened at the Veterans' Home and described the car accident afterwards, but against the tragedy of the fire, it didn't seem so important at that moment.

They were watching a group of firemen kicking their way through the ashes when, after a brief discussion, two of the men came over to the group sitting on the grass. One fire-fighter had yellow stripes on his waterproof clothing, denoting he was a sergeant of the brigade. The other was the same man who had asked Brendan earlier if there was anybody still in the burning house.

'We can't find any evidence of someone being trapped in the fire,' the sergeant said to Brendan accusingly, without any preamble. 'Everyone says there was somebody in the flames, just after you two escaped.'

Brendan looked up at him for a moment, then dropped his head wearily. 'There was no one else in the house,' he said.

'Jeff here says he asked you, and you said there was no one.'

'That's right.'

'Then who did we see? They saw someone standing in the middle of the fire.'

'Hey, you're the experts,' Brendan told them, trying to sound angry. 'You tell me what it was. As far as I know, there wasn't anybody else in the house.'

There was a silence, then the sergeant said to his companion, 'Maybe we should ask the police to look a little harder. I've got a feeling there's something wrong here,' he added, without caring that the others were listening.

'But there's no evidence of a body. Not a thing,' the other fire-fighter reminded him quietly.

Warden interrupted them. 'Guys, whoever heard of someone standing in the middle of a fire? Wouldn't they be running around, or trying to escape? It must have been some sort of freak anomaly caused by the heat.'

They stared at him hard. 'We are the experts, pal, don't forget. And I've never seen anything like that in my whole damned career,' the sergeant said harshly.

Warden shrugged and tried to stay calm. 'I know these people well and if they say there was no one else in the house, then that's the way it was. In fact, if anybody should have been in there, it is me.'

'And who the hell are you?'

'Just a friend.'

At a loss for anything more to say, the sergeant abruptly turned on his heel and walked away, his companion following. Moments later a policeman squatted down on Gwen's side.

'Have you folks got somewhere to stay?' he asked kindly. 'We can drive you there, if you like.'

'They'll be staying with me,' Warden said quickly, before Gwen or Brendan had a chance. Then he asked Gwen, 'You got some keys?'

Brendan's car was a burnt-out wreck, but Gwen's, parked behind it, looked comparatively untouched. However, she shook her head and waved vaguely at the smoking ashes. 'In there somewhere,' she said wryly.

'A ride to my house would be good,' Warden said to the policeman. 'It's been a bad day—I trashed my own car this afternoon.'

The policeman showed a moment of surprise. 'Okay, give me a few minutes to clear things up, then I'll come back to get you. We can take some details off you on the way, too.' He rose and walked away.

Warden waited until he was safely out of hearing distance before he spoke. 'So I suppose we have to say the *Setris* saved your life?' he said quietly.

'Got us out before the gas tanks blew and everything,' Gwen nodded, although Warden already knew this.

'Oh, I doubt he would have any knowledge of things like gas tanks or stoves,' Warden said. The firemen had already told them the fire appeared to have started in the kitchen. 'They didn't have a lot of those in ancient Egypt. He saved your skins from the fire, that's for sure, but if you'd stayed in there much longer, there would have been nothing he could do about any exploding gas tanks. Remember how we talked about that? The twentieth century will beat him one day, you'll see—' Warden stopped, suddenly realising what he was saying.

'So, I'm out of the fire and still in the frying pan?' Brendan murmured darkly. 'Or in my case, out of the fire and still in my own, personal fucking nightmare. Maybe I should have hung around and gotten myself killed in the explosion? It looks like getting killed is the only way out of this mess for me.'

'Don't talk like that,' Gwen told him sharply, but with exhaustion creeping into her voice too.

'Why not? Look at it from my point of view. I can't kill myself, and that leaves me with a lifetime of being haunted by some sort of a monster. For all we know, he started that fire just to have some fun, for God's sake! How long will it be, before they stick me in a padded cell, too?' He stopped and stared moodily at the burnt-out house. After a moment he added savagely, 'And now, just to make it worse, it looks like I owe the bastard one.'

24

Warden lived in a two-storey, brick townhouse in an expensive part of town. The street was normally quiet and lined with impressive gardens. Vehicles parked at the curb were BMWs and luxury sports cars. There came a muted roar of an expressway quite close and passenger airliners passed low overhead, but the house was air-conditioned and well insulated. Warden had no qualms about keeping the place shut tight to leave the noise outside and running the climate-control system almost all year round.

The spare bedroom was fully furnished with a

large double bed and an ensuite. As he showed them he explained, almost apologetically, 'I've had this joint designed for visitors. Have a shower and just make yourselves at home. I'll have a rummage around and see what clothes I've got to lend you.' By the time he returned with an armful of clothing the shower was running and Gwen and Brendan were obviously in there together. He quietly put the things on the bed and went away. The next time he had the opportunity to peek through the door his guests were both fast asleep on the bed underneath a single sheet. Warden resisted the urge to pull an extra cover over them, but he did flick the light off and gently close the door. At the last moment he saw a faint glow in the room and realised it was coming through the window—the slightest, gentle pink colour. He squinted at his wristwatch, feeling his tired eyes burn at the effort and nodded to himself. It was, in fact, late enough for the dawn to begin impressing itself on the night sky.

Not surprisingly the next day started late for all of them. Warden was the first to awaken, late in the morning. He crept past the spare bedroom and went downstairs to make himself coffee and read the paper, waiting for the others to stir. At the sound of a shower and footsteps on the ceiling above him, he began to cook a full breakfast of bacon, eggs and tomatoes for all of them and made a pot of fresh coffee. Not long afterwards he turned to see Gwen, attracted by the smell of frying food, finding her way into the kitchen. He wished her a cheerful good morning and got a weak smile in return.

'Chasing ghosts must be a profitable business,' she said, gesturing at the comfort around them. Her smile widened to show she didn't want to offend him.

Warden pointed at the coffee percolator, inviting her to help herself. 'I wish it was,' he said, with a chuckle. 'Then I might be able to do it all day and every day. But it's the software company paying for everything you see. It's a crazy business with high prices and even higher fees. I'm only cashing in, before everyone comes to their senses—if they ever do.'

'Then you must be going broke at the moment. All you've been doing is looking after us. We owe you so much.'

'Hey,' he turned from the frying pan and spread his arms. 'This is the spook story of my lifetime! I'll probably never get this close again, so it's me who owes you guys for letting me in. In fact, I may have to retire from the ghost-hunting business after this. Nothing will ever be the same.' Warden was surprised when Gwen suddenly came over and gave him a quick kiss on the cheek. Without saying anything she went back to making two coffees, after checking that he still had some left in his cup.

'Besides,' he added, a little flustered. 'I've got a few business things happening at the moment which will just keep running by themselves. I often have times like these, where I can take it easy for a while.' He shrugged self-consciously and grinned. 'It's the price of success, I guess.'

There was a silence between them, while he flipped the bacon and Gwen tinkled a spoon in the coffee cups.

'Where's Brendan?' he asked.

'Coming down in a second. He wanted another shower, too. You can still smell the smoke, like it's in our skin.'

He nodded. 'And what do you think you'll do today?'

'God knows. What the hell are you supposed to do, the night after your house burns down with everything in it? Get busy with the insurance people and everything, I suppose. Hell, neither of us even got our wallets out of the house. We've got no credit cards, cheque books or anything,' she finished with a sigh.

'I think you two could leave all that for another twenty-four hours, don't you? Give yourselves a break. Hell, I can get you some cash. Why don't you just go down the shopping centre and buy some clothes, that sort of thing, and forget the rest until tomorrow?'

'We could,' she agreed, nodding slowly. 'But I really must go into the hospital. I can't avoid it and I won't be long. Will you look after Brendan for me?'

Warden was surprised by her sudden intensity and even more puzzled by the way she glanced towards the doorway, as if worried Brendan might come through and hear her. 'Sure,' he said, frowning and wondering how much he should pry. 'I was going to call up a hire car for the day. You can borrow that.'

It was Gwen's turn to be confused for a moment. She had forgotten Warden was involved in his own personal tragedy the day before, losing his car in the accident. 'We'll pay for half,' she offered. Warden looked about to argue, when Brendan came into the kitchen.

Warden asked him with a loud cheerfulness, 'Hey, how're you feeling, champ?'

Brendan gave him a soft slap on the shoulder as he passed on his way to stand near Gwen. 'Normal,' he announced quietly. They looked at him, surprised, and he shook his head. 'No, not *that* normal, but I have a feeling everything from yesterday is under control again. I don't know why, but I don't feel so—so unstable anymore, I suppose.'

'Well, that's something,' Warden said, covering the moment of disappointment which had come with the misunderstanding. 'Just don't go anywhere near Robert Lawson. Hey, I hope you guys are hungry, because I've got the best breakfast in the world coming right up.'

They helped him move plates, cutlery and glasses of orange juice to a dining table. There, Warden again raised the subject of what they should do for the day. He was glad to hear Brendan readily agree to taking it easy for a while longer. He didn't even protest about Gwen's trip into the hospital and Warden figured he was used to Gwen's concern and commitment to her work even on the day after their house had burned down. For his part, Warden said he would be doing some business from home while he kept an eye on Brendan. Again, Brendan didn't have any objections.

Not long after breakfast he started to look fatigued and depressed once more and announced he would probably spend most of the day catching up on some sleep.

The hire car arrived just before lunch and Warden insisted Gwen use it. He had no special plans, he simply wanted transport on hand, in case they needed it. By this time Brendan was already asleep in the spare bedroom. He hadn't seemed interested in buying new clothes and some of Warden's older stuff fitted him okay anyway. When she was leaving, Warden followed Gwen out onto the small front lawn and watched while she stuffed money into the pocket of her jeans, which she had washed and dried first thing that morning. The brown singe marks from the fire didn't look out of place with the frayed, faded denim and one of Warden's shirts appeared fashionably baggy on her.

'Why are you going into the hospital?' he asked her, aware he might not get a truthful answer. 'Wouldn't a phone call do?'

'I'm going to get something,' she replied simply.

'Care to tell me about it?'

Gwen hesitated. 'Only if you promise not to argue about it—and you won't say anything to anyone. You might even help me, if you like.'

Warden looked at her a long time. Gwen was really starting to show signs of stress and lack of sleep. But there was also something else—a stubborn determination that wouldn't be refused. He knew that he had a choice. He could agree to her conditions and at least be able to keep an eye on her and maybe help. Otherwise, she might do something bad or crazy when his back was turned and he would live to regret that for the rest of his days. He took a deep breath.

'Okay,' he said.

'Promise me first—a real promise, Warden.'

He tried a smile, but it didn't work. He held up two fingers. 'Scout's honour. That's the best you can get from an old scout like me.'

Despite the joke, Gwen saw he was serious, so she quickly told him what she was doing.

Listening, Warden reflected it was a good thing he'd promised to keep quiet. Still, he wondered if it was the right thing to do.

25

This time it was Brendan who awoke in the middle of the night. He was sleeping restlessly, because his exhaustion during the day had kept him mainly in the bedroom dozing. His mind was still feeling strained and in need of peace, but his body had had enough of resting. He opened his eyes and stared at the wall next to him. There was little comfort in the unfamiliar room. He could feel Gwen at his back, curled against him and asleep. He considered getting up, going downstairs and fixing himself a warm drink. Warden had a selection of books down there and Brendan would easily find himself something to read until he felt tired enough to go back to bed. But the gloom of the room also tempted him to lie where he was and wait to see if he got drowsy again. He had no sleeping pills. Presumably, they'd been destroyed in the fire with everything and no one had considered getting a replacement prescription. Brendan hadn't mentioned it. Luckily, there were no signs in his drowsing consciousness of the nightmares returning, and there hadn't been all day.

Five minutes later, he gave up and eased himself out of the bed. Gwen didn't stir. Brendan was only wearing his underwear and normally he would have stayed that way, but being in a strange house he felt around on the floor until he found his jeans. Concerned the rustle of clothing might disturb Gwen, he carried them outside the bedroom and put them on in the hallway. Bare-chested and hopping on one foot as he pulled at the jeans, he noticed the door to Warden's room was slightly ajar, making Brendan double his efforts to stay quiet. He wondered what time it was. He wasn't wearing his watch and the cheap alarm clock in the bedroom didn't have illuminated numbers. Shrugging that it didn't matter anyway, he worried about negotiating the stairs in the dark instead.

In the kitchen he made himself a hot chocolate drink. The timer on the microwave told him it was well after midnight. Brendan took the liberty of lacing the brew with a liberal dash of Warden's brandy taken from the lounge room. Everything he did sounded unnaturally loud and he kept worrying about waking the others. The microwave beeped so loud he punched the button to open the door too hard and made more noise that way, anyway. He tried to stir his drink without letting the spoon touch the sides of the cup. Finally, armed with his hot chocolate and a handful of biscuits raided from a jar, he made his way into the lounge, putting his supplies on a small table beside a large single leather armchair. He left the bright overhead lights on while he searched the bookshelves for something to read, but once he had two books he thought would keep him entertained for a while, he switched over to the reading lamp beside the chair.

He immediately felt uncomfortable about the deep shadows in the room where the reading lamp's low light didn't reach and he considered turning the main light back on. He stood in the gloom and tried to reach out, feeling at the air around him. His instincts told him it wasn't bad. *It's all in your own fucking mind, half the time,* he told himself savagely. *That's what the damned* Setris *is all about, right? Fucking with your mind. Well, screw him tonight. He can look after me for a change.* Unaware he was doing it, Brendan's hand went to the charm hanging around his neck and fingered the metal for a few moments. He felt a small surge of relief.

He sat in the chair and let it rock back to a comfortable angle. The chill leather closed against the bare skin of his back, making him gasp, but it quickly warmed. He carefully took a sip of his drink, holding it out over the edge of the armrest so there was no chance of spilling any on the leather, which he figured would be harder to clean than the carpet. Then he opened the first of the books and flicked slowly through the pages, looking for something to grab his attention.

Some time later he had finished the drink and even let his head nod tiredly towards the pages once, telling him it was time to return to the bedroom. He decided to have a quick scan through the second book, which should last long enough to make him just a little more weary. He put the first book gently down on the floor in front of him, then bent sideways to retrieve the second one from beside the coffee table.

He realised someone—or something—was in the room with him.

He looked over his shoulder, a cry coming to his lips. But the direction he looked meant he also stared directly into the lamp and he was blinded to the room beyond by the glare. All he saw was a tall, menacing shape looming behind his chair and moving close, before Brendan could struggle out of the embracing leather.

Then he saw it was Warden.

'Christ, you scared the hell out of me,' he said.

'Sorry, pal,' Warden said. He was wearing a strange smile. 'Sorry about this, too.'

He reached out, gripping the back of Brendan's

neck with a fierce strength. Brendan let out a cry and tried to twist away, but Warden's grip was too strong. Unbidden and suddenly uncontrolled, the hold on his neck brought back a terrifying memory from one of his dreams. The ritual killing scene on the steps, in the bright sunshine, where the high priest had slit a man's stomach while he gripped him by the neck like this, then shook him like a rag doll to make his entrails spill out.

Instead of grabbing for Warden, Brendan's hand went automatically to his belly, expecting to feel the knife probing for his gut. He felt himself lifted out of his chair effortlessly and carried forward, feeling his neck wrench with his own weight. Then he was sent sprawling forward onto the floor until the carpet fibres were being crushed against his cheek. Pressure came onto his back and something else pinned one of his arms down. He was yelling hoarsely now and trying to fight back, but it was useless. Warden was too powerful.

Brendan began to feel strange and, at the same time, a fatal resignation. For some reason he accepted he was going to die, even though it was his friend attacking him. All the strength ebbed from his muscles and a curious numbness took its place. The sound of his blood pounding filled his ears and, with a fresh spasm of fear, he could hear it wasn't a regular sound—his heartbeat was erratic and unsteady. It was getting harder to breathe, too. *Oh God, is this what's it like to die?* he thought desperately and in a sudden reversal wanted to survive. *Am I dying? God, don't let me die yet!* With frightening speed he became completely paralysed. A warm wetness leaked from his groin, his bladder control fading, and he found a moment in his terror to feel a hot shame. Dragging air into his lungs became harder and black spots began to appear in front of him as a lack of oxygen made itself felt. Then he felt someone grip his shoulder and roll him over onto his back.

He could still see enough to make out two faces staring down anxiously at him. Gwen was beside Warden now. Relief registered in Brendan's mind faintly, but he was already too far gone to experience even emotions properly now. The last thing he thought was that Gwen didn't appear to be trying to help him or stop Warden.

Uncaring of where it went, other than it landing somewhere no one would tread on it, Gwen tossed the used syringe into a corner of the lounge. Then she leaned forward and professionally checked Brendan's pulse and breathing.

Warden breathed, 'God, I hope you know what you're doing.'

'I know the damned theory, that's all,' she replied grimly. She explained more, her voice rushed and shaking, talking to fill the silence and keep control of herself. 'It's called Suxamethonium, or Scoline for short. It's a fast-acting muscle relaxant they use at the beginning of almost every surgical procedure. Without it, they couldn't get tubes down patient's throats or anything like that. Usually it only works for about three minutes, then wears off. By that time, an anaesthetist will be injecting a different sedative and you'd have machines attached to breathe and pump blood for you.'

Warden's face was pale in the gloom, but he managed to look even more startled. 'You mean, he should be connected to life-support stuff?'

'I told you—it's a muscle relaxant. The heart's a muscle and so are the lungs. He'll go into respiratory collapse and soon after that, without fresh oxygen, his heart will stop. With the double dose of Scoline I gave him, the drug won't be wearing off for about five minutes.' Gwen paused to peer at her watch.

'In about ninety seconds, he'll be dead,' she announced.

She stared up at Warden, daring him to say something, but he was speechless. Behind them, unseen in the darkness of the kitchen, the air began to shift and swirl, and a shape started to form out of nowhere.

26

There was complete blackness, which for a moment was almost reassuring in its familiarity. At first Brendan feared he was back in one of his old nightmares, wandering the catacombs of some tomb in ancient Egypt, but without the torch to light his way. He put a hand up in front of his face, near enough so he could feel his breath against the skin of his palm. He still couldn't see it. Then he remembered his near-death experience when he was under hypnosis and, with a sickening swoop in his gut, realised that he'd returned to that same place, but because he was supposed to be here this time.

He couldn't be anywhere else. Memories of his last moments alive came back to him.

Gwen didn't get to me in time, he thought, tears coming unseen to his eyes. *It's finally happened—I'm dying, or I'm already dead. This is what it's like.*

He expected to feel some sort of relief or even a happiness at passing from one life to the next. Everything in life, every lesson, every religious tenet, suggested that death offered a release. Certainly not this emptiness he felt in his heart, like a despair or a feeling of being cheated and the lack of any direction, such as a guiding light or any awakened instinct telling him what he should do next. Instead, just the impenetrable darkness.

Brendan sensed someone—or something—close by, but before he could react a cold breath washed over one side of his face and a woman's voice whispered in his ear.

'Who are you?'

He jerked around, trying to follow the sound, but it was useless. He couldn't see a thing. He called out nervously, 'Who's that? Where are you?' His words were curiously flat, as if he were in an immense space with nothing around for the sounds to echo from. He thought he heard a dry, humourless laugh in the distance. The chill presence came past his other side.

'Which way do you walk?'

'What? Where are you?'

'Tell me, which way will you walk?'

'Which way? What the hell do you mean?' He spun around again. Brendan was torn between anger and fear at the taunting whispers. The next voice he heard was unexpectedly loud and commanding, like a stern teacher addressing a misbehaving student. It seemed to come from directly in front of Brendan, making him step backwards in surprise.

'You can't stay here. Haven't they told you that? If you stay too long, you'll be here forever, like us.'

'I don't understand,' Brendan called into the darkness. 'Where am I? Won't you tell me?' He cried out suddenly when he felt something rub against his legs, but even as he jerked away he recognised it. It was the warm, furry sensation of an animal—perhaps a cat—pressing itself against him. It let out a tortured wail—another soul lost in the darkness. 'Where the hell am I!' Brendan asked again, becoming more unnerved. The authoritative voice answered him.

'Your time has come. You are on your way. You must choose between the Light and the Dark. Everyone has that choice, either now or before they come here.'

'What do you—?' Brendan stopped, because in that instant he became aware of a light in the distance, burning with a blue intensity like an arc-welder's torch, but unwavering and not harmful to look at. He was sure it hadn't been there a moment before. He knew what the light represented. He had a good feeling just looking towards it. At the same time it confirmed his fears about exactly where he was, what had happened to him. A deep sadness filled him.

'I have that choice myself? How can I?' Despite the facts in front of him, doubts remained in his mind. He still felt the whole thing was strangely unreal. He had a sense that everything was just too fantastic. And surely dying wasn't meant to be this cold, almost clinical transition? It should be an uplifting, even wonderful sensation.

'Make sure you choose what is right, because you cannot turn back. You only have time to go towards one or the other and if you are wrong, you will stay here like us—and that might be the worst choice of all.'

'But I don't understand. I know what the Light is. Why would I choose the—the other way?'

A figure appeared in front of him. Brendan struggled through a moment of shock as he recognised his mother. She was young again, exactly as she appeared in the wedding photograph he'd had on his mantelpiece, and she literally glowed with some inner health. Automatically he moved towards her, his arms reaching forward, but it needed only a few steps for him to see he couldn't get any closer. She regarded him with an impassive, curious look.

'You don't have much time, Brendan. Which way will you walk?'

'Mum, I don't understand,' he told her haltingly, tears coming to his eyes again. 'What's happening to me?'

'This the last test for the Unfaithful,' he heard

her say, matter-of-factly and apparently uncaring that she was instructing her own son. *'You must choose between the Light and the Dark—but you must choose what you believe you deserve. In your life you did not embrace any god to judge you in this moment, so now you must face the most critical judge of all—yourself. Have you lived your life so you deserve the Light, Brendan?'*

Before he could answer, the commanding voice spoke.

'What you choose is not what you may be given. The Light can lead to Darkness forever, if you are undeserving. The Darkness may lead to the Light, in time, or you may remain there for your sins.'

Brendan looked towards his mother. 'Which way should I go?'

'I can't tell you. You have to judge yourself.'

A sudden anger got the better of Brendan. 'This is crazy! I don't even belong here! I shouldn't be—'

His mother had vanished.

Again, he felt the cold presence brush close to him and the woman's voice hissed near his face.

'Which way will you walk?'

'For Christ's sake, leave me alone!'

He heard a girlish giggle fade into the distance. Brendan faced the blue light, which still glowed with an intense, unmoving glare. Everywhere else was the same blackness and on an impulse he put his hand in front of his face again. Strangely, he still couldn't see it. The beckoning blue light didn't illuminate anything.

'Damn you!' he called loudly, and started walking towards the light. 'Damn you all, whoever the fuck you are! I've *been* through Hell lately. I can judge that for myself!'

Brendan hated what he was doing. There was a finality about what was happening—something that he couldn't return from. He believed, deep inside, that this was all some sort of mistake. He shouldn't be here yet, shouldn't be making this choice. *But then,* he thought reluctantly, *that's what some people say ghosts are. The spirits of people who won't accept death. Is that what'll I'll become?* He strode through the darkness, drawing strength from his anger.

He had no idea how long he walked or how much distance he covered. The blue light stayed elusive in the distance. His anger continued to grow and he was thinking the whole thing was some fantastic trick—he'd had no thoughts of the *Setris* at all, until this occurred to him. The chill presence of the taunting spirit passed by him several times, whispering into his ear, but now he couldn't understand any of the words. Sometimes he heard the giggling laughter. He ignored all of it.

Then he saw someone, a man, sitting in the blackness in front of him. He was curled into a ball, hugging his knees. Brendan approached him warily.

'Who are you?' he asked, from a distance. Beyond the man, still no closer, the blue light burned. At the sound of Brendan's voice, the man raised his head and looked towards him. Brendan could see he was very old, then with a shock noticed bright red blood matted in the old man's thinning hair and running in a trickle down the side of his face. He was naked. More rivulets of blood were appearing from somewhere near his wrists to run freely down his wasted legs. Slowly he raised one arm, his fingers spread, in a beseeching gesture. Brendan went closer.

'What happened to you? Can I help you?' he asked the old man. The gaunt limbs with their unhealthy, pale flesh stood out starkly against the pitch black surrounding them. Brendan saw a ghastly puncture wound on the man's wrist. It was pumping out blood at an alarming rate, spurting into the air. He had no idea what to do, or if the image was even real. As he approached, too late he realised something else. The old man's begging stare wasn't fixed on Brendan's face, but on the golden charm hanging around his neck on its leather thonging.

With an agility he shouldn't have possessed the old man snarled an animal cry and sprang towards Brendan, his hands clawing at him. Brendan was taken completely by surprise and would have been hurt, but his attacker's hands were clutching for the charm, not him. With luck more than judgement he managed to grasp the thin wrists and wrestle them aside, but the old man's momentum carried him on, sending them both backwards. Next he was on top of him, the blood on his face dripping down onto Brendan as he fought to keep him off. The old man's yellowed teeth began snapping at his throat, like a savage dog, and the stench of his breath made Brendan gag. The wounded wrist was slick with blood in his grip, slithering and threatening to escape. Brendan realised, as he fought, that the old man was trying to bite the leather around his throat—to release the charm. Then, as suddenly as the attack began, the old man stopped, frozen in his posture, suspended above Brendan and with a stare of terror on his face. Brendan felt the man being drawn away from him and he tightened his grip, afraid the withered hands would claw at him for support and pull him along, too. It was as if the old man was dangling above a hidden bottomless pit and he was slipping through Brendan's saving grasp. Incredibly, the lower part of his naked body began to disappear, drawn into the hole in the darkness. He started screaming, a high, unintelligible sound that raked at Brendan's ears. Hauled inexorably by some undeniable power, he slipped from Brendan's blood-slickened fingers and vanished, his terrified screeching cut off in an instant.

Brendan lay there panting and frightened, smelling the blood on him and the old man's own unclean stench. He heard someone laughing and it sounded familiar, but he knew the laughter wasn't directed at him. He suddenly understood the attack hadn't been directed at him, as much as it had been a torment for the old man.

Galther, he realised dimly. *That was Adrian Galther. The* Setris *was having some fun with him, for a change.*

As if uncaring, or even unaware of what had happened, the coldness swept past Brendan again.

'Which way will you walk?' the voice whispered.

On an impulse Brendan snarled, 'Go away, you bitch!' He heard the female giggling again. Someone else spoke. This time the voice was gentle and sad.

'It's mine, you know. I should still have it.'

Brendan twisted around and stood at the same time. From somewhere behind him had come a young soldier, his uniform in tatters, his skin pale and lifeless. Brendan recognised him from the three wounds across his chest. It was the soldier who had appeared in his lounge room that day, only to wither and turn to dust in front of their eyes.

'*Who* are you?' he asked.

'The charm is mine. I took it, then it was stolen from me.' The spirit reached one hand towards Brendan as the old man had, but with his palm upwards. *'I can take it back.'*

The ghost's image moved Brendan to such pity that a lump formed in his throat, stopping him speaking for a moment. 'Tell me who you are,' he asked again.

'It doesn't matter—it only matters that the charm is mine, so I own the demon that lives in it. Give it back and I will take him, too.'

The conflict that had festered in Brendan about

owning and wearing the charm made itself felt now. As much as he'd prayed for an end to the nightmare that had become his life, now that an answer was offered he still couldn't bring himself to take the charm off. It would be like giving away a part of himself, or losing his most precious possession. He faltered, unsure what to do or say.

'I don't know if I can,' he said weakly.

'You have to. Look at me—look at Galther. Is that what you want to be?'

'No, but—' Brendan clamped his eyes shut and tried to find some courage. He lifted his hands and his fingers played with the leather thonging. Then another voice swept past him in the darkness. It was his mother again.

'Run for the light, Brendan. You haven't much time.'

Brendan opened his eyes and looked around, but he couldn't see her. The soldier's ghost was still in front of him, his hand held out. From the corner of his vision he thought he saw the blue light flicker for a moment.

'Run for the light, Brendan! Run for it now!'

With a feeling that wrenched at his heart, he grasped the leather and swept it over his neck, offering it in front of him. The soldier was impassive and didn't move. Brendan took a step towards him and, as with his mother before, discovered it didn't bring him any closer. 'Take it!' he cried, feeling suddenly wretched. 'Take it now, for God's sake!' He ran a few steps forward, but still the spirit came no closer. Then Brendan was running wildly, straight towards the soldier. It didn't make any difference. The soldier's image kept fading into the distance in front of him, tantalisingly near, but never close enough. Tears blurred Brendan's vision as he ran. Voices still echoed in his ears and the coldness slapped against his face.

'Run for the light, Brendan!'

'Which way will you walk?' the girl's voice asked, now with a delighted laughter.

'Brendan, listen *to me. Run for the light.'*

In front of him he thought he could see a wistful smile playing across the soldier's face. He stopped suddenly and, predictably, the ghost stopped too. The distance between them hadn't changed. Feeling beaten, Brendan looked at the spirit.

'You aren't close enough,' the soldier said oddly.

Brendan saw the blue light wink out and wasn't prepared for the feeling of crippling despair that overtook him. Now the chill presence wrapped itself around him, as if embracing him, and the girl's voice whispered triumphantly very close to his face.

'Now you are one of us.'

Still holding the charm in front of him, he took a final, hopeless step towards the soldier. He stepped into an unseen abyss and began to fall, the darkness whirling around him.

27

The first indication Gwen and Warden had of something materialising inside the house with them was a croaking, ruined voice coming from the kitchen.

'Leave him alone, you slut!'

Gwen looked up and Warden whirled around, both of them frightened. Jodie Seager's corpse stood in the doorway, glaring at them from hate-filled eyes in a ravaged face. Her burial clothes hung in rotting rags from her thin frame. Where her skin was exposed they could see it was grey and decaying with shreds of bruised, dead flesh peeling away. A stench was filling the room. Gwen let out a small scream, having managed to choke most of it down at the last instant. She stood and put herself protectively in front of Brendan's body.

'Let him live. If he dies, we are doomed to exist like this forever. He must take his own life. Keep your murdering hands off him, you whore.'

Gwen's voice shook as she replied. It took all her courage to stare her dead friend in the face. 'I'm not killing him, Jodie. I'm reviving him. But it must be done now. Jodie, for God's sake, let us do this. Don't try to stop me now.'

'Keep away. You've done enough, bitch.'

Warden whispered to Gwen, 'What can she do? How can she stop us?'

'I don't know—'

'We've only got less than a minute, according to your calculations. If we don't start artificial respiration then, it'll be too late.'

'I know . . .'

Gwen looked desperately down at Brendan lying on the floor. He had stopped moving altogether. There were no fluttering eyelids or twitching spasms. His breathing was obviously stopped and Gwen worried that she had been distracted at the wrong moment and now didn't know exactly how long his lungs hadn't been working. She came to a desperate decision and suddenly dropped to her knees beside him.

'I have to start now,' she said, pinching Brendan's nose closed and tipping his head back, to open his mouth. Warden braced himself, not knowing what could happen next, but ready for anything. Gwen took a deep breath and clamped her lips over Brendan's, expelling the air again and watching his chest slowly rise and fall from the corner of her eye.

The corpse screamed, a horrible and terrifying noise that chilled Warden to the bone. She leapt forward and tackled Gwen, dragging her away from Brendan. Suddenly, Gwen found herself fighting for her life. At first, the shock of grappling with the loathsome body, feeling her fingers dig into the rotting flesh and having the smell of decay choking her, meant she could do nothing but listen to her instincts and fight blindly back. She was pinned to the floor with Jodie above her. The corpse was trying to free her hands so she could scratch at Gwen's face with hooked fingers. They were curled into claws now, ready. Gwen could see the black dirt of the cemetery caked under the broken nails. She didn't notice she was screaming herself, frantically trying to get the corpse off her.

Warden was shouting, too. He had tried to pull the shrieking thing away from Gwen, but when he tried to encircle the dead woman's waist and drag her upwards his arms broke through the image as if she were tendrils of smoke. He tried again and again, becoming frantic himself at the sound of Gwen's terror, but he dimly realised the corpse was also some sort of ghostly spirit and was attacking Gwen only—he couldn't touch her. In fact, coming into contact with the apparition struck him ill in the stomach and made his head swim. Helpless and distraught, he forced himself to think of a way to do something—anything. Then he heard Gwen was trying to tell him something.

'Brendan!' she yelled at him, her voice breaking as she both fought her dead friend and tried to make herself understood over the corpse's terrible screeching. 'For God's sake, Warden! Revive Brendan! It's what she wants. I can't hold her off much longer. She's too strong!' As she battled to get the words out her concentration lapsed and Jodie's spirit slipped a hand free and raked it down Gwen's face, leaving behind three cruel lines of broken, bleeding skin. She screamed with the pain, but managed to recapture the spirit's wrist, grabbing it with such fierce, desperate strength that she felt a bone crack under her palm.

Warden nodded dumbly. Cursing over and over again, he knelt as Gwen had beside Brendan and prepared to give him mouth-to-mouth. He knew what to do, but it was a long time since he'd been taught. It was nearly impossible to concentrate on his task with the other madness happening in the room. 'Come on, buddy,' he muttered, before administering the first breath. 'For God's sake, don't take too long.' After giving Brendan three lungfuls of air, Warden quickly swapped position so he could press down on the breastbone, massaging Brendan's heart. As he moved he saw Gwen throw off the screaming corpse and manage to jump to her feet. She backed warily away from Jodie, who advanced mindlessly towards her, her fingers clawed and ready again.

'Three lots of three pumps,' Gwen snapped at Warden, who marvelled she had the presence of mind to worry about what he was doing. 'Then give him breath again. Repeat that over and over.' The blood was running in thin lines down her face and into her eyes, making her blink. She found herself backed up against the dividing counter between the living room and the kitchen area. She saw a heavy, copper-based pot within reach. Grasping it by the handle, she readied herself for the next attack just in time. Jodie launched herself at Gwen again, who brought the pot down in a short arc and smashed it squarely onto the dead girl's head. There was a horrible crunching sound as her skull shattered, but all it did to Jodie's efforts was send her stumbling backwards for a moment. Recovering, she advanced again.

Gwen began bludgeoning her repeatedly, pounding the corpse's face and head into an unrecognisable mess. Gwen was sobbing with what she was doing, but she had no choice. It had no effect on Jodie's attempts to attack her, except to keep her at arm's length. The problem was, Gwen was becoming exhausted, and wasn't sure how long she would be able to hit the dead woman hard enough to drive her back. From the corner of her eye she could see Warden relentlessly giving Brendan artificial respiration and cardiac massage. Gwen had no idea how long it had been going on, and a cold fear in her own heart was saying they might have left it too late—Brendan wasn't going to revive.

'That's it, pal!' Warden yelled encouragingly. He had seen a flicker of pain crossing Brendan's face, then suddenly he coughed horribly. A moment later he was breathing again in short, shallow breaths.

Gwen was distracted, seeing Brendan revive. The corpse flung itself at her and Gwen dropped the pot and threw her hands up in time to save her face being ripped at again. She was slammed back against the room divider and her head caught the sharp corner of a cupboard. It was enough to stun her completely, making her vision swim and a roaring noise fill her head. She felt herself slipping to the floor and could do nothing about it. She expected at any moment to feel Jodie's fingers clawing at her, digging into her face and skin.

But Jodie's spirit abandoned the fight and moved towards Brendan. Acting on a reflex, Warden rolled away from her, then shamed by his cowardice and realising he was leaving Brendan at her mercy, he reached back at the ghost and tried to push her back. But at the first touch the same, sickening feeling flooded through him, stronger this time, and he had to fall back again. He could only watch in horror as she lowered herself onto Brendan.

She started making soft, loving sounds. Her rotting hands caressed his face, urging him back to consciousness.

28

Brendan's vision started to clear, but it began with a blurred, spinning light. His chest hurt, he realised, and he had a headache that was truly agonising. There was a weight on top of him, pinning him down, and it took him a moment to understand someone was lying over him.

'Gwen?' he croaked, the effort of one word sending a lancing pain through his skull. Something else was wrong—there was a smell that shouldn't be there. An offensive smell that would have had him holding his breath, if it wasn't so painful to do. His eyesight recovered some more and he saw a face above him. He concentrated, willing his eyes to focus and slowly the girl looking down at him became clearer. Brendan found himself staring into Jodie's dead face. Every detail of her rotting, deathly features was only centimetres away from his own eyes.

He screamed, and it worsened the pain in his lungs, making him buck in reflex. The awful image shimmered briefly, then vanished, the weight on his body going with it.

Two long minutes passed. The three of them lay where they were, each lost in their own dazed thoughts. Warden was the first to move. He was confused and still feeling sickened, but not hurt like the other two. Slowly he crawled over to Brendan and touched him on the shoulder. Brendan flinched and turned his head to stare at him wildly.

'It's okay, Bren,' Warden said, softly. 'I won't hurt you any more, believe me. You can *trust* me. There's only us left now. She's gone.' He watched as his friend visibly unwound from his panic. 'Come on—Gwen's hurt. She needs help.'

He didn't wait for Brendan to get stronger. Warden stood weakly, went over to where Gwen still sat with her back propped against the room divider and crouched down beside her. He was surprised to see her look at him—the blood on her face made her injuries appear much worse.

'Are you okay?' he asked her.

'Head hurts,' she said weakly, but nodded at the same time.

'Don't move for a second.' Recovering with every passing second, Warden went into the kitchen and found a towel, dampened it under the tap and returned to Gwen. Brendan was beside her now, squatting down and holding both her hands in his and watching her anxiously. He looked unsteady, crouched there. They all ignored the acid, urine smell of his soiled clothes. Warden used the cloth to gently wipe away the blood on Gwen's face. She winced as the material touched the raw wounds of the scratches. Next he carefully tipped her head forward and felt the back of her scalp. He found a sizeable lump and Gwen cried out when he touched it, but his fingers came away dry. There was no bleeding there. When Gwen let her head fall back again, Warden saw she was crying. Her eyes were filled with tears and a single fat drop was rolling down her cheek.

'What the hell are we going to do now?' she asked, her voice catching. Then she said again in a low, despairing whisper, 'Just what the hell are we going to do now?'

Warden tried to think of some encouraging words, but had to admit to himself he felt beaten and exhausted. He managed to say, 'Don't worry, we'll think of something.' It sounded weak and unconvincing, which was also how he felt.

Then Brendan spoke, and Warden was surprised to hear him sound sure and confident with his words, even though he was obviously physically weary and unwell.

'I know what I have to do now,' he told them, looking at each of them in turn. A cold smile came on his lips. It did nothing to relieve his haggard appearance. 'Someone told me,' he added oddly.

29

Gwen couldn't go, because she didn't have a passport and they didn't want to wait any longer than they had to. As it was, there was going to be a delay—while Brendan replaced his own, which had been lost in the fire. She was going to stay behind in Warden's house until the two men returned.

Three days later—days filled with nervous hours and sleepless nights—Brendan and Warden flew out of the country, bound for Zimbabwe. It was the quickest, if not the most direct, route to their destination. From Zimbabwe they caught a flight straight to London, then a shuttle across to Paris and, finally, a rough flight plagued by bad weather to Istanbul. In all, it took them the best part of thirty-six hours with some seemingly interminable waits in international airport lounges. Although both men had travelled overseas before, the deliberate non-stop journey halfway around the globe was exhausting, despite the fact that much of it was spent simply sitting in an aircraft seat.

Brendan carried the charm in a soft leather pouch in his top pocket. Warden watched him carefully the entire journey, which was the reason he had come along. Gwen had given him a handful of tablets, similar to the sleeping pills, which would dope Brendan to insensibility within minutes if things got out of hand. Warden was determined to administer them by force if necessary and hope no one who saw them got the wrong idea. The two men passed the time mostly discussing what had happened. It seemed to help Brendan's state of mind and keep them constantly aware for any possible danger.

'Where is it now, do you think?' Brendan asked Warden at one stage, as their aircraft was cruising through the night. Most of the passengers were dozing.

'Our evil friend?' Warden thought for a moment. 'You know, at first I thought it was in you, like a possession. But now I think he's around you. You're wearing it like a cloak. The *Setris* is like a bad companion you can't shake off.'

Brendan automatically glanced nervously around the plane. 'So, why doesn't he do something? Surely he knows what we going to try and do?'

'I don't know. Maybe not. It could be it's confused or unsure what's happening right now. Don't forget, with being locked into Adrian Galther for sixty years, then lost in your cupboard for about another twenty, it's been transported from an early twentieth-century Arab country to the modern day western culture in a comparative fraction of time. It might even be a bit of a shock for the damned thing, really.' Warden thought about it a moment more and broke into a chuckle.

'What's so funny?' Brendan said.

'I was just thinking,' Warden kept smiling, 'We're dealing with a demigod, or demon, who has roamed the earth for thousands of years seducing people into killing themselves so he can drag them to his own personal hell. He comes from a religion that believes in the Underworld, right? A place physically under the ground.'

'I still can't see any humour,' Brendan told him. 'I lost my sense of humour about two weeks ago.'

Warden waved at the aircraft around them. 'Well, at the moment I figure we've got him about thirty thousand feet above his home sweet home. I wouldn't be surprised if he's not happy at all.'

It was ridiculous, but it brought a smile to Brendan's face. Later on, although he had said it already several times, he asked Warden again.

'I'm right, aren't I? We have to go there.'

Warden nodded, patiently. 'If it's going to work, it'll work there. It makes sense.'

From Istanbul the next step was a two hundred kilometre bus ride. They had to wait another six hours and they sat around the departure lounge of the bus terminal. The place was filthy, compared with what they were used to back home, and had a variety of odours which were unpleasant to most visitors. Local travellers, many of them dressed in flowing Arabic clothing, were scattered around the terminal as well. They regarded the two Westerners curiously and made Warden feel nervous. Both he and Brendan were desperately tired now, but neither could sleep. Warned by friendly customs officials, Warden bought several bottles of water for the coming bus trip which, they were told, was short on convenience stops and facilities. He also bought two heavy sleeping bags and some winter clothing for them both. They were advised it may even snow where they were going.

When they climbed aboard the bus, they were surprised to realise it was close to midday, local time. Hurriedly they occupied a vacant double seat near the front, barely squeezing in with the sleeping bags, extra clothing and their luggage under their feet and on their laps. A large Turkish woman glared at them from a nearby seat for quite some time, before she apparently decided they weren't worth the effort. Brendan was glad when she finally turned her head and stared out the window at the passing city instead. An hour later the bus had left the outskirts of Istanbul. The countryside was cold and arid, bracing itself for the coming winter.

Then, for the first time during the entire trip, things started to go wrong.

Brendan, his face suddenly turning pale, nudged Warden. 'Something's going to happen,' he said. He sounded scared.

'What? How do you know?' Warden twisted around and searched the bus, but there was nothing new to see. The other passengers stared back at him with blank expressions.

'It's like when I know I'm going to have a bad nightmare,' Brendan explained quickly. 'I can just feel it.'

'Damn it, we're getting so *close*, too.' Warden almost snarled, digging in his pocket. Then he rummaged amongst their luggage and came up with a water bottle. He held out four tablets.

'But they'll knock me out for hours,' Brendan protested weakly.

'I don't give a damn. I'll carry you off the bus, if I have to,' Warden said, grimly. 'What we don't want is you getting us thrown off the bloody thing here.'

Brendan could see Warden wouldn't listen to any arguments. He took all four pills, then while the unfamiliar Turkish countryside rolled slowly past, Warden made him recite the most inane things to keep his mind occupied, until they took effect. He went through all the names of his past girlfriends, the addresses of where he'd lived, his old schoolteachers—meaningless lists that needed concentration. Finally he became drowsy, then suddenly dropped into a sleep so deep Warden was afraid he'd overdone it with the pills. He was quietly relieved to see Brendan was still breathing.

Carefully, he watched him sleep. Brendan began to twitch and expressions of fear and pain crossed his face. Once he moaned something incoherent, but he didn't wake.

The sun was low in the sky when they arrived at a small town, the jumping-off point for the Gallipoli Peninsula. Brendan was awake, but barely aware of his surroundings and what he was doing. Warden propelled him around like an automaton. He managed to find a tour operator with a dilapidated minibus who, for an outrageous price, agreed to ferry them across the straits and drive them to Anzac Cove that evening, rather than wait until morning. A similar amount of money had to grease the palm of the ferry's operator. They completed the water crossing without incident and drove through low-scrubbed hills for about twenty minutes. The road began to hug a beach line some ten metres down a shallow cliff-face, then the bus pulled over to the narrow verge. The driver twisted in his seat and looked at them.

'Hey, where are we?' Warden asked, suspiciously. He felt dirty, tired and he ached all over. He was sick of sitting in seats—aircraft, buses or anything. Brendan stirred next to him.

'Anzac Cove,' the driver said in heavily accented English. He pointed at the narrow strip of sand below, then towards the road up ahead. 'Graves,' he added. 'There, the Shrines,' he swung his arm. He went on to explain haltingly he would be returning the next day with a load of tourists and they could catch a lift back, if they wanted. Also, camping was frowned upon, but many people did it. There were many old firesites Warden could probably rekindle for warmth.

The two men piled out of the bus and stood in the glow of a sunset, their possessions around their feet. Hardly had the last baggage come through the door when the minibus puttered away in a cloud of noxious fumes. 'Look,' Warden said, pointing at the beach. In the fading light the black circle of an old campfire stood out against the pale sand.

They eased their way down the sandy incline and dumped their stuff on the beach. Brendan had to lie down again, his body still rebelling with the drugs, but Warden set about quickly gathering a collection of driftwood and managed to get a good fire going as the last of the sun's rays disappeared below the horizon. It started getting very cold and they sat close to the fire. Warden produced two cans of beef stew, which he heated over the fire. After they'd eaten he scurried over to the water's edge, washed the tins out and came back. He refilled them with fresh water from their bottles, dropped a tea-bag in each and put them back on the fire.

'All the modern conveniences in this camp,' he

said. Brendan watched him with red-rimmed eyes and didn't reply.

With nothing left to do, Warden pulled out two more pills and held them towards Brendan. 'Last time, buddy, with a bit of luck.'

'Do you think I need them now? We're here, aren't we?'

'Let's not make a mistake on the last lap,' Warden warned. 'Tomorrow we'll look around and figure out what we're going to do. Tonight, we should just rest.'

'Okay. God knows, I hope it works,' Brendan whispered, taking the tablets.

They got into their sleeping bags and moved as close to the fire as they dared, then lay staring up at the stars. After a while Warden said, 'Hey, Brendan. We're actually on Anzac beach—*the* Anzac beach. I never thought of doing it before, but now I'm here, whatever the reason, I'm glad.'

Brendan didn't answer. Warden rolled over to look and saw in the firelight that his friend was again in a deep sleep. Warden returned his attention to the stars and thought about everything that had happened to them. He supposed he should have felt a little frightened, lying on this beach at night-time, thousands of kilometres from his native land. Instead, he felt curiously at home.

The dawn, rising from beyond the cliffs behind them, was slow in coming. Warden awoke in the grey pre-light aware something was wrong. He jerked up into a sitting position and stuff fell away from his body onto his lap.

It was snow. A light fall had occurred in the night, blanketing everything with a clean whiteness. Warden looked for Brendan and was alarmed to see he was gone, his sleeping bag a crumpled heap half hidden under the snow. Warden's eyes followed a set of tracks leading towards the water. Squinting, he could just see Brendan standing in the gloom about a hundred metres away.

There was someone with him. A drab, wasted figure dressed in ragged khaki. Brendan was holding something out to him and the figure slowly took it. It glinted a pale gold in the low light. There was a moment when both men seemed to be staring at each other. Warden thought he could feel the tension from where he sat.

Then the khaki figure faded away.

30

Brendan had awoken at the first touch of snow on his cheek. He stayed like that, lying on his back and waiting for the stars to fade with the rising sun. As soon as he could see the ocean lapping, eating away at the layer of snow on the beach, he quietly got up, brushed the snow from his head and shoulders and walked down to the water's edge. The morning was absolutely still. Only the sound of tiny waves hissing against the shore filled the silence.

Then Brendan heard the voices starting to buzz in his head. It sounded like an unseen gathering crowd coming closer. He ignored it. Something moved at the corner of his vision—something ugly, but he didn't turn to look. He pulled the leather pouch from his pockets, took out the charm and let it dangle from his fingers, his arm outstretched.

This was what he'd travelled so far, in such a short time, to do. There was no point in waiting any longer.

'Hamilton,' he called softly—the name Warden had told him. 'Ben Hamilton!'

The response he got was a savage hissing inside his head.

'No! He is dead! He is already mine!'

'Ben Hamilton!' he called again, shutting his mind to the inner angry voice.

It became like he was trying to fight a swirling mist inside his head. A mist that shouted and screamed abuse, clawing at his mind with jagged fingernails for acknowledgement. Brendan kept it at bay by concentrating on the image of a young man he'd seen twice now, once in his home and again in a frightening half-world on the threshold of Eternity. The ghost of a soldier who had told Brendan, *'The charm is mine. I can take it back.'*

Someone appeared in the distance, further up the waterline. It was a man dressed in a worn khaki uniform. Brendan held his breath and didn't call again. The figure began to walk slowly towards him, leaving no tracks in the fresh snow. As he came closer, Brendan began to hear other sounds inside his head. The sounds of braying mules, shouting men and odd, crackling noises which he knew to be gunfire. Underneath these was the noise of something screaming with outrage, trying to pull his mind in another, different direction and demanding his attention.

Ben Hamilton stopped an arm's length away. His pale, wasted face looked infinitely sad. His bare feet and hands would have been cruelly cold, if he'd been alive. The three bullet wounds across his chest had aged to dirty brown flowers. Hamilton held out his own hand and spoke. His voice was a whisper amongst the other sounds in Brendan's head.

'It's mine. I didn't take my own life. The demon failed to protect me.'

Brendan concentrated on everything he loved. Gwen, now Warden, and his own life, to give himself the willpower to ignore the raging inner voice and listen to the soldier's spirit.

'Yes, it's yours,' he choked out, with a trembling nod. 'Take it. Take it now, for God's sake.'

Hamilton's ghost reached out and closed its hand over the dangling golden charm. The leather thonging pulled easily through Brendan's fingers. They looked at each other for a long moment.

'And—thank you,' Brendan whispered.

The ghost turned and began to retrace its steps up the waterline. As it got further away, it began to fade. So did the sounds of men and gunfire.

And so did the screaming, angry voice in Brendan's mind.